WRAITHS AND RAIDERS

BEN GREEN

Loamseed
PRESS

To boys, young men, and men who risk being vulnerable and compassionate. You are a powerful force for creating a better world. Onward!

ROYAL CRAFTS

GOLDCRAFT

PHYSICAL AUGMENTATION
METAL: GOLD
BODY & FORM

SILVERCRAFT

MENTAL AUGMENTATION
METAL: SILVER & NICKEL
MIND & SPIRIT

SHIELDCRAFT

PROTECTIVE AUGMENTATION
METAL: TUNGSTEN & LEAD
PROTECTION & HEALING

INDUSTRIAL CRAFTS

COPPERCRAFT

ANIMAL DOMINION
METAL: COPPER
ANIMAL CONTROL & COMMUNICATION

TINCRAFT

PLANT DOMINION
METAL: TIN
PLANT CONTROL & COMMUNICATION

IRONCRAFT

ELEMENTAL MANIPULATION
METAL: IRON
FIRE, WATER, AIR, EARTH, SHADOW, LIGHT

BUDGECRAFT

SPATIAL MANIPULATION
METAL: ALUMINIUM
TELEPORTATION

MODERN CRAFTS
(REQUIRES GESTURING)

MECHCRAFT

MECHANICAL MANIPULATION
METAL: TITANIUM & PLATINUM
MACHINE CONTROL & MANIPULATION

BLUECRAFT

ELECTROMAGNETIC MANIPULATION
METAL: COBALT
COMMUNICATION & ENERGY

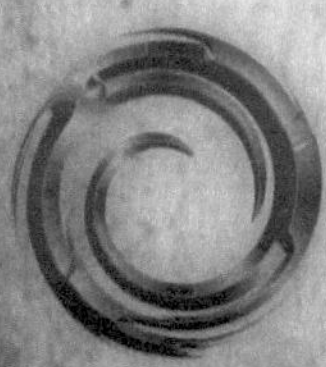

TIMECRAFT

TEMPORAL MANIPULATION
METAL: MERCURY & CHROMIUM
SLOW TIME & SPEED TIME

PROLOGUE
RENSIRA

RENSIRA SILVERLAMP STANDS *at the edge of a glowing pit, eyes squeezed shut. The dull light obscures the splatter of freckles across the bridge of her nose. Her lily-patterned dress would be a beacon of sunlight anywhere else, but here it sits on her like a damp cloak.*

She's not watching as the snaking line of people throw their budges into the unholy, melting churn below, not watching as the aluminum sea bubbles like a primordial soup, not watching Vor, his crown glowing all the more as he controls the people.

But when a man cries out, she opens her eyes.

Vor is smiling softly, standing next to her. He's always smiling. If he's not, then he's shouting. And that shift can happen faster than a daychange in Tungsten City. Sira trembles against this worry.

The man she heard cry out is not old or young. He wears a startled look and a bright red shirt, threads of sharp cobalt swimming along the seams. With two short breaths, he steps back from the pit, clutching a bundle of budgecraft objects to his chest.

He angles back toward the crowd. "What is this? Why am I—"

Vor's smile shifts. "Tas!"

The tall Dura man behind Sira moves forward closer to the pit. "What?"

Vor growls. "Don't do that, Tas. Don't say what. Are you blocking my control?"

Tas replies with a single word. "No."

At the lower landing, the crowd stirs. The man's disturbance hasn't gone unnoticed. Whenever Vor loses control of someone, even for a second, he blames Tas. He wouldn't blame Kel because, like him, she is too dangerous to upset. He can't control the Dura. But they follow him —for now.

"Maybe it's Ara?" Sira says. But these words are a risk.

Vor fires a stare at Sira, who trembles. He knows what she's thinking.

He doesn't smile or shout at this, which is even more dangerous. He adjusts the crown on his head. The crowd surges forward, forcing the man and his objects dangerously close to the edge of the pit. Vor will kill him to make a point.

"Stop!" Sira yells. "Please don't!"

"No?" Vor says. "Was it you? Did you give your craftprint to Tas?"

"You know I wouldn't," she says.

Tas slides closer to Sira. "Vor, enough."

"No, I don't think that is enough, Tas."

Vor tightens his control on the next three people in line. The wave of clarity and revelation—the silvercraft from the mithrium crown—crashes into Sira. Even peerless, she feels its pull toward complete obedience. They grab the man in the red shirt, yanking the bundle from his grasp and hoisting him into the air.

Sira closes her eyes. "Please! No. No, no, no, no, no."

"Open your eyes, Sira," Vor commands.

She resists for two seconds, but the familiarity of silvercraft calls to her. She opens her eyes. Someone hefts the man's bag of budges and throws it into the molten metal. It will all melt down in the pit, leaving behind only the aluminum. The group eases its grip on the man.

"We have his objects," Tas says, glancing at Sira.

Vor nods slowly. "Fair. That is fair. There must only be a few more people who can still resist the crown. Who knows, maybe this guy is like you, Sira; maybe he's peerless of silver. I can let him go..."

Sira's shoulders sag. This time, she wouldn't have to take the guilt for a death. This time, she would sleep tonight.

There's a startled intake of breath from the crowd as the three closest people push the man from the landing. His body drops into the heavy liquid aluminum, which squelches like it's only a layer of mud. Sira turns her head, but Vor turns it back. She closes her eyes. He tries to open them again. With a scream, Sira presses her eyelids together. When they open again, only a sliver of the man's red shirt flashes below.

Vor produces a metallic clothespin. Sira's back straightens, her tears dry, and her breath quickens.

"You need time to process this," he says.

Sira backs away, clinging to Tas' arm. "I don't. I'm okay. I understand. Please."

"You know it's too late. You can't say or do anything. Think about what you did."

Vor closes the distance between them, clipping the clothespin to her finger. She doesn't resist. How many times has he done this? When was the last time he sent her to the tomb to think?

She budges into darkness, surrounded by clammy stone. The clothespin vanishes. Vor knows what budgecraft does to her. For a moment, she feels all around her body. Is her skin attached? Her hair? She can't see her freckles but hopes they are still there. Then she retches until she has nothing left. Her arms find their way around her knees, and she draws inward.

She sobs. "Clayson, why did I leave you?"

There's nothing but stone to comfort her.

GUARD OUR ACREAGE

FOR ME, starry nights awaken the imagination. The moon must be far past the horizon because the sky is alive, a billion sharp pinpricks stitched into a gossamer blanket. My dad has a name for these brilliant, cloudless nights—star soup. No matter the circumstance, I don't tire of this part of surface life.

I park the four-wheeler in the green-dark orchard and turn off the headlights. Slowly, the sound of insects overtakes the hum of the engine. This late in the summer, surrounded by the forest, there's no breeze to rustle the silky leaves of the pear trees.

My thoughts kept me awake last night. It's early, but work helps me focus.

As my mind uncoils, I unbuckle the hose attached to the water tank on the four-wheeler. It's been hot and dry in the Blue Ridge Mountains for the past few weeks. The dwarf trees we planted this spring need a good amount of water. It's a task I'm well acquainted with.

The events since Ara arrived last autumn seem like they've been lined up like dominos. My decisions have trapped all of us on the surface. Sometimes I come out here to hide. In the dead of night, I can pretend it's still my dad and me at the cabin. There's no Vor. There's no mithrium. Ruined underground cities powered by massive artificial suns—yeah, that's not real. None of it. This is real. The stars. The forest. The feel of waxy leaves brushing against my hands.

Halfway through watering the saplings, someone clears their throat at the tree line. I turn, expecting Jeiahlir, my intuitive and uncommonly beautiful girlfriend. I'm expecting her sharp blue eyes and a conversation about the stupid thing I said to her yesterday. But it's not her.

In a way, Andalynn, my sister, the queen of Whurrimduum, looks the same as when I first met her in Gamgim. She's wearing green, though this time is just a cropped t-shirt, not a glimmering gown. Her hair is bound in a loose bun, but the thin strands of malleable silver hair mirror the night. Somehow, this makes her even more regal. She looks at me expectantly for far too long, her chin raised in a question.

Then a smile breaks on her face, and she steps into starlight. "Clay, Clay, Clay. How did I know where to find you?"

"I'm not hiding."

"Liar." The playful smile on her face is an accusation and forgiveness all at once. How does she do that so flawlessly? She glides over to the four-wheeler and leans against it.

"It's four in the morning, Sis. No one should be looking for me." I go back to watering.

"Thought you might want to talk about what you said to Jeiah."

"She told you?"

Andalynn shrugs. "In more of a question than a verdict. She wanted to understand why you—"

"Let's talk about something else. Rugnus is coming back tonight."

Andalynn sighs. "I should teach you some subtlety. You'd make a terrible politician. But yes, he's *supposed* to come home tonight."

The water in the tank runs out as I finish tending the last

sapling. "He *will* be back tonight. It's Rugnus. He doesn't know how to fail."

Andalynn helps me wind the cord around the tank and abruptly hugs me. Her arms wrap tightly around my shoulders, pinning me in place. Still, I sneak my forearms up and squeeze her back. This hug isn't meant to console me. Something's wrong.

I kiss the top of her head. "It's gonna be okay. Rugnus is fine. I know it."

"I know. That's not..." I feel her take a deep breath, and she steps away. "It's Mom. She's falling back under again. I can feel it. It's just like before when she'd pace the castlestack late at night. Back then, I had to keep a guard on her."

This isn't something Andalynn talks about, not to anyone. But I've noticed Mom changing too, settling into her worries like an old comforter. For the past couple of weeks, Mom's been wandering the property late at night, wringing her hands.

I know what it's like to watch a parent fall apart, but I can't come up with the words to help Andalynn through this. "I thought after we destroyed Yinzar's dungeon... you know? Like the moment we were all together, before..."

"Before Vor destroyed everything? Yeah. She had hope in her eyes. And now her father and husband are missing." Andalynn looks toward the distance as if Rugnus will come wandering out of the grove. "Dad is her strength, even though they've been so distant."

I swallow hard. "Do you think Dad's still..."

"I hope so. In his way, he tried to warn us." She smirks at this.

I can't help my half-grin. "You mean by dropping impossible hints and keeping everything secret?"

"Okay, so *tried* is a stretch."

We both laugh at this because what else can we do when the whole Loamin world is being held captive by a man with a crown forged of mithrium and silvercraft?

"He really believes in ending craft," Andalynn says. "Could

you imagine what he thought when he heard your champion name like the rest of us? Wraithking."

"Mom's AMP has been two points away from championship for a long, long time. It's like he already grieves for her."

Slowly, Andalynn nods. "And now you. I guess it makes sense, especially knowing what we know about Dura, Vor, and Ara. They don't remember their lives as Loamin."

Neither of us connects the final piece out loud. When I die, my soul, my life, whatever you want to call it, will generate a dungeon forged out of my consciousness. I make an effort to unfurrow my brow, reaching behind Andalynn to shake a bucket.

"I brought some scraps for the chickens."

Andalynn stretches. "It's close to dawn. They'll be out soon."

With a nod, I jump back on the four-wheeler and turn the engine over. Andalynn squeezes in behind me, tousling my hair. Something in my chest loosens a bit, and I give a silent thanks for having a sister like her.

The grove passes by in darkness, the headlights igniting the path with sharp, bright light. Is this how an animal sees the night, all edges and crisp lines, without the hidden shades?

"Watch out!" Andalynn shouts.

I skid to a halt. Koglim's standing in the path in pajama pants, shirtless. There's a pale scar on his upper arm from the removal of his silver tattoo. His eyes are frantic, his dark skin slick with sweat. In a manic squeak, he says, "Rugnus! Trouble on the road in!" He leaps onto the four-wheeler.

The front sinks into the dirt. Andalynn and Koglim grasp a long aluminum handle on the side, budging us to the edge of the property. The road is split by energy from the mithrium shield Ara set as our protection. The one she can't come back for, and we can't move.

My dad's flatbed is hurtling toward the entrance, Rugnus in the driver's seat. I didn't teach him to drive that fast. We jump from the four-wheeler. To my right and left, Andalynn and Koglim look fierce. I hear the barking of Nox, Gem, and Stone, Hemdi's three labs, catching up to us.

"In or out?" I ask.

My question is answered when four figures appear on the road. Darksmiths—Vor's willing henchmen. They harass us whenever we leave the safety of the shield. We've had some close calls.

Koglim screams a battle cry and surges through the protection of the shield. Golden light blossoms over his left fist and encloses him from head to toe. One massive haymaker pounds the closest darksmith into the dirt like a nail into a two-by-four.

Andalynn isn't far behind. As she passes through the shield, she yanks the hair tie from her head, smoothing down the threads woven of tincraft. Fingers of barbed ivy whirl out of the forest, entrapping a second darksmith.

Two more darksmiths appear. I curse. The only craft I have is a spool of lead for healing. I hope I don't need it today.

Jeiah budges in front of me. "Here." She presses a metallic cup forged of iron into my hands. "Time it to my mark."

I blink. How is this supposed to help? I've only seen Rugnus use this once, and it tore up a half-dozen trees on the edge of the grove. Then I remembered what else it did. From inside the shield, it created a gap—a big one. We had tried it from the outside, but just like everything else, the effect broke against the shield.

If Rugnus is going to make it through the shield without stop-ping, I'll need to make a gap big enough for the flatbed to drive through but timed not to let anyone else through.

"Do it," Jeiah says. My words from the day before intrude on my thoughts, but she's already moved closer to the shield. "Back here in seven!"

I start the countdown. Six. Five. Andalynn and Koglim break from the fight and sprint toward Jeiah. Four. I scoop gravel into the cup. Three. Two. Jeiah reaches for Andalynn through the shield. One.

My continued motion launches the gravel from the cup. It becomes a towering cyclone of dirt and wind, shattering against the inside of the shield. Half of the darksmiths dive to the side of the road. As the truck hits the shield, two darksmiths disappear entirely. Rugnus guns it straight into the ironcraft whirlwind.

The truck slows the moment it crashes into the whirlwind. It's lifted twenty feet in the air. Their momentum carries them through the shield. I exhale. They made it. The energy field flickers back to life, and the whirlwind dissipates, dropping the truck to the dirt.

I turn to run, but the truck hits a pocket of protective craft and slows. A soft white energy pulses around its wheels. It's enough to break the fall but not enough to halt its forward motion. Rugnus slams on the brakes. Only now do I see Hemdi, a thin necklace in his clenched fist. The dogs swarm his legs, barking at the truck as it hurls gravel and skids to a halt between two trees.

Andalynn and Koglim are sweating, but they both made it back through the shield. Jeiah stands with a grim, satisfied expression, though she watches the remaining darksmiths closely. I have to refocus my attention on the truck because I'm thinking about her lighting eyes, the way they evaluate everything around them with cool efficiency. There have been just as many moments where they've been as soft as a summer sky.

Ide keep me. I really messed things up between us.

Then two people tumble from the passenger seat of the flatbed. I rush forward to help them, immediately recognizing the father and son. They'd been on their way into Bluebottle last year when Jeiah, Rugnus, and I went searching for a connection between Lagnar Emberfence and the attack on StoneYoke.

"Wraithking." The boy whispers, eyes as wide as the truck's tires.

The father gives me a thankful nod, but Hemdi intercepts them.

"Welcome to Spangler Acres," Hemdi offers a wide, kind

smile, glancing at the shield. "Why don't we get you over to the main house for the night."

The father, Tredigfal, nods once more but looks back at Rugnus. He's still in the driver's seat, his hands stiff at the wheel as he takes deep breaths. "He okay? We owe him our lives."

I check the shield before I answer. The remaining darksmiths on the road test the shield and argue, but it's back to full strength where I ripped the gap. We're all safe again. "Yeah. I think so."

The father and son follow Hemdi and the dogs back down the road. I come to the driver's side window, Andalynn right behind me. "Hey. Close one."

Rugnus' knuckles are white. His tumultuous dark eyes stare upward. Finally, he sees us. "Sorry, I thought I saw... never mind."

There aren't a lot of situations that rattle Rugnus' focus like this. I lean closer. "What does that mean? Something besides the darksmiths trying to kill you?"

He shakes his head, a smile breaking through. "It's nothing." The door pops open, and he hops from the truck, rubbing his head and stretching. He clasps my shoulders, but only quickly. His smile widens as he sinks into Andalynn's open arms. They stay molded together long enough for Koglim to clear his throat.

Finally, Rugnus says. "Found the source of the distress call. You were right. They were holed up a few miles outside Whurrimduum—just a carved-out sphere in the rock—for two weeks. Ran out of food yesterday. No budges, nothing. Just a basic bluelink connection. But we did it."

With a long, hard glance over Andalynn's shoulder, he finally lets her go. He strides over to the shield face-to-face with the darksmiths on the other side. He straightens the hem of his bright neon t-shirt. "You tell Vor I'll see that crown of his melted down for scrap."

Koglim is at his side. "And pass him this." He makes an obscene gesture he must've learned on human television.

Two darksmiths finally break the other man free of the barbed ivy. The one closest to the shield breathes through some sort of leadcraft machine strapped to his back to counteract the surface effects. The rest of them look none the better when it comes to fizzblood. One's about to puke. They can't stay up here without better shieldcraft. We have the safety of Ara's mithrium shield, forged with Ergal, the ring from Wolfstaff Dungeon.

The man peels away the mask, taking a labored breath. "Vor won't need the crown when the people finish building their prison."

Rugnus scowls.

"What does that mean?" Jeiah says, coming to stand next to me.

"Means what it means," says the darksmith. "Vor will be free to do more important work, like melting all the dungeons down to blackened rocks. Starting fresh."

Koglim cracks his knuckles and growls.

The darksmiths are gone in a flash of brown light.

"That's gotta be a joke," Koglim says. "They can't melt any dungeons, right, Rugnus?"

Rugnus shakes his head and sighs. "No, Koglim."

Jeiah nods. "They'd need Clayson for that. I mean... I don't mean it like that. Just a fact. Anyway. I'll go help Hemdi with the new arrivals. Glad you're back, Rugnus."

Koglim winces, but he follows Jeiah, starting a conversation with, "Did you see how hard I punched that guy?"

I don't hear Jeiah's response, but I hear her laughter.

Wraithspit, I'm dumb.

Rugnus finally brings his attention back to me. He snaps his fingers and points to the truck. "Almost forgot. I snagged these near Whurrimduum. Should help Winta and Jeiah make their monster machine."

He pulls a jingling bag from the passenger seat.

Inside, I find a few bluecraft items shaped like frisbees. "I'll bring them to the shop."

"Great." Rugnus breathes deeply. "Man. Good to be back."

"What did the darksmith mean, a prison?"

Rugnus rubs his face. "Just need a minute or two. Okay? Then a debrief. I'll find you. There's a lot to say. Might as well tell everyone all at once."

"Fair. Hurry, though."

Leaving Andalynn and Rugnus, I head to the shop, the darksmiths' words hanging on me. But Vor is like Ara. He can't enter the dungeons. If he can't enter them, he can't break them. The man had to be exaggerating or flat-out lying. But this prison...

The day peeks through the grove in pink and gray. No clouds, a slight breeze; it'll be a perfect day. The kind of day that forces me to the cliff to climb and overthink.

As I walk back, my mistake with Jeiah settles over my body like a cold steel trap. The moment near the garden yesterday will continue to haunt our relationship for a long time. It's carved into my brain. The icy tension is still stuck on my skin, despite the summer heat.

We escaped to a deep patch of shade against the pines near the garden. Everything seemed perfect. We joked about Andalynn and Rugnus, then about Winta and Hemdi, and compared babysitting notes. We agreed Echel is absolutely adorable. The way he fixates on every word you say and how his hands stay in fists as his little arms move in jerky movements. We imitated the little guy and laughed. Winta says Echel looks more like Hemdi, but Jeiah and I secretly disagreed. He has his mother's sharp eyes.

We laughed until my cheeks hurt. We leaned on each other and plucked little strands of grass between our fingers, rubbing that summer smell from each blade.

That moment... it was pure contentment. For once, I was staring into the distance, imagining the future instead of worrying about the present.

Jeiah said something, but I didn't hear through my thoughts.

I replied anyway because I'm an idiot. "Yeah. Sure. Okay."

"What?" she asked.

A single-word question. I blinked. That got my attention.

"I said, I love you, Clayson," but her words became procedural, investigative.

I choked. "Oh."

"Oh?" She waited a few seconds and stood. "I'm going to the shop, I guess. Sorry."

Why did *she* apologize? Why didn't I tell her to wait? Or call out to her to tell me again. I said her name softly, but it didn't keep her next to me.

That's what I gave her yesterday. *Huh. Yeah. Okay.* Followed by, *Oh.*

On my way to the shop, I mutter, "Great job, Clayson."

I move off the road when I catch the gleam of the mithrium shield. Unable to budge with us to the surface, Ara had sent us here with the shield. We're grateful for it, but it's stuck. She can't come and get it. Trapped like the rest of us.

The thought brings me back to the bridge connecting the two sides of Geum Ide. The conjurers had built it. I imagine my grandmother lashing ropes around wooden beams, working alongside my dad. Now he's missing, and her body lies far below the bridge in the ravine. Vor's crooked sword flashes through my mind.

I touch the glowing source of the shield, but as always, it doesn't move. It's a medium-sized triangular buckler with a pointed bottom edge. It had once protected Geum Ide in the same way, throwing out an impenetrable physical border around the city. Without the shield, none of what we've been doing would work. We'd have been caught and brought under Vor's control.

The buildings around me come alive as dark outlines. Spangler Acres comprises the main cabin, the workshop, the barn, and a half-dozen sheds spread out over the property. The newest feature belongs to Andalynn and Rugnus.

Koglim named it the ministack. It's a two-story stone building. A castle basically. Rugnus' original design had ten stories. I convinced him the shield might keep darksmiths out, but if the distant neighbors saw a skyscraper castle on the horizon, they might come asking questions.

There's a pool next to it. Rugnus says it's for me, but he uses it more than anyone, attempting to face his fear of swimming—with the assistance of a few ironcraft relics.

The person I can't convince to build smaller things is Winta. A shiny new radio tower rises into the sky from behind the stout workshop.

I pull the wooden door open and hear the flare of a welding torch behind the makeshift partition. Winta is already awake. She and Jeiah have been hard at work searching for a way to connect bluelink to the internet. Every day brings crates jammed with machine parts, industrial-strength cooling fans, computer towers, and things I've never imagined. We set up a PO box to budge everything here. No need to let anyone through the shield.

But this machine, it's like a monster waiting to come to life. I might wake one morning to a creature made of craft and computing—electrodes and all—wreaking havoc over my chicken coop.

Every time I ask Jeiah about their progress, she gives the same answer: closer.

I expect them to split an atom in the next few weeks. All I've done to help us is clean out the workshop and, most mornings, bring Winta eggs, bacon, and the blackest coffee on earth. I'm pretty happy with my support role.

There's a break in the torch's buzzing, and on this side of the partition, a soft coo drifts from beyond the center table. Echel. He's squirming in an infant bouncer, plush space rockets and plastic mirrors dangling far out of his reach. His bottom lip curls into a frown, and in milliseconds, he's crying. Winta issues what sounds like an exhausted sigh from somewhere in the shop.

"I got it," I call. Setting the bag of bluecraft plates down on the table, I undo the buckle—a plastic tiger's head—and hoist him up, blanket and all, tucking in his legs and arms.

"Clayson?" Winta whispers.

"Yep."

She peeks around the partition, waiting to pass judgment on my babysitting skills, but I draw her son in all the tighter. I hum something Loamin, something my dad used to hum to me. Satisfied, Winta returns to her work, but I point my chin at the bag on the table. When she opens it, she grins from ear to ear.

Rugnus? she mouths, not wanting to cue Echel's tears.

I keep my voice soothing and aim it at Echel. "Yep, he made it back. Didn't he? Uncle Rugnus picked up two more refugees and some more glass for the monster."

Winta clutches the bag and disappears behind the screen, but my focus is squarely on this side of the room. Jeiah's side. The place almost mirrors her office in Bluelink Tower. She's been gathering evidence into five distinct sections. I shake my head as I pace around the room with Echel. There hasn't been a day when Jeiah's intelligence didn't leave me speechless. And I've gone and screwed things up with her.

Section one is a large corkboard plastered orange, studded with pushpins connecting the names and images of all the Dura she can account for. Vor had been a Loamin champion, as had Ara, Tas, and Kel. If there are ninety-three dungeons, in theory, there must be ninety-three Dura. She's found sixty in bluelink records, but many were killed in mithrium explosions during the wars.

As terrible as it is to view that as positive, it means Vor can be killed.

Vor's image is pinned to the top of the board, a polaroid Jeiah took from a paused bluelink video. He's standing behind my dad at a council meeting. Next to him is a drawing of Onrix, Sira's metal knife. She'd used it to control her father, but long before that, it had been the heart of Vor's dungeon. By touching it, he became self-aware. That happened during Erikzin Brightstorm's time. We're the ones that made it worse when we forged the knife into a crown using mithrium. The moment he took the crown, he remembered everything his Dura body had lived through, all the way back to the dungeon. And now he's able to control whole populations.

Ara and Kel have pictures below his, connected to their unique relics, the shield and the wolfstaff. Between the pictures of these two women, there's a long strip of construction paper that reads: TAS AND ICHO. FOUR DURA, FOUR RELICS.

The board next to it is yellow. Individual letters are taped to the board reading: PROTODUNGEONS. Below that lay the words, DUNGEON HEART. Three pushpins wound with yarn are connected to those words, the yarn tracing back to the other board: Tas, Ara, Vor.

Kel was connected to a known dungeon—one I broke this last Spring when I tore out its heart at Torlina Wolfstaff's request. We suspect the three relics are also from broken dungeons—protodungeons that existed long before Loamin settled the Rockies.

I boost Echel to my shoulder, and he grabs a few loose strands of my hair. I wince, but I let him pull on them as I come before the next board.

MITHRIUM. Erikzin Brightstorm. Exralt Blackmug. Both men lived over a thousand years ago. They were friends. Blackmug had tried to leave the ring—Ergal—in Wolfstaff Dungeon, but the dungeon had claimed his life. He had left the knife and Icho to Rugnus' ancestors. Rugnus' mother, Rusela, had loaned the knife to Silverkeeper for his research, but it ended up in Sira's hands and, by extension, Vor's.

Rugnus says it's nearly indisputable that Erikzin and Exralt knew about the mithrium. The timing of the appearance of the protodungeon relics almost matches the appearance of the mithrium. I think he's right. Jeiah, on the other hand, has scrawled out dozens of questions. She's even tried to make some educated guesses about answers, but even those answers, scribbled on index cards, have large question marks next to them.

The last board is green. LAGNAR EMBERFENCE. Bluekeeper. It's like I'm still watching the mithrium leave my hand as I throw it to him in the exit lobby of Mithriumbane Dungeon. He escaped. The last piece of mithrium is out of Vor's hands for now. Vor and Ara have been unable to come to the surface since touching their items.

Finding Emberfence has been our highest priority, alongside relocating refugees to safe houses around the country. We can't do what really needs to be done—finding the power to face Vor. The moment we budge close to him, he can control us using the crown. It's a non-starter in all our planning meetings.

Echel is breathing deeply on my shoulder. I kneel next to his baby bouncer and slowly lay him in place, snapping the little buckle around his thick thighs. Time to go check on everything else. But as I stand, Echel takes a huge, startled breath and wakes, arms jerking. His face sours, and he starts to cry.

There's a sigh from the other side of the room, and Winta appears again. "Ide keep me. Where am I going to find better babysitters?"

"I—sorry, Winta. I can watch him, really. It's not a problem. I just thought he'd stay asleep."

"Sleep? I didn't realize we were still doing that kinda thing. Echel sure didn't get the message. And"—she looks at a wall clock— "you were up before I even thought about sleep." She nudges past me and hefts Echel into her arms. "Go find Jeiahlir. Kiss and make out."

I stifle a laugh. "You mean make-up?"

"I said what I meant." She gives me a knowing smile. "And ew. Make-up is gross. Don't mention it in my presence again."

"As long as you stay out of—"

"No deal. Go." She pushes me out the door.

I find an orange-pink morning waiting for me. My shoes collect dew as I trudge to the chicken coop. I have no intention of searching for Jeiah this morning—not until I can think of something to say to her that will make a difference. Something better than, *yeah, sure, okay.*

Hemdi finds me after chores, around ten, and delivers breakfast. Rugnus follows ten minutes later. He pops his head around the corner of my room as I'm using the quick clean.

"Good idea. Gonna need you at the ministack. Debrief."

I screw the golden lid back on the little iron flask. "I could use some focus, anyway."

He grimaces. "Jeiah's there. Just an FYI for no particular reason."

"Right," I scoff. "Andalynn told you. You know, the more everyone else talks about my stupidity, the harder it will be for me to finally talk to her."

"It's only been a day." A slow smile spreads on Rugnus' face. "Complete latcher, by the way. She loves you. Gotta feel good about that. Even if you screwed it all up by putting your foot in your mouth."

He throws an arm around me and draws me from the solace of my room.

AID THE STRANDED

THE CENTRAL SPACE of the ministack is designed to hold a council. Everyone gathers on couches and tables facing one another: Mom at a back table; Andalynn and Rugnus sit close together with Tredigfal and his son across from them; Winta, Hemdi, and Echel are on a low bench; Brig is at a table with Koglim; Jeiah hovers at the edge of the room. The large bay windows diffuse cheery light through the room, and bunches of fresh-cut flowers sit in glazed pots half a loam tall. Not a single flower is wilting.

Beautiful. Welcoming.

But my hands grip the table's edge, applying so much pressure I might leave a dent. Rugnus and Tredigfal slowly drain the life from the room with every word they speak.

"Vor moved Whurrimduum's foilgrips to Tungsten City," Tredigfal says.

"He forced the people to move them," Rugnus says, bristling.

Tredigfal nods along with this. "He can go anywhere he wants. Simply drags them along with him. Then he forces the budge-smiths and other craftsmen to do what he wants done."

Jeiahlir takes a position against the same wall as the window. "Why take the foilgrips?"

Winta steps over a bluecraft figurine on the mantle by the river stone fireplace. She sets it on a small, flat square of titanium and stands back. A map of Tungsten City ignites in the center of the room. The exterior windows tint automatically.

Koglim stands and whistles as she zooms into a flattened spot in the apex, near the heart of the city. It's a gorge lined with hundreds of waterfalls extending a mile deep.

"Everfalls," Winta says. Rugnus must have gotten her up to speed. "Built out of ironcraft and foilgrips. The water starts at the lip of the gorge, falls in a series of cascading waterfalls, runs through a massive expanse of grates into a billion budgecraft receptors, and then it's budged back to the top. Vor's adding to it, digging deeper, forging something powerful."

"A prison." The words come out through my clenched jaw.

Koglim frames the image with his fingers. "Stronger than Keelcrawl. I've been to the bottom of that thing before. It takes hours to navigate down to the drains. And the budges at the bottom are forged to only budge water. There's no way out but a long climb. Gotta be a million stairs."

Jeiah makes a soft noise in her throat. "About half that. Four hundred thirty-six thousand, three hundred and fifty. But good guess."

"Wraithspit," Brig whispers, and for once, Jeiah doesn't slap him for swearing.

He's right; it's a lot of stairs.

"It's not just this thing he's making," Tredigfal says, "it's what he's doing to people. Working them to exhaustion—starvation."

"He's torturing them," Rugnus says grimly.

Tredigfal nods and adds, "He says he's just waiting for Clayson."

All eyes fall on me. My mouth goes dry. "How can you know that? I mean... makes sense, but—"

"Oh right," Tredigfal's head quirks like he's shaking something loose from his brain. "That's the thing, my uncle was in the ironheads, see, he has all this surveillance stuff, uh, like the plates Rugnus brought you—I hope that helps—anyway, they were in the knights' barracks, some of the darkmages, and I heard them talking."

Rugnus scratches his face. "Vor thinks you'll try to face him sooner or later."

A fire sparks in my bones. "He's not wrong. We're coming for him."

Ontrea finally squeaks out a question. "Wait. If Clayson leaves, will we be safe?"

But his fear only stokes the fires of my vengeful thoughts. Ontrea deserves better than to be trapped on the surface for the rest of his life. So does Echel. "For now, I'm staying put under the shield, but—"

Tredigfal holds up a hand, faces his son, and says, "We talked about this. This is only a stopping point. Rugnus is taking us someplace even safer. A new home."

I sigh, earning me a look from Andalynn. This part of the conversation isn't unexpected. Each time we take in someone new—we're up to about thirty—we listen to them, feed them, and then house them far away from the shield but still under its protection.

Rugnus produces an incandescent light bulb. "Know what this is, Ontrea?"

He shakes his head.

"We call it a graybulb. Can you see what type of—"

"Shieldcraft. That's tungsten."

"Smart. Yeah. The filament in this light bulb was forged kinda like foilgrip. You know what they do to make anti-budge, right?"

He nods. "They bring it right next to the brightstorm. It's one of the only types of craft made that way."

"Yep, and that's why it's so powerful. But see this tiny piece of tungsten? We wrapped it around the mithrium shield out there. Did you see the shield when you came in?"

The boy's eyes widen, and he gives an eager nod.

"Made about twenty of these things. There are families just

like yours, families we've helped find a new place—safe from here but connected to the shield through this bulb. Make sense?"

"I think so."

"And you know who came up with this recipe?"

"Who?"

"None other than Clayson Wraithking."

Somehow the boy's eyes widen further as he turns to me. "You forged this?"

The bulb was my idea. And I might have even forged this piece of the tungsten filament. We'd been trying to access Ara's shield outside the radius to carry its effect. In the end, we couldn't transport it, but we created static places of refuge that borrowed from the shield.

I didn't agree to use them for the refugees. Rugnus knows exactly how I feel about sending these families away. I think we should let them stay with us, but I was outvoted. He's not trying to rub it in, but for a brief second, that's how it feels. There's no need for me to bring this up. This family wants hope, not anger.

"I did. And it works just like the shield I made."

"Cool," Ontrea whispers.

His father pats him on the back. "Then we go. I'm sorry there's not more I can tell you about the Everfalls and Vor, or the darksmiths, or—"

"Are you kidding!" Koglim says. "More info than we've gotten in weeks."

There's a pause, and Andalynn stands. "Let's get the two of you ready to go. Rugnus will budge you to your new home once we go over the logistics."

"Can Clayson come too?" Ontrea asks.

"Son, I'm sure Clayson has a lot of other responsibilities."

I put my hand on Ontrea's shoulder. "But nothing this important. Of course, I'll come. Right, Rugnus?"

Andalynn trades a look with Rugnus. They don't want me to leave the safety of the shield. But I don't like being treated like a latcher.

With a shrug, Rugnus says, "If he wants to come, he's welcome."

Andalynn leads the father and son to the den to give them more instructions about the graybulb and supply deliveries. Jeiah and Winta quickly disappear, trading ideas about how to use the bluecraft plates. Koglim stays behind, evaluating the map of Everfalls as if it is the next dungeon he's gotta figure out.

He zooms out, and for a moment, all of Tungsten City is on display. Loamin aren't meant to live on the surface. The shield, the graybulbs, are a finger in a dam that could break any moment. What if Vor sent everyone to the surface? It would be a mass execution.

A hand grabs my elbow, and I find my mom attached. "If you're going out there, please be safe. It takes a minute or so for Rugnus to get the graybulb set up. If the darksmiths find you before—"

"They won't. On the surface, they have the same bluelink connection issues we do. It will take them days to track the craft in the graybulb; by then, Tredigfal and Ontrea will be safe behind their piece of Ara's shield. I should tell *you* to be safe. Every time we turn one of those things on, we lose some of the circumference of the shield."

"Just promise you won't do anything rash."

"Done."

Her hand stays connected to me, and for a second, I want to ask her about her late nights. Maybe I could help. Instead, I say, "I left a few buckets in the barn I need to clean up."

For the next few hours, I focus on scrubbing down the barn. It's possible it's the cleanest it's ever been by the time Rugnus comes around to collect me for the relocation.

We stand in the cabin's living room. Rugnus has Icho. These relocations have been the only time we've used it outside the shield. They've become almost routine.

"Ready?" Rugnus asks everyone.

Tredigfal draws his son next to him. "Ready."

I feel no nausea when we budge. After taking the heart of Wolfstaff Dungeon months ago, I became peerless in budgecraft. I became a champion. The idea of being trapped in a dungeon of my own creation when I die makes me nauseous.

We move in an instant. One moment we are standing in the cabin, the next on the winding driveway leading to a spacious mountain home somewhere miles outside Flagstaff, Arizona.

I stare at it in wonder. Surrounded by pines, the spacious house sits back from a rocky precipice. Large windows appear as we walk toward the house. The eastern side of the driveway is lined with pines, the other with white-flowered scrub bushes. Through the massive windows, I catch a modern interior with vaulted ceilings and an open floor plan.

We had to convert a lot of metal and ferrum into cash to buy this place. But our reasons lay well beyond its charm. It's just a stopgap, but it has six bedrooms and four bathrooms. Perfect for a few more families stuck on the surface. Once we get the gray-bulb installed, it should be able to hold a few more.

It's beautiful, but I can tell the surface effects are already weighing Rugnus down. Ontrea is having trouble making it up the driveway. I let him lean on me and unwind a thread of protective craft to help with the surface effects. The moment I connect with the metal, I hear a collective sigh of relief.

Rugnus opens the main doors and waves us in. "Clock's running. I don't think the darksmiths can detect us, but we need to get going."

As I enter the foyer, Rugnus' cell phone rings, and he answers it, his breathing labored. The phone he uses to connect to bluelink is another example of Jeiah and Winta's innovations. It uses no craft. It's the type of thing they are trying to duplicate on a large scale. Rugnus pulls the cell phone away from his ear and presses a button. He sets it on the entryway table.

"—thing's good here." Andalynn's tinny voice carries from the phone. "Just hurry. The shield will have to adjust once you turn on the bulb."

Rugnus pulls a ladder from the closet behind the stairs and places it in the center of the vaulted entryway.

"Will it work?" Ontrea asks as Rugnus hands me the graybulb.

Tredigfal says, "It will, my love." But the look he gives me seems wary and resigned to whatever comes next.

The light above me is off, but one of our failures during the first attempt taught us a few tricks to ensure the craft turns on once I screw in the bulb. "Is the fuse off?" I ask.

"Of course, it's off. Come on, quick."

I fill the only empty light socket on the chandelier.

Rugnus budges to the fuse box, reappearing a second later, but not before the graybulb activates.

Waves of gray light ripple outward from the bulb. The other bulbs in the chandelier switch colors as the effect spreads. My hands, then my whole body, become colorless, like the set of some black-and-white TV show. Below me, Rugnus' soft brown complexion becomes something out of a noir film. The father and son stare at each other, stealing looks at their gray skin, then at one another's dark eyes.

This new color scale will be their permanent life experience if we can't find a better solution; if we can't find a way to end Vor's tyranny. Outside, the gray tones spill like paint over the patio and the landscaping.

Rugnus whispers, "See?" He calls out to Andalynn on the phone. "How're things on your end?"

Andalynn takes a long moment before she responds. "Koglim says we lost about a fifth block."

My mind estimates the Loamin measurement in standard English, and my throat goes dry. "Five hundred feet. Th-that's half of the grove." I don't say it aloud, but it's also dangerously close to my favorite climbing spot.

But then I hear Ontrea take a deep breath. The surface effects are gone. The house and surrounding property are protected by an extension of Ara's shield. Even hundreds of miles away. I step off the ladder and clasp Ontrea by the shoulder. "It worked!"

Rugnus is still a ball of tension, bringing my mind back to our property. "You guys still there?" he asks Andalynn. "Hello?"

The phone crackles "...hear me? This is Brig. They got through!" Then he rambles something about the shield, Koglim, the ministack. "...Rugnus. Under attack!"

Rugnus snatches the phone from the table. "Repeat. What did you say?"

"Ho, you're there," Brig says, relieved. "It's those darksmiths. Jeiah says they must have gotten through the shield with the truck. I don't know! Just—"

Rugnus' jaw tightens. "What?"

The phone crackles again. Jeiah's distant voice says, "Brig! Get back here."

We wait for her to come back, but nothing happens. "Jeiah? You there?"

Nothing.

Rugnus growls again. "We've got to go."

"Go," Tredigfal says. "We'll be fine. Just go!"

I blink, and Rugnus has budged us back on the gravel road facing the ministack.

A large wall of thorns blocks the castle's front door. "That's... not good."

"Help!" Andalynn shrieks. We follow the piercing sound to the edge of the new wall, where I see her hair intertwined with thorns. Her head and torso burst from the wall in a pulse of green light.

As we run toward her, the cuts along her arms and face come into focus, festering with acid. She screams again, but before we reach her, she pulls herself half free and tumbles to the gravel. A long sword, made of white glass and speckled tin, clatters to the ground next to her.

Rugnus tries to pull her further from the twisted wall, but she is attached to it. A long vine extends from the wall into her abdomen like a tether, the end of it speared through her left side. I can only stare in shock.

Her teeth grinding, she cries, "Get it out of me!"

I'm frozen, but Rugnus places a hand on the thorny vine and turns a small portion to ash. Breaking it, he flings one side back toward the wall and starts drawing the rest from her body like a loose thread.

"Heal her!" Rugnus commands.

As the top of the vine shrinks into her body, I put my hands on her shoulders and pour every ounce of healing I can into her. I can't help thinking about Silverkeeper and how I watched him die or when the feral wolves attacked Koglim and my bracelet did nothing. Even with this doubt, her flesh knits back together at the exit wound.

She screams as Rugnus draws the rest of the vine out of her stomach. Blood follows, but I close the wound, feeling the movement of the shieldcraft around her torn muscles. "It's working."

Andalynn takes a shuddering breath. "Ide keep me, that was..." she searches the wall of vines. "Where is he?"

Rugnus squeezes her hand. "Who?"

"The darksmith. He didn't get past the... there." She points to a patch of flesh visible through the vines.

Rugnus' face turns as hard as stone. He adjusts the bracelet on his wrist, the one I gave him before StoneYoke, and the entire wall—except the section where the darksmith is trapped—turns to ash and embers. Using the sword, Andalynn attempts to unwind the vines from the man, but he's covered in them.

He collapses to the ground.

"Heal him," Rugnus says. "We can get information."

I reach out, but there's no life to heal. "He's dead."

"Clayson?" Before I can face the voice, Jeiah's arms are around me. Brig comes to her side, followed by Hemdi and Winta. Echel must be inside. My mom strides toward us, furious.

"I'm okay," I whisper to Jeiah. "What happened?"

Mom winces as her hands reveal a swath of golden blood. She points upward. "The second darksmith."

I scan the sky and see a tiny person floating away to the east.

"Made him much lighter," she says, a deadly edge to her voice.

The sound of the ATV draws our attention behind us. Koglim parks, whistling. As he steps off, he counts us silently. He stops at Winta, frowning, but hears Echel's whining from inside. "That's all ten of us alive. We're good, right? Shield is... functional. Check. Darksmiths..." He looks up. "That will be a long way to drop if he doesn't burn up in the atmosphere. And this one—"

"Dead," I say.

"Dead," Koglim confirms. "Another successful refugee transfer."

Winta huffs. "Bet you wish you still had your tattoo."

Koglim shakes his head. "Still nope. Omens did us exactly zero good."

"That was too close," Rugnus says. "We may have to—"

Something blue flashes in my mom's hand. I follow the path of Jeiah's eyes to a coil of cobalt glass. "Mom?"

Brig scrunches his face and looks it over. Jeiah produces her beholder and scans it, then looks at Winta. "She grabbed this off the darksmith. Some type of bluelink blocker. That's why we didn't see when they got through the shield. They've been here all day just waiting. Makes my skin crawl. But maybe this could be useful."

Winta lifts the blue glass from my mom's hands. "Could be the last piece we need."

"For the contraption?" Koglim asks. "Come on. You guys have been—"

Both girls shoot him a glare.

Rugnus steps closer to them. "Not essential. We need to—"

"This is exactly essential," I say flatly. "Today proves that. Look, we could barely defend ourselves. And how many more people can we help anyway? How much further can we stretch

Ara's shield? We need a permanent solution. We've got to stop chopping at the branches and get to the root."

Winta makes a sound in the back of her throat. "As bad as Clayson's metaphor is, he's not wrong. Getting blueweb up and running could make the difference in finding Lagnar. Which could lead to the last piece of mithrium, which could help us make something to stop Vor."

Koglim shakes his head. "This leads to that. That leads to this. Everything feels like a melted side mission to nowhere. I just want to go melt that piece of brick latchmage. I mean, what if Lagnar is already dead?"

My mom takes Echel from Winta. "He's not dead. He's too smart for that. But if he has the last piece of mithrium, he could be useful."

Rugnus looks sick. "Andalynn almost... and we have a body here. Can we just... I need a second."

Andalynn places a hand on his arm. "Rugnus isn't wrong. We need to regroup, but I also"—Rugnus groans— "I also think we need to act quickly. Winta and Jeiah, see if that thing has enough bluecraft to power the machine. Make sure it's safe before plugging it into everything. Koglim and I can clean up the body."

She says this, but her face looks pale. I might be able to heal her, but I can't replace lost blood. Rugnus shakes his head. "You, go lay down. You lost a lot of blood. Get fluids."

Mom steps over to me and holds her palm up. I heal the cut, but golden blood stains her skin. I glance back to the sky. The darksmith has become a black speck. She used the same craft that let her conceal my identity the night I met her in the RV park. It turned that darksmith's body into a balloon. Every time she uses that golden ring box with the translucent candies, I understand why other Loamin find her frightening.

"I'll stay with Andalynn," she says.

I nod. "I'll go with Jeiah and Winta."

"Me too," Brig adds, moving to my side as if proximity to me will help everyone take him seriously.

As we split up, something hangs in the air: a feeling of discomfort and worry. For a second, it's as if no one wants to move. We've all lost too much and don't want to be separated anymore. Still, our small group—Hemdi, Brig, Winta and Echel, Jeiah, and me—start toward the workshop. I hear Koglim and Rugnus position the body, and then they budge to find a place to bury it. I'm half-tempted to tell them to throw it in the forest beyond the shield and let the birds and wild animals pick at it.

It's more than the darksmiths deserve.

When we reach the workshop, Brig holds the door open for everyone, taking Echel from Winta.

On Winta's side of the shop, a huge water tank glows with cobalt light. Thousands of shards of blue glass tumble in a whirlwind of refraction, suspended in the thick, bubbling liquid. Three copper rods cut through the center of the tank. Winta dumps the coil of blue glass on the table, covers it with a piece of canvas, and smashes it to pieces. The sound draws my attention away from the tank.

Jeiah's eyes are glued to mine.

"How does it work again?" I ask.

Jeiah purses her lips as if considering an explanation or maybe whether I'm worth giving an explanation to. My breath catches as I wait for her to speak, but Winta interjects.

"We've been trying to reach a level of saturation in the saltwater solution. We needed enough bluecraft to catch the electrons in the water, to interact with the copper."

"Why coppercraft?"

"It's not craft," Jeiah says. "It's copper wiring, human metal. That's what connects to the power supply, which connects to the converters, which connects to the server farm." She gestures to the three server towers at the other end of the room.

Winta sprinkles the shards in the tank like fish food. "That will do it. Time for the beholder."

Jeiah grimaces but pulls her beholder from her side pocket. For a second, I think she means to shatter it along with the other relics, but she slips it into a long vertical tube near the servers. She seals it shut with a series of clasps and vents the air inside of the container with the click of a button.

Then she and Winta climb into matching gaming chairs at a control panel like they're readying for a NASA test flight. Winta swipes three fingers across the screen, holds down a key, and says, "Execute blueweb."

Music.

I don't know if it's part of the program or just Winta being Winta. They've both developed a fondness for trance music, and the synthesized tones fill the room. Jeiah's slow, cool voice is overlaid against the melody:

> *What's more than a night?*
> *What's more when you've got that feeling?*
> *You can't get in silver*
> *Or the pulse of the light.*
> *Everyone get ready, everyone get ready, everyone get ready.*

I glance at her, and she looks away.

"Right?" Winta says over her shoulder. "We're trending all over social media. Don't worry, Clayson, we're untraceable... anyway, Jeiah, take it away."

Jeiah taps her keyboard, opening bluelink. No, that's not right. This is more—this is bluelink connected with the Internet. Something both human and Loamin. Something new. Blueweb. She lifts her arms, palms flat like she's calling an audience to rise. Screens flare to life on the sidewall.

I can't believe my eyes. "Trollbrick, you did it."

Winta spins around and leans back, eyes wild and excited. "Yes, we did."

I step toward the screens, searching. It's mostly camera footage and other surveillance, but some of it scrolls impossibly fast over pages and pages of the news, searching for keywords. "Can you search for Lagnar? How long will it take?"

"Depends on how much Emberfence knows about using data trafficking and satellite surveillance," Jeiah says.

"More than we think is my bet. If we find him—"

An alarm goes off, and the wall of screens blanks out.

"Already?" I ask.

"Not Emberfence," Jeiah says. "But yeah, something."

Above us, a host of projectors send blinking streams of light down to the floor, creating a ghostly three-dimensional picture. It's nothing like the augmented reality of bluelink. Saying it's three-dimensional, is generous. It's more like someone took pictures from twenty different angles and put them together like a cardboard cutout.

Winta side-eyes the facsimile with disappointment. But the scene in front of us is clear: it's a convenience store.

Two customers crash through a snack food display, scrambling away from the specter that's passing through the candy aisle. Not *down* the candy aisle, *through* the candy aisle. Made of a hundred shapes and strange angles by the Blueweb machine, the figure glows with neon gold and silver veins. An itch starts at the back of my brain. Why does that seem familiar? Have I seen this type of craft before?

The figure lumbers forward, passing a foot away from a man picking out a soda. The man freezes, and then bolts the other direction as the figure crosses the store, opens the ice cooler, and climbs inside.

Koglim and Rugnus appear at the door. Koglim's jaw nearly comes unhinged. "Spit and bones, what is that?"

"You're asking me?" Winta says. "Ide, I don't know. The program searches for craft energy. This is what it picked up."

I scoot closer to the projection. "That's craft?"

Echel whimpers as Hemdi comes to stand by Brig. "It's a wraith." He's looking at me, not the projection. "You can't tell?"

"I-I... that can't be a wraith. They can't exist outside of Gamgim and the dungeons."

Hemdi juts his chin in its direction. "Yeah, but that's a wraith."

Rugnus says, "Is this real-time?"

"Yes," Jeiah says, "and there are ten other incidents like this one, all in the same city in Colorado. Denver news reporters are calling him the Brain Killer. Everyone he touches becomes a vegetable. None of them have recovered."

I follow the camera back to the man with the soda.

"Ide keep us," Hemdi whispers. "How did we not pick up on this earlier? We have to stop this thing."

The wraith—if Hemdi's label is right—crawls back out from the cooler carrying a few bags of ice. The light strikes its head and shoulders.

"It can't be," I say.

"What is it?" Jeiah asks.

"I... rewind a few seconds. Yeah, right... there. Back. Pause it."

A haggard and deathly face appears under a cloak of darkness.

I utter a name. "Landred."

Rugnus glances from me to the projection. "You're right."

"Who's Landred?" Winta asks.

Koglim's answer enters my brain with the consistency of mud. "Landred Wolfstaff," he says. "The only son of Torlina Wolfstaff. He's the wraith from the dungeon Clayson broke. Looks like the rules changed again."

HAIL OLD FOES

THE THIN SYNAPSES holding together my understanding of craft and mithrium and dungeons and wraiths—all things Loamin—experience a cascading failure. As I try to mend the pieces of my understanding, Rugnus sits next to me.

When did I sit down?

Rugnus and Hemdi call my name. Koglim thumps my back like I'm choking.

Finally, my brain strings the words together. "How could Landred be alive? I destroyed the dungeon. Now he's floating around on the surface, sucking people's brains out?"

Jeiah's expression matches my utter confusion. Even she can't put the pieces together.

Rugnus taps Icho against his leg. "Must be what happened when you destroyed the dungeon. You freed Torlina Wolfstaff. Then her consciousness—or whatever—found its way to Kel and joined her other form—her Dura form. Landred was the only wraith in her dungeon. Torlina's consciousness didn't die. Guess Landred's didn't either."

Koglim pokes the hologram with a long piece of metal he must have grabbed from the table. Landred rummages through the convenience store freezer again. "Why's he getting ice? Sports injury? Startup Juice Bar?"

"I don't know," I say. "But we've got to do something."

Winta looks offended. "This is not why we made blueweb." She raises her fist and starts to number the reasons. "One: Find Emberfence, so we can get the mithrium back—which you gave to him—so we can make something to kill Vor. Two: Protect us from Vor so we see his darksmiths coming—also so we can figure out a way to kill Vor. Three: *Stopping* Vor. Am I wrong?"

"No," I say. "You're right. But what if Vor finds Landred? What if Landred helps him? Vor's trying to free the other Dura. I'd much rather we solve this mystery before he does. I'm going to Denver."

"Another side mission." Koglim sighs. "I'll back you up. I could use some excitement."

"You're thick as spit," Winta says. "We don't know what it's capable of. A regular wraith can take your highest craft with a single exposure."

"It could be even more powerful," Hemdi says.

This I can agree with. "That's why I have to do this alone."

This is met with half a dozen groans. "Yeah, okay," Jeiah says. "Anyway, who are we sending on this side mission? Clayson might be right about investigating this, but he's not going alone."

"I'm serious," I say. "I'm immune to wraiths. I need to go alone."

Jeiah shakes her head. "There are a few dozen darksmiths still out there, trying to kill us—you particularly. Probably half of them just standing outside the shield, trying to break it down as we speak. And you want to budge out into the open, accost a wraith, and then what? What does that accomplish?"

Pointing to the image of Landred, I say, "There's a good chance this can give us a better understanding of the dungeons. It could help."

Winta circles her ear with a finger.

I ignore her. "Wraiths were trapped in dungeons the same as

the champions. And... and I know Landred. I've spoken to him. Maybe he still has a connection to his mother."

"You're being stupid, Clayson." Winta says, "Torlina Wolfstaff —Kel—betrayed every Loamin exactly three minutes after being given a conscience. She was fickle and mean in life. It didn't change in death."

"What does that say about you?" I ask. The second the words leave my mouth, I regret them. The temperature of the room drops to the level of Winta's blood.

"Out of line, Clayson," Jeiah says.

Before Winta kills me, I hold up my hands. "That was... I didn't mean that. I'm sorry. I just... I don't know."

"Stress?" Koglim comes to my defense.

Rugnus stands. "We're all stressed. Ten minutes ago, Andalynn almost... Maybe we can all be just a bit more forgiving."

"That sounds like Andalynn talking," Winta says. There's an approval behind her voice and reluctant forgiveness for my stupidity.

"But this," Rugnus continues, pointing to Landred, "this can't wait. And I don't want Andalynn thinking she needs to do something about it."

Koglim readies something on his belt, dancing excitedly. "I get to come, right? Who's going?"

This is not going the way I want it to go, but Rugnus is right. "If you won't approve of me going by myself, then at least let me be the first to approach him."

"Deal," Rugnus says. "Who else is going?"

"I'm in." Koglim sets the metal pointing stick down. "What about you two?"

Hemdi and Winta both shake their heads. Hemdi says, "We're good."

"We don't need everyone going," Winta adds.

"I'll go too," Jeiah says.

The shop door opens, and Mom enters. "Go where?" As the

door squeaks closed, she stares at the floating image of Landred. "What is that?"

Rugnus catches her up with a quick summary, pushing past her shock into another question. "How's Andalynn?"

"Good enough for me to chaperone this trip, so I'm going. Brig, keep an eye on Andalynn."

A crestfallen Brig, who had obviously been waiting his turn to volunteer for this mission, starts drifting toward the door, arms hanging limply at his side.

"You're sure she's okay?" Rugnus asks Mom.

Mom produces her small golden candy box. She flips it over in her hands, opening and closing the lid. It's empty, meaning she used one recently. I think of the darksmith currently floating higher into the atmosphere. I repress the urge to step back, thinking about how she used it to change my appearance the night I fled with my dad.

A month ago, she saw Koglim eyeing the box and shut him down. "If you eat one of these," she had said, "your limbs will detach from your body."

This only encouraged him until she explained the amount of blood involved and how quickly he would lose consciousness and die.

"Andalynn will be fine. Are we ready?" she asks.

Jeiah and Koglim step toward us.

"Remember," I say, "I go in first. We don't know what effect Landred still has outside of the dungeon."

"Clayson," Koglim says. "Can you use your bracelet for me too? I've got a lead coin, but it's nowhere near—"

I slide over to him, and he rests a hand on my shoulder. "Anyone else?"

Jeiah takes my hand. Her fingers are cool even on a summer's day. She squeezes gently. I try not to attach any meaning to it— maybe she just needs the protection of my bracelet—but her hand feels good in mine.

A second later, we appear in the parking lot of the convenience store. Everyone except Koglim and Jeiah sags under the weight of the surface effects. Mom seems to be weathering the change in symptoms the best. Maybe it's something in the piece of candy she ate earlier.

Rugnus always has the worst symptoms. But he manages with a coil of tungsten made from the same spool used for the gray-bulb filament, though not connected to the mithrium shield.

"You first, Clayson," Rugnus says, already out of breath.

I can't see Landred through the windows of the convenience store, but the clerk looks catatonic. When I break contact, a weight settles on Jeiah's shoulders, and Koglim hunches over. I start to peel off the bracelet to leave it with Jeiah, but she stops me.

"You may need the shieldcraft in there."

Reclasping the bracelet, I nod. "I'll be as quick as possible."

Approaching the window, I spot movement from two customers—a young man and his mom, perhaps—peeking around corners. I forget how young human teenagers look. The young man catches me watching them. His face is ghostly pale.

When I reach for the door, he shakes his head imperceptibly. The door chimes when I pull it open. Behind the counter, the clerk, his eyes half-closed, stares at the register. His hand hovers over the open cash drawer, frozen. I motion for the young man and his mother to come toward me, toward the door, but the mother seems incapable, gripped by an invisible fear.

Landred is nowhere to be seen.

Quickly, I close the distance between the two humans and me. Even hunched over, they both seem impossibly tall. "Is she okay?"

It's as if the woman snaps from out of a trance. "What? I... where is it?"

I haul the young man to his feet. "You need to leave. As fast as possible. Go."

Coming to herself, finally, the woman snags the young man by the shirt and flees, screaming and sobbing as the doorbell rings behind her.

The soft squeal of a swinging freezer door brings me back around to search the aisles. "Landred? It's Clayson."

The freezer door shudders again. The word ICE is stamped in big letters over the top. Through the glass, I can see him without the filter of the Blueweb machine. Unlike in the projection, here, Landred has shape and definition. His skin is like rough-hewn marble, a patchwork of white and grey, but the surface ebbs and flows in tiny crystal avalanches. His neon veins pulse in silver and white. His eyes are pure golden light.

"Landred?"

I'm close enough to hear the crunch of ice chips. He's eating them like a rabid dog tearing through flesh. It's so like the crunch of bones I shiver. My throat bobs as I reach out and ease the door open. "Landred?"

His eyes shoot upward, glittering like golden diamonds. His skeletal stone jaw hinges open to form a word. Nothing comes out. But I see the sound wave if that's possible. A strange resonance pulses in my direction.

Lost. Need.

The words are so startling inside my mind that my grip slips on the handle and the freezer door slams shut. Before I can work up the courage to re-open it, Landred's whole body quakes into particles, and he slips through the top of the freezer, somehow making the bags of ice in his hands as immaterial as him.

Need. This time it's a desperate moan. He clutches the bag of ice closer to him as if he's afraid I will take it.

"Alright. Relax. You need… ice? Why do you need ice?"

You made this.

This catches me off guard. "What?"

Forged connection. Recipe.

"Like to make something? I don't understand."

He becomes material again. *You know! You caused this! You did!*

Remember. He bares his glistening teeth at me, swoops down, and seizes my shoulder.

Pain sears through my temples. I remember every unpleasant thing that has ever happened to me and some that haven't: A bruised knee. A broken ankle. The feeling of a rock smashing my thumb. My mother being unable to speak with me. Am I even walking yet? My father cries, sitting on the edge of his bed. Night stars. The burning of a brightstorm. My flesh glowing with fire. The tip of a knife protruding from my chest. Gamgim, with its mismatched trees and thin oxygen. My thoughts freeze on Gamgim.

I come to myself, gasping for breath.

There. Landred says, sitting on the floor with bags of ice in his lap.

I catch my breath. "The day I left the cabin. The day I met Rugnus."

His form disassembles and reassembles itself again. *Need.*

"There are other wraiths there. Is that—"

He buries his face in the ice and crunches.

"Should I go to Gamgim? What's there? Would that help you?"

His figure flutters again. His eyes flicker and disappear. Hollow sockets stare back at me. A white flame starts somewhere inside his skull. *Need a guide.*

I step back involuntarily just as the door chimes again.

Landred careens forward, and I feel the searing pain in my head again. I hold up my bracelet, but it has no power here. The pain increases. Something is terribly wrong. That's when I realized I'm not immune to this creature's power. What had the news called him? Brain Killer.

I'm a champion. Will it create a dungeon in this convenience store if I die here? What will be the heart of my dungeon? I glance over my shoulder, hoping no one else has chosen to die with me, but I find a familiar face.

Lagnar Emberfence sits in a motorized wheelchair, oxygen

mask whispering. The surface effects have wreaked havoc on him. He looks worse than when I first met him in his workshop with Rugnus. Baggy-eyed, skin sagging, his normally smoothed vest is rumpled, and he's missed a button.

He squints. "It can't be. Well, spit and slateworms, Clayson Brightstorm. Coming here was an enormously stupid thing to do. Looks like I came just in the nick of time."

He motors forward. With an aluminum foil hat, a tin bucket in his lap, and gold earrings, he looks like someone you could find on a street corner somewhere predicting an alien invasion. He grabs a muffin and hurls it at the wraith. "Alright, you devil, now back up. Go on. Get!"

For reasons unknown, Landred's eyes dim. Then he floats toward the back of the store, snapping his jaw as if he were a tamed lion.

I stumble back toward Lagnar. "How did—"

"Wraithbait," Lagnar says. "Seems to work the opposite way with this new breed. I'm calling them wraithlings." He jangles a few tungsten bracelets on his wrist.

I scan all the objects hanging from him. Sure enough, he's wearing every craft type. Wraithbait.

Lagnar snarls. "Thing doesn't like being controlled."

The rest of my party comes tumbling through the door. Rugnus takes one look at Lagnar and tries to use the lapel I gave him last year as if he will melt the wheels on his chair, but nothing happens.

Lagnar laughs heartily, but it turns quickly into a wheeze. He opens a valve on his oxygen tank and puts on the mask. "Who's there? Rugnus, no doubt? Not a very nice welcome for the guy who just saved your buddy's life. You can't use craft around these wraithlings." He gestures to the back of the store.

"Cool name. Wait, what do you mean you can't use craft?" Koglim digs in his pockets for something to test. He pulls out a tin coin and scrunches his face, but nothing happens.

"Not gonna work," Lagnar says. "If you—" He stops when my

mom shifts around Koglim. "Queen Azbena. I-I didn't know you were here." His voice is softer, and his respirator kicks into a higher gear.

"Former queen," she says. "You look horrid, Lagnar."

Looking back and forth between them, a creeping suspicion enters my mind. They know each other. More than that, they knew each other. He's roughly my dad's age and would've lived in Whurrimduum about the same time. In all our discussions about Lagnar, she's never mentioned it.

Rugnus strides forward. "I don't need craft to deal with you."

Lagnar reaches under his wheelchair and pulls a shotgun from some hidden location. He pumps it, chambering a round.

"Nuh-uh. Not unless yours is bigger. Got guns? That's how the surface works. See, up here, bullets and dollars are more important than a good AMP score. So, I'll be leaving. You guys might wanna get ahead of me. When the wraithbait gets out of range, the wraithling might get some ideas about making y'all brain dead."

"Ide," Koglim whispers. "That *really* is a good name for this thing."

Lagnar gestures with the shotgun for everyone to move toward the door.

The grit of my sneakers tugs against the floor. "We can't leave. Not yet. We came for answers, Bluekeeper."

Jeiah ruffles at my use of the name. It was only a few months ago that Langnar's cousin, and Jeiah's mentor, had use of the name as the keeper of Bluebottle Dungeon. But he was killed in the attack on StoneYoke. When Lagnar took over his job, he took the name. None of us call him this, but it's an olive branch. He's also the only one who knows where the last piece of unused mithrium is, so I need his cooperation. This is our only lead.

I continue, "You're the only member of the Keeper's Council on the surface; we request your assistance."

After a second, Lagnar points to me with the shotgun. "Fine. How can I be of service? And don't bother asking for that bright little cube of metal you threw to me outside of Mithriumbane. You ain't getting that back. The way I see it, you screwed up your chances when you made Vor that stupid crown—yeah, I heard about that—and now we're all stuck here because of you."

"Fair enough... for now. But if we need it to stop Vor, then—"

Lagnar laughs long and hard, nearly choking himself. Rugnus stands close to him, ready to help bury his body. "What world do you live in? There's no coming back from this. Vor is in total control. Best we can do is live as many days as we can on the surface until the effects put us all in an early grave."

"Lagnar," my mom says. "You're here. It's not a coincidence. You're trying to do the same thing as us. You're trying to help. I know you."

"This?" He gestures to the many objects he wears to help neutralize the wraithling. "This's just a quick patch job. Figure these humans don't deserve to have their brains sucked out."

"How'd you find the place?" Jeiah asks.

His eyes shift over us. "I watch the news."

"So, you're still living in the area?" Rugnus pries.

"Enough!" Lagnar says. "Okay, little Therias." A pang of guilt hits me at the name. He smiles under the oxygen mask. "What crazy idea are you having?"

I step away from the bags of ice on the ground and glance at the back of the store. "He's back in the freezer. The wraithling. His name is Landred Wolfstaff."

"So that's what happened when you broke open the dungeon? The wraith meandered topside and started rampaging. Good job. Any idea what happened to Wolfstaff herself? Think she passed on permanently?"

Lagnar doesn't know Wolfstaff is now Kel.

Rugnus shakes his head. "Let's not worry about that. What's the plan?"

Is it right to keep that from Lagnar? He's been my family's enemy for a long time, but still... something about how Mom speaks to him leaves room for doubt. "I'm going to talk to

Landred again. When he blocked my craft, I felt him in my mind. He showed me a bunch of weird events and all the times I've felt worried or afraid. He showed me Gamgim."

"The night we met?" Rugnus guesses.

I shake my head. "It was daytime. I think it was something that hasn't happened yet." I don't tell them about envisioning a knife through my chest. I still can't be sure what that was about. If it was my future, maybe I can still change it.

The air becomes still. My mom looks at me. Jeiah looks at me. Rugnus keeps his eye on Lagnar, who's looking at me.

"I don't know what it means, but maybe Gamgim holds the answer. There are wraiths there, maybe like Landred."

Jeiah considers this, shooting me a knowing look. "That could confirm some of our other suspicions about… things."

She has her back toward Lagnar. She must want me to connect the other dots. Those wraiths could be from the protodungeons. The ones we think belonged to Ara, Vor, and Tas.

"I can reach him," I say slowly. "It could be the piece we're missing."

"Wraithking," Lagnar whispers. Then, back at normal volume, he says. "Alright then. Talk to him if you think it will help us. I'll be right behind you. He shouldn't attack when the wraithbait is close. At least, he hasn't before."

I start back toward the freezers again. Lagnar trailing me, everyone else trailing him. "Hasn't before?" I ask.

Lagnar clears his throat. "May have tried to stop him the last time."

Koglim mocks him. "Switching to hero now, huh?"

"I wouldn't expect a person of limited intelligence like yourself to understand the ethical parameters I set for myself."

"Watch it," Rugnus says. "Still not sure we couldn't maybe just kill you and make a run for it."

Lagnar pats his gun. "Try it. It'll be a blast."

Ahead of me, behind the freezer door, I find Landred waiting, dug into the ice.

"What's with the ice?" Jeiah says. "Got to mean something."

"Not everything has a meaning, Jeiah," Koglim says.

"This might," Mom says.

"He told me it was about a recipe. A lot of recipes use ice, though."

Jeiah glances down at all the ice. "Could he mean Yinzar's recipe?"

"Maybe. Landred?" As I reach for the freezer door, Koglim sucks in an audible breath, like we're jumping into a pool. "Landred? Are you okay?"

His cracked stone face focuses and unfocuses on Lagnar, and a broken scream echoes inside the freezer. He shifts, and small pieces of stone break free from his arm, melting against the ice like phantom snowflakes. *Make it stop. Guide me there.*

"You're dying," I guess. "I'll help. Tell me about Gamgim."

At the mention of Gamgim, the tiny grains that shape his face tighten into something almost Loamin. For a brief second, he's the gaunt, sad-eyed young man desperate not to be separated from his mother. I wonder if he knows she returned to Kel's body.

His golden eyes dart to Lagnar.

The craft must be hurting him. As clear as anything spoken by the living, he repeats the name, *Gamgim*. In a last soundless scream of pain, he vanishes. The bags of ice shift from his absence.

Rugnus immediately turns his hands into molten fire and lunges for Lagnar's gun. He's using Sular, my dad's lapel pin. I throw my shield up and block him.

I snap. "Calm down! We're not doing this!"

Instead of being angry, Rugnus looks almost relieved. Lagnar lowers his shotgun and squints at me, confused. "Protecting me?" Lagnar asks, disbelief in his eyes.

"If there's a way to stop Vor, it's what we all want. No matter what else we have between us. If there's a way to stop him..."

"Okay," Lagnar says, tucking his shotgun out of sight. "Sure, I'll bite. So, Gamgim? We start there?"

"Good a place as any," I say.

Koglim's eyes widen so fast I think I hear them snap. "Well, count me out. Besides that, this is just one more side mission. I don't mind a wraith or two skulking around a dungeon during a raid, but you're talking about a small town full of them. Gamgim." He says the word with reverent fear. "No one—"

"I can. Wraiths don't affect me."

"This one did," Mom says. I hear the protectiveness in her voice. It's different from my dad. He mostly wanted to protect my freedom so I could do what I wanted; her fear is more visceral. She can't lose me.

"Landred was different from the other wraiths. He *wants* me to take him there. I could do it. Maybe there's a connection between the change in Landred. Or maybe we can understand how Torlina Wolfstaff became Kel. Or who Ara once was." The second the information is in the air, Rugnus and Jeiah cut angry looks toward me. But I'm done with trying to cut people out of the equation. We need as many Loamin on our side as possible.

Lagnar takes the mask away from his face. "Did I miss something? Wolfstaff became Kel? Come again?"

Rugnus closes his eyes, probably so I can't see how far back in his head they roll.

I clear my throat. "Vor, Kel, Ara...all the Dura, they're—they were—former champions."

Emberfence blinks and shakes his head like he has water in his ear. "Run that by me again. That's a new one."

"Wolfstaff is Kel. Vor is—"

"Clayson." At first, I think Jeiah's trying to get me to stop talking, but when I look at her, her eyes are searching for something far away. She squints, rubs the air like she's cleaning a mirror, and then squints some more. "We've got company."

"Well, pull up the display," Koglim says, though his eyes wander to the sandwiches sitting under the warmers.

"I can't," she says. "We haven't gotten Blueweb to run that way."

"Blue what?" Lagnar takes out a blueish-metal key and holds it up, staring. "What is it you're looking at?"

"Someone shut him up," Jeiah snaps. "I think darksmiths are coming down the road."

Rugnus risks a look out the window. "Can't see them. Does it say—"

Lagnar whistles. "You did it. That's how you found the wraith. You must have connected bluelink with the human wideweb."

"Internet," I correct.

Lagnar waves off my comment. "No wonder she was Bluekeeper's Paladin. When this is all over, you want your job back? I could use a head paladin."

Jeiah's lip curls. Somehow it makes her even more attractive. "Not if it's run by you. I'm still not clear about your involvement in StoneYoke. In the true Bluekeeper's assassination."

He winces. "I didn't understand what Vor could do with a craftprint. But if you wanna have someone to blame, fine. Fair enough. Get in line."

"Jeiah," Rugnus says. "Come on. How close are they? Does it name them?"

Jeiah clinches the air, shakes something invisible, rubs her thumb, and forefingers together like she's trying to separate stubborn pieces of paper. "There's maybe five or six of them. Their names are all garbled. Like looking at static. They're trying to break into my Blueweb connection."

"Can they?" Koglim asks.

She shrugs. "Who knows? Haven't worked the bugs out yet. We better go."

"Bluekeeper," I say, grabbing the back of his wheelchair. "You're with us."

"I—no. I don't want to." He reaches back and tries to peel my hand off the wheelchair handles.

"It's the safest place," I say.

Mom looks directly at him. "No arguments, Lagnar. We have the mithrium shield. We don't even feel the effects of the surface there."

He clears his throat. "Shoulda led with that. Sounds nice."

Rugnus takes out Icho, but Jeiah's hand flies to her mouth. "Rugnus. I think it... no, he wouldn't. It's—"

Six individuals stride out from behind the filling stations toward the convenience store. Five wearing grotesque golden masks. The sixth person stands a distance behind them in a brown jacket trimmed with small white beads, his head bowed.

Rugnus gapes. He gropes for words. "I did see him. He was... I thought I saw a flash of gold. It was him on the road. Bhogda Grimflail." Then his fist comes to his mouth shaking. "That one is... that's my mother. I'm sure of it."

He could be right. The build is close. But she's wearing a warped golden mask, ill-shaped with scratch marks raked across the eyes and mouth. Her hair and clothes are unmistakable. In fact, it may be the same thing she wore the day we fled from Vor. Whoever this Grimflail is, I'm getting a sinking feeling we need to run.

Four other people wear similar masks. All different shapes but with unique scars. None look as though they were made by the same hand, only with the same dull gold element.

"Grimflail," Rugnus says. "I'll kill him."

A soft squeak comes from Koglim. "He's got Hardkeeper, too, and I think—no, no, no—that's Brude, from my raiding team."

Jeiah shakes her head. "We need to go. Like now."

Through the glass of the large windows, I watch the skin along Rugnus' mother's arms turn thick and gray. She lowers her head. They're coming for us.

"Rugnus, now!"

His nostrils flare. "We're not going anywhere. He's got my mother."

"And my friend," Koglim returns. "But we both know we're not prepared for this. For him." He aims a thick finger out the window at the person Rugnus called Grimflail. With his other hand, he grabs Rugnus' shoulders and shakes him hard.

With audible disgust, Rugnus tucks Sular away and retrieves Icho.

The transition from the Rockies to the Appalachians is seamless. We're standing right next to the floating shield when we appear. No one is physically hurt. In fact, with the surface effects gone, everyone breathes a sigh of relief. Even so, an unnatural quiet settles on the group.

"What was that about?" I ask. "Was your mom gonna attack us? She can't be under Vor's influence. So far, all the darksmiths we've come across have been sadistic monsters, people willing to kill us on sight. But your mother..."

Winta and Hemdi wander out of the shop. They must have been watching for us. They stop dead in their tracks the second they see Lagnar. Hemdi backs up a few steps, swinging Echel to the other side of his body.

"You found him?" he says.

"That's not all we found," Koglim adds.

With a monstrous roar, Rugnus throws Icho as far as he can. I reach for him, but he brushes me off, marching into the grove.

Winta whistles. "That's new. What's with him?"

Koglim whispers the foreign name again. "Bhogda Grimflail."

Winta steals a glance at Rugnus as he disappears into the trees. "Brick."

FORM NEW SPECTERS

No one will say a single word about Grimflail.

Not Winta, who leans in close to Hemdi and whispers something. Not Koglim, who insists we let Rugnus tell that story. And not Hemdi, who only says, "I did make potatoes and grilled lamb. Perhaps a late lunch first?" Leave it to Hemdi to take care of everyone, to want to feed us as a solution.

Lagnar eases the valve closed on his oxygen tank, removes his mask, and draws in a deep breath. "Y'all have lamb, and friends, and Ide's blessing over there"—he points to the mithrium shield — "shoulda let you find me earlier." He hoists himself from the wheelchair and takes a tentative step. "And my sight is already improving. That shield…"

I don't want to let this go yet. "Okay, come on. Mom? Andalynn? Someone has to know about Grimflail."

Andalynn shrugs. "I don't know enough to explain. Rugnus doesn't talk about it."

"Can we do this over food?" Lagnar says. "I'm starving."

Hemdi and Winta reluctantly lead him back toward the ministack. As soon as they open the door, Gem and Nox sprint out, barking at him. Lagnar doesn't so much as flinch. He crouches down and grabs one in a playful headlock, scratching the thick fur on its head. "And who are these good boys?"

Winta commands, "Down." Gem listens immediately, but Nox takes another gentle pull. "Gem is a girl," she snaps.

As we enter, Lagnar takes a huge whiff of the aroma hanging in the air. "Smells right nice, Hemdi. Where's the kitchen?"

With everyone else content to eat, I wander into the den. I find the remote and turn on the news, just to have something to mitigate my thoughts. Vor is one thing, but the fact these darksmiths are willingly following him sends lava through my veins. And now he's using our friends and family against us.

When mom enters the room a few minutes later, I haven't even sat down.

"I can tell you what I know," she says. "It's not much."

"Until Rugnus is ready to talk, I guess that's all I can get."

She motions for me to sit and then takes a chair across from me. "Bhogda Grimflail is a known murderer. He was brought before the council on charges of corruption of craft a couple years ago, and he was sentenced to life in Palecloak prison."

"Palecloak? I thought Keelcrawl—"

"Keelcrawl is unbreakable, leaving its occupants in perfect suspended animation. Palecloak, though, is a house of torture. As much as your sister and I have tried to shut it down, the council maintained that the handful of its prisoners deserve worse than death."

"But what did he do? What's corruption of craft?"

"You saw what he does. He enslaves people with the use of those gold masks. He has full control over them. I don't remember the details, but a girl was killed. It must be this friend Rugnus mentioned."

"Valifra Hollyhelm," I say, remembering. "She was part of Rugnus' team. A goldmage. She died a while before I arrived in Tungsten City. Someone mentioned her before the Keeper's Social last year. Rugnus didn't want to talk about her then either."

"So, we wait."

We watch the news together for a while. After a report on a flood in the southeast and wildfires raging west of the Rockies, she sighs deeply and says, "Sometimes it seems just as bad up here."

My mind goes back to StoneYoke, making quick pit stops in Thiffimdal and Gythanstyan, the ruined city once wrapped around Geum Ide. "It's not. And I hope it never gets that way."

Out of nowhere, she says, "Will you try to go to Gamgim?"

The thought had been rattling around in my mind. "If I do, I'll go alone. We don't know what effect those wraiths will have on anyone else."

"Your father did a lot of things alone."

"No. He did them in secret. There's a difference."

"This is how it started, you know."

"What started?"

She laughs so gently, with such sadness, my insides twist into a giant knot. My dad's absence—wherever he ended up after the confrontation with Vor—looms between us.

"We used to tell each other everything," Mom says. "But when he started working with my mother and the conjurers, we started drifting apart."

"You two are not... you're not like your parents." I've tried to get Mom talking about what Vor did to her mother, about Yinzar being gone, but she's changed the subject every time. Her parents didn't seem to have a glowing relationship, and now her mother's gone. Killed by Vor.

She shakes her head and dabs a tear away. "I know. We're not. I love him, miss him so much it hurts. He'd never be cruel like my mother or purposefully absent like my dad. He loves me. Us. He'd do anything for his family. Anything. And I want him back as much as I've ever wanted anything in this world."

Lagnar clears his throat and walks into the room, holding a plate of roasted potatoes. "I'm betting he feels much the same." He sits down and leans back on the couch, putting his feet on the coffee table. He takes another bite and says, "I was there when he first laid eyes on you. The new keeper in status for Silverlamp, the daughter of an Everbloom—just a sight to behold. That was a Keeper's Social to remember. Even though Therias was the prince of Whurrimduum, he still didn't think he could win you over."

"You know he didn't have to," Mom says. Her hands are glued together in her lap.

"Either way, you two were meant for each other. Lost my friend to you fair and square. He never looked back."

"You were friends?" I ask. "Somehow, I can't picture that."

"Eh, picture what you want, but friends we were. How else do you think we came around to the high level of animosity we currently enjoy?"

Something simmers under my skin. "Maybe it's because you killed my dad's parents. Unless I have that wrong."

His head weaves from side to side, more of a solemn dance than a firm no. "I've tired of saying this, but King Brightstorm himself ordered me on that mission."

"But you used the mithrium. You murdered millions of—"

"I followed my orders. Then I was banished for it. And if you didn't catch it down near Mithriumbane, I'm pretty sure Vor orchestrated the whole thing. With craft, you never know what's real or imagined."

"Death toll seemed pretty real to me," I say. My mom rests a hand on my forearm.

Lagnar inclines his head and turns to the TV but continues speaking. "That part's real. Therias... I can understand why he won't forgive me."

"It's the day he joined the conjurers," Mom says. "He started working with Glaris to find ways for Loamin to live without craft. He went at it with the same passion he had for ending the war. That's just who he is. A dreamer, to steal a human phrase. It's why we need him back. If anyone can think of a way out of this, a way to defeat Vor, he can."

"Now *that* I believe," Lagnar says.

The conversation remains suspended in the air, so much left unsaid. But something mysterious tumbled out in these short minutes. It's nothing like my dad's secrets. I know the timeline from the end of the Mithrium Wars—anyone with bluelink knows that much—but hearing it from them is like peeling back an old wound.

Andalynn's voice floats over from the doorway. "Rugnus is coming back up the road." There's a sense of worry in the words that go beyond Andalynn's usual weight-of-the-world aura. One of the darksmiths almost killed her this morning. The pink of her round face hasn't fully returned.

Mom is the first up, then Lagnar, then me. We all wait in the large living area. Winta switches tasks with Hemdi, hands him her phone and takes Echel on her lap. She taps the phone screen and gives Hemdi a quick look.

Rugnus comes through the door, taking only a few steps into the carpeted area.

"Nice. Everyone's here." There's an edge to his words, but I can't read any anger in them. When our eyes meet, I find something fierce and determined, like we're about to walk into a dungeon without any relics. "This isn't going to be... not going to talk about Valifra. Right now, cooler heads are needed. Have to work through other problems, stay centered on Vor, but—"

"But," Andalynn adds, "Grimflail is one of those problems."

"He is," Rugnus acknowledges. "He's helping Vor willingly. And if he's out there searching for us, for me, then any quick budge to Whurrimduum, to Tungsten City, the dungeons, spit, even the surface—is now many times more dangerous, potentially deadly."

"There's no way to remove the masks?" Mom asks.

"You can't. That's how people... no, there's no way."

Lagnar purses his lips. "Then Hardkeeper, your mother—"

"Brude," Koglim adds.

"—they ain't coming back?"

Rugnus nods, blinking rapidly. His voice catches. "No. But

when we end this, when we defeat Vor, when we're free to go back home, justice will catch up with Bhogda Grimflail."

Brig smiles almost cruelly. "A thousand lifetimes in Keelcrawl oughta do it."

"Not quite," Rugnus says. This statement drops the temperature of the whole room, and Rugnus lets everyone sit with the implications for a long moment. "Until then, we've got work to do. Koglim and I will recheck the perimeter. Jeiah, Winta. We're up to thirty-five refugees spread over five locations. Send a notification. Explain what happened. The graybulbs should keep them safe, and the food and supply automation should still be in effect. They'll have to make do."

"Agreed," Winta says.

His shoulders relax. Maybe he was expecting to have an argument, but he's not wrong about lying low. His posture changes too, head bowed, face pinched tight, fighting off tears.

"We'll stop Grimflail, Rugnus," I say. "And I'm not giving up on your mother, Brude, or even Hardkeeper. You didn't have the mithrium shield when you faced him last time, when he took Valifra from you. And you didn't have me."

Emotion threatens to overwhelm my friend. Then, all at once, Andalynn wraps her arms around him. I charge across the room and pull them both toward me.

"Group hug!" Koglim shouts with glee.

He and Brig join the circle. Winta reluctantly comes toward us, Echel in her arms. Hemdi is close behind. I hear Lagnar curse and go back to the other room. Jeiah graces my back with a soft hand, then grabs Winta and heads for the door, to Winta's obvious relief.

Rugnus pulls away and motions for Koglim. "Come on, you big idiot. Let's check the perimeter."

Koglim chuckles but follows him.

The world reshapes around this one moment. We have each other.

Mom checks on Lagnar while Andalynn returns to her room upstairs, leaving Brig, Hemdi, and me.

Hemdi looks at me strangely, then down to Winta's phone. "Who wants to help with dishes?" he asks.

Brig coughs. "I better help Koglim and Rugnus. Or maybe Winta with Echel. Yeah." He scoots out of the room.

I eye Hemdi with suspicion. "Okay, you never need help with dishes. You enjoy doing them. What's up?"

Hemdi takes one more look at the phone. "What happened with Landred?"

The question brings me back to my moment with the wraithling, with Landred. I walk Hemdi through everything that happened, only leaving out some of the more personal memories Landred showed me and the vision of myself with a knife sticking out of me. When I tell him my theory—that Landred might be dying—Hemdi purses his lips and glances back at Winta's phone.

"Why the recipe? What's the connection there?"

"Something about Gamgim? And I think—once we get a team together—"

"No." Hemdi shows me Icho. I had forgotten he picked it up when Rugnus threw it. "Only us. We must bring him to Gamgim."

"You mean now? Rugnus just said we should be careful. That we needed to regroup."

"That's fine and good in theory, but Landred is in pain. He told you. When I saw him—that image—I felt it. Eventually—in an hour, a few days, or a week, you will start thinking the same thing. So, we need to go now."

"No, we need a plan. We need to talk to everyone else. Leaving? That's how I will get in trouble."

"Jeiah will forgive you."

"It's not just... look, we can't be rash. Grimflail is out there."

Hemdi shakes his head. "We get Landred. He can protect us. Then we go to Gamgim. Simple."

"And how many more wraiths are there in Gamgim? It's the

only place outside the dungeons they're known to exist. It's too dangerous."

"Not for us. Wraiths can only take your strongest craft."

"Yes, Silverlamp's brothers took tincraft from you, but we don't know that another wraith can't take something else. If anything, I should go alone. I'm Wraithking. And Landred asked me."

"No one has ever had two crafts taken by a wraith."

I wave this comment away. "Unfortunately, no-one-has-ever is the kind of territory we're in."

"Can you just... I need to do this." He tightens his grip on Icho.

"This isn't like you, Hemdi."

"I understand. I... I know that. But I also know how I felt when I saw Landred's pain. It's the same pain I feel when I want to heal something in the garden or speak to a flower. His loss is mine. Will you come with me or not?"

There's no talking him down. Hemdi, the consummate peace-keeper of the group, has found a mission that requires his unique empathy. We're perhaps the only two Loamin in existence who would care about what happens to a wraith. "Did you at least tell Winta?"

He shakes his head.

"Forget the wraiths, then. I'm dead even if we live through this."

Soft footsteps land behind me. Hemdi looks toward the entryway.

"Have you guys seen Winta's phone?"

Jeiah walks toward us.

"Clayson," Hemdi says softly, his eyes pleading to leave. He's right. It's now or never. My mistake is looking back at Jeiah, who can read faces as easily as I can read the path to the top of a fifty-foot cliff.

She rushes forward, eyes pleading, but her hands scramble for something in her pocket.

Without a nod or acknowledgment from Hemdi, I reach for Icho. I hear Jeiah snap her fingers at the exact same moment. Something small, metal maybe, clicks against Icho just under my hand, but we budge.

I don't feel the added gravity. I don't get nauseous from the effects of a budge. Except, this time, there's a sinking feeling in my stomach. Silently, I add this choice to the things I will need to apologize to Jeiah about. I scan my surroundings. Headstones litter the ground, some at crooked angles. Thick-rooted oaks fill all the other spaces—layers of old leaves and muddy tufts of grass.

I ease Icho from Hemdi's hand.

He peers around me. "Did Jeiah—"

Jeiah's voice drops over my shoulders like ice water. "Yes, *she* did." She wanders out from behind a scrub oak. Leans over and retrieves a single aluminum coin from the ground. "*She* is a paladin of Tungsten City and can follow you into the heart of Ide itself and not lose your trail." She jabs a finger at me. "This was a stupid idea. Whatever *this* is."

"It's my fault," Hemdi offers.

Jeiah glances at him, features doubtful. "This was your idea? Where exactly are we?"

"Followed Landred's location data, I think," I say.

Hemdi agrees with a nod.

Jeiah looks between us, no doubt gathering a case for when we return.

"And you two latchers think you can't be affected. That's a leap, Hemdi. This won't get us any closer to stopping Vor."

"I'm not sure that's accurate," I say, but I stumble at the daggers Jeiah sends me. "Um, well, it's not exactly related to our mission, but if we can understand what Landred is, it could be one more tool we use against Vor."

"For once," Hemdi says, "I'm not thinking about Vor."

"The risk from Landred is less for us," I tell her.

Jeiah only smiles dangerously. "Winta's going to kill both of you."

We both respond. "We know."

Something shifts in her stance. Her body relaxes. "So, what is this place?" Her eyes flicker between headstones. "Some kind of memorial?"

"A cemetery," I volunteer.

She steps back, scanning the ground, then shifts forward again like she's trying to avoid stepping on anything. "So, there's..."

"Dead humans? Yeah."

"Melt me. I thought Loamin traditions were weird. Do they at least make sure they're dead?"

"Well, yeah. They take all their organs out and..." I glance around the graveyard abruptly, uncomfortable with the tone of our discussion. "...they make sure."

She shivers. Maybe it's the wind whipping around the patches of scrub oaks.

Oak trees. Something's strange about the presence of oak trees. About the headstones. Jeiah interrupts my thoughts.

"I don't like this," she says, "But if you're going to do this, you need wraithbait. Not that I *want* to agree with Emberfence, but it was effective last time."

Hemdi answers. "Clayson said it hurt him, drove him away."

"But Clayson got answers."

Whatever direction my mind had been going about oak trees, I switch back to the here and now. "I'm not looking for answers anymore. I know what has to be done. If he stays tangible enough to touch, then I can bring him to Gamgim."

Jeiah surveys Icho again. "Can you use craft that close to him?"

"Icho is bound to work." I pause. "What do you think we should do?"

With a quick shrug, she says, "You've already decided to take him to Gamgim."

"I'm trying here, Jeiah. I mean it. What should we do?"

"Of all the insane things... I might actually believe Landred won't hurt you. But... I'm not sure about Hemdi. And I'm *definitely* not safe around him. How far away is he?"

Hemdi already has Winta's phone out, scrolling and pinching the screen awkwardly. Of all of us, he has been the person slowest to use human technology. "Not far. That way."

"I don't think he knows he's hurting anyone," I add. "But if this works, it will be for the best. He can't keep wandering. He's hurting people. I'll try to help him understand."

Jeiah sweeps an approving arm outward. "Lead the way."

I nod. "When we get close enough, I'll give my bracelet to Hemdi. If Landred comes your way—"

"It won't protect her," Hemdi says. "But if Grimflail finds us..."

"Right, and there's that."

Hemdi leads us closer to a thick grove, the floor of leaves transitioning to something muddy and trampled. Here and there, I see pieces of headstone scattered on the ground as if something recently smashed them. The oaks, the stone... something connects in my mind.

I point to the broken pieces of the headstone. "Would you say this is onyx?"

One side of the chunk of rock is still polished and inky black, but ribbons in the middle are a rough yellow-brown. "Onyx?" Jeiah says. "I... yeah. Do you think he's still looking for pieces of the recipe?"

"It has to be. Ice, at the convenience store. Onyx, here and... and..." My head swivels toward the grove. "Oak. Those are oak."

"What else did you code into the recipe for a mithrium object?" Hemdi asks.

"Amethyst dust, a silver bucket for the ice, the pieces of oak are slimy... not sure what that's about. Oh, and gypsum. Any reason a wraith would be concerned about a recipe that turns mithrium into a usable object?"

"None whatsoever," Jeiah says, "but I would lead with that. Get Landred talking."

We come to the edge of the oak grove. The trees are bushy, but a single large opening leads inside. I slip my bracelet off and hand it to Hemdi. "If anything happens, run. I can get back with Icho. Jeiah, do you have another budge?"

"We've got this part, Clayson. Go find Landred."

"Sorry you got dragged into this."

Her face softens. "Dragged into this? I'm a paladin. It's nice to feel like I'm protecting something. Even if it is just a couple of idiots."

Her smile sends a thrill through me again. That's all I want: for her to be happy. To spend a lazy afternoon in the clearing or the orchard. But that's not the hand life dealt us.

At least she's talking to me.

I enter the grove. These aren't the majestic oaks you find guarding a palatial estate. They're scrub oaks, twice my height, but leaning and feeble, more branch than trunk.

I find Landred in a small dead-grass clearing at the heart of the grove, tearing the oaks to pieces. I'm not prepared to see him eating them like the ice chips, his white stone body half crumbling, half broken. Flecks of stone float in the cloud around him as if most of it could be stripped away with a good breeze. He's draped in gold neon. And I make another connection. White stone, gold, and silver neon. It's the colors of Wolfstaff Dungeon.

"Landred?"

The buzzing cloud of granite pieces collects along his skin, protruding in crystalline forms, desperate to stay connected to him. His face turns, eyes piercing into mine.

"Are you working on the recipe? Landred? Hey. Listen. I get it: the ice, the onyx, the oak. Is that what you're doing?"

The two golden orbs shift from neon gold to a haunting silver, dangerous and hate-filled.

Through grinding breaths, a moaning voice reaches my mind. *This keeps me.*

"Keeps you what? Alive?"

Suddenly he's confused. The features on his face sharpen. Shaking his head, he says, *Only thing I could do after I failed. At first, I tried to enter there, but it wouldn't let me enter. This helps.* He unhinges his stone jaw and places more oak inside.

"Enter where?"

After a quick swallow, his lip curls, and the expression is so alive I forget for a second what he is. *Gamgim.*

I take a step toward him, but his face instantly changes again; his eyes sockets and his mouth fill in with stone. More flakes of light lift from his shoulders like reverse snow, dissipating in the air. He circles to the right, pieces breaking off and reforming, suddenly looming over me. This could end badly. "Landred, whatever's happening, we can help. You need to trust me."

For a split second, Landred's face is visible, carved into the stone. *Connection.*

He lunges for me. I stumble backward, but he catches my wrist.

Pain shoots through my skull. Even worse than our last encounter. The fear isn't my own, but it's strong. I'm seeing myself through his eyes. My heart is dragged across hot coals, burned and bruised, then floats back and inhabits my body. Something is coming. I see a blazing light in the form of two figures burning, becoming nothing but particles of ash floating away. I'm surrounded by dark trees and strange shadowy geometric shapes.

A knife explodes out of my chest. My skin erupts, roiling like the surface of the sun. Now, I'm only bones as I search for solace, wandering the forest of Gamgim. What am I seeing? A gasp expands my lungs, and then it's over.

Landred has materialized in front of me, more real than he has ever been. *The forest is sour with evil, but it's the only way for me. I feel it.*

Searching his eyes, I find no fear, no anger, but an icy judgment.

"You're not afraid of going to Gamgim." I say. "You're afraid for me. Why?"

You have power over them. They want it back.

"This has to do with the curse, with being Wraithking. You called Gamgim evil. Aren't they wraiths like you?"

He shakes his head. His features soften, and he drops the oaks in his hands, almost looking alive again, as the stone softens into something closer to skin. *I regret tending to my mother. She was horrible to others in life, and she taught me to do the same. She molded me into a wraith long before I was trapped in her dungeon.*

"I'm sorry, Landred."

The dungeon only turned her into more of what she was in life.

"Do you know she's still alive? She's different now. And she doesn't remember her life as a Loamin. What's left in her memory is only her life as a Dura and her existence in the dungeon. She may know of you, but from the way I understand it, she doesn't remember anything before she died."

Then it's best if I just let go.

I place a hand on Landred's shoulder. The flashes of shadow and light, of what I fear is some future vision, flicker for a second, but I focus on Landred's eyes. "I will. But I brought two others. Please... we don't know if you can take their craft."

I will leave them be.

With Icho in my grip, I reach out for Hemdi and Jeiah. They appear next to me, and we budge to Gamgim. We don't appear in the forest but in the chamber where I was supposed to have my summation last year. My dad's wish, the tradition of the royals, might end with me. The space stretches into two darkened corridors. Behind us, the room is lit by dusty sunlight from the stairwell, but this side is lit only with torches. Landred is gone.

"Where is he?"

"Landred?" Jeiah asks. "Did you—"

"He's here somewhere," Hemdi says, but his thoughts must be far away. His voice is distant, and he stares up, up, and up.

Beyond the basin, tendrils of thin wires rise to the earthen ceiling far away, mercury dripping along the strands, accumulating in the basins, slow, steady, running droplets from the tree roots above into the basins. I step into the pool of mercury and trace my fingers over the woven metal, as high as I can reach, where the metal frays into individual wires. Above me, the wires are like a giant root system.

"I didn't understand this place when Dad sent me here. I understand it even less now. How can a wraith live outside of a dungeon? How can these wires hold craft so far away from the Foundation? Nothing made the trees above us."

Jeiah glints at the basins. "Gamgim is one of the true mysteries of the world. Even with everything we've learned about Loamin and Dura and the dungeons, this is different. These roots are metal, but the trees above appear normal."

"That's where he is," Hemdi says. "Above us, in the trees."

I step away from the basin. "Let's go, then."

Jeiah is about to start up the stairs, but I say, "You should stay behind us in case—"

She flashes a smile. "Trying to protect me still? I'm a paladin. I'm fine." She takes the steps two at a time.

I follow her. Hemdi follows me.

The surface is exactly like I remember it. A rock wall stretches away in both directions. Gravel extends from the base to the forest, like someone was trying to create a barrier between the two worlds. One world of hope and excitement, of childhood, and the other of loss and fear. One stone and grit, the other sunlight and nature.

Landred hovers at the edge of the forest. In front of him, the forest of Gamgim looms like a specter of something unholy. It's spun together from a thousand types of trees: beeches and oaks, firs, maples, and willows. My skin prickles as though something might rush out from under the boughs and drag me deep into the twisted tree roots below.

"I've never actually been here," Hemdi offers, the words

seeming as out of place as the large ponderosa next to the willow tree. "They say the wraiths come only at night."

Luckily the sun is still high. Though this forest shouldn't fit at the top of Pike's Peak. So much of the Loamin world exists inside strange places, expanding the limits of reality.

Landred is half form, half swirling broken pieces, gazing into the forest. *Home to things both living and dead, a dungeon spun of starlight and crystal.*

Jeiah tosses me a confused look. "Are you communicating with him?"

In answer, Landred's cold eyes find her. "Something you cannot see. But Clayson, I can show you... and this one..." His gaze falls on Hemdi. "He knows loss. He has room to accept the truth."

I repeat Landred's words to the group.

"Knows loss? And I don't?" Jeiah asks.

Landred's eyes burn dark as obsidian.

"He's talking about my lost craft," Hemdi says. "I don't think you want to see what he can see." He steps closer to Landred before I can stop him. "Show me."

Landred's smile is cold, but something behind his eyes is distinctly alive.

His arm morphs into a sharp stone of light, and he stabs it through the back of Hemdi's skull. Jeiah screams and jumps forward, but I catch her. This isn't an attack. At least, I hope it isn't. In quick succession, the dagger of light withdraws from Hemdi, and he falls toward my arms. I think of the dagger sticking out of my chest as the cloud enters my torso. Is that what that vision meant?

I gasp as a trail of light pulls from my body.

Gamgim is no longer a forest but a valley glowing with scattered crystalline trees. At the center, strange blurry shapes rest in what can only be a man-made pattern. A settlement? An ancient, unknowable feeling permeates the whole place. Strands and bursts of light hang suspended in the air, and everywhere I look appears as a reflection, a ghost of what this place once was.

"Clayson, answer me!" Jeiah screams. "What is it? What's happening?"

The desiccated form of Landred is gone. He's Loamin again, radiant and transparent. Healed, but still somehow ghostly. He smiles. *Now we can see Ide for what it truly is.*

Hemdi nods his agreement. "Or what it once was."

NEAR THE TRUTH

This is the Valley of Ide.

The weight of this unnatural knowledge arrives sharp and unwelcome. It's similar to the moment I heard the name Wraithking for the first time. And yet, this feels deceptive, a half-truth, as if the forest holds something back, something important. It's this withholding that moves my empty hand toward my bracelet.

Instinct. Defense.

Hemdi is awestruck, tears of shimmering light stuck in his eyes, hurt and healing competing in his expression. But that light reflects the forest. This determination, fierce in some certainty he's carrying, stands as another warning for me—don't let your guard down, Clayson.

Beside me, I can almost feel Jeiah's eye scanning the world, scanning me with powers of discernment that go far beyond any craft. It's an ability woven into her DNA. I see past the radiance washing out her features down to the beauty in her very bones. I can't lose her. We shouldn't have come here. It's too dangerous. I shouldn't have let Hemdi talk me into this. I read the same fear on Jeiah's face.

"Do you feel that?" Hemdi asks in wonder.

Jeiah breaks eye contact with me. "Feel what?"

"It's beautiful," he mutters.

Landred walks toward the forest. Instead of the statue-man, all sharp angles and glowing seams of silver and gold, he's flesh and blood. I blink, trying to understand how he can look so alive. "Now you see," he says, his voice clearer than ever. "We have to get to the center of the valley."

Hemdi moves to his side, but my gaze returns to the forest. That's when I notice—nothing. Nothing stirs. There's no movement. No swaying of the trees. There's no sound coming from the valley. This realization, more than anything else, draws my worry out into lines of stark fear. "Jeiah? Is there any way to... I know you don't have the beholder, but..."

She rubs a reflective button on her pants pocket and shakes her head. "I wouldn't even know what to look for, but there's no evidence of craft. Explain it to me in detail. What are you seeing? Whatever Landred did to you. I'm not seeing the same thing."

"No craft?" Hemdi says, blinking for seemingly the first time. "That's... wrong. I can feel it filling my body. Sunlight. Warmth. That only comes from one type of craft."

"Tincraft?" I shake my head. "That's not possible. Is it?"

Hemdi digs into his pocket, revealing a small thimble. But the moment he lifts it toward me, he shakes his head. "I could have sworn I could use this again. Don't you feel it?"

"No," Jeiah and I say together.

Landred's voice comes out a desperate whisper, sewn together from longing and loss. But it's rounder and more alive than anything he's ever said to me. "I do. Craft is all around us."

Maybe I don't feel what Hemdi does or what Landred is talking about, but I do see the forest. "I wish you could see this," I tell Jeiah. "You would know what to do."

"Describe it."

"It's a valley. There are trees here and there, but nowhere near what Gamgim was like. And they... I don't know, glimmer, almost like they're made of starlight. I'm not sure what to make of it."

"What about behind us?" Jeiah asks.

I glance back. "Still the wall and the doorway leading to the summation chamber."

She's thoughtful for a few long seconds. "How close is one of these trees?"

"Here." Hemdi points. "There's one right here."

She lifts her hands in a calming gesture. "Slowly... take me there. I'll follow behind you. Maybe something matches in the real forest, even if you're seeing an illusion."

Hemdi shakes his head. "Maybe Gamgim was an illusion. Not the Valley of Ide."

"The valley of—is that what it's called?"

I clarify. "We heard its name in our mind."

"Interesting," she says. "But how can we tell what's an illusion and what's real?"

Hemdi sighs, uncharacteristically impatient. "I just feel it."

Landred places a hand on his shoulder. "The girl is slowing us down. I want to go to the center of the valley. Something is calling me. If she won't help us, then she's useless." He takes a quick step toward her, but I'm quicker.

"Stop! Landred, we have a deal. You can't harm my friends." He flinches, then returns to Hemdi's side but stops. He can't move further. "And... If you could get there yourself, you would have already left us. Am I wrong?"

He crosses his arms but doesn't deny it. "We must hurry."

"No. We take this slow. Jeiah follows behind us."

Each step takes us closer to the nearest tree, but now that we are walking into the illusion, reality, or whatever I'm supposed to call this double world, our feet find patches of shimmering dust over the ground. In all the life this place seems to hold, it's ghostly and misted as if it's the cloak Ide wrapped itself in and not Ide itself.

We stop at the foot of the closest tree. The bark is a smooth swirling layer of brown and gray, but it shines so brightly you can hardly see the texture until you get up close.

Around one side, we find a fallen branch. The edge of the broken branch and the wound on the tree where it has broken from, shimmer like sapphires. As Hemdi crouches for a closer look, Jeiah pauses, confused. With a sigh, she leans to her side, apparently bracing herself against some unseen tree in Gamgim.

I extend a hand to where the tree might be, and she shakes her head.

"You just put your hand through this willow tree," she tells me. "And you guys have been walking through trees every few steps. It's... unexpected."

I smile. "To be fair, you're leaning on something that doesn't exist."

"Hey guys," Hemdi says. "Clayson, check this out. Does this feel weird to you?"

I crouch next to him and touch the scar in the wood. It's immediately apparent this world's rules must be different. The tree limb is both tangible and intangible. No. That's not quite right. It just feels strange, empty.

"What's going on?" Jeiah asks, keeping a wary eye on an impatient Landred pacing at the furthest point we've come. Does he still look like stone to her?

"Describe what you're doing," she continues. "Remember, I can't see the same things."

I touch the tree again, scooping some grainy sapphire pieces into my hand. "There's a fallen tree branch. And when I touch it, it feels like I'm trying to hold on to water. Like a snapshot of something real, but then it just fades away. Though, I'm still holding it. Does that make sense?"

She stops leaning against her invisible tree. "Not in the slightest."

Hemdi nudges the limb away from me, trying to look at something. As I stretch out my hand to help, the grainy pieces of sapphire scatter, racing back to the wound in the tree. Tiny flares of stark light bounce back at me as the specks hit the wood and swarm into the deep cut, forging a glowing patch.

A pulse of light travels the limb as if it has iridescent veins. Movement. Until now, the whole valley has been completely still, not even a shifting shadow, a brush of wind, but this, this is something. I feel something, not craft, but *like* craft.

Jeiah gasps, and I catch her reflexively extending her hand toward the fallen limb as if she could scan it. "You could see that?" I ask.

"I—you mostly blocked it. A light of some kind? What happened?"

"Tincraft," Hemdi whispers.

"Maybe," I say, "maybe not."

But Hemdi and I must have the same idea. We reach down and put our hands under the branch. It's not heavy. Without another thought or confirmation from each other, we angle the limb against the tear in the tree. The grains repaired the wound; maybe this will work.

Before, the pulse of light was a quick snapshot. This time, the second the limb reconnects with the tree, the world flashes like an overexposure. Hemdi lets go, and I follow. The limb stays in place, but the light is so blinding I look away.

Jeiah suddenly cries out, but as the color returns to the world, she says, "Brick. What was that? I saw... it was a branch, maybe? What did you guys do?"

"We fixed the tree, I think."

She nods. "I need my beholder. This is driving me crazy. How are we supposed to understand this place? I can't measure it. I can't judge it. So, I can't protect us from it."

Hemdi gently raises his chin to her. "Ide will keep us."

That word—Ide. It's almost a sacrilege to hear him evoke it here.

"What we see here," Hemdi says in awe, "it's something you can't measure, Jeiah. Perhaps even what the conjurers always believed. Maybe it's possible—craft without metal."

With the mention of the conjurers, a memory of my dad comes crashes into my mind. One of the first nights I came running to his room as he screamed—it must have been just days after he first swore off craft. A week later, Ara was there with an oxygen tank. I didn't know it then, but every visit she borrowed his craft, he got better. Draining him meant craft couldn't affect him on the surface. Now here we are again on the surface, and the power of craft has taken a new shape.

"What if there's a connection between this place and the surface effects?"

Jeiah looks doubtful. "That's a strange conclusion."

Of course, she would need more evidence.

She must sense my thoughts again. "But there's a precedent."

"Is there?" Hemdi asks, pulling his focus away from the tree.

Jeiah looks back and forth between us. "You can't think of one exception?"

What could have this natural type of power? It hits me. "The mines?"

"Further," Jeiah says. "The Foundation itself. The craft from the Foundation bleeds into the stone above it. That's the only way we can harness it. So yes, there is another place where craft seems to exist without metal. It's the only other outlier. So, we put the outliers together, and a pattern forms. Perhaps. Craft. The Foundation. Gamgim. The Valley of Ide. The Summation chamber below. The fact Wraiths can live here without a dungeon. All of those things are outliers."

The other pattern here is Jeiah. "But you need more information?"

A smile lights her face. "I'll train you as a paladin yet."

Hemdi's eyes are on the center of the valley. "There *is* more information. Down there. Where Landred wants to go. Let's keep moving."

He takes the lead, Landred at his side, but I hang back with Jeiah. Not even a minute later, she has to stop. Grunting, pushing her arms around something invisible, she looks trapped.

"What is it?" I ask.

She turns, walks ten bars, and then rewinds her way back to me.

"The trees are getting thicker," she calls out. "I'm going to have a hard time keeping up. Meanwhile, you guys keep walking through everything. I can't sort out what might be the illusion." She flexes her hand as if hoping the beholder will appear.

"I'll hang back with you," I offer.

"No. Keep up with Hemdi. I can't even see him through the trees. You said it's a valley, right? How far away is the center?"

"It's close. I can see it from here."

"Perfect. I'll stay where you can see me."

I glance Hemdi's way, but he's pulling ahead with Landred. They're walking into the center of this place. There are few trees left to obstruct them, just dunes of crystal sand, the same material that healed the tree. After another quick look at Jeiah, I realize she's right, but I don't wanna leave her in the middle of Gamgim. "No. This is the worst place I could—"

"I'm fine, Clayson. I'm more worried about what Hemdi is doing. Besides, it's the middle of the day. Wraiths only come out at night in Gamgim. And no one else knows where we are. I'll be fine. You'll be able to see me. I trust you."

The urge to tell her how I feel comes bubbling outward in a wave of emotion. "Jeiah, I'm sorry. You've gotta know how I feel about you. I didn't mean to—"

"Now?" she says flatly. "You don't get to say it now. Oh, Clay."

"What? No, I... Don't I have a choice about when I say it?"

"Yeah. Sure. Okay."

The three words land like a punch to the gut. I'll never be able to take them back. "That's not fair. You can't use my stupid words—"

A smile breaks on her face, brighter than mithrium. "You'll get your chance. I'm not upset. Only... I didn't know how to react. Look, I'll stay where you can see me. Go."

Reluctantly, I call out to Hemdi to wait. He slows to a fast walk. Something is unsettling about his enthusiasm, watching him side-by-side with Landred rushing into the unknown. He's always been the most cautious of our group, the one most likely to call for calm and restraint.

The closer we get, the more dangerous things appear. The few trees become increasingly more broken and damaged until it's clear the center of the valley is some epicenter. The dust of destruction lies under our feet. The trees completely give way to fields of large ruinous gemstone walls, scattered and broken shapes, in dazzling colors, like the twisted remains of an ancient city.

That's when Landred and Hemdi stop.

Landred's eyes reflect the light from the valley but are filled with wonder. His voice is almost swallowed in the emptiness. "We're getting closer."

Hemdi bends near the ground, resting his hand on a jagged, pale ruby the size of one of his dogs. "There was loss here. The tree we fixed was only the edge of this disaster. Clayson, this place, craft is everywhere. Here. Come here."

I put my hand on the same massive red gemstone and feel it immediately—the tightening of my skin. A pulse of light sizzles in the center of the broken crystal. "Goldcraft?"

I move my hand, but Hemdi places his back. "If we can even call it that." Hemdi's pronouncement shifts another worry to the forefront of my mind. I thought this might have something to do with Vor, with the mithrium, but this is all far stranger.

Landred isn't here for the same answers as we are. "You promised to help me," he calls. "We are so close. Can't you feel the draw?" Again, he strains against an invisible barrier. We brought him this far. I don't understand how our movement forward unlocks the way for him.

"You must see what I see." A tentacle of light lashes out from Landred's hand, striking both Hemdi's hand and the stone. Hemdi's body seizes, shaking, his eyes rolling back.

"Hemdi!" My hand shoots out, but Landred pulls back; Hemdi's body stills, his eyes close.

"Whoa!" Hemdi says. "Is this what you're feeling? Whatever is waiting for us is powerful." He grins at me. "Come on, hurry."

"Hemdi, wait!"

But he's already rushing ahead. Ide keep us. I glance back to Jeiah. I can still see her weaving a slow pathway toward us. "We're almost there!" I call to her. But in this place, as unearthly as it is unmovable, my voice can't find a way toward her. I growl and follow Hemdi.

He's sprinting. Alongside him, Landred zips forward uninhibited. More than anything, Hemdi's uncharacteristic behavior is setting me on edge. A thousand wraiths could come charging toward me, and I wouldn't be as worried as I am about my friend. But how could I stop them? I wish Jeiah could see this. I wish she had her beholder and could draw answers from this strange illusion.

I run toward them. Time feels drawn out, and a creeping feeling sticks to my insides. Everything I see is made of broken gemstones. This place was the site of some terrible destruction.

"Clayson, quick!" Hemdi calls.

I find them standing next to a massive tree stump, broken and uneven like a great wind came rushing into the valley and snapped the massive thing at the base. The stump has the diameter of a redwood tree.

"Don't you get it?" Hemdi hoists a large chunk of yellow gemstone from the ground. He drops it over the tree stump, and, in a blaze of light, a small area of the tree stump repairs itself. "We have to fix it."

Landred stands transfixed by the stump, eagerly watching Hemdi add gemstones and grow the tree. But there are too many. There's a valley full of them, not to mention the streams of shimmering powder we saw on the way in. The task would take an army of people to set every particle of gemstone back in place.

What was this? Where are we?

I try to draw Hemdi away from the stump, but he pushes me away. "Hemdi, even if we could fix it, I don't know if we *should*. We don't know enough about—"

"That's Jeiah talking. Or Rugnus. Or your sister. Where's the Clayson who forged the mithrium shield and took the heart of Wolfstaff?"

"You're not yourself, Hemdi. Something's wrong. Just think past what you're feeling. This isn't like you."

"You're the wrong one, Clayson. You promised Landred to—"

"I brought him here, yes! But I didn't—"

"I'll do it myself!" Hemdi finds another large stone and rips it free from the ground. This time, when he drops it onto the stump, a pulse of energy flows outward. A second later, the stump draws in a ring of tiny gems. They clatter onto the stump and reform as part of the tree in a flash of light, sending another pulse of energy outward like a wave, even stronger than before. I brace myself to avoid being knocked over. Landred doesn't move. The only reminder that he's not flesh and blood like us. He's a ghost.

When the light recedes, a tall figure steps from the tree stump.

It's Vor. No. That's only my fear playing a trick on me. This man is Dura, but he looks nothing like Vor. What is a Dura doing here? Did our repairing of the tree bring him here?

His face appears as radiant as moonlight, with a regal pointed jaw, and, under wild eyebrows, angelic eyes hold a warning of darkness. He's flawless, besides a long red scar down the side of his face. The figure is crowned with a diadem of woven branches and flowers. He smiles only with his lips.

"Who are you?" I whisper.

"First, greetings. Second, trying to rebuild this great city is a fool's hope. Nothing you do can change this great act of destruction. You can put down the gemstones."

Hemdi drops the gemstones. "Who—"

"Who am I? Perhaps it would be better to answer a different

question—who *was* I? Before the Destruction, before the rise of the Loamin and the death of the Valley of Ide. I was Jassin of House Anleth, the Loved. The second point of the sixth star."

"I don't understand. You're Dura?"

There's a flicker of anger on the man's face, but it's replaced with a tight smile. "A plain word for our great race. We are the children of starlings. The children of Ide. We hold power in ourselves. Power we *can* give to those who are worthy."

As he turns to me, his body shimmers, almost transparent. His light grey clothing, a uniform maybe, is shredded and torn. As Landred reforms next to me, I understand the connection. The man is not only Dura. When he moves, an outline of clouds shifts with him, and rainbow lights crackle along his skin.

This Dura is a wraith.

Fizzblood. How can a Dura be a wraith? A wraith is a Loamin who's been trapped in a dungeon with a champion. Could a Dura be trapped? Is this the wraith that haunts Gamgim forest? A fresh look around reveals no more wraiths than this man. There are supposed to be many wraiths in Gamgim.

The man's look pierces through me as if I'm the wraith. With one glance at Landred, he says. "You brought us this fallen Vessel," he gestures to him. "We've felt him out there. It's good he has come."

He smiles, but the expression reaches cold fingers into my stomach. "Vessel?"

Hemdi stumbles back into me. I steady him. "What did I do?" He whispers. "This place doesn't feel right. I shouldn't have—"

"I have forgotten," Jassin says. "Of course. You refer to yourselves as Loamin. Not Vessels. Very well. The fallen Loamin."

"What do you want with Landred?" I ask. "Did you draw him here?"

"He is a lesser wraith. Our claim on him is as the tree that calls back its leaves to feed the roots."

"A lesser wraith? But you're a wraith as well?"

Jassin acknowledges this with a nod.

"But how is that possible, you're Dura?"

The ground trembles at our feet. "Cease from naming us with your petty terms." The veneer of his welcoming face cracks again; this time, he makes no attempt to smile. "Those you call Dura do not have our great power."

"Our?"

The man raises his hand into the sky, inviting us to view this place's remains with him. "This was once a beautiful city crafted by true creators. The starlight could step foot on the ground and stay here as if it were our closest friend. There was a host of my people, but we brought the destroyer here—a Vessel, a Loamin."

"When? How long ago did you live?" I ask.

"Before time itself. My people held magic for ages. We were the capstone in the transformation of this world's highest species. Loamin had no power in themselves in that day. They could absorb our craft, magic we couldn't use without them. But sharing power was difficult for some of the Children of the Starlings. It divided us. Some helping the Loamin, others—jealous of their ability to use our power—sought to eliminate or enslave them."

"Wait, so you shared craft *with* Loamin? Like Dura borrow craftprints *from* Loamin?"

"That is a pale imitation of our once glorious power, but yes. Essentially. And with that power, we gave and gave to the leader of the resistance, a Loamin woman—the destroyer."

"I don't understand. Who is this destroyer?"

"We thought we could bring an end to injustice. But it destroyed us. And now we remain trapped here as shadows, and she remains in the first and deepest dungeon. A creation of her own making. Our only connection to the world lies in the dungeons with the other wraiths. We can see what transpires in those places. And we are connected to those who lose their power to the lesser wraiths."

"Like me," Hemdi asks. "Those who have surrendered some form of craft?"

"No, there are two whose status among us is greater. Clayson was marked to be a wraith, but he remained free. Wraithborn. Do you know the Loamin Exralt Blackmug? He came to us by the same status."

A flash of an image from Jeiah's investigation boards enters my mind. Blackmug and Brightstorm were friends. He had the silver knife. He hid Ergal in Wolfstaff Dungeon and left Rugnus' family with Icho. Rugnus is his descendant. But there was more to him than his poems and his secrets. "He was like me."

Hemdi and I look at each other. "And he came here? How? Landred helped us—"

"Three other dungeons were destroyed. One of them held four wraiths. They were very much like Landred. Cursed to drift over the surface and search for things they can never have. Dying. Exralt gathered them for us."

"What else did Exralt want?" I ask.

At almost the same time, Hemdi asks. "Where are these other wraiths now?"

The Dura wraith squints at Hemdi but turns his gaze upon me. "Exralt came looking for a way to fix the destruction brought into this world by the destroyer. We gave him a key to reach her, but he never returned to us."

"What key?" I ask.

"We sense it in the dungeons, still working. But it was hidden under the mountain. In the dungeon of your blood, your family."

"Erikzin Brightstorm? If you know about all that and truly watch the dungeons, then do you know about Vor? Do you know what he's doing with the power he has?"

"Yes. He is a corruption. All *Dura* are. Imitation. Facsimile."

"Do you know how we can stop him?"

"Perhaps he is in league with the destroyer; we cannot tell. We need the key. Give back the power of the wraiths inside you, and we will make a way to bring Vor to an end."

Hemdi stutters forward a step, but I hold him back. If this Dura wraith is what he says, then he's been around for thousands of years, trapped here. If craft worked differently so many years ago—these beings sharing their power with Loamin—then what changed? Something this destroyer did flipped the world upside-down. And whatever that was, how does my power help that?

"What does that mean?" I ask. "My power?" The moment the words leave my lips, images flash in my mind unbidden. I'm bleeding, stabbed through, dying. It's the same thing Landred showed me. As subtly as I can I pull Hemdi toward me.

"You're like Landred in a way, Wraithking," Jassin says. "You are connected to us through the dungeons. But you hold a greater power. We need that piece of us back. We need all the pieces. We will use it to kill the destroyer once and for all. We helped her against our fellow Children long ago. It is time we fixed that mistake."

A chill in my spine warns me not to trust him. "Giving you my status as Wraithking—if that's even possible—that's what you want? And could this help put an end to Vor's power over all the other Loamin?"

"We could help you defeat him."

"At what price?"

"Bring us the key we gave Exralt Blackmug." His words quicken, trembling. "Find it. We will trade power with you to kill Vor. We require the key, your craft, and your status as Wraithking." Jassin can't keep a slight snarl from his lips. His body is quaking. Something's definitely off with this whole situation, and we shouldn't stay here to find out what that is.

The ground beneath my feet shakes violently. Landred moves in front of me, blocking Jassin. "This was a mistake. Leave, Clayson."

Before we can respond, Jassin charges into Landred with a gleaming knife. The same prick of metal he showed me in vision protrudes from his stomach. Landred screams as particles of his form burn away from his core. Hemdi shouts something I can't understand, pulling me even as I fight against him.

It's too late. Landred sizzles away into fractals of smoke.

The illusion of the broken trees and mystical valley vanish. The trees of Gamgim reappear, swarming with wraiths. Some of them are still wrapped in clouds and bursts of light. But these wraiths are different. They're not Loamin victims trapped in the dungeons with the champions. They're taller, majestic, and crowned with gems and bones. They're all Dura.

I scream. "What are you doing? Did you—"

"Kill him?" Jassin says. "Landred Wolfstaff has been dead for millennia. Now he's at peace. And what of you, Clayson Brightstorm? Wraithking?" His voice drips with disgust. Any mask of invitation and welcome is completely gone. "A false name if there ever was. Do you think that will protect you here? Give us our power back!"

He charges us. My legs are frozen in place. Fear takes me as I see a flash of a knife in his hand. I'm going to die here.

But Hemdi is quicker than the wraith. He yanks Icho from my hand, and we budge, appearing next to Jeiah, further out in the forest, away from the wraiths.

"Whoa!" She jumps back. "What's happening?"

"Time to leave!" Hemdi says.

CHOOSE A PATH

The forest of Gamgim lies in complete silence.

Sweat drips down my face. Jeiah, Hemdi, and I wait at the edge of the trees, standing so carefully that even the gravel underneath our feet barely moves. The late afternoon has brought slow clouds rolling overhead.

This is real. But was the Valley of Ide an illusion? No. Landred is gone. Killed.

Jeiah takes my shoulders and angles me toward her, almost shaking me. "What happened?" Her words come between breaths. "Be as specific as possible."

I recount the whole thing. Landred and Hemdi racing toward the center of the valley. Finding that massive, broken stump. Repairing it slowly. The Dura wraith—Jassin—appearing. Hemdi interrupts a handful of times, adding apologies laden with disbelief. I continue with Jassin's description of the Children of the Starlings, their jealousy for the power they could only share with Loamin—hangs in the air, wrapping us all in a fog of confusion. How could the world have been so different for Loamin?

When I finish, Hemdi offers a final, "I don't know what happened to me."

"It must have been something Landred did when he helped you see the valley," Jeiah says. "Don't beat yourself up about it."

"No," Hemdi said. "It didn't affect Clayson the same way. Part of me allowed him in. I let that feeling take over."

"What's done is done," I tell him, not unkindly. I've been in his shoes before. Desperation and craft don't mix.

"No matter your motivation," Jeiah says, "we have actionable information again. We need to get back to the others."

Hemdi looks up from his shoes. "How can I go back? Winta will be—"

"Oh, it's not going to be good," Jeiah says. "But we can't wait around. I know that the wraiths of Gamgim don't come out during the day, but we can't understand the extent of their powers. It's been a little less than half a day. We need to get back before the others send out a search party."

Hemdi scoffs. "Winta is going to kill me."

"I'm sure everyone is blaming Clay anyway," Jeiah adds encouragingly. Bringing her goofy, sincere smile out to compete against Hemdi's despair. He doesn't seem phased by this, but it works on my mood like ice cream.

"True," I say, returning her smile. "I can take the heat, Hemdi."

"Not necessary." He rounds back his shoulders. "Let's get this over with."

I breathe in, and when I breathe out, we're standing between the workshop and the cabin next to the hovering mithrium shield. It's late in the day, by the sun, maybe even past dinner.

"Ide keep us, we're back," Jeiah whispers.

A clipped laugh escapes me. "Now that I know where the word comes from, I'm not sure how I feel about that phrase. I never want Ide to keep me."

"That place is a corruption of Ide," Hemdi says.

There's no sign of anyone in the cabin, where we usually eat dinner, but with Hemdi and I both gone, I doubt they made anything too difficult, if they made anything at all. We check the den but end up in the kitchen, staring out the window at the ministack. Winta turns on the light in the dim room. But Hemdi and I know what it means—she's signaled the others that we're back.

"You and I are the only ones that could have gone," Hemdi says, an assurance to himself more than anything else. He takes a deep breath and laughs. "She's gonna kill me."

"She loves you," Jeiah says.

I don't physically wince at the word *love*, but I wonder once again when the time will be right for me to tell Jeiah how I feel about her. I felt so sure of my feelings when I left her to follow Hemdi in Gamgim. The word buzzes in my mind, but I can't just blurt it out. It's not the right moment.

There's movement in the ministack. I see Brig rush out of the front room. Hemdi moves toward the backdoor, but Jeiah stops him.

"I know that was a risk," she says. "And I know Landred is gone, but if Jassin was telling the truth about Loamin, and the destruction of that place, those are mysteries that have never been uncovered."

"Still…"

It seems like everyone but Winta passes the front window.

Jeiah clicks her tongue. "She'll make your punishment swift and painless. Don't worry, even if it was your idea."

"I'm equally in trouble," I add. "Let's go. Poor folks are probably starving."

"Unless Winta made trollbrick chili."

Jeiah almost gags. "Oh, for everyone's sake, I hope not."

We march out of the cabin. Before we get to the door, Brig steps out. He takes one look at us, laughs, and then yells. "They're ba-ack!" He hustles down the stone steps, nearly knocking over one of Andalynn's flowerpots. "You went to Gamgim, right? What happened? Ho, you're not dead, so that's something? Or are you?" He jabs my side with his fingers.

"Ow, no, we're not dead."

"So, what happened? Did you talk to the wraiths? What did they say about Landred? Did your status as Wraithking protect you? What about Hemdi? We figured he went because he had already been wraithtouched."

Hemdi holds out his hand against the onslaught of Brig's questions. "Why don't we get inside, and we can go over it with everyone at once."

The three of us step over the threshold together, passing through the foyer decorated with glass and plant life. Everyone can fit comfortably in the gathering room and no one is missing. My mom, Emberfence, and Koglim are playing cards around a circular table at the back of the room. Rugnus and Andalynn are sitting hand-in-hand on the couch. Winta sits waiting on a chair, back straight, her nervous energy absorbed into bouncing Echel on her lap.

Everyone looks at me. "Good," I start, "everyone's here. It's kinda a long story."

"Well, it didn't take that long," Winta snaps. "So why don't you give us all a summary."

"A summary?" I glance from Hemdi to Winta. Maybe it's Echel bouncing on her lap, but Winta seems much less upset than I thought she would be. Behind the normal fire in her eyes, all I see is concern. Or maybe she's using the baby as a shield so she doesn't melt Hemdi right where he stands.

Brig must feel he's in the spotlight, standing next to us. He slips past the kitchen counter and scrambles for something in the cabinets. That's when I notice the cereal boxes and the empty bowls everywhere. This was dinner.

Rugnus sits forward. He's angrier than Winta. "No, no, no. Start from the beginning. After our whole heart-to-heart, before you left, this had better be one hell of a story."

Lagnar compliments him on his human swearing.

"I felt," Hemdi says, testing the room's reaction with slow words, "as though Clayson and I were the only logical choices to make an inquiry at Gamgim."

Winta stops bouncing Echel. "It was your idea?"

"We have new information," I say.

"I caught them just before they budged," Jeiah says, but she moves quickly into the kitchen to help Brig find whatever he's searching for.

Traitor.

"Even if it was the right decision," Mom says, "you didn't have to leave everyone in the dark."

I inch further into the room and sit on a chair near Winta, facing Rugnus and Andalynn. "Would you have let us go?"

Andalynn smiles softly. "We're all in this, Clayson."

"And we know," Rugnus says, "there are risks involved in everything. I knew you two would need to go to Gamgim, but you need to know you can trust us."

"You were upset about seeing your mother, and it seemed like everyone was upset about Valifra and Grimflail."

"Oh, no doubt. I'm still upset about that, and now that you're back, I can get back to figuring out how to get the people away from Vor."

A chair scrapes across the tile. Emberfence turns to face everyone. "That's a separate issue. Why don't we let him tell us what happened in Gamgim?"

"Summary first," Winta says. "Then we'll fill in all the gaps."

Hemdi clears his throat, "Gamgim was never what anyone thought it was."

"It's some kind of illusion," I add.

Hemdi takes a deep breath. "Landred helped us to see it with only a touch. It was the wreckage of some long-ago act of destruction. We heard its name—like the name of a champion. Which is strange because we were on the surface. It's like it wanted us to know that it is called the Valley of Ide."

As Hemdi explains what we saw, the truth of his words crystallizes. He's right. It wasn't an illusion. Both places must exist at once. And the act of destruction that caused it... I'm not sure I want to find this destroyer Jassin mentioned.

Hemdi describes that first tree and the way it could be repaired.

Koglim whistles. "Wow."

A cabinet door slams in the kitchen. Brig mutters a curse. "Who took my cereal?"

"This one?" Koglim says, displaying a red box with cartoons.

Brig's eyes turn to stone. "That's mine!"

"I don't see your name on it?"

"Get melted." Brig steps around the corner and reaches for the box. Emberfence, caught in the middle, does what any rational person would. He grabs the box for himself. The three of them squabble over it until a loud voice stops them all in their tracks.

"Stop it." My mom reaches across the table and pulls the box from their combined grasp. She pushes the plastic bag back inside the box—it had nearly fallen out—and neatly folds the top back into place.

"Guess we should have left something for dinner," Hemdi says.

"Continue," my mom says, glaring at Brig and Koglim.

Andalynn comes up from rubbing her temples. "Fate of the world is in the balance, and they're fighting over marshmallows."

Rugnus looks down at the empty bowl on the ground near his feet. "It *is* the best kind."

"Anyway," Winta says with a growl.

"Right." I take a moment to pass Icho back to Rugnus. "Hemdi explained it pretty well up to that point, except the fact that he felt tincraft."

Winta blinks rapidly. "You felt tincraft again?"

"Yes, but not from metal. From the trees, from Ide itself."

"But..." Brig says. When everyone looks at him, he shrugs. "There's always a but."

I nod. "A Dura appeared, Jassin, and this may sound strange, but he was a wraith."

The only sound is Koglim still crunching his cereal.

Even though she heard our first explanation, Jeiah's internal calculator looks overclocked. Her face becomes tight like she's eaten a lemon. "I'm just not sure that can be right. Loamin, who are in the radius when a champion dies, become wraiths in that dungeon. The Dura are different. Thanks to what happened with Kel and the other Dura, we know they are the champions."

"Maybe this is something more ancient," Mom says.

"The whole forest felt like a ghost," Hemdi says. "A whole colony of Dura wraiths lives there. They referred to Landred as a lesser wraith. And Jassin said that before Loamin could use craft, they would borrow it from Dura. Like Ara borrows craft from Clayson's dad."

"Rewind, please," Koglim says. "So, you're saying that way, way, way back. Before like, everything, Dura had craft of their own, and they gave that to Loamin. Which makes no sense because Loamin champions become Dura when they die." He blinks at me and scratches his head.

"Maybe it hasn't always been that way. If Jassin could be a wraith—like Landred…"

"Wait, what happened to Landred?" Rugnus asks.

When I pause, Jeiah answers. "Jassin killed him."

Emberfence clears his throat. "How does this help us? So, there's a bunch of undead Dura living in Gamgim. We've known since the dawn of time that place was different. Did they say anything about Vor or the mithrium?"

"We weren't the first Loamin they'd seen," Hemdi says. "Exralt Blackmug. He entered the valley."

"And," I add, "he brought four wraiths that were like Landred, freed from their dungeons."

"So, all of this is on repeat?" Lagnar says.

"Kind of. Exralt must've had a different experience. They gave him a key to the protodungeons, to find something or someone— I guess the person who destroyed their valley, the one they all gave their craft to."

"That's the part I'm not so clear on," Hemdi says.

"Well, no matter what else the key does," I say, "Jassin said they would help stop Vor if we brought the key back... and if I surrendered my power to them."

"There we go," Emberfence says. He turns to my mom. "Your son needs to learn where to start a conversation. That sounds like something that can help us stop Vor."

"Where is the key?" Koglim asks. "Did they say?"

"In a dungeon."

"One from Clayson's bloodline," Hemdi adds.

"There could be a dozen or more connected to our bloodline," Andalynn says. "It's a start, but—"

"And so, we find this key," Mom says, "But we're not thinking of Clayson going back to these Dura wraiths, right?"

"Absolutely not," Jeiah says. "But whatever Exralt hid, it's likely very powerful."

"Wait," Rugnus says. "Erikzin Brightstorm and Blackmug knew each other."

My mom shares a knowing look with Emberfence and says, "So the key is in Brightstorm Dungeon?"

Emberfence leans his chair against the table. "Uh, y'all know that Vor raised foilgrips around every dungeon under granite, right? So, that's gonna present a significant problem."

"Fizzblooded idiot," Koglim murmurs.

Rugnus holds up a finger. "That's if we use craft to get there. Brightstorm Dungeon has a rare exception."

"I don't follow," I say.

Jeiah answers from the kitchen. "There's another way to get to the threshold of Brightstorm Dungeon. It's not isolated from civilization like most other dungeons. We could start from far away. Budge near enough to it and walk right in."

Koglim raises a pointed finger. "Oh! Right. Whoa! Could we even though?"

Everyone in the room understands this comment but me. Jeiah's wheels are spinning. Koglim and Brig are grinning broadly, and Lagnar looks like he's gonna lose his breakfast cereal all over the living room.

I sigh. There's always something that gets past me. "Would someone please—"

Emberfence violently shakes his head, his jowls wobbling. "No, no, no. The lobby for Brightstorm wanders all around Kalisserl, never in one spot. You couldn't even see the way without... nope. Ide keep me. You'd have to be crazy. I'm not going there."

I step into the center of the room. "Guys!"

Jeiah takes a few steps out of the kitchen. "Brightstorm is located in Kalisserl, one of the dead cities. It's the rare dungeon that wasn't carved out of stone in an isolated location. He died right near his birthplace. We could use two Keeper's keys like a compass to paint an arrow straight to the threshold. No budging required. With your key of Mithriumbane—assuming it still holds craft—and Lagnar's key for Bluebottle, we can find a path through the city."

Koglim starts nodding. "I love this idea."

Emberfence stands, gesturing wildly at the room. "Look around you! Y'all have a nice thing going here. Totally safe. You can live a nice long life. That city? No. I'm not going to Kalisserl. Binary brightstorms. With two brightstorms to use, you know what the mithrium did to that city? Gunked the whole place up. Mechcraft and mithrium combination is nothing to mess around with."

Koglim shrugs. "Come on. It can't—"

"Can't be that bad? You spend an hour there without any defenses, and you start becoming a machine. Literal parts of your body become metal and gear. Not to mention the millions of Loamin who already have. They say they can hear your thoughts, that the machines have even learned to harness elemental craft themselves. Mechcraft automates all other crafts. Imagine a city automated to attack anything that moves. The buildings think and breathe and kill."

"And if none of that gets you," Brig says excitedly, "every ten hours, one of the two brightstorms crashes into the surface of the city, and it has to rebuild itself."

Somehow, my mom must have left the cereal box unguarded because Koglim refills his bowl, and it's the only sound in the room. As he's pouring the milk, he says, "When do we leave?"

Emberfence gathers his used bowl, walks past Brig, and drops it in the sink. Without another word, he passes Jeiah, then Hemdi, and leaves the house.

Koglim's shoulders sag. "Guess that means Lagnar's out."

Rugnus sighs. "Without two keys, we'll never spot the entrance to Brightstorm Dungeon. If we could budge there, that would be one thing, but..."

Koglim takes a bite of his cereal. We all stare at him, but he shrugs. Brig replaces Lagnar at the table and reaches for the box, but Koglim's hand closes around it.

"Keep Ide, Koglim!" Winta says. "It's his cereal. I'll order you some of your own."

Reluctantly he lets go, nearly sending Brig backward off the chair. Jeiah dances a step and nudges him forward. She looks at me. "Without Emberfence, without that key, we can't find the dungeon."

Hemdi finally sits down next to Winta. He lets Echel grab his little finger. "Even if we can convince Lagnar to go, is it possible? We'd have to get through that city, and the moment we get down there, Vor can track our location."

"Found that out the hard way," Brig says.

"He may send Grimflail to find us," Rugnus says. "That means Hardkeeper, Brude—Koglim's friend—and my mother. We're not prepared to face them."

Winta and Jeiah pass a quick look. "We may have something. Something that could keep Vor from detecting our craftprints—if that's what he's doing."

"Maybe," Jeiah says. "It could use a few more tests."

"Tests, test, tests," Winta says. Then she smiles. "Sure. We'll run a few more tests. That's the easy part. Convincing Lagnar not to be a coward... who's gonna do that?"

Koglim stands and stretches. "Whatever you guys gotta do.

Just don't leave without me. Looking at you, Clayson. I want in next time we're leaving for a deadly mission."

Hemdi laughs. "Getting half-eaten by feral wolves wasn't enough for you?"

"When this all blows over," Koglim says, "when we stop Vor for good, my reputation as a raider..." He makes a little explosion sound as he gestures with his hands.

Jeiah frowns. "Maybe reevaluate your priorities a little, but I like the optimism."

I run a hand through my hair. "I'll try to find Emberfence. We can—"

"No. I'll find him," Mom says. "He'll listen to me... maybe."

"Hopefully, he stayed under the protection of the shield."

Brig dismisses this with a breath. "Ho, have you seen how happy he is to breathe normally? He won't go far. I'll help look too. He likes me."

"Cause you're so adorable." Winta uses the voice she reserves for Echel.

"Eat brick, Winta," Brig says.

Jeiah slaps him on the back of the head. "No."

With every ounce of self-control, I push the smile from my face. Jeiah narrows her eyes, and I see her resist the impulse to slap me.

"What?" Brig says. "You said it?"

Jeiah offers a defense. "No, I didn't. I—"

"Yes. Yes, you did. You said: Sometimes Clayson is—"

She clamps a hand over her brother's mouth.

A giggle burst from deep inside Koglim.

"Don't stop him," Winta says. "I've been wondering how you two have—"

With a loud groan, I leave the room. "I'm getting some air."

The heat from summer is a welcome relief to the air-conditioned room. Mom follows me out of the castle. "Hey, got a second?"

"If this is about Lagnar—"

"No. I just... I'm wondering if you want to talk."

My feet stop. "About what?"

"About Jeiah and you."

My eyes go unfocused. Is she trying to offer me relationship advice? Of all the things I need right now, having a heart-to-heart with my mom about my failure to express my feelings is—let's say—very low on my priorities. "I appreciate the thought."

"I *am* your mother."

"True, but I'm going to play my teenage boy stereotype card on this one."

"Fair enough. I think we should check the shop first."

We walk down the road in silence, past the cabin, toward the shield. The sun has already slipped nearly out of the sky, behind the ministack and the woods beyond. Halfway to the shop, the light flips on inside. When we open the door, we find Lagnar fiddling with a piece of equipment at the worktable.

"Come to talk me into throwing my life away?" he asks.

Frustration grows inside of me. "That's not—"

"Not talking to you, Brightstorm."

Turning to me, my mom motions for me to leave. "I've got this."

"You sure?"

She nods. The second I hear the door close behind me Lagnar says, "He's so much like his dad. Makes me sick."

These words, the way he talks to my mom—familiar and antagonistic all at once—send me stomping down the gravel road to the eastern cliff. I spot Jeiah through the living room window, but she's busy talking to Winta about something. Good. I don't want company right now.

I pass the waterfall, but in the middle of summer, it's like the river's on life support. The waterfall barely lives, only a slow trickle of cool water over the stones. It's one of the reasons I prefer spring to summer. There's something about the way the world comes to life again. There's nothing like it in the world below. Everything there is made of sharp contrasts and conflicting viewpoints. Always alive, never dormant. It's a hard place for me, having spent my life roaming the Blue Ridge Mountains.

Once I reach the cliff, I take extra time searching for a new way up. Many of the paths are known, worn by hand and foot, by years of trust. But tonight, I search for the rougher places, the more difficult paths to climb. I still reach the top in short order. I march down the trail, back to the foot of the cliff, and start again. This time the challenge is to use a single hand. Your legs do all the work if you find the right places. Again, I reach the top.

After a couple tries, I pull myself over the lip of the cliff and roll onto my back. The daylight is mostly gone, but I stay long enough for the night to transform, for the stars to deliver themselves into the sky and translate the endless summer day into a vast universe. There's no moon, I realize, and long after the sun is down, I begin to make out a vapor of the milky way.

"Not something you get to see in Tungsten City." Jeiah's voice startles me.

I move to sit up, but she lays down next to me. Her hand finds mine, and she leans into me. Something in my chest fills with relief. The world becomes simple.

The stars. The cool air. Our heartbeats.

She draws her body closer and leans over. Her lips find mine. The kiss is so soft and light I might float upward into the night. Then I kiss her back, trying to draw her closer, but she stops. She settles back to look at the stars.

"It's easy for me to say I love you," she says. "You're kind. Courageous. The way you see the world... maybe you're rash sometimes, but intelligent. You're a good friend to Rugnus, and everyone else. And the way you stand by Brig..."

"Then let me say—"

She puts a finger to my lips.

"I'm not sure it will be enough to make me believe that you actually do."

What am I supposed to say to this? "That doesn't leave me

much of an option. I'm not sure how to prove my feelings to you. And—"

"I don't need that," she says. "I'm a paladin, remember? I already know how you feel about me. You need me."

"It's more than that."

"Is it?"

My chest tightens. My next breath is more of a gasp for air. How can she not see the way I feel about her? I form my next sentences the best I can without using the words she doesn't wanna hear from me yet. "I just know there's this space inside of me that's empty, and all you have to do is sit next to me or say a single word, and... it's as strong as any craft I know."

Her eyes catch something of the stars as she blinks and stares at me. "That's exactly enough for me, Clay. Can we just not worry about what words either of us uses right now?"

We stay there, unmoving for as long as the night will let us.

"Do you think Lagnar will go?" I ask.

"No. The part of him—the general from long ago—that's all gone. He doesn't have a bone of bravery left."

"I don't know. I'm never sure we can know what he's thinking. I mean sure, maybe with silver, but even that has its limitations. We can't know what he'll decide."

"He'll keep himself comfortable. Live out his days under the protection of the shield. However long that lasts."

"I don't suppose that makes him the greatest keeper in history."

Jeiah closes her eyes. I know her well enough to guess what she's thinking about. Who she's thinking about. "Bluekeeper— the real Bluekeeper—what was he like? I only met him once, but you said he was like a father to you."

"He taught me to see the room. To judge efficiently. To exploit every possible avenue until—" She stops abruptly. Her breathing changes.

"What is it?"

"That's it. Clay, that's it. Lagnar may just do it. Come on." She hops to her feet, pulls me up, and then we're running down the side trail, past the waterfall, and back onto the gravel road.

"Tell me where we're going."

"I can't believe I didn't think of it."

She pulls open the door to the shop, revealing Rugnus and Winta in the middle of an animated conversation. At least they both seem excited about something. Emberfence is sitting in Jeiah's chair, watching them like a ping-pong match.

Jeiah comes to the center of the room. "Everyone, listen."

The conversation screeches to a halt. Lagnar swivels around in the chair.

Jeiah extends an arm out to him as if to test strengths. "If you won't go, give me your keepership over Bluebottle. Clayson and I can find Brightstorm Dungeon without you."

SHIFT INTO GEARS

LAGNAR'S ADAM'S apple bobs as he swallows. Leaning back in his chair, he laces his fingers behind his head. I'm unsure if that's to cover a deep feeling of being insulted or if he's genuinely at ease.

"That's a mighty tall order," he says.

Mom is gone from the workshop. It looks like she couldn't convince him of anything. So much for being old friends.

"But she's right," Rugnus says, realization in his eyes.

Winta saunters next to Jeiah. "It makes a lot of sense. She could lead a team through Kalisserl and find the dungeon. She's been a paladin for Bluebottle. Lagnar could surrender the key to her willingly."

"Been a couple of centuries since someone gave up a keeper-ship," Rugnus says.

Jeiah points a finger of judgment at Lagnar. "After what you did... with the whole world turned upside-down... you'd keep this from—"

"Relax, sheriff." Lagnar stands from the chair and cuts the distance to her in half. "The queen and I talked it out. Figured you'd come asking."

Winta's mouth nearly drops open. "So, you'll do it?"

"Mostly," Lagnar says.

"What does that mean?" I ask.

"Means someone oughta go get the monarchy. Princess included. I want the best silvermage to oversee this oath."

"Lagnar." I lace his name with a warning.

"Nothing sinister. Just a teensy promise. The moment she leaves that dungeon, or heaven forbid, dies before you guys get out, the keepership returns to me."

He draws a thin trapezoidal disk from his vest pocket. He flicks it twice and the edges glow blue. A tiny metal key surfaces on the disk.

Jeiah smiles with satisfaction. "Fine."

"Not finished. After that, you work as my chief paladin in Bluebottle."

"No." The smile is gone from her face. "No. You can't withhold your key for... for that."

"Well, if you won't promise..." He starts to put the key away.

"Wait. Fine. Brig, go get Andalynn."

"Why do I have to—"

I barely have to glance at him for his mouth to shut tight. The door clatters behind him. No one says a thing. The computers buzz and ping, but we don't have to wait long before Andalynn enters, followed by Mom. I can tell by the look on Andalynn's face that Brig's already filled her in. Mom leans back against the door, letting Lagnar take the lead, but this must have been her plan.

Coming between Lagnar and Jeiah, Andalynn says, "Are you both absolutely sure about this?"

Jeiah clears her throat. "Unless Lagnar will stop being a coward and go himself."

He purses his lips like he's considering it. "No, thank you."

"Test strengths."

They clasp each other's forearms.

With a simple silver dowel, she taps their knuckles. Ribbons of light appear around their heads like halos.

Lagnar speaks the words of an oath. It's clear he's thought this through. "I grant you temporary keepership of Bluebottle Dungeon, with all its powers, until your life is ended, or you exit Brightstorm Dungeon safely, with the additional promise to serve as Bluebottle's chief paladin, under my keepership forever thereafter. Swear it?"

"By my blood and by silver, I swear." Jeiah squeezes his arm.

A swell of silver-grey light plumes around them. Lagnar releases her. He hands her the card, shaking his head. "Alright then. Now just gotta wait around for you to die... then back to the status quo."

"We won't let that happen," I say.

"As foolish and wishful as your father."

"When do we leave?" Brig says. "You know, for Kalisserl."

Winta laughs and wraps her knuckles on Brig's head. "You? Never. The rest of the team..."

"Did the last test work?" Jeiah asks her. "Are they ready?"

"Are what ready?" I ask.

Lagnar points to a table filled with electronics. "Some more of Winta and Jeiah's human-Loamin hybrid specials."

I pick the closest one. It's an old pager. But the hint of blue glowing along its seams is distinctly Loamin. I hear the door, and Koglim steps in.

"What did I miss?" he says. He looks down, spots the pager in my hand, and scrunches his face. "What's all this?"

"These," Jeiah says. "Should scramble our location from any AI in the city."

Koglim's mouth opens wide. "We're on for Kalisserl!"

"These new objects should block some effects of the fallout as well. More importantly, it hides our location from Vor and Grimflail."

Winta presses a button on a second pager, and blue light appears at the seams. "With any luck, nothing in the city or out of it will sort out your location." She nods toward Koglim. "Too bad you don't have your neckless or at least the tattoo."

Koglim waves the comment away. "Why? So we can just ignore all the bad omens? With this group of raiders, I've learned to just go with it."

Winta chuckles. "I'd take the warning if it were me."

"Are you not coming?" I ask. "We'll need all the mechcraft we can get."

"Jeiah may not have the same mechcraft AMP, but she's better at all the puzzle stuff. I mean, melt me for admitting it, but this was her idea. As was connecting the human internet to bluelink in the first place. I can't leave Echel. No, let me be clear. I have no intention of leaving him without a mother or father, for that matter. We have to stay."

It's a reprimand of Hemdi, as clearly as Winta can give him. She's not risking her life; he shouldn't have, either.

"Fair enough," Mom says. "That leaves six of us."

"Seven," Brig insists.

"Not a chance." Jeiah grabs him by the shoulder and pushes him toward Winta. "Keep an eye on him, too, would you?"

Koglim fiddles with a flip phone from the pile of electronics. "Wraithspit, let's get going then."

"We have everything we need," Andalynn says. "Is there any reason to wait?"

"I don't have the keeper's key with me. The one from Mithri-umbane Dungeon, it's in my—"

Mom taps the key on my shoulder. "Figured you'd need this. You and Jeiah should take the lead."

"Thanks. And you're coming with me?"

"With Grimflail on the loose, it will be good to have a gold-mage with you."

Koglim keeps flipping his phone open and closed. "So, how do we use them?"

Lagnar laughs. "You guys are mech food, for sure."

"Zip it, Lagnar," Rugnus says.

Lagnar waves him off and returns to fiddling with the machinery on the table.

Brig smiles. "Ho, Clayson. This is why you need me. I know all the ins and outs of craft, and dungeons, and—"

Rugnus pats Koglim on his shoulder. "We've got one database. And he's actually been in Brightstorm. Even knows how to work the keeper's key as a compass. Besides, he's been in every dungeon, if I'm not mistaken."

Koglim blinks at Brig like an innocent kid waiting for a lollipop. "Too true. Well, besides Mithriumbane, which you guys destroyed before I could raid it even once."

"The key, Koglim," I say.

"Right," Koglim says. "Well, the pattern inside Brightstorm is simple: up and toward the sharpest light you can find. So, finding his dungeon from outside—"

"Is opposite," Brig says, trying to keep himself relevant. Winta laughs, but Brig continues. "To find the dungeon, you go down and into darkness."

"And the keys?" I ask.

A sudden look of panic grabs Brig. He freezes.

"The keys," Koglim says, "should guide us toward Brightstorm with the opposite pattern from anywhere near the dungeon threshold."

"Sounds straightforward," Mom says.

After a pause, Rugnus adds, "I know a budgeport on the city's periphery. Well... it's sixty percent reliable. Which is just about as good as it gets in the ever-changing fallout of Kalisserl."

There are nods all around. Rugnus takes Andalynn's hand. "We'll find the dungeon and get the key the Dura wraiths gave to Blackmug. Hopefully, it will help us find a way to defeat Vor. And we can fix this world."

"It will," I say. I clip the pager to my belt.

Andalynn picks up a wireless heart rate monitor and attaches it to her necklace. Jeiah grabs a touch watch. Koglim has already been waiting with his phone, and my mom grabs an identical one, which she tucks away. We all watch as she takes the golden ring box from her pocket, with its royal velvet inside. She lets a golden candy dissolve in her mouth.

Koglim begins his pre-mission jig. "I know this is just another side mission to hopefully lead to actually attacking Vor, but spit and bones, this is exciting. The fallen cities always remind me of old times surveying for Quimdem with Rugnus."

Rugnus takes out Icho with a flourish.

I catch one last glare from Brig, and then we budge.

The second we arrive, I feel my body pulled forward by the floor. We're inside a dark tunnel, firelight reflecting off the grimy metallic walls. The floor moves all of us in a single direction toward the only light source—a wall of flame.

"Not good," Koglim says, backpedaling... or no, striving to stay in one place on the moving conveyor belt of a floor.

Within a few seconds, we all set a pace moving us toward the back wall, but it feels like an uphill walk. What we assume to be a wall ends up being more darkness. This whole hallway is a treadmill nightmare.

"What now?" Mom says. "We won't be able to keep walking like this forever. Hold it. Something is there." She points down the corridor into the darkness. I squint in that direction but see nothing.

"You sure?" I ask.

Koglim points to her eyes. They have a golden color mixed with green. "Bloodcraft."

"Attunes my physical senses," she says. "The thing I'm looking at is getting closer. I think... yeah, whatever it is, it's alive. It's small, but wait..."

"Through the firewall," Rugnus shouts.

All of us but Mom immediately stopped walking. We know to trust Rugnus. But she calls out again. "Wait! It's—"

As the thing emerges from the darkness, more details appear. The figure on the floor is not some unholy creature made of mithrium fallout. It's a person struggling to get his feet under him.

Brig.

"You little brittle-boned latcher," Jeiah charges over to her brother, hoisting him to his feet. But he can barely stand.

Koglim asks, "How did you—"

Brig is breathing heavily. His eyelids keep closing. "...used... Icho's... signature."

Andalynn shakes her head, confused. "Can he even do that?"

Rugnus can't take his eyes off Icho. "New one to me."

"I used... Blueweb... knew you wouldn't... let me come with you."

"Well, whatever you did, it cost you," Mom says. "You can barely breathe."

Brig nudges Jeiah's hands away. His feet find a steady rhythm. His breathing normalizes, not without effort, but we all know he's trying to prove he can hold his own.

"Just as easy to send you back," Rugnus says, leveling Icho. The second he frowns, Brig smiles, holding up his digital watch.

"Ho, nope. I slaved this to Icho's signature. Send me away, and it will just bounce me back."

Still walking in place, I move diagonally to intercept Brig. "Then turn it off. We're sending you home."

"No," Jeiah says, grabbing my arm when I reach for him. "That's not how this works. The devices offer protection from the effects of the fallout. If you take it off, the city will see him, and Vor might too." She whirls back to Brig. "Wipe that smug look off your face, you idiot. You just made our mission more difficult. Now we have to take care of you."

He takes another step back, the flames at the end of the hallway reflecting in his eyes. "I can take care of myself. In fact, back there's a dead end. I'm gonna lead us through that hologram over there." He points to the wall of flames.

"Hologram?" I ask.

"Oh," Koglim says. "Yeah, that's probably true. Hadn't thought about that."

"Getting old, raider," Brig says, letting Koglim catch him on the moving floor.

"Get melted."

"Is he right?" Mom asks.

But as we all draw closer to the fire, we realize it's not giving off heat. Brig smiles as we allow the floor to move us through the flames. He's right. It's just a hologram.

The walls fall away, and we let our feet rest. The floor still moves, but we are high on top of a mechanical structure, the world alive with machines around us. Sparks rain down over half the city from the cavern ceiling. Two brightstorms—balls of molten power—orbit each other in the sky, moving like clockwork. Swarms of what look like truck-sized light bulbs hover nearby, filaments glowing. A forest of mechanical stalagmites drip chunks of copper upward, defying gravity. They form on the ceiling into rust-green stalactites.

"You weren't kidding about this place," I say.

Jeiah scans the horizon, the keycard in her hand. "Follow the darkness. Does anyone see a darker spot than that hole?" She extends her finger down to the base of the cavern, but I don't see anything until I take out my key.

I follow where she's pointing into the depths where the darkness seems to be a living thing.

"What hole?" Rugnus says. "The darkest place I see is near the base of that massive building." The others glance where he indicates. The whole base of the building opens into a ravine, but it's not dark—not like the other place.

"Clayson?" Andalynn says.

"I see what Jeiah's seeing. We go there."

Rugnus hands her Icho. "Lead the way."

Together we budge the whole group into what I assumed would be darkness, but we arrive in a stark world of contrast. Bright swaths of UV black light cut columns through a maze of pure midnight. Here and there, the UV lights shift in the shadows, revealing stone walls.

A scream strikes out from my left. Rugnus clutches his hand.

"Rugnus?"

"Get back!" He yells. "Stay out of the light!"

The closest UV spotlight dances toward me languidly, but I step out of the way, moving toward Rugnus in the dark. When I get to him, he doesn't appear hurt or in pain, but he holds up his hand. His thumb has been transformed into metal, glass, and gears. He wiggles and bends it, making sure it still works like a thumb.

"Keep Ide," Koglim says. "That looks... permanent."

I try to heal it using my bracelet.

"Don't bother," Jeiah says. "Koglim's right. It's permanent."

Andalynn takes Rugnus' hand and looks it over. "I thought the electronics were supposed to protect us!"

"Oh, they do," Brig says. "But there's still the innate mechcraft from the fallout. The city has learned to harness other crafts by itself. And if the city could see us, it might do that to all of us—on purpose."

Koglim takes another large step away from the closest column of light. "Trollbrick."

"Let's move," Jeiah says. "I think we can avoid the lights for the most part. I can see the darker spots."

"We're lucky one of us didn't budge straight into the light," Koglim says.

"I don't want to think about it," Andalynn says as Rugnus tucks his hand out of sight.

Jeiah and I lead the others through a maze of darkness and stone, wall-by-wall, light-by-light, holding back in a few places but more often rushing through a gap in the lights. No one else tries to take charge. No one argues. Brig is the most close-lipped I've ever seen him.

"Just beyond this light," Jeiah says.

Once it passes, we move quickly. Halfway there, the light changes pattern, heading back for us. Koglim notices the same time I do, but he's closer to the light, Brig's in front of him.

Koglim grabs the back of Brig's shirt and tosses him forward. Then Koglim's simply gone, a column of light in his place.

Rugnus stands ten feet away, Icho in his grip.

Andalynn searches for Koglim "Where's—"

Rugnus breathes out slowly. "Budged him."

"Spit and bones I—" Koglim, another few steps ahead of us, pats his hair. A few ends have become gold wiring. "That was too close."

"Down the stairs," Jeiah says.

Andalynn pats Koglim's back. "Maybe you can just cut it."

"Oh, it won't grow back like hair," Brig offers. Andalynn throws him a warning look, but he continues. "It will be wire forever. A new look for Koglim Felsight—golden-haired professional raider."

Koglim considers this. "I suppose that could work."

At the end of the stairway, it opens into a hallway of yellow neon. To our right, pulses of purple light lead up another stairway.

"Is that music?" Koglim asks.

"Unmistakably," Brig says. "But I heard those who find the source of the music in Kalisserl never stop hearing it."

"This way," Jeiah points down the yellow hallway. An unnatural black cloud hangs against the far end of the long corridor.

We follow Jeiah down another stairway. At the bottom, an ominous wall of mirrors waits. No, that's not quite right. They're not mirrors.

"Interesting," Jeiah says. "They're screens."

"Are we still going in the right direction?" Mom asks.

Jeiah purses her lips. "I think so, but here I don't see anything dark. Not like before. Clay?"

Even as she says my name, I sense something through the key. Dread. I know it's not a feeling that belongs to me. It's something the key is pumping into my nervous system. A sense of darkness and evil. "It's more of a feeling. Can that be right?"

Brig mulls this over. "Could be. Jeiah was *seeing* darkness. You might be *feeling* it."

"Great," I mutter.

"There," Koglim says. "A break in the screens. Maybe an entrance."

We follow him cautiously toward a break in the mirrored screens. He's right, but the opening leads to another hallway filled with screens on every side.

Koglim waves an indifferent hand. "If we can handle the mirror market, we can deal with a little maze."

"Mazes have a clear path to a clear end," I say. "Somehow, I doubt the city is built like that." I squeeze the keeper's key. There is a spot on the far side of the maze. It's trying to draw me toward it. "But this feeling... I can almost pinpoint it. It's maybe a block or two that way."

"There could be multiple paths," Jeiah says.

"Or none at all," I say. "Are we sure we can't go around it?"

For the next ten minutes, we search for another way forward, but the wall of screens dead-ends on both sides. Eventually, we gather again at the only entrance. As Rugnus moves forward, my mom stops his movement with an outstretched arm. She unweaves a needle from the hem of her shirt and holds it up. When she pokes her finger, everyone gathers around to watch the result. She pools golden blood into her hand, perhaps an ounce total.

Koglim and Brig are the only ones who act squeamish when she dips her finger into her palm and then traces a line across everyone's chin.

"So, this makes us... what?" Rugnus asks.

"My blood should allow everyone to pass through the walls. But hold on to each other. Do *not* let go. We'll form a rough circle, Clayson at the head." She holds out a hand to the screen, and it mirrors her. When she presses it to the wall, it sinks to her wrist.

"Okay, then," Koglim grins. "We can walk through walls. I love goldcraft."

"Stay together," Jeiah says. "I—" She blinks, and I see something cross her face. Her usually investigative pupils swim in uncertainty. "Do you see that?"

She points to the bottom of a screen. Her reflection stares back at me, but there's something else in the bottom corner. A number and the symbol for ferrum, Loamin money.

Rugnus slides next to us. Points to his reflection and the number beneath it. "I think that's my account balance. How does it know how much ferrum I have?"

Mom urges us closer. "We need to move before the goldcraft wears off."

Rugnus grunts, and we huddle back together.

We hold fast to each other as we slip through the first wall. The next room is filled with screens, half of them simply mirroring us, but the other half runs video of a host of other people. The videos loop, but each has the same stamp at the bottom corner. This time the number next to the ferrum symbol slowly ticks downward.

Koglim glances at his reflection, admiring himself, but I watch the number under his video tick down by two ferrum, then two more.

"What is this place? Brigs says. "It's not taking ferrum from my account... is it?"

Rugnus pushes closer to me, ignoring his reflection and the number ticking away. "Move. Faster."

We cross through another wall into an even larger section of screens, the walls towering a few stories. A billion holographic ferrum signs dance above us like rain. My reflection appears before me. At the bottom of the screen, the number drops by multiples of twenty. Understanding slowly dawns on Koglim's face. "Wraithspit. Something's collecting our ferrum?"

"Not just ours," Jeiah says. I think it might be anyone who's ever been here. Or who had ever lived in Kalisserl."

Brig whistles. "That's a lot of ferrum."

"It's a trick," Mom says. "Remember, the city is alive with mechcraft. It can automate everything. It must have bluelink access."

"Bricks and bones, that's greedy," Koglim says with a low whistle. "Keep Ide. What does a living city need with my ferrum?"

The number beneath my mirror picture continues to count down. But we keep running. Before we cross through the next wall, I glimpse a video I know must be impossible.

The second we enter another room, I spin around to face everyone. They nearly run into me. I gasp out the name. "Hardkeeper. In one of the videos."

"What?" Rugnus says.

"It was him. I saw him in that golden mask. I think—"

"They found us!" Koglim shouts.

Figures burst from around the corner, Grimflail at their head. He laughs, satisfied. "Hello, Rugnus!"

I push to the front of the narrow hallway and ignite a shield using my bracelet. It spills between the walls and rises through the ceiling. Grimflail launches himself at it. His golden nails scrape into the shield, sending sparks flying outward at Hardkeeper and the others.

Rugnus is beside himself, his face contorted. "Mom!" He growls, throwing fire at this side of the shield.

"Stop!" I yell. "You'll weaken it!"

"I'll kill him!" Rugnus screams. He charges forward, but Koglim grabs him.

Grimflail's nails scrape deeper into the shield, and he bellows with joy. "You'll wear a mask!" he yells. "I swear it, Rugnus. You and everyone you love will wear my masks."

Beside him, Hardkeeper produces a cast iron ball. The small figure among them, Brude, steps next to him. With a click of something on the ball, Brude disintegrates into sparkling smoke. Hardkeeper gathers the smoke into the ball.

"Now!" Grimflail shouts.

Hardkeeper slams the ball into the shield. The white energy flickers and the cast iron globe drops to the ground, rolling toward us. In a billow of smoke, Brude reappears, his face covered in the same scratched golden mask. He lurches toward us, grabbing Brig. Jeiah sweeps Brude's leg out from under him and pulls her brother away as Brude comes crashing to the ground.

"Through the next wall," she shouts. "Clayson, what are you waiting for?"

I snap to attention as Koglim drags Rugnus back into our reformed circle. We move through. I half expect the goldcraft to fail, but we charge through wall after wall.

Ten walls later, we emerge from the maze of screens into an identical hallway to the entrance, and for a moment, I think we've only come back around. Down a new set of stairs, a dim red light waits.

Jeiah points in that direction. "The darkness is back."

Rugnus kicks a screen. "We have to face him!"

My mom shakes her head. "No. We go on. The bloodcraft worked. They can't hope to catch us. We need to move forward."

Andalynn touches Rugnus' arm, and more tears swell around his eyes. "She's right, Rugnus. Hey, look at me. She's right. And we will find a way to face him. But not on his terms."

"Yeah," Rugnus whispers. "Okay."

Koglim takes one more look at the screens where Grimflail's image flashes. "Well, at least the city is taking their ferrum too."

As we spiral down the stairs, the red light grows deeper and deeper. We follow a series of long ramps winding back and forth on the side of a ravine of rotting metal and slime-wet stone.

In the near dark, Brig whispers, "I can't stop thinking about how much ferrum the city has collected. Where does it keep it all?"

"If I had access to that vault account..." Koglim says, but he leaves it to our imagination how he might spend the ferrum. Probably food.

Around the next corner, I stumble into ankle-deep water. I've been following Jeiah, but I draw the key out to check. Dread immediately washes over me. "We're definitely going the right way."

"Through here," Jeiah says.

The next room is vast, like a great cathedral or the inside of a grand train station. The bright red light gleams off clusters of metallic surfaces. It takes me a few seconds to translate the metal walls, tables, and the hilly floor into something I can understand.

"I think we found all the ferrum," Mom says.

The spacious chamber is filled with piles and piles of glimmering ferrum. The small rectangular coins form great towers and mounds, as far as I can see. One massive hoard of coins.

"What's that?" Koglim points to the center of the room, where the red light emanates.

I recognize the towering, glowing gemstone. It's a mindhive. Similar to what Jeiah showed me in Tungsten City months ago when we spoke with the soul of one of the ancient azdeth. This one is peppered with various rocks and metal shards and rests on a gunmetal base.

"A mindhive?" Brig asks. "Here?"

Jeiah continues. "I've heard of this one. The Gem of Worms. The minds of all dragonkind—or many—are contained in this thing."

"Guys," Koglim says softly.

I focus closer on the gemstone. A large piece of the collapsed ceiling sets next to it, but it must have hit the gemstone when it came crashing down. As I pace around the side, I see the chasm in the gem's surface. "It's broken."

"Um." Koglim's voice sounds like he just stepped in a pile of trollbrick. I'm about to check on him when Jeiah stumbles away from the Mindhive.

"That..." Jeiah nearly chokes on the words. "It can't... it means the minds of all those dragons were released. The minds of the dragons made something down here."

"Guys," Koglim squeaks. "I think I know what's collecting ferrum. Worm!"

Jeiah shakes her head, her face frozen in fear. "Dragon."

Energy settles on my skin, and all my hair stands on end. Red lightning courses the heights of the vaulted ceiling, revealing a tangle of metallic flesh and limbs. It crawls from a black vortex on the far side of the chamber.

More branches of lightning sizzle through the air, and the slithering entity fills the entire ceiling with a cover of chrome and titanium. When the lighting strikes again, the limbs shift with the sound of a thousand car crashes, and a massive bulk drops to the floor. All its mechanisms shift, and the world trembles.

It speaks with the voice of hundreds of jealous monsters. "You smell of wealth!"

ASSEMBLE THE PUZZLE

Lightning strikes next to me, scattering electrified ferrum like a shotgun blast. My bracelet drops a glowing energy shield between the dragon and me. A handful of sizzling rectangle shapes break through, one passing close enough that my hair lifts slightly with the electrical current.

Hands pull at my shoulders, and I retreat with Jeiah, Koglim, and Rugnus behind a wide tower of glinting ferrum. Mom, Brig, and Andalynn huddle behind a nearby pillar.

"Bright ideas?" Koglim asks Jeiah.

She shoots him daggers. "Don't look at me!"

"I just thought... you're from Hngaal. Your people know a lot about wormkind."

Under another barrage of lightning, Jeiah slaps Koglim's chest. "My people? Latcher! I'm from Tungsten City!"

"Focus," Rugnus snaps. "Options?"

The monster roars a cacophony of grinding gears. I glimpse around the column, staring back at the pulsing hole this thing climbed out of.

Darkness and downward.

I grab Jeiah, finding her blue eyes in the dark. "The hole that thing slithered out of, that's our destination."

"Spit! You're right." With a breath, she peers around the pile of ferrum we're hiding behind, but more red and white lightning blasts the thick column. Ferrum rains down from above us, but my shield holds.

The dragon roars again, like the spinning of a thousand gears. "Koglim Felsight!"

"Don't answer it," Jeiah says.

Koglim growls. "You think I'm a complete idiot?"

The whole room shakes with mechanical laughter like someone recorded the sound of a thousand grandfather clocks and ran it through auto-tune. "Koglim! Hmmm. Your vault is so full, so full. Tastes... new. Where did you earn your ferrum?"

I glance at Koglim. "What if I go out there? Distract it."

Koglim pins me to the wall. "Latcher move, bro."

"Agreed," Rugnus says.

"Right," Jeiah says. "But a distraction could work. I have an idea. Koglim and Clayson—with me. Rugnus get everyone else into that opening."

Rugnus nods.

Under his breath, Koglim says, "Knew she would figure something out."

She pushes him in front of her. "You'll be bait."

Before I can object, Jeiah and Koglim drag me out between the piles of money.

"Great one!" Jeiah calls out. "We want an audience with you."

"What are we doing?" I whisper.

The massive creature coils, readying a strike. The dragon's snaking body folds over and over, too long to truly fit, even in this vast cavern. Deep-set, double-slitted orange pupils bear into mine.

"I'll speak with the wealthy one." Its words shake my bones.

"I'm his accountant," Jeiah says. "What do I name you?"

The dragon purrs. "Name me... Lennox."

"Lennox. We've come to you for a loan."

Lennox's laugh is like a million nails drawing across a tin roof.

We curl into ourselves reflexively. "And what type of loan do you seek?"

Koglim steps next to her. "Oh, uh, high interest. Really high. It's only fair, Great Lennox. Your wealth is insurmountable, more than I could have ever imagined. That's why I've come."

I see Andalynn leading the others to the back wall. They're almost there. Just another few seconds.

"That seems reasonable," Lennox growls. "But loans are boring. I think I'll murder you now. I can make ferrum out of your bones."

Lennox's body glows at a million seams, crackling with electricity. The hair on my head stands up, and my fears turn to cold dread. Behind Lennox I see Andalynn and Brig standing near the exit. Everyone else is through.

Suddenly Rugnus is standing next to me, Icho extended. "I don't think so, worm." We budge to the exit.

The swirling vortex pulls at my clothes. It wants us to enter.

Jeiah shoves Brig through the gaping entrance without another word. She locks eyes with me, and I feel our tether of trust become something unbreakable. She jumps in.

Then Koglim screams.

Lennox extends a sharpened claw, groping toward Koglim.

My bracelet flares to life, casting a sheen of white around Koglim's torso. At the same time, Andalynn draws the white glass sword speckled with tin. It's the sword she took off the darksmith from the cabin. She thrusts it into the air, sending thick barbed vines around the claw. She draws the sword back like a fishing rod, and the vines tighten. Lennox howls in pain.

"Lennox!" Andalynn shouts. "I'm offended you don't know of my wealth. I'm the queen of the Kingdom of Rimduum. This city is the home of my forefather Erikzin Brightstorm. You know of the royal coffers? You know what I can offer. Let us through and protect us from our enemies, and I will offer you a most generous payment."

The beast's eyes widen. "You would wound me and seek an offer?"

"Wound? That was barely a scratch. Take my deal. You can have half of the royal treasury."

The myriad of its moving parts click shut, silenced. Lennox slithers higher. In the quiet, I hear muffled voices in the adjoining hallway. Grimflail. Lennox glances toward the door.

"Enemies you say?" asks Lennox. "Sixty percent."

"Done."

Another laugh from Lennox shreds the rest of my nerves.

"Good luck." Lennox turns toward the other hallway.

"In!" Andalynn shouts at the three of us.

I jump into the entrance. My feet fall from under me, and I plummet down. The stomach-dropping feeling only lasts as long as it takes me to hit the water below. Pain shoots through my shoulder joint and down my arm as I sink. With one good arm, I swim upward. Painful. Slow. Finally, I break out of the depths, panting. Stone encircles me. I've landed in more of a well than a lake. Rugnus, Andalynn, and Koglim splash down next to me.

"There!" Mom calls out.

The light is dim, but the edge of the well isn't far. I swim the rest of the way and pull myself onto the rough stone. My arm's throbbing, which makes climbing out of the well look like I'm the first sea creature to crawl on land: a brutal, air-grasping, painful experience.

Andalynn and Rugnus come out of the water as one, steadying each other. Brig is still struggling to reach shore, but Jeiah finds him and pulls him along with her. Sometimes I forget how bad Loamin are at swimming, so afraid of water they bathe with craft instead.

I'm still nursing my arm, pumping shieldcraft into my shoulder. Better, but not great.

Jeiah turns back to the water in full lifeguard mode. "Koglim."

We wait. One second turns to five. Five seconds to ten. He doesn't surface. The others ignite two bright spotlights, illuminating the water. There he is, sinking slowly, eyes closed. Before anyone else moves, I dive back into the well.

Luckily, I'm faster than his descent. My shoulder burns, but I ignore it, kicking and pulling myself down toward him. My hand touches his foot, but it slips away. My lungs are screaming now, but finally, I grab him, pull him close, and get my injured arm around his head and arm. If we weren't in the water, I don't think I could move him. I give as much as I can to each scissoring movement until finally, thankfully, air reaches my lungs. I sputter and gasp for breath as Rugnus and Brig help hoist Koglim from the water.

Rugnus produces a black iron spoon. He pulls Koglim's mouth open and sets the spoon in like he's force-feeding him. Andalynn hovers over them.

With a start, I move forward. He needs CPR. "What's—"

Jeiah grabs me. "It's ironcraft."

After everything Koglim has lived through, after all the traps he's narrowly dodged, this can't be how he dies. I don't care how hydrophobic Loamin are; Koglim Felsight can't be drowned. I don't accept this. Dropping to my knees, I place my finger against his neck, searching for a pulse.

Then Koglim sputters, coughing water. Rugnus shouts in relief, throwing his arms around Koglim's shoulders. I stare in disbelief.

"Ide keep me," Rugnus swears, "you old raider. Don't do that!"

Koglim coughs again. "After the feral wolves, you thought a little bit of water could stop me?"

"Koglim the Invincible," Brig says with awe. "Or Koglim the Indestructible."

Jeiah laughs. "Picking your raider nickname?"

"Hey now," Koglim says. He coughs, but he sounds almost back to normal. "I'm not picking it. I put Brig in charge of that. And he gets to leaf my biography."

Jeiah says. "Brig can't leaf anything but statistics."

Koglim smiles with a shrug. "That's all he'll need."

"Your biography is going to be a leaf on statistics?" Andalynn asks.

"Why not?"

"Not to rush us," Mom says, "but with Hardkeeper under his control, it may not take Grimflail very long to get past the dragon."

"And Brude Bogsmoke," Koglim says, standing up, "is excellent with mechcraft. I hate that Grimflail can just..." he growls.

"Come on," Rugnus says, moving forward. If he's thinking about how Grimflail is controlling his mother, he's not letting any of it spill into this conversation. "We're in the lobby now. The threshold is in the next room."

This is news to me. "This is the lobby?"

"Usually," Brig adds, "it's an easier swimming experience. Then right to the threshold door. A simple lobby."

"Why water?" I ask. "I thought Loamin feared water."

"You don't know?" Jeiah says, surprise in her voice.

"Know what?"

"He's a hydrophile. Loves water just as much as you."

Koglim shudders and makes a retching sound.

"You make it sound so terrible," I say, but somewhere in my bones, I feel a deeper connection with Erikson Brightstorm. An uncountable number of generations stand between us—though I'm sure it's documented in an equally uncountable number of leafs—and yet there it is, a commonality.

Jeiah smiles and shakes her head. She's said before that she finds my knowledge gaps endearing for whatever reason. There's something about the way she looks at me... another reason I love her. No *"yeah, sure, okay"* about it.

Rugnus and Andalynn lead the way down the tunnel. They find each other's hands even in the relative darkness. Somehow, they make relationships look easy, even though there's so much difference between them. Somewhere between the extremes—he for Tungsten City's radical democracy and she for the honored traditions of the monarchy—they found their mutual passion for serving the people. Nothing else mattered. They became one.

Jeiah and I could still have that. I imagine us trading curiosities and beautiful things, sitting someplace peaceful with a long vista stretching into infinity. I wanna find her hand and let her know how much I care for her, but I can't shake the feeling that Vor will never let me have that. This world filled with dangers and dungeons will never be safe.

In the next room, a dim light and a single door greet us. The metal door is painted yellow and carved with a white sunburst. The door is bound by stone and flanked by window boxes. Succulents thrive in the planters beneath. It seems like we've stumbled onto someone's porch, not the threshold of one of the greatest Loamin in history.

"This is a home," I whisper, trying not to disturb the family inside. They could be playing together, eating a meal, or telling stories around an unassuming hearth. I thought the door to this dungeon would be shining like a brightstorm, something regal and majestic.

Jeiah's eyes widen. "You had a whole season before the council restricted you from entering dungeons, and you never came to your own ancestor's threshold? How did I not know this?"

"I... no." Why hadn't I ever come? I could've. But I know the reason. After Silverlamp last year, after Ergal, Sira, and the mithrium, I felt like stepping into a dungeon caused some great desecration. The council was right to forbid me from entering any other dungeon.

Then all at once, my thoughts turn to Erikzin. His consciousness runs this place. Though how that works, I still don't understand. Like Vor, he has another body waiting for him to be free. Would it be wrong to take him from this home? Will I find the heart of his dungeon in there? What about my oath to the council?

I take a firm step back. "My oath with the council."

Andalynn rests a hand on my back. "They can't hold you to that under these circumstances."

My mind races. What if the dungeon holds me to the oath? So much could go wrong inside. "I can't go in there."

Rugnus finds my eyes. "Hey. No. You'll be fine. We're not going for the heart of this place. We'll let Erikzin rest here. That's not why we've come. We're here for the key Blackmug left. That's all. And you have *us*."

My gaze wanders from person to person. My mom and my sister, Jeiah and Brig, Rugnus and Koglim. These are people I love, people I must keep safe. "You can't promise I won't mess this up."

I see Jeiah's concern even before she speaks. "Clayson, we all love you. You don't have to put this burden on yourself. We're here. I'm here. Got it?"

I try to let her words in. I try to believe nothing bad will happen, but that type of hope doesn't materialize. After a moment and another few breaths, I say, "Got it."

But I'm far from trusting in myself or in Erikzin Brightstorm's dungeon. Every threshold is a roll of the dice.

Mom places her hand on the doorknob. "Jeiah's right. Besides, we all have a stake in this, Clayson."

She pulls open the door.

Jeiah takes my hand, and I follow her in. With my first step into Brightstorm, the world becomes a single piercing light, and I am weightless. Everyone around me floats in the same light-clouded space.

Koglim tries to grab my shoulders but accidentally nudges me forward.

"Whoa!" he says. "I know this one. We need to find the dungeon marker and aim for it—straight line. There!" He points to a splotch of green light high above us. "Come on!"

We float through this world. The further we get, the more speed we pick up until we're hurtling through the air like rockets. The thrill isn't lost on me, even with everything terrible happening. Brig whoops and laughs, triggering a cheer from every one of us.

The green marker turns out to be a stone cliff. We land next to a copy of the threshold door with same yellow paint and white sunburst. This entrance has no quaint plant life. No torch-filled window boxes. The long exterior windows appear as narrowed eyes. It's impossible to see what's inside.

"Koglim?" Rugnus says.

He shakes his head. "Not sure until we go through the door."

Rugnus glances at Jeiah's little brother. "Brig?"

He purses his lips. "Can't say I've seen this… but they say that if you find a threshold duplicate in a dungeon…"

"What?" I ask.

"It will have a strong connection to the champion's life. Many times, something unknown to the world at large. Something personal or secret."

Rugnus points at the door. "So, this could be a connection to someone he knows."

That clicks something into place for me. "Someone like Exralt Blackmug,"

I crack the door open. A cluttered house waits for us, with leaf-filled shelves, woven rugs, and steam rising out of the kitchen. We cross the threshold, and nothing changes. We're safe. We haven't been moved or split up. Erikzin Brightstorm, the soul running this dungeon, has kept us together.

Andalynn smiles. "This cottage reminds me of something."

"It's how Hemdi describes his home in Firas Andem," Rugnus says. "Before Whurrimduum—the Knights of Shale—drove them out."

As I look around the cottage, a rough stone drops into the pit of my stomach. The braided rugs, the mended metal objects, the simmering hearth: this is what Hemdi lost. How can he be such an optimistic, kind person? All at once, I know another place this reminds me of—the cabin.

My home.

I picture the evening Bazalrak and his knights came and tore down the peace of that place. At least they left it standing. From what I know of Hemdi's stories, the knights collapsed the whole cavern where he and his family lived, a neighborhood of tiny homes.

"Sharp contrast between this place and Kalisserl," Rugnus says.

"Actually," Brig says, "King Brightstorm—Erikzin—chose Kalisserl for two reasons: one, the binary brightstorms were his crowning achievement—Kalisserl used to be known for its natural beauty and coloration. And two, before he invented the brightstorm, before he took his place as king, his family lived close to this cavern in a cottage just like this one."

Koglim whistles. "I may know the dungeons like my dearest objects, but you sure know the history of Rimduum better than any bluelink channel."

"Thanks," Brig says. Everyone understands this to be the highest compliment Koglim could pay the kid.

The small area is so unlike other dungeons that I don't even know where to start. There are no other doors, visible challenges, or enemies. "So, how do we find where Blackmug hid the key?"

Koglim strokes his chin. "Not sure about Blackmug's key, but this challenge... I think I've seen it before. It's ancient. Why is it that when Clayson comes into a dungeon, he pulls some ancient challenge out of nowhere? Cool, but tricky as spit. This one... it's almost too simple." Casting his eyes around the room, he taps his skull like it can call back a memory. "We're looking for a small chest. Something you would use to hold ferrum before the vaults."

"Okay," Andalynn says. "A treasure hunt. The dungeon likely knows our purpose. Maybe if we find the box, it will lead to the key."

Koglim says, "There could be multiple boxes."

We fan out. I move to the kitchen, where a vat of steaming water rests embedded in the countertop. As we search, I'm careful to leave things in their place. The cupboard is stacked with silver pots and pans, but there're more items made from wood than I would expect in a Loamin cottage. Where did they get wood? Before the brightstorms, their cities contained no forests. Did they have to grow them one by one using tincraft?

The cupboard is stocked with jarred food and glass in so many colors I wonder if every craft is represented. A cornucopia of pale carrots, dark cabbage, and lumpy potatoes fills an entire shelf. Onions in braids and strips of dried meat hanging from the rafters. This is Erikzin's childhood, and my dad would approve of the lifestyle—minus the craft.

A hand finds my shoulder. It's Andalynn. "Strange, isn't it?"

"Actually, no. Feels a bit like home."

"Ha! I guessed you would say that."

"Must have been a simpler time."

Andalynn pulls down a blue jar of something thick, maybe jam. "People during this period had lower life expectancies than a typical Loamin today, forty at best. The brightstorms, modern leadcraft, and so many time-saving inventions... all helped to change that. Erikzin's work was critical to the advancement of civilization."

"And then someone discovered mithrium."

"Yes, that was during his time."

"It's like I can see all the pieces are connected, but... I don't know. Blackmug. The protodungeons. The brightstorms. The appearance of the mithrium. Vor working behind the scenes, pushing things into place."

She sets the jam back on the shelf. "The day I met you in Gamgim, I... my life changed forever. I think everyone here can say the same thing."

My mouth opens before my brain can construct a response. Can she mean that? "But—"

Andalynn smiles. "You may have knocked things into motion, but the world is built out of glass. The way the council hurts people, the way mob justice in Tungsten City hurts people. All of our systems have been overreactions to world events. But you look at something and say, 'This way is right,' and forge a new path."

"Okay, but—"

"What I'm saying—Jeiah says this to me a lot—is that you see the world differently. Just"—this one word reveals how much she's adopted Rugnus' worldview— "know that you don't have to take on the weight of the world."

Brig takes this second to wriggle past us. "Excuse me." He nudges everything out of place. The jars clink together. Apples spill out of a bag sitting on the shelf, thudding against the stone floor. "Ho! I've got it."

Something scrapes against the stone shelf, then Brig lifts an item like a trophy, his smile gleaming as much as the gilded metalwork embellishing the box. Sneaking between us again, he sets it on the kitchen table. We all gather around.

Koglim shakes it like a mysterious gift and sets it back down, frowning. His hands glide over the surface of the box. "No lock."

Rugnus tries next and shrugs. "Clear seam, but..."

"Think this through," Jeiah says. "If Blackmug left behind a key, maybe he left this box, too. The dungeon is only presenting it to us. What made Blackmug unique?"

Brig picks up the idea. "He was the only other person we know of to see the mysterious Valley of Ide."

Jeiah weighs this in her mind. "Right. Anything else."

I point at Rugnus. "Rugnus is related somehow."

Rugnus snaps. "And, he had Icho. Maybe..." He picks the box up and takes a deep breath like he's steeling himself for something bad to happen.

Then he draws Icho.

The lights across the room—in the hearth, flickering in candles and lamps, even through the two slanted window boxes —fade into embers. The temperature drops.

In a pulse of darkness, Rugnus, Jeiah, and Brig disappear.

In the time it takes for Andalynn to reach for the place Rugnus was, something shakes the door.

Thud. Thud. THUD.

With the last loud smash, the yellow wood splinters. Koglim charges and drops the bar over the door. Koglim and I scramble to the windows. We both slide out a simple wedge that holds the window covering in place. One covering swings down. Koglim clamps it into place, but as I swing the second cover into place, something metallic slips through the crack before I can clamp it shut.

Koglim knocks me to the floor, forming a shield around me with his body.

One—the sound of the wind. Two—an ear-splitting tearing of wood. Three—Koglim's teeth grinding together. And then silence.

Koglim rolls off. I pull myself to my knees. The right side of the room is covered in sand.

Andalynn helps me up, shouting, "Look out!"

I whirl around. One of Grimflail's masks, dull and haunting, glimmers in the lamplight on the far side of the room, the side I failed to secure. It's Rugnus' mom, Rusela Whitechin. She charges Koglim without a sound, a jagged knife in her hand. It looks so much like Vor's jagged sword I have no doubt he wanted us to see it.

She's quick, but Mom is quicker, a streak of golden light. Rusela's knife strikes downward, and Mom blocks it. Koglim grabs Rusela's left arm while Mom uses her block to pivot and grab on, wrenching back the other arm at the wrist. The knife clatters to the floor. With an extended leg, Mom brings down our assailant. She reaches for the mask.

"No!" Koglim shouts. "If you take it off, it will kill her."

He flips Rusela over and pins her down. Rusela struggles against him, but she makes no sound as if she feels nothing but the drive to kill us. I'm not certain I would prefer a scream to silence, but the quiet feels wrong. I'm suddenly glad Rugnus isn't in the room with us.

"That's how Grimflail's relic works," Koglim says. "That's how Valifra... that's how she died."

Mom's hand had been wavering, but now she withdraws it. "Can we keep her restrained?"

Koglim wrangles her arms even more. "Can you get any other relics off of her?"

Searching her, Mom shakes her head. "Nothing. Why would they send her in with only a knife?"

"How did she... I almost had the cover in place. She didn't budge in?"

Someone outside hammers the door. The bar shakes but holds.

Andalynn searches the pile of sand lining this side of the cottage and grabs a small ball of wrought iron and gold. "Hardkeeper's work."

"Should you be..." I gesture to the fact she's holding it in her bare hands.

"It will be fine. It's not engaged."

"What are these things?" I ask.

Koglim's eyes are saucers. "Packing husk. They used to transport soldiers in these things by the barrel full. Or they'd use them on the battlefield...could throw a person at your enemies like a grenade. They'd pop out and do the up-close, dirty work."

The cover over the window rattles.

Whatever Rugnus did with Icho and the box, maybe it wasn't connected with this attack. Rugnus' mom makes another effort to free herself, but Koglim stands her up, keeping his arms around her. Silver light seeps from his forearms, and her eyes flicker shut. She slumps downward. Koglim sets her gently on the ground.

He pulls the collar of his shirt, where he's woven in a thread of silver. "That will give us a few minutes."

"So"—I look around the room—"where did Rugnus and the others go? And did opening the box somehow bring Grimflail here?"

"I'm not sure what to think," Koglim says, "I've heard of this task, but it never included a group competition, just searching for the box. I think their attack was just bad timing. Could be a good sign that Brightstorm didn't give them an easier way in."

That's a thought. Brightstorm watching over us, maneuvering our party as close as we can get to the key. Now the bars on the door and the window covers seem more intentional. But Grimflail and the others got past Lennox, which means they can get past this.

I move back to the box on the table. But something is different. A smooth metal disc, like a coin, is pressed into one side.

Andalynn sees it too. "What's that?"

Shrugging, I pick up the box and press my finger to it.

The lights in the cottage return. Andalynn vanishes from my side. I blink, and Koglim, Mom, and Rusela are gone. The sand from the husk is gone too. Suddenly, Jeiah, Brig, and Rugnus appear, startled by my sudden presence.

"That's curious," Jeiah offers, the corner of her mouth twitching up.

"Ho, Clayson, what did you do? I mean, glad you're back, but—"

"Back? You three are the ones that left. Wait. Quick, bar the door!" I rush to the door and drop the bar into place. As I seal one window, Rugnus seals the other.

There's a clink of metal against the window cover. Did Hardkeeper try to get another husk in through this window? Could he be in both places, in front of both doors, at the same time? A loud thud against the threshold answers my question.

Rugnus stops me from pacing. "What's going on?"

"Will the door and windows hold?" I ask.

"In a cottage from the Discovery Era?" Brig scoffs. By his reaction, I can tell this may be something I missed out on from Loamin grade school. "Trollbrick, have you read *any* of our histories? With the doors and windows barred, you couldn't break into one with mithrium."

"That's an exaggeration," Jeiah says.

"Okay," Rugnus says. "Gonna tell me what's happening?"

"You three disappeared, and then—we think Grimflail tried to—"

Rugnus grabs my arm. "Grimflail! He's outside the door?"

"He sent your mother in through the window in a husk, like how he got Brude through my shield. He had Hardkeeper do that."

"Another husk?" Jeiah asks.

"Yeah. But Rugnus, she's... she's okay. We've got her subdued for now."

"And Grimflail?"

"Trying to bust down that door," I point backward. "Weird, this is the same room, but..."

"Let me try something." Rugnus takes the box from me. Nothing happens.

When I take it back, my finger grazes the plate surface on the side, and the room returns to darkness. Rugnus, Jeiah, and Brig are gone again, but Andalynn hugs me.

A second later, the banging resumes at the door.

"What happened?" Mom asks.

"Hold on," I say. Gently, I set the box on the table, waiting a moment, then lift it again and press my finger to the plate. Again, the room switches like a light, and the other three appear.

Brig looks at me, questions swimming in his eyes. Jeiah appears much the same.

"Okay," she says expectantly.

"Seems like I can go between rooms." Another loud bang drowns out my words. "And I think I'm bringing Grimflail with me no matter which room I'm in."

I survey the room. Both cottages are the same: a single yellow door, now barred, two windows, now covered, the central room with its fluffy, comfortable-looking chairs and a few small tables, the kitchen and pantry, and the sleeping area, plush with hammocks and oversized pillows.

"So, what's the challenge here?" Rugnus asks.

"I'm not sure. The room hasn't changed at all."

Jeiah's ears perk up. Her eyes adopt that ever-so-familiar confidence that somehow draws me to her. She's a bright flame against a cold, intolerable road ahead. "You've said exactly the right thing, Clayson. It hasn't changed at all. Brightstorm—Erikzin—used the same words a long, long time ago. It was something I found while I was doing my initial investigation about the Bluelink disturbances before StoneYoke."

"Translation," Brig says, "when she was obsessed with you."

"Brig," she says firmly. "Turn off your mouth. Besides, it's a mutual obsession now."

This stops me short. My breath quickens.

Rugnus smiles, that wide dangerous smile of his. "Not wrong."

I widen my eyes so he understands that I want him to stop talking.

"What? Come on. In what world is love a bad thing?" Rugnus asks. "Certainly not this one. We can use more of it."

"You sound like my sister," I say.

Another smile. "I'm okay with that."

"Anyway," Jeiah says. "I'm trying to tell you that I think Brightstorm left a hint about what he and Blackmug left here. He was close to death, so no one wanted to be around him for fear of being caught in a dungeon as a wraith. But someone interviewed him through bluelink. When the topic came around to his childhood home, he said: *I'll give you a clue. It hasn't changed, only a few stones out of place.* It was a strange response. He planned on dying here. He planned the location of his dungeon. They moved everything and everyone out of the radius."

"But Erikzin wouldn't have known what anyone would find in his dungeon," I say.

Brig shakes his head. "Some champions believed they could control what formed, at least to some extent."

"And," Rugnus continues, "If he told Blackmug what he would

make, then Blackmug may have come in here with the key knowing exactly what to look for."

Brig immediately scours the walls and floors. We join him, fumbling over the stones, making every attempt to pull or shift something out of place. Rugnus works systematically from ceiling to floor, yet after testing nearly all of them, we have nothing to show for it.

"It has to be something about stone," he says. "Spread out; look for anything out of place."

Three canvas hammocks stretch across the sleeping room, one of which is made for a child—Erikzin's childhood bed. I duck under the two longer ones and move to the back corner, where the child's hammock is slung crosswise. But it's been flipped over. As I nudge it to the side to check the stone wall for anything movable, my hand bumps into something inside a pillow.

It's cold and rough, about a finger's length. I withdraw the slim stone and immediately recognize the rich black of obsidian. The small rock is even on all sides except one. When my finger passes over the surface, symbols appear.

WRAITHBORN AS ME

"Guys! I found something."

Ducking back under the hammocks, I make for the table.

The pounding at the door recommences, but we ignore it. I think Brig was right about this cottage being impenetrable. I just didn't seal the window fast enough in the other room.

"What did you find?" Jeiah says.

I hand her the stone. She turns it over and over again.

"Wraithborn," I say. "That's got to be something."

Rugnus takes the stone from her and flips it over. "It's just a rock."

I pull it out of his hands, fearing that the words are gone by some craft. But they're there. I point. "It says, *Wraithborn as me.* None of you can see it?"

Brig pries it from my hand, looks over it once, and shakes his head.

"It must be Blackmug's key."

Jeiah takes back the stone. "Then maybe that's why you can read it and we can't. You're both wraithborn."

"Weird way to phrase it," Rugnus says. "*Wraithborn as me.*"

"It sounds almost... poetic," I say.

Brig snaps his fingers. "Didn't Yinzar find the recipe for the mithrium objects in some old poetry of Blackmug's?"

Rugnus claps Brig on the back. "That's it. There will be another piece that fits into the jagged part. It should form a line from a poem."

"It's a puzzle," Jeiah says, eyes dazzling.

"And I bet," I say. "The other room has another piece."

MARK THESE STONES

THE OTHER TEAM waits for me in the kitchen. They've already found a stone. It's nearly identical, but this one's jagged puzzle edge is on the left side. After a hasty explanation of Jeiah's theory about Blackmug hiding the box and my apparent ability to read invisible messages, Koglim collects the stone from the counter and hands it over.

"Thought it was kinda weird," he says.

They all watch as I turn it over. Andalynn says, "Anything?"

But my attention is drawn away from the stone. Rusela.

She's tied up—unconscious—slumped over the side of a leather chair. Another thud sounds against the door. I shake my head and focus on the stone. As before, strange symbols appear.

I mutter what it says. *"Must open the box."*

Koglim keeps one eye on Rusela but glances at me. "Does that mean something?"

I tell them the phrase from the other rock. "Where did you find this one?"

Mom points up to a shelf. "Koglim says he looked in this cup before we found the box, but Andalynn double-checked, and there it was. Perhaps the stones showed up after we found the box?"

Andalynn rubs her temple. "The message doesn't make sense: Wraithborn as me must open the box."

"Maybe there's more. I should go back and forth between the two rooms."

Koglim rummages through one of the lower cabinets in the kitchen. "BleakYam's rule of raider inspiration says: two heads aligned, and you won't be blind."

"Great," I say. "More poetry."

THUD.

Koglim slaps his forehead. "Won't matter. I can't process anything with all this noise. You'd think Grimflail would realize he can't break in."

"What are we going to do when she wakes up?" Andalynn asks. She's watching Rusela but clearly thinking about Rugnus.

After everything Rugnus and I have been through, I can't let him down. "We will get her out from under that mask."

Koglim dusts off his hands. "Well, I'm going to recheck a few places. I'm betting that cup was for a kid, meaning it belonged to little Erikzin Brightstorm."

He moves to the sitting area of the cottage, opening a large trunk filled with blankets and pillows, some lined with copper piping and foil backs. I step over to help him just as he draws a stack of blue glass leafs from under a gold-woven blanket. Right on the top of the stack, there's another piece of the obsidian puzzle.

"As easy as Summation." He checks over the stone, but then passes it to me. "Well, maybe not your summation, wraith boy."

My mind flashes back to my first attempt in a dungeon, to Landred Wolfstaff, his gaunt face, and the party of people speaking behind his back. I remember their flashing goblets and rude words. The memory stings as it transforms into a flash of light and the pinprick of a sharp knife. Landred turns into particles scattered in the air.

Andalynn nudges me. "What does this one say?"

Descending out of my thoughts, I flip the stone over and nearly drop it in surprise.

Mom steps forward, alarmed. "What is it?"

"It says, *Vor's secret*."

Andalynn takes the stone and tries to connect it to the other one we found.

No luck.

"So," Koglim says. "That's: *Vor's secret, wraithborn as me,* and *must open the box*. That makes no kind of sense."

"None of these are connected to each other," Mom says. "There are at least three more based on the edges."

"Did you check in the pillowcase? That's where I found the stone in the other room."

"Yeah," Koglim says. "No double dipping. Each stone must be in a unique location."

Behind us, there's one loud *thud* against the door. This time the wood splinters inward. Not enough to create a hole or bend the iron bar, but enough to bring our attention back to the invaders and Rusela.

"Is there a way we can find these a little quicker?" Koglim says.

"I'll go back to the other room. Give you a break from Grim-flail over here."

Andalynn hands me the box. "Tell Rugnus... never mind. Be careful. Hurry back."

I scoop up the stones and move to the other room.

As I adjust to the higher light level, I hear Brig say, "Finally."

There's a scraping noise and one of the window covers shudders slightly. A second later, the same thudding from the other room starts here.

"Great," Brig says. "You brought them back with you."

Rugnus steps over from the kitchen. "How are the others? How's my mom?"

"Others are okay. The door is holding for now. Your mom is

still unconscious. We're not sure what she will do when she wakes up, but... they have her restrained."

He grunts softly.

Jeiah's standing over by the brick-laid hearth. She waves me over. "Come see this."

I step around the table to the hearth, which is the most foreboding thing about the room. It's larger than a typical fireplace and protrudes into the room like the exposed belly of a giant. The embers deep in its center pulse with orange-white light. Wood ash is smeared around the base near the mouth. If I wanted to, I could duck under the stone and stand inside.

A rectangular groove holds one of the obsidian stones in the cobblestone above the opening. More than that, it's a frame for all of the pieces. It reminds me of the wooden puzzles I would do as a child—no room for guessing or error.

The fireplace already has another stone.

IN THE SUN THEY

"The other pieces?" Jeiah says.

I hand them over. Rugnus and Brig gather to watch us assemble the puzzle. Each stone we've collected can be connected to another stone, but none match. Between each line, there's a gap.

"Trollbrick," Rugnus says. "How many are there?"

"Let's start from the top," I say. "Wraithborn as me... then blank... then blank again... must open the box... then blank... then a whole empty line."

"But that one's shorter," Brig says.

"Could be a single piece," Jeiah adds.

"Could be. Then Vor's secret... then blank... then a longer line, so two blanks... in the sun they... then blank."

Brig whistles. "What now?"

"Keep looking for more stones. I'm gonna move back and forth between rooms."

As I move toward the table, I look back at Rugnus. He swallows. "Clayson, tell Andalynn to be safe. If they have to take the mask off—"

Brig's mouth drops open. "You said that would kill her."

Rugnus continues. "If they have to stop her from hurting someone..."

I shake the warning voice from my mind. "It's not going to come to that."

Taking the box, I move to Andalynn's room.

At first, no one sees me; they're scouring the room. A new stone lies on the table. I grab it and move back to Rugnus' room.

"That was fast," Brig says.

Setting the other stone in the puzzle box, I stand back. "We've got a full line. This one. Says: Vor's secret and the ancients unlocked."

"The ancients?" Jeiah says.

"Could be a reference to the protodungeons," Rugnus says.

Jeiah nods. "Blackmug was looking for the protodungeons. The key he got from Gamgim may have unlocked it."

"Do you think Blackmug reached the protodungeons?" Brig asks.

"The mithrium," I say. "The mithrium had to come from the protodungeons."

"Maybe," Jeiah says. "But if this key lets us into the protodungeons..."

The possibilities float around inside my skull. Could we find even more mithrium? Who is the destroyer Jassin spoke of? Vor? If we got more mithrium from the protodungeons, could we use it to free more champions? Change the hearts of their dungeons into powerful weapons? What would the wolfstaff be if we turned it into something of mithrium? What would Icho be? How many more hearts and pieces of mithrium could we get? Would any be like Ara? Would they support Vor or us?

My mind won't stop jumping from fear to fear. My hands shake. Is this what a nervous breakdown feels like? Why can't I get enough air into my lungs? Someone calls my name and shakes my shoulder. I try to swallow but can't.

"Clayson," Rugnus shakes me even harder. "You alright?"

My thoughts bounce from worry to worry. "Sorry. I just—"

"It's okay," Jeiah says, squeezing my arm. "It's a lot to process. Try to stay focused on the key, on the puzzle. You don't need to solve everything at once."

I nod, but my mind is still connecting the dots.

"Check on the other room," Rugnus says. "We'll keep going."

The box is still in my hands.

In the other room, Andalynn and my mom discuss something, but they stop when I appear. Mom hands me another stone. It has no jagged edges. It's the single line near the center of the poem.

"*Never again to be alone.* That's what this one says."

"So," Andalynn says. "*...must open the box, never again to be alone.*"

"Does it mean the box won't be alone?" Koglim asks.

Andalynn leans back. "Or the person who opens it won't be alone. I don't know."

Rusela groans but doesn't wake up. My mouth almost works open to tell them Rugnus' request, but I can't do it. The door creaks under the weight of another barrage of strikes. Thud. Thud. THUD.

Instead, I say, "We need to think of a way to break the curse of these masks."

"Good luck," Koglim says. "I don't think there's anything that can be done. The goldcraft in the mask latches on to the person's physical features. It reads who they are, down to their bones."

The new information pulls at something inside my mind. "Mom, that's it. It reads who they are. You changed my face. The day I left the cabin. You used bloodcraft to change my whole physical appearance."

Koglim waves his hands in the air. "We've tried a concealer. Tried complete physical change using goldcraft. Brick, we even tried animal features with coppercraft. Nothing worked."

"Mom?" I ask.

She squints at Rusela. "But my bloodcraft concealer is… strong."

"Yes, ma'am," Koglim acknowledges. "But still."

I catch his eyes. "I don't wanna ask this, but…"

"You want to know who took the mask off Valifra. It was Rugnus."

"That doesn't matter," Mom adds. "*How* did he take it off?"

Koglim tilts his head. "What do you mean?"

"Quickly or slowly?" she clarifies. "I'm sorry to bring this up. It's just—"

"It took hours, and we thought we had it. We thought it would work."

Mom glances at Rusela. "I could try. If it seems like it may not work, I'll pull back. But we can't have Grimflail controlling her. Not here. It's too dangerous."

"We have to be sure," Andalynn says.

Mom hesitates for only another second. "It will work."

She produces the glimmering ring box from her pocket and everyone tenses. In the dimness of the room, it gives off its own light. I have a strange sensation where I remember what it was like to live in a world without all these things. A world where no goldcraft was needed because no one was after me. Where Andalynn couldn't make me magically feel better with a strand of the metal in her hair. Where the dead weren't trapped in dungeons under a hundred thousand layers of rock and dirt.

If I had that world right now, I wouldn't know my mom. Andalynn couldn't pass a determined smile to me, and Jeiah wouldn't be waiting in a parallel room to help me solve another mystery.

The little box opens, and my mom draws out the single glittering piece of candy.

As she places it on her tongue, Koglim asks, "What does it taste like?"

My mom puckers her lips as if savoring the tiny gem in her

mouth. "To me? Strawberries. To anyone else who tries to eat one... let's just say it would be bitter."

Koglim eyes the box and taps his head. "Got it leafed. No touchy."

She leans down next to Rugnus' mother. When she helped conceal me, she used a pin to slightly prick her finger. In order to get us through the maze of screens in Kalisserl, she used an even thicker pin, drawing more blood. She sets the fleshy part of her palm against the rim of the sharp lid of the ring box, pulling it over her skin as quickly as ripping off a bandage. Blood dribbles from her palm into another cupped hand, and a pool of thick liquid forms like gold-glittering craft glue.

More thundering at the door, frantic as if Grimflail knows what we are about to try.

As her blood overflows, she rubs her hands together, coating her skin in the liquid. It's an eerie, otherworldly scene as she reaches under the mask and spreads out the liquid. The mask lifts ever so slightly with a soft wet sound, flesh peeling back. Spare drops of golden blood drip on Rusela's shirt and the surrounding floor, mixing with the sand.

Rusela's fingers curl around the chair. A low scream builds into a guttural cry, and thin, painful-looking veins redden her eyes as she snaps awake. It's the type of pain no person should witness in another.

"Stop," Koglim shouts. "You'll kill her."

The door splinters against the weight of another onslaught. This time the bar bends inward. But it holds.

My mom's hands shake. She sucks in a breath. Between gritted teeth, she says, "No! It's working."

But Rusela's cries become deafening. Something inside me, a mix of terror and sympathy, rages to step forward and save my friend's mother. Rugnus lost his whole city. He can't lose the woman who raised him. "It's not working. Mom, stop!"

She looks back at me. The blood on her hands darkens, turning red but still dripping. Whatever power lay in the goldcraft has been drained. My mom's face is white ash, her eyes shot through with red. She draws one hand out from under the mask. Rusela sags in the chair.

More pounding at the door.

Koglim whirls to face the entrance, preparing himself.

As she withdraws the second hand, my mom plants her first hand on the mask itself. Her head flies back, hair billowing under some unnatural power, and she shrieks as she rips the mask from Rusela.

Rusela jolts upright, taking in as much air as her lungs can hold. She coughs. The mask falls to the floor, my mom's slick red-gold handprint smeared across the dull, scratched surface.

The thudding at the door stops.

"Where"—Rusela's voice is a whisper— "what's happening?" She blinks, and then her eyes focus on me. "Clayson Brightstorm? Is Rugnus... where's my son?"

"He's okay."

With the pounding at the door silenced, Koglim turns to Rusela. "What do you remember? Under the mask... do you remember anything?"

There's an urgency in his voice, an uncharacteristic desperation.

Rusela glances at the mask in the sand. "I remember being under Vor's control before the mask. The whole world... the things people are doing... Grimflail... he's exactly as Rugnus described him. Vor forced me to put on the mask, but Grimflail..." Her face twists. "He's doing this because he wants to. There are darkmages Vor doesn't even have to control. They are just hurting people."

"But," Koglim says softly, "what do you remember under the mask?"

Rusela nods. "Everything."

Koglim's face falls.

Anger coils deep within me. Why would anyone wanna cause this type of suffering?

"In a population of millions," Andalynn says. "Murderers, oath breakers... there are probably hundreds of Loamin eager to do damage where they can. The population of Keelcrawl prison alone. But Grimflail..."

My head spins. "The world is burning and—"

"He'd help it burn." Andalynn wrings her hands. This is the type of world she has spent her life battling against, a world heavy with chaos and death, filled with hate and revenge.

I take her hand. "We find the key, defeat Vor, and make the world into something greater. We follow your vision."

A mighty crack ricochets from wall to wall. Our heads snap toward the door. There's a big enough hole that Hardkeeper could throw in another husk. How many people are outside this door with Grimflail?

Koglim grabs a coffee table and charges, plugging the hole. "Go to the other room! Grimflail will leave us. We can keep searching. Don't come back until you absolutely have to."

Both my mom and Rusela can barely hold up their heads. I quickly heal the cut on my mom's hand, but it doesn't fully seal—must be something about the goldcraft. Taking the only new stone this team found, I grab the box and return to the other room.

The others are crowded around the hearth.

"Ho, finally," Brig says. "Found three more. We need your expert translation skills." His face falters when our eyes meet. "What happened?"

The attacks resume in this room.

"Rugnus, we... Rusela..."

Rugnus' hand flies to his mouth. He closes his eyes. "What is it?"

"My mom's concealer, it—"

"Tell me you didn't try to remove the mask?"

I nod. "It worked, Rugnus. She's okay."

The hand at his mouth trembles. "Ide keep me. Clayson." His voice catches, and tears spill from his eyes. Then he clears his throat and focuses directly on me. "Did she remember? Being under the mask... does she know what she did?"

"Yes. She remembers."

Rugnus' shoulders sag. He groans. "Everything?"

I put my hand on his shoulder. "I'm so sorry, Rugnus. We will get him. Grimflail will go down. I promise."

Rugnus blinks hard like he's trying to hold back tears. "Well, let's figure out the key, then."

"Here." I add my stone to the puzzle box. "Looks like only one is left."

Rugnus stares for a second. "Out loud, please."

"*Wraithborn as me, read this stone: Two descendants must open the box, never again to be alone. Vor's secret and the ancients are unlocked, but not for the makers of...* here's the last blank and then... *In the sun, they place their bones.*"

Jeiah has me read it twice more, then shakes her head. "That doesn't sound pleasant. Who has to place their bones in the sun? The two descendants?"

"It's probably a metaphor," Rugnus says.

Jeiah doesn't look convinced.

"The first part," I say, "is just a reference to me: I can read the stones. But two descendants? Blackmug's descendants?"

"That would be me," Rugnus says, shrugging, "but I don't know another descendant of Blackmug. Or... no, my mother."

Jeiah traces the stone. "This is Brightstorm's dungeon. He died first, then Exralt Blackmug. What if it's one descendant of Blackmug but another of Brightstorm?"

Rugnus locks eyes with me like a wire connecting to a live circuit. "That makes more sense." He glances at the box in my hand. "*Two descendants must open the box.*"

He inches forward when I hold it out and takes the other side. He finds the metal plate on the opposite side, and we both stand, waiting for something to happen.

Brig throws his hands in the air. "That didn't work. So much for poetry."

"Maybe the last piece of the puzzle..." Jeiah offers. "We've searched this place top to bottom. My guess is that it's in the other room."

The door bulges and strains against another attack.

"If I go back there... Grimflail can break down their defenses. There's a hole in the door. They're only safe because I'm here."

Jeiah weighs this. "But how long will it be before he breaks this one down?"

"We'll look a while longer here," Rugnus says. "Our door is still in okay shape."

Another *thud* against the door. "For how long?"

We scour every place we can find, turn over every pillow, move the furniture, and peel the rugs away from the stone floor. So far, all the puzzle pieces they've found were near items made for a child: a small cup, a pillow, and a large plush dragon in a bronze chest. I try to picture the other room, but that room is dark and half-covered in sand, which was my fault for not covering the window quickly enough.

The sand.

The living area in this place hasn't been covered. In one corner, I find a box of simple metal connecting blocks, but there's no stone.

Jeiah's still searching the kitchen. I call to her. "Did you find one in here?"

She pauses along the side of the table and looks over. "No. You would think we would have. It fits the pattern. What about in the other room?"

"They could've missed it. When the husk opened, it filled half the living room with sand. If they didn't know what to look for..."

After a short discussion, we agree; I'll go back to the other room, but only for a second. I can give them instructions and come back.

The second I appear in the other room, Koglim—who's been waiting by the door—grabs the coffee table and presses it against the breach just as I see movement through the gap. "Be nice if you could give a warning!"

"There's a toy box under the sand. Have you found it?"

"No," Andalynn says. "We'll get it."

In a blink, I'm back in the other room.

"They hadn't checked there. Or if they did, they didn't dig deep enough."

"They'll find it," Brig says with confidence. "Exciting, huh? Do you think it's a physical key or—"

"Don't know," Rugnus says, "but the more I think about those lines, the more I think it means Clayson and me."

We look at the hearth where the poem sits. Jeiah has me read it again. Rugnus has me slow down so we can think about each line one at a time. Between each line, I hear a thud against the door like a thumping heartbeat. Rugnus and I attempt to open the box together a few more times.

"Maybe it has to do with the two rooms?" Brig offers. "Two descendants in two rooms."

Jeiah shakes her head. "But the box doesn't exist in both rooms at once. There has to be something else that opens it. Best guess? Something will happen when we place the last stone. Then the box itself holds the key."

Rugnus, deep in thought, leans against the kitchen table. "I don't like this. It doesn't seem right. And that poem... *place their bones in the sun...*"

I wait only another minute and then return to the other room. Andalynn stands ready with the stone. "Here."

This stone seems heavier than the others. I read it out loud. "Of the crafted rock."

Koglim growls. He's pushed back from the door. My mom moves to help him.

"I'll take it back."

"Wait. How many more?"

"That should be it."

"Recite it. Quick."

I've repeated it enough times that I know it. "Uh, with the last phrase, it says:

The color drains from her face. "Blackmug didn't want or expect anyone to come for this... ever."

"We think the two descendants could be Rugnus and me."

The world erupts in waves of water, and Brude appears, eyes set on me. He charges.

"Go!" Andalynn says.

I return to the other room. My arms and shirt are wet. My breaths come in short bursts. What did I do? I shouldn't have stayed that long.

Jeiah sinks her fingers into my shoulder. "Clayson. Clayson! What happened?"

"I think it was another husk. Koglim's friend appeared. He attacked."

Thud! Thud! Thud! Thud!

"Let's get this over with," Rugnus says. He's already standing by the hearth.

Hands shaking, I throw him the last stone. He places it in the puzzle frame as I catch my breath. The second he steps back, the mouth of the hearth triples in size. The embers inside brighten into beams of light strong enough that we all look away. There's a blast of hot wind.

Rugnus yells over the shrill sound of the windstorm. "It's what I thought!"

I shield my eyes with a hand. The hearth is large enough to enter.

Inside, there's a glowing brightstorm.

"No!" I scream toward Rugnus. "No!"

But he's a black silhouette against the eternal, burning sun.

In the sun, they place their bones.

I rush toward Rugnus, but he's already crossed the threshold. It rebuilds itself as I move, leaving only an arm-sized gap. I tear at the stones, but they won't move. I scream through the gap. "Rugnus!"

He turns toward my voice. "I know what we have to do! Two descendants. It will open the box, the key. Vor's secret is unlocked... but not for us! We place our bones in the sun. This is what we have to do."

The weight of a boulder—no, a building, a city—crushes me into nothing. This is not a game Brightstorm has played with us to be watched and viewed by Loamin sitting in Kel's Lounge. This is not a challenge where we break off pieces of ourselves and heal with leadcraft. Blackmug must have planned this challenge to require the deaths of two people. Only that would be a great enough witness that the key was needed.

I understand this. It's attached to the structure of my very body, into the strands of my life that keep me sewn together, that rebuild me. But there will be no rebuilding this time.

My resolve firms into a reflection of what I see on Rugnus' face. He knows what's being asked of us. "Okay."

"Hey," he says softly. "This time, *I* made the rash decision. And it's the right one."

I nod. I don't fight the tears that fall as I blink. "I'll go to the other room and..."

Oh, no. I'm not the only one who can go into the hearth from the other room. We say her name at the same time. "Andalynn."

Horrified, I say. "She'll go inside."

Rugnus shakes his head. "No. It must be you! You hear me! She's the only one that can piece this world back together. It must be you!"

The box. I dropped it on the floor somewhere. My hands feel

for it, numb. Slow hands. Here. There it is. I grab it. Jeiah is screaming something, but I can't stop. I have to go.

The lights in the other room are back on. No. It's the hearth. It's open.

It *was* open.

My mom is frantic, her face twisted in horror, as her fingers tear at the bricks lining the hearth. Koglim is restraining Brude the best he can, scrambling to pin his arms, reaching over him, looking for a place to lock on. But none of that matters. Andalynn is not in the room. She's not here. And if she's not in the room, she's in the fire. In the sun. I rush toward the opening and scream her name, peering through the impossibly small gap.

A faint response comes as if she's yelling but too far away. "I love you, Clayson. It had to be this way. Make the world what it should be!"

The light envelops her, but I don't look away. I want her burned into my eyes. The past and the future are gone. Missing from this world now. Some horrifying craft has ripped them from me—my friend and my sister. There's a wall I can't break through; there's a weight I can't shift. I sink further and further to the bottom of some vast cavern I'll never return from.

The box clicks open in my hands.

The key is a cold rock made from obsidian. A small shield that can't protect anyone. One side is blank, and the other holds the shape of a Brightstorm crest. I guess at what this is; Brightstorm merged my father's lapel pin—the one Rugnus had just been wearing—with the key that will lead us to the destroyer, the key Erikzin and Exralt left behind, never to be uncovered. They miscalculated.

The two rooms combine. Light and dark. Jeiah and Brig and Koglim. My mother—Andalynn's mother—stricken at the foot of the hearth. Rugnus' mother is bewildered and gaunt. The lock is restored against the door. Koglim's arms are empty. Grimflail is pushed away by the power that runs this dungeon. But it's all meaningless.

The hearth finally, painfully opens. Instead of a destroying sun, there's a glowing door.

Jeiah presses Icho into my hands, but I can hardly hold onto it. We move like shadows into the hearth toward the door. I feel my breath, hear my anguish far away. My mom's golden blood is on my hands. We hold each other up and walk toward the door. Muted questions come my direction from Rusela, but my ears are hard-packed with emotion, with disbelief.

"They'll be okay," I say. "Once we leave the dungeon. They'll be okay."

Jeiah strokes my arm. "I'm so sorry, Clayson."

As she pulls me through the bright threshold door, my shuttered emotions crystalize into a single thing. The terror and fear, the disbelief and shock, it all drops away like flakes of stone. Inside, I find something snarling and angry.

I find rage.

RAGE INWARD

THE EXIT LOBBY of Erikzin Brightstorm's dungeon is black as pitch. He invented the strongest light source under granite, but here, in this place, he leaves us in darkness. It feels right, though. Death is the same bleak pit we find ourselves in now.

How do you kill a champion? It's what Brightstorm deserves —what Blackmug deserves for creating a no-win situation. The whole dungeon—the soft lights and pillows, the childhood memories, the cozy feel of the cottage—all masked this terrible, awaiting sacrifice. Even if I return now, search for the heart of his dungeon and tear it from the stone, he'll live on in another body, like Vor. A villain.

The key cuts into my palm.

The real key may be that is there is no key. This is all a terrible illusion. It must be.

Rusela keeps asking about her son, but no one dares answer her. Mom is in worse shape. Her sobs fill the world, deafening. Koglim tries to console her.

"Clayson, we're going back to the cabin." Jeiah's voice and hands reach out for me, but my body goes rigid. "It's gonna be bright," she says.

I close my eyes. I don't wanna see the sun. Not ever.

But we appear on the surface at the height of the day, standing in front of Rugnus and Andalynn's home. I finally break down. My legs lose strength, and I crumble into the gravel road. I don't know if I cry, or if I scream, or if I stop breathing.

Next to me, Koglim whispers. "This can't be happening."

My hand closes around the sharp key, digging the cut deeper until it bleeds. I keep the fist for a long time. Someone moves me to the cabin. Hemdi maybe. I'm glad it's not the ministack. Winta is asking questions. Then she's yelling questions. Something flies across the room and breaks. Did I throw it? Did Winta? Our eyes meet, but... I can't. I can't look at her.

My legs push me upward, knees bending, muscles tensing.

I make for the door as I hear Hemdi echoing Koglim's disbelief. "This can't be happening."

Well, it is.

The key drops out of my hand, bloodied. I leave, and no one follows me. The heat is oppressive. I have no destination but the trees. I don't take any path and can feel the brambles against my legs and hands. No, fists—they're still fists.

The day is lost to this: wandering, hurting, hiding, avoiding. When I hear movement or see someone searching for me, I find another place to exist. I don't go to the cliff, fruit trees, or the shop. I go to the most forsaken places on the property.

Late at night, I wander back to the cabin and find my room. I don't wanna sleep, so I sit at my desk. At some point, my mom comes and stands in the doorway. Her eyes are red, but she doesn't say anything at first.

How much time passes?

Then she enters the room and sits next to the chair and cries and cries.

"I need your father here." These are her only words before she crawls into the bed and falls asleep.

The sun comes up, and I haven't slept.

I return to the woods, and the sun goes down.

On the third day, I head back to the cabin. At some point,

someone must have determined that the obsidian key belongs on the kitchen table. They've washed my blood from it. I swallow and move to the living room, only to find Koglim and Rusela sitting across from each other, quietly talking.

"He'd want that," Koglim says.

"Want what?" I ask.

Koglim stands clumsily, his eyes grief-stricken. But he didn't cause this—I did.

"Clayson. Hey, morning. We were, uh, we—"

Rusela scrutinizes me, her eyes set in firm resolve. It feels like she's challenging me. "We're holding a celebration tonight for my son and Andalynn."

The blood drains from my body through an invisible cut somewhere, center mass.

"No. We're not." The bones in my jaw force my teeth together tightly.

Koglim's chin tips toward the ground. "Clayson, I... look. This... it's awful. No one feels right. Even if we can't—I can't— believe what happened—"

"I can believe it." My anger and rage crystalize into sharp words. "They're dead. Say it. Rugnus, he's dead. Andalynn... they're not coming back. I don't know what there is to disbelieve. So, no! No celebration!" My voice is reverberating off the pine boards now, loud and out of control, but I don't care. "There's nothing to celebrate. How about this? How about we burn their castle down, rip out all of Andalynn's plants, and tear down every stone. Then maybe—"

"Clayson!" Jeiah calls a warning to me from the door. She's just walked in. Winta is standing behind her, holding Echel. Winta's on my side. I can see it in her eyes. But she has to be careful now. She has to be kind, or she might just join the revolution I'm about to start. Everyone else is trying to sweep them under the rug. There are two sides. Those who want to lay them to rest and me.

It's the first time I've looked Jeiah in the eyes since our return.

The last three days have merged into a single, non-event, a nothingness. My chest heaves. My mind circles more angry words. I won't be able to stop if I keep going. My words will expand out and destroy even more things.

I expect Jeiah's words to be hard, but they're as warm as a comforter. "Leave the cabin, Clayson. Please. Go."

All the air leaves my lungs like a punch to the stomach. I can't breathe. Almost at a run, I flee the den, exiting through the kitchen door.

Lagnar stands against the post. He follows me off the porch. "Young Brightstorm."

I whirl on him. "Don't call me that."

"Whew, sure thing. Don't you worry. Hard to be responsible for something like this. Trust me. I know. Your father's father... this is the type of thing he asked of me. Duty and order... don't make it right."

I grab him by the shirt.

"Whoa, whoa. Take it easy. Come on now. Just calm yourself."

"Stay the hell away from me." I shove him.

"Oh, we're using taffy swears." He laughs but doesn't follow me when I storm off toward the woods. "You gotta come to grips with this *Brightstorm*. This is the way of craft, the way of kings and kingdoms. Look, I'm sorry for you." His voice rises the further away I get. "I'm sorry about them, but everything wants a piece of your soul! So, what do you do? Are you gonna run away from this? Huh?"

The words fade, but I can't get them off my skin. I run. My legs pump, my hands whip the undergrowth, and the trees create a tunnel. There are so many paths through the grove, but I've worn them all down to dirt.

When I finally burst past the trees, I nearly run straight into Hemdi. It's an open clearing full of sunlight and bright summer grasses.

He takes one look at me and nods. "Help me with this, will you."

He's got a good size sapling in hand. The roots are canvas-wrapped, the small limbs tenderly folded outward. I open my mouth to make an excuse, but he hands me the sapling. Following the end of the shovel, I find a large hole. We move together, unbinding the roots and spreading them over a small mound of dirt at the bottom. This will give the roots room to breathe and grow. I taught Hemdi about this, but he's a quick study when it comes to plants.

We pat the dirt into place. Hemdi jabs wooden rods through the ground on either side of the tree and ties them off. He has the four-wheeler out. In the back, there's a large water tank. I unwind the hose and prime the pump.

"How much water?" Hemdi asks.

My voice is raw when I speak. "A good soak early on... gotta keep moisture around the roots so they can get established. Make sure you water it tomorrow. Early's best."

"Will do."

"So." I don't hide the disgust from bleeding into my words. "Is this some kind of memorial? Some kind of tribute?"

The light in his eyes shifts from understanding to sadness to knowing. "Just a tree."

I know what this is, though. This is something he's choosing, his way of marking the passing of his friends. Will it have any meaning? The tree will grow and change over the years if it survives. Then like everything else, it too will come to an end.

"Clayson," he says. "You know the garden could use some weeding."

Everyone on the property knows the garden could use some weeding. And everyone knows I like being outdoors. I like walking the paths and climbing the cliff. But they also know how much I hate weeding. How I pass it off to everyone else and take the more complicated, interesting tasks.

"Yeah," is all I offer him.

He nods and returns to the four-wheeler. The engine starts, and he doesn't look back as he drives away. This is Hemdi's way, looking forward. He's dealt with more loss than any of us. As a child, he lived in the Kingdom of Firas Andem, under the mountains of South America. There are only a handful of brightstorms, and many Loamin lived on homesteads deep in the Andes. But now, having seen a similar cottage, the homes of the people before Erikzin Brightstorm, I can understand what Hemdi might have lost when the knights came and invaded his home.

I'm suddenly glad he wasn't with us in that place, with Grimflail trying to gain entrance. How the hearth turned into a gaping maw and swallowed the world.

"Weeding," I murmur. "Yeah, alright."

The walk is short.

Through the trees, I see the brown swatch of dirt ahead. When I emerge, it's clear that we've neglected this chore far too long. The weeds haven't grown tall yet, haven't fattened with seeds, but they've multiplied and multiplied and multiplied. And that sometimes makes it more difficult, easier to put off. Sometimes I'd rather have one massive weed I have to dig out than a thousand tiny plants.

There's a hoe someone left leaning against the tree. Have we had rain? Not good to leave these things out. They become rusted and dull. Had someone else been weeding in the last few days?

The work is oddly calming: the kiss of the afternoon sun on my skin, a mist of sweat on my forehead. There's even a slight breeze drifting in from the mountains. But I hate how good it feels.

The weeds have the barest of roots. Before long, I've cleared half of the garden, breaking up the dirt, raking out the uprooted plants, and leveling everything again. Everything we've planted will have an easier time finding nutrients with less competition.

Jeiah appears in the distance, near the cabin. She waits on the gravel road for a second, then veers in my direction.

What do I say to her? What do I say to anyone?

Ten feet away, she says, "Thought you hated weeding?"

"Just needs doing."

She runs her fingers over the onion shoots as she comes closer. She sighs and looks up. "I'm going to tell you this clearly, for everyone's benefit."

Leaning on the red handle of the hoe, I give her permission with a nod. I can feel what's coming.

She takes my hand as if she's testing my reaction. I don't move. Then she lets go and slips her arms around my sides. I don't want this comfort, but it feels so good I eventually bring my arms up and pull her in, tears stinging my eyes. We stand there for a while until she leans back and takes my hand again.

"You have every right to feel completely awful about Rugnus and your sister," she says. "I know how it is to lose someone. My mother died when I was young, then my father last year. And StoneYoke claimed our aunt and uncle. Brig and I... You can't just float away. You said something to me once about how you make hard decisions. Do you remember?"

I nod. "I said I should let you be my anchor. You help me see what makes sense. But... this is not that. There's no decision to be made here. We can't keep going back and forth between worlds. There's always a terrible consequence. What if... what if this isn't the end of the cost?"

She nods slowly, understanding. "It might not be. But you're wrong. You said there's no decision to be made. How about the way you're treating everyone? Treating me. Even your mom. That's a decision whether you like it or not. And she needs you. If there's any way you can clear your head... any way you can come back to us..."

The weight of losing Rugnus and Andalynn still crushes my chest. "I can't."

Her mouth hardens. With a shake of her head, she says. "What have you eaten in the last few days? Huh?" Her words carry a pointed edge.

"Eaten?" It's a strange question, but I realize the answer. "I—"

"Barely anything," she answers. "You slept till eleven this morning. I've never seen you sleep past seven. And..."

"What?"

"And you haven't even changed your clothes. Did you even realize? You smell awful. You're a mess, Clayson. And we need you back. We don't need you to ignore how you feel, but we need you to help us decide what to do next. Everyone's waiting for you."

"They shouldn't. This is over. We stay here. The key. Vor. Everything. None of those things matter. We can't go back to that world."

She takes a step back from me. "Ide keep me, Clayson. Open your eyes. None of us can stay here. We're all dealing with the consequences of the dungeon."

"Why can't we stay here?"

"You know why not." She jabs her index finger into my chest. "There's so much I love about you, Clayson. But look in a mirror. Clean up. I'm trying here, but you're not giving me anything back. You always want to do things on your own. And maybe that's what you need right now, but we are here. Your mother lost her daughter and her son-in-law. Rusela lost her only son. Hemdi and Winta lost their closest friends.

"Lagnar is my *boss* now. I'm the Paladin in a dungeon where he is the keeper. And I'm sick to my stomach about that, but I'm choosing to try. That's all I'm asking of you. Try. We're having that celebration tonight. Come if you want, but don't judge everyone else because of the way we're grieving."

She stalks out of the garden.

The two halves of me struggle for control. I don't wanna feel anything, but I need Jeiah. She's right; she's been my anchor in the last few months, but I have to let her in. I call out, desperate to stop her. "Jeiah, wait!"

She doesn't stop.

The sun speaks in her absence, speaks in shadows and heat. It's four, maybe five o'clock, plenty of the day left. Reluctantly, I return to the work of the garden. My dad would be astonished at how fast I clear the rest of the weeds. I find a wheelbarrow, clean everything up, and dump all the dead plants into the compost. They'll become something more useful, but it will take time.

I take the hoe and the wheelbarrow back to the tool shed, but once they're in place, I stand in the doorway for an impossibly long time. When the door suddenly opens, I step back, banging my head against the tomato cages strung in the rafters.

Rubbing my head, I watch Hemdi move inside and place his tools away for the day. He looks as dirty and smells as bad as I do. Well, maybe not, but still. Giving me a brief bow of his head, he backs toward the door.

"Hemdi..."

"I need to get changed for—"

"You were there with me, in the forest with those things, the Dura wraiths, Jassin. He said the key would help us find the destroyer. He said the destroyer might help us bring an end to Vor. The key could."

"That is what he said right before he killed Landred."

Something lodges in my throat. "I... do you think the key was worth... worth all this?"

"Worth Andalynn and Rugnus? No, I don't. And neither do you. Except..."

How long has it been since their deaths? The word 'except' might as well be 'accept'. It means we're supposed to move onward. It means we are not allowed to make decisions out of our pain. I won't be able to do this. I raise my hand, hoping Hemdi will stop speaking.

"Except," Hemdi says, ignoring my attempt to quiet him, "there no longer remains a choice to save them and return the key. And now that we have the key—the thing that cost us so much—how can we just leave it there on that table? It insults their sacrifice not to use it."

"That's a terrible thing to say."

"It's a terrible thing to hear. I only heard it this morning."

I scoff. "Who told you?"

"Myself." He pauses, then says. "I'll see you at the celebration."

Once he's gone, I stand perfectly still, fumbling with only my empty hands. The cut from the key isn't healing well. It's an angry red gash, further irritated by my work in the garden.

The key. Just sitting there on the table.

After losing count of the minutes—the one high window in the little shed doesn't help me read the sun—I drift beyond the door, back into the cabin, past Winta and Hemdi sitting on the porch swing with Echel, past Rusela and Koglim in the kitchen weaving paper lanterns with craft, past my mom sitting in the den with Emberfence and Brig.

In my room, Jeiah sits at my desk.

"I'm taking your advice," I say.

She tries to hand me the quick clean Rugnus gave me the day I met him. A real Loamin wouldn't shower, but how can I use the flask after... I push the object away.

"I'll get cleaned up, but I'm not coming to this thing you guys are doing." I can't say the word celebration. I take the first shirt I see, grab a few more things from my dresser, and move to the door.

At the same moment, she stands. She places a hand on my shoulder. "You can get through this. I'm still here."

With a quick nod, I move through the door, lock myself in the bathroom, and shower until the water runs cold. The lilac-scented soap in the shower belonged to my dad. I stare through the eye-level window, parting the curtain to see a sliver of the forest. The evening has opened into something made from orange and red.

When I'm dressed and ready, there's a knock on the door. "Clayson?"

My mom.

"Yeah."

"Come to the celebration." There's an angry edge to her

voice.

I keep the door closed. "No. I just can't, okay."

"No, that's not okay. That's not okay with me."

"I'll deal with this my own way."

There's no response for a long time. Through the door, I hear her breathing, long inhalations and exhalations. Finally, she says. "I can't do this without you, Clayson."

Letting go of the doorknob, I say. "Yes, you can. I'm not important."

She pounds on the door. It's so sudden and unexpected that I recoil as if it slapped me.

"Clayson! Ide keep me. If you... just..." Her voice could cut open steel. The next sound is a desperate groan, a cry retreating down the hallway.

Looking anywhere but the door, I find the mirror above the sink. The broadness of my face looks flat. My stubble is thick. I don't look real to myself. I whisper, "What are you doing, Clayson?"

When I finally leave the bathroom, the cabin is empty, and the lights are off. I float down the dark hallway and switch on the TV.

The current channel details when the next hurricane of the season may hit landfall off the Atlantic. The remote finds a place back on the coffee table, and I watch without really watching. Darkness seeps from the walls as the minutes tick by.

The world is a dangerous and terrible place.

Rugnus and Andalynn wanted to rebuild the Loamin world into something beautiful. Something that felt and sounded like the StoneYoke festival. Laughter. Food. Games. They knew how to rebuild this world. The only thing I know how to do is destroy everything around me.

I turn off the TV and go to my dad's study. A desk, 80s sci-fi posters, a table with oiled shop rags. Something soft smashes under my foot, and I'm surprised to find a makeshift bed—pillows and blankets dragged from my dad's room. Mom's been sleeping here. Has she been as heartsick as me?

Has it really been days since Brightstorm Dungeon?

All of this started with my dad, with his secrets. I return to the den and pick up the remote, but I can't bring myself to turn on the TV. My grip tightens. In a fury, I shove the coffee table with my foot. Not enough. I hurl the remote at the wall. Every impulse sends me searching for loose items, and the world comes apart at the seams.

A half minute later, it's Vor's voice that brings my rage to a halt. *You're the perfect wrecking ball.* I collapse to the floor and scream.

When I'm finally wrung out, I survey the damage I've done. The Spangler crest is on the ground. Chairs are toppled, and the couch lies on its side. A lamp flickers upside down in the corner of the room. I'm lucky nothing collided with the TV, though it's been nudged at an angle. I pick up the crest to start cleaning up and freeze.

A clean-cut square gap in the drywall stares back at me like the threshold of a dungeon. I hoist a chair against the wall to get a closer look inside.

The first thing I see is a teal AMP. I read the name.

THERIAS BRIGHTSTORM

I thought my dad didn't keep any objects in the house.

I glance at the scores. Peerless of goldcraft, coppercraft, and ironcraft. His shieldcraft is an open circle. His weakness. The thought of my dad going with his mother and father to Tinseer Dungeon for his summation seems like text in a history book. Summation recordings aren't public; the dungeons refuse any bluecraft or other recording without a keeper's key.

It's strange, though. Tincraft is one of my dad's lowest scores on the AMP, and yet Tinseer Dungeon called to him. His mother was a Tinseer by birth and craft. She was distantly related to Tinkeeper, whom Vor killed when he attacked the council.

So much history and connections, and Vor severed them one by one.

I set the AMP back and keep digging. A gold ring with a red glass stone, the metal warped around the stone like a dozen sharp claws. An iron dagger bound with a hard wooden handle. Something glimmers in the back corner. I reach into the depths of the compartment.

When I pull the object toward me, I know what it will be, and a dangerous idea forms in my mind even before I spin the aluminum can around to read its label. GAMGIM. It's the same type of energy drink that first took me to Gamgim when we ran from Bazalrak.

My blood thickens. I know someone else must have Icho. They've all kept it out of sight, fearing I will do something rash—for good reason. I'm about to do something rash again.

The ring feels solid in my hands. I tuck it into my pocket. I leave the furniture overturned and the lamp flickering in the corner. In my own room, I find my bracelet on my desk and slip it on. I'm jogging now, back to the kitchen. The key waits for me on the table. Sular. No longer is it made from iron but from stone. I pick it up and will it to do something, but I feel no craft.

The energy drink hisses when I pull the tab. It's as bitter and metallic as I remember. Unlike the night with Dad at the RV park, there's no foilgrip to stop me. Though I'm peerless in budgecraft, there's still a long moment of darkness and the feeling that I'm being reassembled. A few seconds later, I appear in the forest of Gamgim. Whatever I was able to see with Landred around is gone. I've arrived exactly where I met Rugnus, which only hardens my resolve.

Jassin is going to answer my questions about this key.

I push my bracelet onto my sleeve, removing its contact from my skin. I won't be on the defense tonight. I slip on my dad's ring, and my muscles bulk up a couple sizes. Even with an average goldcraft score, this relic is strong. A surge of power hammers like a new pulse in my veins. My hands take on a golden glow as my body rises from the ground. The power comes with an edge of goldcraft sensation—like a sunburn, a tightness of my skin.

I rocket forward like a missile, smashing through a pine tree. Splinters erupt around me as I call to the wraiths. "Jassin, where are you!"

Nothing answers. I fly deeper into the forest of Gamgim under scattered light.

My mind flashes to the image Landred showed me of a knife sticking out of my body. I bury it deeper inside my skull, a place without images or words. A place made only of emotions, both fear and hope.

I call out again, but the dense trees absorb my words.

Winding through the trees, my feet barely scrape the forest floor. I stop in the largest clearing I can find and hold up the key. "I'm here! Speak to me!"

Jassin appears regal and feral-eyed. "Wraithking."

The word is mockery from his lips.

The air shakes with craft: I can't catch my breath; nausea worms its way through my center; there's sunlight and revelation and fear and the prickle of hair at the back of my neck. The swirl of wraiths holds all this power and more.

I don't care. "We make a deal, Jassin! Here and now. You want the destroyer! Fine. I'll deliver. But tell me how to defeat Vor. What can I use against him? I won't leave until you give me something."

He sneers. "You would demand our trust? Exralt made promises too."

"I need this. You tell me how to stop Vor, and we have a deal. I'll swear to it."

The other wraiths begin to materialize around us.

"We no longer make oaths," Jassin says. His grin is wicked, eager.

I don't flinch. "Then you'll never see the key again."

"You misunderstand. You're not leaving."

CONTEND WITH GHOSTS

A GALE-FORCE WIND knocks me from the air. My head slaps against the hard ground. Blackness reverberates through my skull. I groan.

I crawl to my feet, my head pulsing. My hand comes away bloody. When I open my eyes, the trees are swimming with clouds and light—not just one wraith, but an army of them. I swallow and blink, trying to reorient myself. A hive of wraiths swirls before me. The wall of trees is now a wall of enemies.

Jassin's bottom half transforms into a dark cloud, glittering with fireworks. He grows, towering above me. He may be trying to intimidate me, but with my dad's ring and my rage, I gather all my strength to face him. Golden light slips down my arms almost involuntarily as the power of my dad's ring comes to life. But I'm a fool. Something flickers in Jassin's eyes as he looks at the cloud around him—excitement.

Dread. Its familiar power washes over me. Why did I think I could use my dad's power? Why did I think goldcraft would help me? Can they hurt me like they hurt Landred? The vision of the knife through my chest flashes in my eyes. I scramble to move my bracelet into position, but I'm too late.

Jassin flies toward me, his cold hands finding purchase against my neck. He pushes me to the ground, and I hear the forest move as one. The silvery bodies of the Dura wraiths attack me like frenzied animals. There are no dazzling lights, no clouds of mist, only emaciated bodies revealed after eons of drought. Every inch of my skin is pulled outward. They scrape horrifying nails against my body. They yank my limbs in opposite directions. The muscles in my neck tense as I clench my jaw against the pain.

I grasp the key tightly in my hand.

Something pops out of place in my arm, leaving me screaming. I roar until their feasting takes my voice or dampens it. My sweat runs cold. My chest tightens. Jassin reaches his translucent fingers through my skull and pulls something loose. Craft. Maybe I'm immune to Loamin wraiths, but not to these monsters. Our minds connect, forcing me to understand. The other Dura are shadows of these beings. A mockery. Vor and Ara might be able to multiply craft, but these beings can manipulate it further. Subtracting, dividing it. Taking. He's removing my craft in order to take my power as a champion. There's an order to loss.

He rips every power from me, and it feels like another death. The pain from this new loss surges like a tsunami of grief mixed with all the hurt from the loss of my friends.

He withdraws his icy fingers from my skull.

But Jassin's connection leaves something behind. An image, like an old negative from a camera. I recognize the place that flashes in my mind. Edium Fiarie. The House of Ide, where Loamin send their dead back to the earth, melt them into the mountain. The image flutters for a second, and then I'm inside Edium Fiarie itself, the obsidian blockade that divides the Foundation from a ring of lava surrounding it. The stone from the puzzle in Brightstorm Dungeon, the stone the lapel transformed into. That's where I recognize it from—the House of Ide.

That's where the key goes. That's where the entrance to the protodungeons is.

But I won't live to use the key. Jassin smiles cruelly and reaches into my chest. Somehow, I know what he's after next. My invulnerability to normal wraiths, my connection to them. He's searching through my organs; I can almost feel the cold vapor of his fingers glance over my heart. He's getting close. The others are yipping around me like hungry coyotes waiting to clean up after a kill.

Jassin's fears come spilling into my mind. The key is dangerous. It holds a power Jassin doesn't even understand. A connection to the dungeons used by his kind. By Dura. A question arises in my mind—Dura can't go into dungeons. But could they enter with the key?

Jassin tries to hide the truth from me. He pulls back his hand, but his thoughts—our connection—betray him. With the key, Dura can enter the dungeon. With the key, even a Loamin could wield the heart of any dungeon. Even one made new with mithrium.

The shield.

Enraged, Jassin pushes his hand deeper into my chest. His fingers close around my heart. He finds the power I have as Wraithking. I cry out. He can't have that. I need it to use the key. I see that now. His body is still flesh for the moment. I push with everything I have, shaking him loose.

Rolling to the side, I'm met with the hungry faces of the other wraiths. I struggle to my feet, but they swirl around me, no longer corporeal but a force of nature. There has to be a way out, but I can't see through the cloud. Then, there's a flash of light and a shock of lightning through my body. Pain explodes across my back. A prick of a cold metal bursts through my stomach— Jassin's knife. This is exactly what I saw in the vision. My eyes punch open. Everything around me comes into clear focus.

I'm not leaving here alive. Jassin made his threat real.

I've kept my status as Wraithking but traded my life.

My hands reach for the knife, but he's already removed it. They come away bloody. I'm lying on the ground now. The wraiths become silent, or maybe the world becomes muted when you're dying. My limbs prickle at first but then go numb. All the wraiths hiss and tremble, waiting for me to die.

My fist begins to unfurl, showing a sliver of the key.

Commotion.

The sound of distant yelling and the banging of metal. The edges of my vision are sparking with fire. I hear Rugnus and Andalynn. *It's okay. We're still here.*

A lie. They're gone forever, and I'm following them quickly.

Don't give up, Clayson. Ara's voice. But that can't be right; she's trapped under granite. She can't be here. But her voice is as clear as if she was kneeling over my body. *I'm with you.*

A swift shadow appears above me. I barely see its face before... blue. Everything's electric blue. What's blue in a forest so dark?

"It's me, Clay," Jeiah says.

Is it truly her? Her magenta hair brushes my face. My mouth is dry. My words gasping. "...can't be. How?"

"Hemdi and Koglim are using wraithbait. We've got to go."

But this is the end for me. I can't leave without telling her. "I... Jeiah, I—"

Jeiah screams my name, but my eyes are long closed. Muffled pinpricks of faraway light reveal the wraiths are closing in again.

My eyes open for a split second, and I see a blanket of stars.

"Clayson," Jeiah says. "We're back. We made it. Now heal yourself."

"...took it," I murmur. "My craft."

Jeiah screams for help. She screams and screams.

I slip from this world, not into some fantasy, not some ancient ghost of a world; I slip into absolute oblivion.

Can a person exist in oblivion? Do they remember what they were before? Or do they only remember the absence of something? Blood. Is that what's missing? There was blood on my hands—a lot of it. There was the knife, then the forest, then the dark. Then a dream of Jeiah. I never told her I loved her.

How much time passes?

Wake up! Ara's voice again.

In the absence of *something,* I feel uneasy, not like a bad budge, but like what I'd imagine death to be. Is this *that?* Did my consciousness slip out of my body, and now I'm something else?

Wait! Jeiah was there when I died. I'm a champion—Wraithking.

She'll be a wraith.

This is not what I wanted. I found more clues, and I need to give them to Jeiah. She'll put everything together. She'll understand. But I've lost her. I'm either dying, or I'm already dead.

Is she somewhere feeling she's lost me?

Wake up!

There's no waking up.

Clayson, wake up!

No. I'm something else. I've lost a part of myself.

What was it I lost? The wraiths took craft from me, but they tried to take something deeper. I was born with a connection to the wraiths. Deep inside me, I feel that connection still. I didn't lose it. They couldn't take it.

And that clue... I had something.

Edium Fiarie. The House of Ide. That's where we have to bring the key. That's where I can find an opening. A pathway to the destroyer. No, to a way to defeat Vor. Maybe, that's what they were hiding. And the mithrium shield... I can use it. That's new. Or could I use it before they took my craft? I don't know. I have to...

"Please, wake up."

Wait, those words were real. Everything else has been a reflection.

"Please." It's Jeiah.

I must have trapped her here with me in my dungeon. Wraithking Dungeon.

"No!" This is a word from my mouth. I have a mouth still. I

have words. I have a purpose, direction—into the House of Ide to search for... something. I can use the mithrium shield.

"That's it," I mutter.

"Clayson?" This is my mom's voice. Where is she? Did she come to Gamgim? Was she there when I died? Is she a wraith, too?

Clayson.

This voice shouldn't be here. No, not voice... voices. They're dead.

"Rugnus," I say. "Andalynn."

"He's delirious." Jeiah's words echo around me.

I blink. Can the dead blink? No.

I blink again, and Jeiah is there. Jeiah, my mom, and Koglim.

It's Koglim that draws me out of this trance. He grabs my shirt and lifts me up slightly. Pain flowers across my back and radiates through me. This is what the knife left behind. But...

Koglim's face is angry. That's not right. Koglim doesn't get angry. He gets excited; he gets jumpy. He should say something funny. Something with dark humor about how we're all going to die deep in the dungeon I've made.

Instead, he says, "He's alive." He drops me to the bed as everyone else protests his actions. Then he looks me directly in the eyes. "Keep Ide, Clayson. You latcher, stay alive, will you? I can't... I couldn't... if you... I already lost..."

Hemdi comes up behind him. "Hey, Koglim, he's gonna be okay. Give him a second."

But none of these voices is the loudest. Ara. I hear Ara.

Clayson, bring it back. I know you can do it. Bring the shield back.

I set up shakily, but Jeiah and my mom each take a hand and push me back down.

Don't, Clayson," Jeiah says. "Hold on. You might not want to sit up."

"No. Ara wants... help me up, please."

No one moves. I push against their hands until they all step back. "The shield. I need to... please."

I swing an uneasy leg over the side of my bed. I'm barefoot, still in my cargo shorts, and my shirt is ripped to shreds. My feet press against the ground, but they don't wanna hold my weight. Koglim reacts first, throwing an arm underneath me.

I grind my teeth, doing my best to ignore the fever of pain. Mom supports my other side.

"No, no. Lay him back down," Jeiah says. "We can't move him."

"Jeiah." Her name is soft on my lips. Her eyes are rimmed red from crying, but I don't look away. She has to trust me. "The shield, please."

Her jaw trembles. "Fine."

She opens the door and steps out of the room. Koglim and Mom help me down the hallway, through the kitchen, and down the back porch steps. A summer breeze cools the sweat on my forehead.

The small, triangular shield awaits me, glowing softly. Lagnar watches from the gravel road, and Brig, Hemdi, Winta—everyone is watching.

"Right up to it," I say.

Koglim shifts his hand around my back, placing another hand over my stomach to steady me but frees my arm.

"Clayson," Mom whispers. "I don't understand."

"Me neither."

Whispers drape over my mind the moment the shield is in my hands. Connection. The voices of many—of the champions maybe, of the wraiths, the Dura, Ide itself, a vast unknowable chorus—fill my mind. A few soft strands of words call for attention: *We're here.* But I cannot know what this means.

"Who's here? Ara?" Who am I even asking? I don't know.

Clayson? The shield… you're connected to it. I'm in Geum Ide. Bring it to me.

This voice is clear. "It's Ara."

"Ara?" Jeiah shakes her head. "How—"

The shield comes free of its mooring, dropping into my hands.

"Impossible." I hear someone say this, but I can't focus on who. I sense the graybulbs we've made. Lines of power draw back into the shield. Whatever's happening, whatever I'm doing, it's weakening the shield's connection with the graybulbs. The safety we've provided our refugees is evaporating. Ara's shield is collecting its full strength again.

"No." I release the shield. The whispers fade into a dull buzz.

My body has regained some strength, healed by the mithrium shield. I can stand again on my own. Still, my breaths come quickly, sweat building up on my forehead, stinging my eyes. My lips are parched. "I should... I need..."

"Rest," Jeiah says. "We can sort this out later."

I return to my room. I ease onto my bed, lying on my back, ignoring the sharp twinge of pain that shoots down my body. Regardless, I'm exhausted, and sleep comes immediately.

When I wake, the lamp is glowing on my desk, it's night, and Hemdi is the only one in the room. I must have stabilized enough for Jeiah and the others to agree to take turns watching me.

"How am I, doc?" I ask.

"Dead. This is actually your dungeon. Kinda disappointing." A smile spreads on his face, and he laughs. "It's a joke, Clayson. You are very much alive. Well, maybe not *very much*. But alive."

When I first woke up, Koglim was angry, and now Hemdi is making jokes. The world is turned upside down. I bet Jeiah sent Brig on a dangerous mission, and Winta is baking cupcakes for everyone just because.

"Here." Hemdi holds out the quick clean.

They don't know. I shake my head. "I can't."

Hemdi's shoulders slump. "Clayson, Rugnus wouldn't want you—"

"It's not that." How do I tell him? I can still feel the fingers digging through my mind. "Jassin took my craft."

Hemdi blinks, confused. "But these wraiths, they're different. And I thought shieldcraft was your highest. Here, try."

Reluctantly, I accept the quick clean. I remove the cap and

take a drink. Nothing happens. I screw the lid back on and pass it back to an astonished Hemdi.

"You mean all of it. They took all of your craft. Everything."

I nod. "I think so."

"But the shield... how did you move it?"

"I'm not sure. But listen, I feel better—hungry—but better. Can you get everyone to the den? I have a lot to explain, and we have some decisions to make."

Hemdi reluctantly agrees. It takes me a few minutes to get new clothes on with the back injury. It's healed thanks to Hemdi and the mithrium shield, but there's still a sharp pull on my nerves if I twist too far right.

When I enter the den, everyone's there. I don't know why I expect to see things still turned over from my outburst, but even the Brightstorm crest has been restored to its place on the wall.

"Hey." It's a weak start to an explanation. "I'm sorry about—"

"Yep, you're a latcher," Lagnar drawls. "Can we skip to the part about how you moved the shield?"

A quick scan around the room and I find only agreement. "Well, you'll need to know what happened."

I start with how I found the budge to Gamgim and everything else my dad left. Winta and Jeiah share a look when I mention his AMP score. But quickly, I turn the conversation to Jassin, trying to make a deal with him. When I describe how he reached into my mind and took my craft, the whole room goes silent. Hemdi confirms this part.

"Jassin tried to take my status as wraithborn, but I pushed him off. I think that's when he decided it would be better if I were dead. He stabbed me, and then you guys showed up."

"The shield?" Jeiah asks.

"I can hear Ara. She wants me to bring it to her. Though, I felt something else. Taking the shield could break its connection with the graybulbs. And I think, now that I don't have craft, it's like... there's room to *hold* the shield. Does that make sense?"

Brig eagerly jumps in. "Do you think you're as strong as a

Dura? Like can you do that thing she does and multiply its power?"

I shake my head. "Doubtful."

Koglim nods with understanding and excitement. "But we could bring the shield back to Ara. It could let us face Vor. You could even take Vor's crown."

"And what about the refugees?" Winta asks. "Those who are connected to the shield with the graybulbs?"

"That is a problem. And there's more," I say tentatively. Everyone waits for my next words, so I choose them carefully. "When Jassin reached into me, I connected with him. It gave me a glimpse of something."

I stare out the window at the gravel road.

Koglim snaps. "Out with it!"

"The entrance to the protodungeons is at Edium Fiarie. And, unless I'm wrong, Ara can use the key made by the Dura to enter the dungeons. Which means..."

"So could Vor," Jeiah finishes. "That makes the key far more dangerous than we thought. If it fell into his hands, who knows what the result would be."

"Won't Ara's dungeon be like Wolfstaff," Mom says, "uh, Kel's, I mean. Clayson took the heart of that dungeon, and it was destroyed. So, since someone took the heart of Ara's dungeon, Vor's and Tas', then won't their dungeons be broken?"

"You're forgetting about the destroyer," I say. "Something is down there with the protodungeons, or the Dura wouldn't have bothered to try and hide it from me. I think it's a way to stop Vor. And we should bring Ara with us in case her protodungeon is connected."

"We're still jumping to conclusions," Jeiah mutters.

"Even if we can move the shield and bring Ara the key," Mom says, "we don't know where she is at the moment."

"She's at Geum Ide. She told me."

Winta stands and dusts off her hands. "Anything else,

Clayson?" I start to answer her, but she just continues. "Because we have something too." She holds up m dad's AMP score.

My face reddens. "You found that... after I—"

"Melted the place? Yeah. And I bet you don't even know what Jeiah and I can do with an AMP score."

I raise my shoulders.

Jeiah takes something from a pocket, a glimmering flat square of metal. The leaf Silverkeeper left for my dad. Vor had given it to him at Silverkeeper's funeral. My dad had told me he destroyed it, but that was a lie. Ara gave it to me when she banished us to the safety of the surface. We've never been able to open it.

"Now, wait just a minute..." Lagnar says, astonishment edging his voice.

Rusela stands and looks at the leaf. "That is Theridal's mark."

Winta smiles. "It is indeed the mark of Theridal Silverkeeper. This was meant only for Therias Brightstorm's eyes, but an AMP gives us access to biometrics."

"Well, what are we waiting for!" Koglim says.

"Five minutes," Jeiah says, moving toward the door with Winta. "We were waiting for Clayson."

The door opens, and there doesn't seem to be a second thought as everyone files out of the room. Only mom is left. I sit down across from her, still processing everything. She traces my dad's ring sitting in her palm.

"You know, your father wanted you to have this someday."

"The ring?"

"It's a relic. Yavan is its name." She smiles. "The week after Andalynn was born, I gave it to him. A gift for a new father."

She's offering it to me. I nudge her fingers closed around it. "You should keep it. Please, I can't use it anyway."

"Right. Sorry... I'm being insensitive. I—"

"No. Mom, seriously. It's better off with you. Don't give it another thought. You're peerless in goldcraft. Look what you did for Rusela. Though, it was pretty cool to fly around and smash through trees."

"I'm surprised Jassin could even attack you. Yavan should have turned your skin to steel."

"Even as a champion, my score in goldcraft was garbage. Guess it didn't work as well for me as it probably did for Dad." I look away from her, trying to imagine my dad hovering through the air, invulnerable and as strong as any fictional superhero.

She taps the iron knife sitting next to her on the table. "What about Krest—that's his iron knife."

"It's not like he'll take them back. And I can't use them."

"Right. Clayson, I can't even imagine what you're experiencing. The Dura wraiths took everything from you."

"I don't know. In a way, I feel... lighter. Is that weird?"

"No. I can understand that."

"I just don't wanna feel useless. How will I face Vor?"

"Maybe that's not what you'll need to do? Would it be so bad if you didn't get to be the hero? All of us. We're ready. Besides, you can use the shield. So..." She chuckles softly. Her words break off a piece of my stubborn pride.

"I haven't made it easy to be my parent."

Another laugh. "You act like there are parents out there finding it easy. I hear raising teenagers can even be hard for humans, and they don't have craft."

I'm not sure why but her words create a bubble of hope inside me. "Yeah."

Finally, she stands. "Come on."

As we walk toward the shop, a string of whispers emanates from the shield. I've only been able to understand Ara's words so far, but I don't hear her. Maybe Ara will be able to explain the other things I'm hearing.

The shop is crowded. Rusela and Koglim stand near Jeiah's orange board. Lagnar waits on my dad's old shop stool, making no comment as I walk in—which is a first for him.

Hemdi marches in small circles at the far end, holding Echel. Brig's pacing near the glimmering water tank. Winta and Jeiah work at some complex jumble of bluecraft hovering in the center of the room.

"Perfect timing," Jeiah says as she ties one more loop in a knot of holographic blue-silver thread. "Should I start it?"

"Start it?" I say, "There's visual information?"

"Yep, this leaf was designed with a bluecraft core sandwiched between layers of silvercraft—highly encrypted. It's a recording."

Winta smiles at Jeiah, and they knock elbows and then wrists in some secret hacker girl code.

I clear my throat. "No reason to wait."

Koglim squeals and claps like it's the start of the next annual Hundred Dungeon Games. I flinch at the idea that if we don't stop Vor, there won't be another Hundred Dungeon Games. Such a small thing when I hold it up to all we've lost, but it's a reminder of the ideals Rugnus and Andalynn fought for.

The speaker system buzzes, and then Theridal Silverkeeper is standing in the shop, barely recognizable. His body isn't yet tainted with all the craft that Sira used to keep him alive.

Rusela takes a deep breath. "It's been a long time since I've seen my friend."

For my part, my only memories of Silverkeeper are recent. Sira had controlled him and led me into Silverlamp Dungeon to retrieve the piece of mithrium hidden there by my mom. But Rusela and my parents knew him long before this. Even Lagnar squints harder at the image and shakes his head. Did he know him too?

I can't help imagining them exploring one of the ruined cities or combing through a dungeon in search of relics. Rusela Whitechin, Theridal Silverlamp, Lagnar Emberfence, Azbena Bloodfeign, and Therias Brightstorm. Strange to think about. How close were they?

On the recording, Silverkeeper adjusts his copy of the leaf on a holographic table. A forge flickers behind him. There's something familiar about the room.

"Look, if you're seeing this... I didn't make it out of Wolfstaff.

And I'll get to that. But... well, the last time we spoke... I think I owe you an apology. Maybe you were right to hide the mithrium... to live away from all of this." He grins mischievously. "Though, I hope you're not becoming completely fizzblooded."

Silverkeeper must have made this after my dad was on the surface with me.

"Anyway, I'll leave this—the leaf—with Vor. The kind of thing I'm about to tell you... I'd only trust to a vacant. No other Loamin should know about this. Sorry, that's pretty cryptic. Out with it, right? I'm rambling again."

Rusela almost laughs. "Ah, Theridal. You sweet man."

Theridal swallows hard and holds up a bronze cup. "I found this. It's Exralt's. It's a cipher for his poetry. There are maps and diagrams in those words, as vivid as... I don't know, but they're clear to me now—this bronze cup he made. He talks about three relics from the protodungeons, even names them—Ergal, Icho, Onrix. And Therias? This is one of them." He holds up Sira's silver knife. "Exralt passed it down to his family. Rusela, she was his descendant. She helped me track two of them down, but she's keeping the other one. Sworn to secrecy, though I didn't tell her any of this. The club she kept, Icho, it's a budge— powerful. And this is probably the most dangerous piece of silvercraft I've ever held."

He shakes a chill from his back. "They were all Exralt's. Also, the poems, and the cipher, point to Wolfstaff Dungeon. I think he hid one of them there. And... well, you know of his friendship with Erikzin. I think, maybe, they worked together to hide something even more nefarious inside Brightstorm Dungeon. Whether he did this after Erikzin's death, or whether it was woven into the dungeon when Erikzin became a champion, isn't clear, but what *is* clear, is that it was a key. The thing they left in Erikzin's dungeon.

"And, if I'm interpreting his poetry correctly—with the cipher —the key may open the way to the protodungeons. I mean, they had to have used it to get these items. If it's true? I don't want to speculate—okay, I do—but there are three of these relics: there are three pieces of mithrium... just saying. Okay, that's a stretch, but still."

"Therias." The name is more of a sigh. Then he sits down on the floor and stretches out his arms reluctantly. A little blonde-haired child comes crashing into him.

"Play with me, pleeeease." It's Sira.

Theridal strokes her golden hair. "One second." Then, almost like he's facing me directly, he says. "I wish you were down here with me. I'm gonna go looking for the ring Exralt left in Wolf-staff. This information is dangerous, my friend. I'm making myself the only keeper of it." In one hand Theridal holds an iron ring. He lifts the cup above it and lets it drop. The cipher disintegrates in a flare of light as it passes through. "There. If all goes well, I'll meet you at the crossroads at the end of Gem, and you'll never see this recording. Until then, keep Ide, you brick-headed fizzblood."

The recording ends.

Rusela stands from the couch. "This... this was my fault." She rushes from the den, with Lagnar and Mom calling out for her.

Lagnar leans forward, ready to stand.

"Hold on there. Maybe we need to give her a moment," Koglim says. "Besides, we have some serious choices to make here."

"This evidence corroborates what we've already accepted," Jeiah says. "The key will open a way to the protodungeons. What Clayson heard from Jassin seems confirmed. But also, each item is the heart of one of those dungeons. Silverkeeper didn't know that. But the mithrium could also have been from behind the door in Edium Fiarie—we can't confirm that possibility."

Winta takes Echel from Hemdi but raises her eyebrows at him. He steps further into the den. "I know where this is all going, so we might as well have it out there—Clayson believes he can take the shield. He will use it to protect himself from Vor as he searches for Ara. Then what? Does Ara go with you to use the key? Check on her dungeon? And what happens to all of the refugees on the surface. Winta and I... won't be coming with you this time, Clayson. What happens to us?"

Lagnar nods at this. "The key and Ara's help. Those things ain't guaranteed to fix problemo numero uno: Vor. We need to slow things down. How long would it take us to get things shuffled around and move the refugees?"

I scratch my head. "There's nowhere—"

"How long would it take?" Lagnar asks more firmly.

"We have Icho," I say. "A couple days."

"My place it is, then."

Mom gives him a sidelong look. "Your place?"

"The hub. An old radio building east of Alamosa, lined with foilgrip and just a slight touch of shieldcraft, sends out false bluelink location data across half the United States."

"You old raider, you," Koglim says. "You do have a hideout."

"And you're volunteering to help?" I say, not trying to hide my disbelief.

He nods.

"To let people stay with you?"

He nods again. "I mean, they've got ferrum, right?"

Mom slaps him on the shoulder.

"Yes, yes. Bring who you want. Gonna be tight, but how I figure it, you either break the whole melted world down there under granite, or Vor takes over everything, and we're all fizzbloods forever."

I scowl at him. "Or we stop Vor, and Loamin can return to Rimduum."

"Sure, kid. Whatever helps you sleep at night."

The weight of this conversation hangs in the air for a moment, everyone drifting off into their thoughts. I rub my wrist where my bracelet used to sit. What good am I to everyone without craft? Even if I try to help with the refugees, I have a feeling Jeiah will want me to rest, getting healing sessions from Hemdi until they stop working.

"No one has to come with me," I start, "but I won't stop you either. We have to find Ara in Geum Ide, open the way to the protodungeons, and then figure out how to use whatever's down there to stop Vor."

"And avoid this destroyer person," Jeiah adds.

Winta holds Echel a little tighter.

Koglim leans against the counter, hands behind his head. "You know I'm in. The side mission is the new mission."

THE TOMB OF THE UNKEPT
RENSIRA

THE TOMB *of the Unkept houses ten thousand nameless bodies.*

Sira sits against the cold stone, just inside one of the hallway's entrances, staring placidly at the black-smudged floor. She sighs. There are no flowers to pick here. No one to talk to. Nothing beautiful to look at. She used to think the punishment was fair. That Vor was helping her to learn control and keep her emotions in check. After all, she had had to hide from everyone to keep them from knowing the truth about her father.

For as long as there have been dungeons, there have been keepers. And in those thousands of years, some keepers have been judged unworthy of rejoining the earth, of melting with their relics in the fires beyond Edium Fiarie.

Her father, Theridal Silverkeeper, had almost lost his bones to this place. But, of all the people who came to his defense when he died in Silver-lamp dungeon, Andalynn Everbloom had spoken the loudest.

Tears prick Sira's eyes again. Since her mistake on the bridge at Geum Ide—when she betrayed Clayson—there hasn't been a day without sobbing.

She screws up her face in anger. "Stop it!" She balls her fist. "Stop."

With her next breath, she draws in as much air as possible. In—shakily—through her nose, out through her mouth, more even this time. Another time. Another.

She looks around, grounding herself. The central canyon of the tomb rises to an arched ceiling of porous rock. The walls are a honeycomb of entrances that lead to the twisted maze of tombs. Sparingly lit with unnatural, pink torchlight, the tombs glare at the dead and all who dare seek entrance here.

A flare of brown light draws her attention. A man's face catches only a sliver of the pale light. Vor? No, he wouldn't have left Tungsten City. He'd lose control of everyone. Besides, he never, ever comes to get her this quickly.

Tas steps into the light.

"Tas?" Sira jumps to her feet and throws her arms around him. She sobs into his shoulder, then holds her breath to make herself stop. "Does Vor want me to come back now?"

He shakes his head. "You need to know something."

Sira blinks, sensing one of those moments that she won't understand, where someone will be revealed to be... just horrible, where she'll cry again. "What?"

"Vor's not coming."

Sira wipes her cheeks. "I know that."

"You don't—he's never coming."

"But he'll send someone to—"

"Not this time."

"He sent you."

Tas shakes his head. "I had to tell you."

"Vor always comes back, and you... you wouldn't have come without—"

"He's close to finishing the Everfalls... but something's off. I don't think he intends it to be a prison anymore. Maybe he never did."

"You're not making any sense."

"Vor thinks Clayson is coming." A warning floats through his words.

"Clayson wouldn't risk getting trapped."

"Rugnus and Andalynn were killed in Brightstorm Dungeon. I'm not sure how. It may have been Grimflail. It may have been something else, but they're gone."

Sira's breath catches. The sorrow deep inside her turns to something sharp and cold. "Then Clayson will come for me. He'll burn Vor into ashes. He'll tear down the whole world to get to him. And then he'll come for me."

Tas' jaw tightens. "If Vor moves from the city, I'll come back for you. We can find Clayson together. I-I made a mistake helping Kel and Vor on that bridge."

"We both did, but it's not our fault Vor—"

"It is our fault."

A fresh round of tears finds its way out, and Sira's skin is painted with shame. She had thought Vor would make things safe, make people kind. She should have known better.

Tas wraps her in his long arms. "We can't fix what we did, but we don't have to let Vor and Kel push us around anymore."

Sira straightens. "I can be like Clayson. I can push back."

DANCE BEFORE DANGER

Two days.

It takes two days of healing with Hemdi using the bracelet, but I recover. Granted, there's still a large pale scar on my back where Jassin ran me through with his knife. My movements are still slow and deliberate to avoid unnecessary pain. No one lets me near the shield, but its call grows stronger the more I recover—like a siren drawing me into deep water, complete with alluring whispers.

I ignore them, moving with a heavy heart toward the ministack where my friend and sister had begun to build a life for themselves. We honor their sacrifice tonight. It's the celebration everyone has been waiting for but postponed when I went missing. The one I didn't want.

I'm the first one there. The four-wheeler sits on the gravel outside the door, covered with a canvas drop cloth. A few dozen fresh-cut lilies are laid out almost reverently, their spotted orange muted by the deepening light of evening. Nine black-tar candles sit next to the lilies.

The door to the cabin opens, and everyone else crosses the gravel road to stand next to me. My mom lights one of the tar candles without a word and hands it to Rusela. She lays it at the threshold of the ministack, standing for a few quiet seconds before she returns to the group. She takes a lily and presses it into Mom's reluctant hands. Mom waits for me to receive mine, then we both approach the threshold.

Only a few months ago, Rugnus and Andalynn participated in another ceremony. One that bound their lives and craft together. They lost their lives in Brightstorm, but they went together, and there's something all at once bitter and strangely beautiful about it. I lay the flower at the door.

Mom wipes a tear from her face. "I lost a distant cousin to Bearcloak Dungeon when I was a few years younger than you. We went to the family's castlestack, to the door of her room, and... we left our thoughts there, captured into the silvercraft hinges of the door so that if she ever drifted back into the world, our memories might lead her back to us. That's the tradition."

We stand back. Everyone, in turn, leaves these tokens on the threshold. Last year, when Rugnus and I helped to lower Silverkeeper's body into the lava at Edium Fiarie, the day had felt so distant. I didn't understand who Silverkeeper had been or who he was in life, but his end was final. I still remember Sira's screams for help as all the craft she had built up to protect him failed when he entered the dungeon.

They had gotten his body back for a funeral. With Rugnus and Andalynn, there was nothing left. I watched them burn in that furnace; it was something deeper and more all-encompassing than dropping their bones into the earth's deepest fire.

It's a simple ceremony, calling back lost loved ones from the dungeon. I try not to let the bitterness into my heart. I heard their voices calling to me as I lay dying in Gamgim. Was that real?

Hemdi stops next to me. Instead of saying anything—because maybe his emotions, like mine, are too close to the surface—he puts a hand on the back of my neck and pulls our foreheads together.

No one goes into their home. We tread the rose-bordered, stone path around the side to the patio, where I find Koglim and

Lagnar already manning the barbeque, serving burgers. Winta and Jeiah are chatting quietly over a cobalt disc sitting on a table. They agree on something, tap the disk, and immediately upbeat music starts playing from the speakers mounted above the patio.

Hemdi hands me a plate "Clayson, didn't you tell me your first meal from Tungsten City was a burger?"

Koglim points a spatula at me. "That's right! Funny he gave you taffy food first. Would have thought he'd take you to Kel's Lounge for the soup."

The conversation wanders a hundred directions as we move to tables bordering the pool Rugnus built with ironcraft—his attempt to normalize the difficulty of living on the surface. He spent hours training to breath underwater and to shoot balls of ice at unsuspecting trees.

Across the yard, Brig is trying to balance a horseshoe on his nose. Mom is watching Echel lying on a blanket on the lawn. At some point, after my second burger, Rusela marches over to Koglim.

With a flourish, she produces Icho. "It has been in my family long enough. I think he would want you to have it, Koglim. Besides, you're going with the group to Geum Ide tomorrow. You'll need it."

The music hits a lull as everyone glues their eyes on them.

Still wearing his apron, Koglim stands, his mouth hanging open. His knees bump on the picnic table, shaking everyone's drinks.

"Please," Rusela says, plying the relic in his direction.

Koglim wags his plastic spoon at her. "No. No. I-I… Rusela, I can't."

"Do not deny me, Koglim Felsight." She smiles. "You haven't been able to keep your eyes off this thing. Take it."

Slowly, he sets down his spoon and comes around the table. He eases it from Rusela's hand like he's taking Echel from Winta. "I—it's perfect. I'll guard it with my life."

"If it comes down to it," Lagnar says, "keep your life."

"I couldn't agree more," I say.

Koglim unties his apron with one hand and pulls it over his head. He glances at Brig, who nods encouragingly. Suddenly, Koglim budges next to Brig, grabs him, and budges again. For two seconds, nothing happens then a feral cry of glee breaks the air.

"Cannonball!"

Brig tucks himself into a ball, but Koglim slips out of form and hits the water with an audible smack. A wave breaks from the pool, hurtling an impressive distance, showering our picnic table. I wince, remembering Koglim's near drowning day before. What is he thinking.

"Trollbrick," Hemdi says. His plate is flooded with water. He rarely swears, but his tone is one of disbelief and amusement.

Brig emerges from the pool and flexes his muscles in a peerless imitation of Koglim. "Whew! Ho, that was something!"

Koglim floats upward. When his head breaks the surface, he groans. "Bad idea." I help pull him out of the pool, and he lays on his back with his legs still in the water. Then, suddenly, he's laughing, the same way he does every time he escapes something terrible in a dungeon. It's this high-pitched squeal, bursts of energy and joy.

From where I sit, I still hear him whisper. "Face your fears."

Winta spins up the next track from her playlist, and Brig whoops again.

From this moment, the knot between my shoulders unwinds. We eat and tell stories about Rugnus and Andalynn. Many of them are new to me.

At one point, I find myself sitting with Rusela and Mom when the song changes from Tungsten City's current hits to a popular ping-chant. The rich tonal sounds of vowels blend with horns and rattles in a song with only a spattering of rhythm, where the melody runs quick then slow, quick then slow.

"Booh!" Koglim says. "Ping's the worst. Change it, Winta."

As she starts to gesture a change to the song, both mothers shout. "Wait!"

"Is this…" Mom says.

Rusela bends her ear toward the music. "Durin's Bow?"

Mom shakes her head. "Andalynn found this on Bluelink when she was about ten. Used to play it over and over and over. I couldn't stand it. I think… yes, the council even banned this one." She laughs softly.

Rusela nods. "Even stranger, Rugnus—the week of his summation—would play this every night during his practices. I hated it."

Winta groans. "It's the worst kind of ping. How did it get on my list? I feel like it's pulling parts of my brain out and hitting them with a hammer."

"Agreed," I say. "Leave it on."

Winta makes a quick gesture, and the volume rises to a mind-pummeling level. Everyone cringes, but one by one, they stand and dance with jerking movements and twitching muscles leaving me sitting at a picnic table as the day slowly ebbs away. Koglim cries out for more music, and Winta provides. After passing Echel off to me, she takes Hemdi by the hand and leads him out to dance.

The sun hasn't completely disappeared when Brig and Rusela make their way around the pool, lighting torches. The music changes to something slow tempo. The smooth horns of something from out of the Whurrimduum underground scene fill my head like intoxication.

Koglim comes to my side. "Little latcher's pretty heavy. Will your back hold out?"

I shift Echel closer to me and bounce him on my knee. Small twinges of pain run the length of my back. "I'm fine."

But I'm watching Jeiah dance and laugh, and I can't keep my eyes off her.

Koglim plops down on the bench. It sends a jolt through my

back. His voice is just louder than the music, "She loves you, you know."

I scan the makeshift dance floor, but no one looks over at us. "Keep your voice down, would you?"

"Why? It's not a secret. Not going to surprise her if she hears it."

"I know. I know that," I whisper.

"Okay, so? How do you feel about her?"

"Melt me, Koglim. Look I... I feel the same way. I just get so... my brain stops working, I start overthinking everything."

"How many times did you even tell her how you feel?"

"Plenty," I lie.

"Like with words." Koglim rolls back his shoulders. "Let's practice. I'll go first. I'll be Jeiah." He bats his eyes at me. "Clayson, you're so amazing. I love you."

"Koglim, come on. This doesn't seem the right time to—"

"Time is meaningless when it comes to love. Now, say it."

"Fine. I love you."

"Like you mean it."

Groaning, I try again, but can't keep the smile off my face. "I love you, Koglim."

"Not me, dummy, her. But thanks. That's sweet of you. Oh, here she comes. Act natural."

Blood rushes to my face. Jeiah squints at us, and I wonder if she's using craft to investigate the impact bouncing Echel is having on my wound. But her hands are empty. Her eyes are their normal color. Even without craft, she can see through me.

"I'll take this guy," Koglim says, snatching Echel from my hands.

Jeiah sets her drink down and replaces Koglim, careful not to jostle the bench. "I've heard this one," she says. "It's by Elwa Ringkettle."

"You wanna dance?" The words leave my mouth unexpectedly, like a bird realizing the cage is open.

"You're still injured."

"I can manage."

She stands and offers me a hand. "The dance floor awaits."

I blink rapidly. Why didn't I think this through? "Fair warning: I can't dance."

"Uh-huh. And do you mean before or after this injury?"

"Haha."

"Come on, fizzblood. I'll take care of you."

"I know."

The song switches to something even and steady. Good. My pulse needs a pattern to follow. The evening transforms all at once into something comforting and mystical. Even the fireflies arrive with startling incandescence, dancing around us. After a few painfully slow turns, I hold my head up higher and embrace the moment, this time spinning Jeiah around. When she faces me again, I catch a flicker of investigation behind her eyes, and I watch her as she listens to the lyrics of the song.

We couldn't go back,
We're copper for the night.
And when the day comes
We're upside down.
No upside now.
Feed the forge,
Until the kings say, "How?"

She spins me a bit too hard, but the stretch feels good this time. When I come back around, she's there. The same as the day I met her at StoneYoke, her head turns slightly, and her eyes are dangerous slits. She pulls me closer and puts her head on my shoulder. We sway together. I allow myself a contented sigh, soaking in the cool, electric scent of her.

The song ends. When I try to let go, she pulls my face toward her and kisses me. Which pushes all other thoughts to the fringes of my mind. I kiss her back. Need is the only thing driving me.

Somehow, I didn't mess this up with my stupid words. *Yeah. Sure. Okay.*

Finally, I open my eyes but keep her face close to mine. "I…" The phrase simply won't leave my body. "I'm sorry for not hearing you."

"Okay."

I can't decipher the meaning of this word. "I don't wanna lose you,"

"You couldn't if you tried. When this is all over, and Vor is locked up, when the world becomes safe again, I don't have to guess where I will end up."

"Where's that?"

"Standing next to you."

I refuse to let this take me off guard. She means this. And there's no reason to believe that she doesn't. It's almost too much to hope that we will find some sliver of peace left in this world and live to share more moments like this. I force myself to imagine it. Then I choose to say something stupid.

"Yeah. Sure. Okay." But I stare at her, trusting her power to read my mind. I change the meaning of these words that have cursed me. I make them mean I love you. I carve them into a tree far in the future where nothing dangerous will compete for my attention to her.

Jeiah and Clayson.

And she catches this meaning, smiling. "Yeah. Sure. Okay."

There's a buzz from the speakers, and Rusela announces the end of the party.

"Get some sleep latchers!" Winta shouts. "Big day tomorrow."

I try to start cleaning up, but Jeiah sends me on my way. "I think a few dances are enough activity for the night."

I half-bow, though my back nearly refuses to return to a standing position. My feet find the road, and I cross over to the cabin. Before I get to the porch, I feel someone behind me.

I turn and find Winta stopped in the center of the road. She's smiling. I shake my head in disbelief. The longer we stay up here, the happier she gets. I've only seen her this way in the pilot seat of a Behemoth mech or revving the engine of my dad's truck.

"What?" she asks.

"You're happy."

She frowns. "Shut up, Brightstorm."

"Sorry, things are strange, I guess."

"Like what?"

"I saw Koglim angry for the first time, I mean really angry. Hemdi actually said *trollbrick*. Did you hear him? What's next?"

"Hey," she says like an idea has struck her out of nowhere, "maybe you don't make rash decisions anymore. Could it be?"

"Not likely."

"Figures. What about Jeiah?"

"Observant as always."

"Good. We need someone consistent through all this."

"Yeah."

She steps toward me in the dark, and a shadow of something heavy falls on her shoulders. "I want to make Vor pay for what he did. If you're going to try to stop him—"

"I will stop him."

She's thoughtful again. "I could leave Echel with Hemdi, but... I don't want to. You're right, Clayson. I am happy. But that seems wrong. Rugnus and Andalynn... I shouldn't get to feel happy."

"You deserve to be," I say. "Don't feel guilty for—"

"I need to know you can do this without us. We'll go with Lagnar to the hub with the rest of the refugees until the time seems right. Then we can find a place of our own. But I need to know that you can finish this."

This challenge stirs my blood. "I'll swear by silver if—"

"No. On your life."

My heart turns to metal. "I swear on my life. I *will* stop Vor."

Satisfied, she punches me.

"Ow! I was already injured. What's that—"

"If you screw things up with Jeiah, I will melt you."

Rubbing my shoulder, I retreat up the stairs. "Message

received."

"Good night, Clayson. Keep your promises."

Her words follow me to my room and linger even after I change for bed. Can I do it? Can I kill Vor if the opportunity arises? Hemdi appears at the door and interrupts my thoughts. He doesn't say much as he takes me through another round of shieldcraft with the bracelet.

"How's that?"

I twist at the waist and raise my arms. "Much better."

"Might be as good as it gets."

I roll out to the floor and do a few drawn-out crunches. "Good as new."

"Okay. See you in the morning." He leaves the room, and I return to bed.

I don't recall falling asleep after that, so I'm surprised when I open my eyes to the muted light streaming through the windows. I glance at the clock. Nine AM. I haven't slept this well in weeks.

Hemdi has breakfast waiting—homestyle hash browns, Spangler eggs, bacon, and coffee. "How early did you wake up?" I ask.

He responds with a simple answer. "Echel. You're the last one up. But Jeiah told me not to wake you. Nightchange in Geum Ide was only a few minutes ago."

Everyone else is gathered around the shield, even those going with Lagnar. They stand together in groups off to one side, preparing various budges. Stone, Nox, and Gem weave in and around them, barking for attention. I approach the group with Jeiah, Koglim, and Mom.

"We didn't want to rush you," Mom says.

Koglim shakes his head, flipping Icho in his hand. "Yes, we did. We just didn't."

"You ready?" Jeiah asks.

Without any craft, I feel a bit naked, but the shield is waiting for me. From this angle, I see a corner of the ministack. I wish for Rugnus and Andalynn to be here with me one more time.

I let the whispers back in, and for a brief second, I can almost make out the word *here* among the jumble of sharp sounds.

The whispers grow stronger as I step toward the mithrium shield, somehow becoming even more indistinct. I hear Lagnar order his group to prepare themselves, and they vanish. When my hand touches the glowing metal, it comes free from its long-held position. There is no pulse of shieldcraft, only a blanket of acceptance, a feeling of relief.

Instinctually, I lift my face toward the sky as if the glare from the shield will connect with the sun. But it's not the sun I connect with. It's the brightstorms—all of them. How is that possible? The sensations of all ten crafts embrace every cell in my body. A million foreign thoughts take over my mind. I'm in every place where there's a brightstorm, throughout the Kingdom of Rimduum and beyond: Hngaal, Brimwok, Dashen. Everywhere.

I reach for Geum Ide and pull.

It feels different than budging, more disconnected. But the mithrium shield has a power of its own—as Ara once told me. When I lower my gaze, we're standing in what was once the conjurers' oasis.

No smoke plumes, no fires rage over the ruins of Geum Ide, but still, the sight reaches into my stomach and hollows out an endless vortex of regret. Shattered chunks of red granite lay in massive heaps, scorched black with some unholy fire. Any building not made of stone is only a scar of ashes against the ground. I can't see the Great Barn from here, where my grandmother, Glaris, first brought us.

It seems like so long ago.

The four of us carefully step along the littered road toward the bridge.

"Ide keep us," Mom says in a harsh whisper as we descend into what's left of the conjurer's utopia.

The word Ide holds no more meaning to me. As Hemdi has told me, it is a word meaning the earth itself. Does it relate to the origin of the valley where the Jassin stabbed me? Maybe it's only ever been an expression of something profane. In that case: Ide.

Double Ide.

Jeiah holds out her beholder, reclaimed from her Blueweb machine, and begins scanning the wreckage.

Koglim's face puckers in confusion and revulsion. "What's it saying? No, I've got this: Vor is a deranged psychopath." He kicks a piece of rock out of the wreckage of the road. "Well, am I right?"

Jeiah takes a deep breath and finishes a slow three-sixty but keeps the rod in her hand. "The more information we have, the better. I can tell what craftprints he might have used, if any. I can tell who helped him of their own choice and who was forced by Onrix."

"And?" I ask.

Jeiah shifts her eyes between Mom and me. She settles on me. "It's all your dad?"

"You mean Kel absorbed his craftprint and—"

"No. I mean Vor forced him to destroy Geum Ide one building at a time."

The meaning of that settles over the whole group. Vor keeps proving his flair for unique revenge and hatred.

"You know," Koglim says. "I never agreed with your dad about conjuring, but what Vor did... it's... I can't..."

"Yeah," I say.

Clayson. Ara's voice startles me.

Mom reacts when I jump back, scanning the horizon.

"It's alright," I say, tapping the shield. "Ara."

Lowest level. Other side of the ravine.

I glance at Mom. "How do we get to the lowest level? Across the ravine."

Jeiah and Koglim trade a look.

"Are you sure it's Ara?" Mom asks.

"Why does this feel like a trap," Jeiah says.

"I'd welcome a trap," Koglim says. "We have the shield. If Vor tries anything—" he smashes his fist into the palm of his hand.

"What about Grimflail?" Mom asks.

Koglim's face hardens. "Even better."

"It's her," I say. "I'm sure."

Mom weighs something unseen, then says, "Follow me."

A minute later, we cross under the broken ruins of an entrance to the lower level. A lookout for the ravine is on our right. Jumbled light falls cut brilliant lances of white across the deep red stone on our left. The light is evenly spaced except where the ruins of the city block them.

It seems as if we are heading to my parents' house, but we turn sharply away from the ravine down another layer. The light-falls fade the deeper we go. After a half dozen twists and turns, we find a winding stairway undisturbed by Vor's—no, Dad's—attack on Geum Ide.

Jeiah and I take the side stairway together. There's no railing in the center of the column, but Jeiah still walks on the outside of the winding pentagon stairway. Koglim counts out each flight as we descend. At the bottom of the stairway, we enter a large room swimming in light. At the far end, we emerge at the bottom of the ravine, the shallow river cutting deeper into the rock.

My mom cranes her head back. "The bridge is there."

Far above us, I see the bridge that separates the two halves of Geum Ide. Mom's face goes ashen, and I know she's thinking about Glaris. When Vor attacked us, everything happened so quickly. But I'll never erase the memory of his crooked blade rising from my grandmother's torso or how her body limply tumbled from the bridge.

Jeiah steps around Mom, coming between her and the bridge. She points across the river to a small opening. "There."

Jeiah wades knee-deep into the river. Through the doorway, we find another pentagon-shaped stairway. The citybarrel itself is that shape. At the bottom of the stairs, there are three pathways.

"Okay, Ara." I'm not sure I expect her to respond, but she does.

Her voice gives us the next direction. *Right.*

The next room has four paths.

"Tricky," Koglim says.

Far left.

We pass dozens of open doorways and stairways, each time waiting for Ara's instructions. The walls become rough, narrow tunnels. Until Ara tells us to stand still. The room is strangely dark as if there were no corners, but it still feels small.

A murmur of whispers ripples around us. I flinch against the sound, bumping into Koglim. "What is this?"

Jeiah's voice reaches out, tentative. "Who's there?"

The murmur stills. Though there's something like the rustle of clothing, of soft feet. Abruptly, the shield pulses with light, then all at once the darkness lifts.

Dozens of people skim the outside of the oval chamber, their faces as shocked as ours must look, their eyes glued to the mithrium shield. It was some craft that kept us in shadow. From the way their bodies shift away to the way one father squeezes his daughter closer to him, I understand why. These people are hiding.

Mom moves to the front. "Ara?"

Ara is unmistakably taller than everyone else. Her welcoming eyes soften her sharp beauty. There was a time she used to intimidate me.

"I almost came to you when you arrived," she says. "I felt the shield move."

It's still strange when Ara's glance finds me. Our eyes lock. When she first grabbed the shield and came to rescue us from Vor in Thiffimdal, I couldn't wrap my mind around the change in her personality—as abrupt as a daychange in Tungsten City. She's developed a new relish for eye contact, as if she can look right into my mind. I know it shouldn't, but her glare reminds me of the moment when Vor killed Glaris. He looked right at me, watching for my response as he pushed his sword through her body.

Ara moves closer to the shield. "How did you get it to work for you?"

Jeiah takes a deep breath through her nose. Koglim hangs his head.

At first, it seems like a strange reaction, but then I understand —they're still grieving the loss of my craft. I don't see it that way. "I no longer have craft."

Another ripple of whispers begins around the room.

"Any craft?" Ara says. "I thought—"

"The rules shifted," I say, "again. That's why we're here. We need your help to—"

"Azbena?" A disheveled man with a brown-gray beard appears at an opening behind the crowd. The shield feels suddenly heavy in my hands, and my arm drops to the side.

"Therias," Mom says, disbelief coloring his name.

He drifts out from behind the crowd, cautious. He's worn so many masks over the years it's difficult for me to read this new one: I settle on distress. By keeping Vor's sentience from us, including Mom, it's easy to blame him for everything that went wrong in Geum Ide, but Mom still rushes to him. Gently, he kisses her and takes her hand.

I raise the shield between us. "How did you get away from Vor? He can't control Ara, but"—I look around the room—"did all of these people escape from him?"

For a second, his face falls, but then he says, "Yes, ah, many of them are silver nulls, so their minds can't be controlled. Very rare. Others weren't in Tungsten City or Whurrimduum when Vor claimed everyone else with his crown."

He's been gathering refugees too.

"And you?" Jeiah asks.

Good. Someone is as skeptical as me. It was a previous life when I trusted him. He's made it impossible to know who he is or what he wants. It's time that changed.

His voice falters. "Vor—he... I always treated him like an equal. He doesn't want to control me."

"We know he made you destroy Geum Ide," I say, "so I'm not sure I can believe that."

My dad's jaw flexes. "You're upset."

"I'm upset? That's not even... you're responsible for what he did, Dad!"

His face hardens. "I told you the mithrium was dangerous."

A dry laugh escapes my mouth. "You can't put this on me. If you would've—you know what? Forget it. We didn't come here to see you. I mean, how long have you been here? This whole time? And you didn't think to come to the cabin?"

"I didn't think you would want to see me. Looks like I was right."

"We came to get Ara. We don't need your help."

Suspicion colors his eyes. "Get Ara? For what?"

Mom comes between us. "Clayson found an entrance to the protodungeons. Maybe even a way to stop Vor. But we need Ara's help."

My dad's smile is genuine. At least I can read that much. "That's amazing! How? Where? And where's Andalynn? When Ara said the shield was on the way... I thought she'd be with you. How is she?"

All of his secrets, and he thinks he can ask that question.

"She's fine." The words tumble from my mouth, and I can't put them back. The effect on Mom, Jeiah, and Koglim might as well be silvercraft. Their open mouths immediately close. They all straighten their backs and trade glances. I've done something that I can't take back.

I've lied.

My dad thinks his lies protected me. My lie is not meant to protect him but to hurt him. A pang of regret forms at the back of my throat, but it only ties the lie down under another layer.

"Good," he says. "Maybe I *should* come back to the cabin with you. I'd like to see her." When no one answers, he continues unabated. "Though, now that we have the shield, there's another thing we need to talk about. Follow me. I want to show you something."

His tone has shifted. It's wilder and more dangerous. The

crowd parts and lets us down a corridor. He keeps facing forward, speaking slowly. "So, in thinking about it, the problem when we faced Vor last time... it was craft. The mithrium shield against the mithrium crown—even. But Vor had Kel's added power, and Tas... we didn't stand a chance. So, we've developed something of a solution."

Ahead of us, metal clinks against metal.

In the space between my dad's comments and the end of the tunnel, Mom leans toward me and asks, "Why did you tell him that?"

"You could've said something."

She shakes her head and sighs. "Only you can do that now. There are already enough lies between all of us. You shouldn't have—"

The second we emerge from the tunnel, my dad's awful plan unfolds before my eyes. Three Loamin work a forge at the back of the large space. Steam sizzles up at one of them, a woman clad in leather and thick clothing, drops a metal shaft into a trough of water. A stone's throw from that, a man attaches lengths of metal to cross bars.

"Wait," Koglim says, blinking. "What are you making here? It's ironcraft, right? I thought—"

"No, no." My dad lifts a recently forged two-handed sword. "This isn't ironcraft."

"You're making weapons?" Jeiah says. "Human weapons?"

He smiles. "Indeed, we are."

The *click-click* of someone loading a rifle echoes from the back of the room. There are swords and knives and axes, but laid out on even more tables, I see piles of canvas-strapped rifles, the same mold and caliber the conjurers wielded. These are the crude weapons of industrial societies finally going to war. It's an arsenal forged for a single purpose—to slip through the barriers of craft and pierce Vor's black heart.

ADJUST MY AIM

It's a plan borne of absolute madness.

My dad spools out a roll of parchment, pinning it down on the table with knives. He explains how the math of the craft adds up. Vor's crown and Ara's shield are represented by infinity signs, one over the other, like a balanced chemical equation, like the pressure needed to distill biofuel. Ara's shield cancels out Vor's crown. He adds the bullets and the manpower against the darksmiths. He adds and takes away until reaching the center point and jabs a sharp finger into Vor's name.

My head feels numb. I've only caught pieces of his plot. I can't put it all together like he can. Instead, I'm focused on the point of a single longsword. Then I bounce that thought toward a memory. Vor's blade, jagged and sharp, Glaris attached to it, and then she's falling from the bridge.

"Dad, where's Glaris' body?"

"What?" This abrupt change in the conversation catches him off guard. "Oh. I-I couldn't leave her in the ravine. There's a place up by the Great Barn. She liked to sit out there and look down on Geum Ide."

I rest my hand on the hilt of a sword. "How many people could die?"

"There would be a cost. It won't be easy to stop him. He's clever. But Everfalls is the key." He taps a crude drawing of cascading waterfalls near the center of his master plan. "He's been building a trap, but we're going to turn it against him."

"I missed that part somewhere in the math," Koglim says. "We used Ara's shield to budge to Geum Ide. Couldn't Vor use the crown to budge?"

My dad shakes his head. "By our calculations, Vor has made Everfalls the strongest anti-budge in the history of Rimduum. He's connected it to the brightstorm over Tungsten City, and the brightstorm is somehow growing stronger."

"Are we sure it's the Everfalls messing with the brightstorm?" I ask. I'm afraid of the answer. The moment I brought us here with the shield it was clear it had become connected to the brightstorms—that I had become connected with them, with Ara.

Ara narrows her eyes at me.

"We're not sure," my dad says. "We've relied on incoming refugees for intelligence gathering and a few bluelink readings, various veilcraft objects, and the like. All we know is that the brightstorm has grown twenty percent in just the last few days. And the anti-budge he's using in Everfalls is connected to that power."

Koglim stares at the ground. "Wraithspit."

"And you think Vor will voluntarily trap himself down there?"

Ara and my dad trade glances.

My dad taps the image of the Everfalls. "If we use the right bait."

There. This is my place. Protector of the weak—a shield. "Me."

He nods. "If there were any other way..."

Mom shakes her head. "What? No."

"I'm not sure it's worth the risk," Jeiah adds. I can't tell if she's calculating the balance of craft between the two forces or if she's concerned about me. Probably both. Though she would not want me to throw myself down as a willing sacrifice again.

"And there's no need for the risk," I say. "Look, Dad, I know you grew up at the end of the Mithrium War. There's an acceptable amount of death and destruction you're willing to allow."

"That's not fair. That's not what this—"

"Whether that's your intention or not, it still has the same outcome: destruction. We've found a way into the protodungeons. We don't know what's down there, but I believe it will give us another option to stop Vor, maybe even a peaceful option. The Dura wraiths took my craft—all of it. Maybe there's something—"

"Dura wraiths?" my dad and Ara ask simultaneously.

Koglim jumps at this. "I'll sum up. So, Clayson and Hemdi went to talk to the wraiths in Gamgim. Turns out they're some kind of ancient breed of wraith—don't ask me. They stole all of Clayson's craft and nearly killed him—well, not the first time he went there. The first time they told him about the key. And... we got it." Koglim's voice falls flat with this short phrase, and I know it's Rugnus and Andalynn weighing on him.

Jeiah picks up from there. "The key leads to Edium Fiarie, to the House of Ide. It should bring us to the gateway into the protodungeons. But, by our figures, they should be destroyed like Wolfstaff. If Ergal was the heart of Ara's dungeon, then that's true. But there must still be a way into the dungeons if the Dura wraiths believed we could find a way to the destroyer by going through them."

"And that's why you need Ara?" my dad surmises.

"When the Dura wraiths took my craft," I add, "I sensed something. I know Ara can get back into her dungeon. And if that's true, then we can get into Vor's. We can find what we need to stop him."

My dad looks down at his plan, rubbing his thumb against the edge of the scroll. "I don't get it. You're just guessing. How is your plan any less uncertain than mine?"

"Perhaps it's not," Mom adds, "But the cost of failure is minimal comparatively."

After a moment of silence, Ara finally says, "The choice is easy. If I can use the key, then we should see where it leads."

There's a flash of blue light, and Jeiah holds up her hand. It's one of Andalynn's rings, the type she gave me when I first met her in Gamgim, nearly a year ago. Then I see the patterns coming from it. This is not just one of Andalynn's rings. It's the one Andalynn uses to communicate with all the others. Somehow Jeiah ended up with it. Who did she give the other one to?

"Uh, Jeiah?" I ask.

"Quick, a reflection," she says, and my pulse triples. Something's wrong.

A worker gestures to the water in the trough. "Here."

"Is that Andalynn's ring?" my dad asks. "Why does she have it?"

Shrugging off the question, I come to the reflection. Jeiah touches the ring, and Lagnar's face appears.

He's running, eyes wide and frantic. "Clayson!"

Everyone else crowds around us.

"Lagnar?" my dad says.

"Clayson, Vor's gonna know about Edium Fiarie any second now. My defenses... he sent everyone. Grimflail. Kel. All the darksmiths. Do you understand? They walked right past the foilgrips."

Mom grabs the edge of the trough. "What?!"

"Where's Winta?" Jeiah asks. "Why are you using the ring?"

"She's—I don't know. But we're"—the whole image shudders, but he keeps sprinting. "Hemdi took Icho when the outer warning... but..."

"Why doesn't Rugnus have Icho?" my dad demands.

"Not now, Dad," I say.

Lagnar eyes widen. "Clayson, Kel's bringing it to him. She has the mithrium I hid here. She knows about Edium Fiarie. She knows you're in Geum Ide. She used one of the darksmiths' craftprints, some silvercraft. She took all that information from our minds. He'll know soon, and he'll be coming for you. They all will. Get ahead of him. Use the key. Rusela. Winta and Hemdi... I —we'll get there the moment we can. We still have Icho. Ide keep us."

"Don't bring Icho here. Stay away. Hear me, Lagnar. Stay away!"

But the image breaks. I stumble from the trough. "We need to go. We need to go now! Ara, can you get us all to Edium Fiarie?"

"Wait!" my dad shouts over everyone. "Where are they, Clayson?"

I'm trying to ignore the question because I'm unable to answer him, to soften the blow. There's no time. My mouth works open, and I look at him, then at Mom. I beg her to tell him. It has to be her. It can't be me.

But my dad senses something. His questions sharpen into an accusation. "Clayson! What happened to Andalynn? To Rugnus?" Each word is a sharpened blade opening my reluctant flesh.

"They're dead, okay! Killed in Brightstorm Dungeon. In exchange for the key!" I shove him away, tears flowing from my eyes. "They're gone. Both of them."

"I—no. No." Tears spring to his face. He begs Mom with a look. She can't give him anything but faltering words. He falls to the ground weeping, but we don't have time for him to mourn.

Jeiah knows this. "Ara, we have to leave before Vor can get here."

Mom crouches near my dad. "I'm so sorry, Therias."

Now Ara is shouting. "We can't abandon these people! Vor will take them!"

Koglim is shaking. He snaps his fingers. "That's it. Vor will have to leave Tungsten City. Might even leave people there. We go there. Protect everyone with the shield."

"He'll only follow us," Ara says. "We need to act now." She squeezes my hand. "Sorry, Clayson. If we leave, Vor will only take more of these people. We'll have to face him here—now. There's no other option." Ara stands and orders the Loamin to arm themselves. The few Loamin in the room do just that, hastily grabbing weapons, hands trembling. And then an alarm reverberates around the room.

Everything's going too fast. Then everything's incredibly slow. There's a hard clot of people who struggle to pass through the door, then all at once, they flow through, filling their hands with these toys. That's all they will be to Vor.

I hold the shield out to Ara. "Here. You can at least counteract the power of the mithrium crown."

She takes the shield. A wave of safety, like a plush comforter, is tossed over everyone in the room. The line straightens up, and the people square their shoulders, arm themselves, and march out. The flow of Loamin keeps up as Ara leads us out of the room, Mom practically dragging my dad over the stone.

A boy with long dark hair and thick eyebrows marches up to Ara. Something about him reminds me of Rugnus, and I find myself staring at him as he says, "Are they here in the tunnels?"

"No," Ara responds. "Not yet. The shield is working. When he arrives, the objects will cancel each other out. But I'll know the second he's in Geum Ide." Then her face furrows in concern, and she reaches for the wall.

We steady her because that's all we can do. She holds the shield, so we hold her. And for some strange reason, I breathe a sigh of relief. I don't have craft, and no one is expecting anything from me. I wash the thought from my mind. Craft does not equal who I am or who I'm not.

Ara speaks. "There's a challenge at the entrance by the ravine. It's Kel. She has everyone pinned down." She knows this without looking. She's using the shield to extend some type of protection to them.

"Do you know anything specific?" Jeiah asks, her beholder gathering information.

"I feel Kel's intentions, and I'm blocking them. It's some type of attack. People are fleeing across the river as fast as they can."

"Let's get to the exit," I say. "Can you—"

Jeiah grabs my arm. "Wait. Someone else budged down here. A few tunnels away. They're scrambling their data."

Mom finally turns from my dad. "Where?"

Jeiah points behind us, away from the direction we're heading. "If Kel is outside the cave and Vor isn't here yet, then who did he send?"

Koglim sniffs the air. "It's definitely a trap."

"It's coming toward us," Jeiah warns.

Ara moves around us to the back of the party and levels the shield. Koglim scrambles in his pockets, producing a small cast iron coin, swearing softly and repeatedly, and gathering a ball of ice in his hand. The second someone emerges from the adjoining cavern, Koglim growls and hurls the shimmering sphere. Ara sends a wave of shieldcraft out to block it, and Koglim's attack evaporates. The emerging figure stumbles back into the others behind them.

But the man that emerges is holding something. No, some-one. A child. No, that's still not right.

It's Tas, the Dura who once lived in Geum Ide. The heart of his dungeon was Icho, and when we had him touch the relic months ago, he, along with Kel, had helped Vor defeat us. Now he's standing in front of us carrying... Sira. Her head and limbs dangle over his arms.

She's hurt. My hands and mind reach out instinctually, but so do Koglim's. I find a wary look as he grabs my fist. We've been burned by Sira too many times. Still, if there were mercy at my fingertips, and if I still had craft, I would have already healed her. Her body doesn't twitch.

Jeiah's beholder is wild with blue light, and she stands like a sentinel near Ara.

Tas recovers from almost falling backward. "Be careful, Koglim Felsight. You could hurt one of us."

Another figure emerges from the tunnel behind them.

"Yinzar?" Jeiah says.

My mother's father, Yinzar Copperoath, Mithriumbane,

strides forward, his brawny hands grasping a familiar object. The wolfstaff—a relic of deep gray metal. We gave this to Kel the last time we were here in Geum Ide. Though she couldn't use it, one touch of this staff drew in her wandering soul. How does Yinzar have it?

Mom gasps. "Dad?" She darts forward and pulls him in.

I need no other evidence than Yinzar's presence to know that Sira has traded sides again. She's with us for the time being. "Ara, can you—"

Ara passes a wave of healing from the shield, and Sira sputters awake, nearly choking until Tas stands her up. She retches, but nothing comes out. That's when I realize they must've just budged here. My mom lets her father go, and he steadies Sira.

Sira stares at me with a sad smile. "We have to leave."

"With you?" Koglim gestures at both Sira and Tas. "Never."

Sira blinks at Koglim, takes another breath, and says, "Koglim, don't. We just got free of him. I'm trying to help."

Koglim scoffs. He prepared another ball of ice but drops it to the ground. He rolls his eyes so hard that he almost falls over.

Yinzar steps around them. "We need to leave." He squints at Ara, perhaps predicting our intentions. "Whatever the plan, I don't think you can win."

"Maybe not, but if Tas is here to help..."

Tas lifts his chin upward. "I'm sorry about the bridge. I followed Kel. I should have followed you."

How do I know if I can trust Tas, let alone Sira? The fact they've seemed to convince Yinzar is beside the point. "And you and Sira... you're coming to us only now. If you both felt so bad—"

Sira opens her mouth, I'm assuming to defend herself, but instead takes a breath and closes her eyes.

Yinzar steps in for her. "Vor left Tungsten City moments ago. I came out from under his influence, and they were ready. Now come on. We don't want another draw between the shield and the crown like we had on the bridge."

He's right. Even if my dad's plan could work, and the conjurers can stop the darksmiths with good old-fashioned bullets, the cost is too high. And we have a better option: the path to the protodungeons is open.

"Ara, we have to go. Now!"

She shakes her head. "I'm blocking Kel's attacks for now. But when Vor gets here..."

"We kill him." All eyes turn to my dad. He doesn't use craft, or I would say there was an actual fire in his determined gaze. His face has soured. His body tenses. I know what this is. I know because the same rage boils in my blood, rising to match my dad's.

"This ends now." That's when the orders tumble from his mouth, a knee-jerk reaction grown from his years as the king of Rimduum. "Ara, Koglim: triangulate Kel's position. Then budge everyone possible up to the ruined settlement and attack. Don't take her alive. Tas: if you're here to help, follow Ara's orders. But first, absorb Sira's craftprint—the one from her silver knife. Sira: you're staying out of this. Clayson: you and—"

"No." I force the rage and frustration out of my thoughts. "You're trying to lead your people into battle. And you're doing it from a place of pure anger. I know because I just got back from that place. But more death and destruction aren't going to fix this, Dad."

"And this key will? You don't know that, Clayson."

"Key?" Yinzar asks.

A wave of protective craft starting from Ara reinforces the whole room. It must be her way of warning me. "Stop, Clayson. If I went with you... Vor will hurt these people. He's expecting you to be here. He's doing everything possible to find you. And if he doesn't get what he wants..."

I look to Jeiah and Koglim for support.

"Even with Icho," Koglim says, "we can't budge enough of these people. There's nowhere for them to go."

And just like that, the whole world slips through my fingers.

All my hopes spill out onto the stone. I don't know if I'm wrong or right. I don't know if my dad's plan will work or fail. I don't know if there's anything in the protodungeons that would help us stop Vor.

Jeiah speaks. "Clayson. It's okay. Don't get lost in there. We had a plan. It won't work. These people need us. We can't let Vor take them all."

My teeth grind together, making it impossible for me to speak, so I nod.

"Good," my dad says. "Jeiah: stay close by me. I need you to calculate the balance of the craft between our side and Vor's, like the great arithmetists of the Mithrium Wars. We must end this. Everyone is depending on us."

Immediately Jeiah takes out her beholder, taps Ara's shield, and begins scanning through a maze of multipliers and exponents. Brick. The type of math they did during the Mithrium Wars held people's lives in balance and left behind the ruins of a hundred cities.

I'm going to be sick. Still, my voice reaches out to my dad. "Then, what do I do?"

"You have no craft. I'd say take up a rifle and join us, but that's what Vor wants. You're the tool he'll use to crack open the rest of the dungeons. We'll hide you. Yinzar can stay with Sira and Clayson." Satisfied, my father turns to his wife. "Azbena: stay by my side. Keep the darksmiths away from Jeiah and me." He takes her hands and stares long and hard at the gold ring on her finger. "I don't know how you found that, but... I'll take my ring."

My mind reels. Is he going to use craft?

"Therias..." Mom says. "This all feels wrong."

"Bena, the ring. Please."

She gives it to him and follows him out of the hallway.

Jeiah's words seem hollow as she leaves. "We've got this."

By the time they disappear from sight, Sira wraps her arms around my neck. She pulls me in for a tight hug. No matter how I feel about what she did, I know it comes from a life of pain. I know what she needs is a feeling that she's safe. So, though my back and arms stiffen at first, I hug her back.

There's a warmth and security about being able to take care of her. Something inside me thrills at her need for me. I've sensed it in Jeiah too, but her feelings are not so desperate, grasping and lonely.

"That was nice," Sira says, dabbing her eyes. Her face is still gaunt, but she tries to smile through her obvious discomfort at having recently budged.

When I face Yinzar again, he raises his wild white-orange eyebrows. "Two things: what's the key, and why don't you have craft?"

I clear my throat. "The key opens some type of gateway in Edium Fiarie. It should lead us to the protodungeons. Exralt hid it in Brightstorm Dungeon. We think he used it to get Ergal, Onrix, and Icho. But there may be a way to defeat Vor hidden there too. Exralt got the key from the wraiths at Gamgim. That's who took my craft."

Yinzar looks me up and down. "Interesting. They took all of it?"

"They're not like wraiths in the dungeons. They're Dura. Killed long ago when some great destruction brought about the Foundation. I'm not sure I understand what happened, but..."

"So, you're powerless?" Sira says. She has somehow grown paler.

"I can use the shield. I suspect I can use the crown as well."

"Strange indeed," Yinzar says. "There's always been a connection between mithrium and the creation of the brightstorms. They say that mithrium could even be made of all of the crafts put together. I wonder if Exralt's discovery of mithrium came before or after Erikzin forged the cradle and made the first brightstorm."

"I—" Harsh voices lance through my skull.

Gather.

I squeeze my temples. I gave Ara the mithrium shield. Why is this still happening? "Gather. Gather what?" Whatever the wraiths did to me must be connected to the brightstorms and the mithrium.

Yinzar grips my arm to steady me. "Clayson?"

I don't have time to respond. Something clinks against the stone at our feet, and Yinzar reacts with a wild kick. The thing hurls back the way it came and bursts, filling the tunnel floor-to-ceiling with sand.

"Husk!" He pushes me in the opposite direction and grabs Sira. "Run! Now!"

We sprint down the corridor. Grimflail has found us. I try not to think about what would have happened if Yinzar hadn't kicked the husk, but it's impossible not to. I'd be buried inside a wall of sand with no craft to protect me. We have to find a way out of here.

Sira lags behind. I turn briefly to see two things: Yinzar desperately urging Sira forward, and the glimmer of golden masks rushing at us from down the tunnel. Hardkeeper comes into clear focus. The former member of the council is a deadly enemy even when he's not being controlled by some darksmith hellbent on revenge.

"I can't," Sira pants. "Just leave me." She drops to her knees.

Yinzar stops dead, whirling around in the tiny space and cracking his black staff on the stone. The reverberating clang almost shatters my teeth, but it stops Hardkeeper in his tracks. Grimflail appears behind him and whispers something.

The same moment Hardkeeper hurls another husk in our direction, Yinzar transforms into a beast. His arms and hands become furry and clawed. His orange hair grows into a coarse shock of a mane. A thick tail drops from his lower back to the floor, and his face grows a wolfish snout. In one deft movement, he swipes the husk from the air and peels it open like an orange.

A blast of sand shoots back toward Hardkeeper. Yinzar charges forward and grabs Sira like a doll. He depresses some switch on the husk, and Sira turns into a pillar of glimmering particles. Yinzar presses the husk to her form and vacuums her in. He hands it to me.

"Go," he barks. "Find Therias. You'll be safer around more people."

I stare at the husk in my hands, shocked.

"Go!" he growls. A pale-yellow ring forms around his irises, and he bares his teeth at me. "I can only give you so much time."

I leave him. For all my hope to protect those I love, for all the power that came from being peerless of shieldcraft, I can only run away. What am I supposed to do? Vor didn't come. He left everyone in Tungsten City—every Loamin under granite—he let them go. Why? And why isn't he here? Would I sense it if he were?

The brightstorm responds with more indistinct whispers.

Focus. I stumble through the darkness. Think. Which tunnel did we come down? There! No, there. I see a flash of gold. Brick. Run, Clayson. Run.

With another blind turn, a slant of stark light appears at the end of the tunnel. Gasping for breath, with a lance of pain extending from the scar in my back through the center of my body, I push myself forward with everything I have.

The brightstorm is a searing light high in the citybarrel above, leaving spots on my vision. But I'm out of the cavern and into the ravine. When the spots clear, I shudder at the sight in front of me. Kel had been blocking the exit of the cave, trapping people inside. Several dozen bodies encumber the floor of the ravine. The arrows sticking from their bodies glow with the rust-colored light of ironcraft.

I grit my teeth. This has to stop.

The current is slow, but one body breaks loose from the shore and starts floating away. Instinct takes over, and I grab the woman's hand, pulling her back to shore. But I can't wait here. I don't know how long Yinzar can hold Grimflail and the others in the caverns, but it won't be long, even with the Wolfstaff.

I cross the ravine, winding up the stairs. The distant report of faraway gunfire hastens my footsteps. I crawl back up to the surface of Geum Ide where the brightstorm sheds light against the massive piles of rubble left in the wake of the settlement's destruction.

It's so bright that it steals away all shadows. Too bright. It was never crystalline. I risk looking straight at it. It's smaller and dense with power. Suddenly, it flickers. A single whispered word shoots through my mind—*gather*.

The word shakes my bones. It came from the brightstorm. How?

In response, the brightstorm blinks again. I stop walking and squint up at the giant orb.

"Clayson Brightstorm," Vor's sing-song voice, reaches me from around the next pile of rubble. "I know you're out there!"

My pulse quickens. I stop walking.

"Do you like what we've done to the city!" Vor calls out.

Where's my dad and the others? If Vor is out in the open, they must be planning something. I need to give them time. Without any way to protect myself, without backup, I march into Vor's view.

He has my friends. My heart sinks.

Rusela is there, furious. Winta and Hemdi stand close together, Echel in their unified arms. Lagnar and Brig both look ready to spring into action, but their bodies are frozen in place, facing Vor with snarls like a deadly game of red light, green light.

The darksmiths have captured Yinzar somehow, probably by forcibly budging him from the caverns. Wolfstaff is in the hands of some grinning darksmith. Next to him stands a tearful young man I recognize—Quilgist Brightkeeper, my distant cousin and keeper of Brightstorm Dungeon. He helped us find our way to the cradle last year. Of course, Vor would exploit that.

Grimflail crouches in the rubble behind him, surrounded by his team of gold-masked slaves. Hardkeeper stares at the ground, a husk in his hands. Koglim's friend Brude watches the horizon. The other two figures are still a mystery.

Vor smiles, producing the cube of mithrium. "You know, six hundred years ago, this place—what was it called? Gythanstyan! That's right—it was a lot nicer. I can't even remember how I found a way to destroy it. Someone helped, of course. Someone always helps."

He sighs deeply, tossing the remaining piece of mithrium in the air and catching it over and over. "Opportunity comes knocking at the threshold, and my patience is rewarded. You're going to tell me what you're doing to the brightstorms and why, or—just like Gythanstyan—someone will help me kill your friends one by one."

CHANGE THEM GOLD

VOR DOESN'T KNOW.

Above us, the brightstorm bursts with a tongue of energy. A wave of indistinct voices explodes in my mind. I glance at Vor. Sweat gleams on his creased brow. My dad said the growing brightstorm in Tungsten City was connected to Vor's construction of the Everfalls, but it's bigger than that. It's bigger than all of us, Vor included.

"It's not us, Vor. Whatever is happening to the brightstorms, we didn't do it."

But even that rings somewhat wrong in my mind. Maybe this is something that the Dura wraiths did. Some punishment. They hold a connection to the dungeons, so why not the brightstorms? For some reason, my mind catches hold of the word *destroyer*.

Vor's eyes widen. "Of course, you think that. But you obviously did something. I wish I could dig it out of your mind myself, but"—he shrugs— "I can't read your thoughts with Ara roaming around here. And probably Tas." He mutters this last sentence but stops and stares at the husk in my hand.

"Who's in there, Clayson?"

I don't answer.

"Oh, come on! Did Tas take her from time-out? It's Sira, isn't

216

it? I should have—she's smitten with you, you know." He tsks. "You raise them the best you can, and they still go their own way."

My hand grips the metal husk tighter. I scowl at him.

"That's *my* Sira in there," he growls.

The word *my* crawls under my skin. He may think he raised her, but he didn't. He groomed her. But something good in her survived all his punishments and torment and belittling. The sweet girl from who just wanted her father to play with her. She doesn't belong to Vor.

Vor orders Grimflail to collect the husk. Without moving, Grimflail sends Hardkeeper lurching forward, his eyes placid under the golden mask. If Hardkeeper, the terrifying and fierce keeper of Hardblaze Dungeon, could break out of this enslavement, Grimflail would find himself trapped in a husk and dropped into a river of lava.

I won't give Grimflail the satisfaction of using Hardkeeper against me. I flip the switch on the husk, and it bursts open, letting Sira drain out in a pile of sand in front of me.

The second she reforms, she pulls herself behind me like I'm a shield.

Vor rolls his eyes. "This again? Sira, come here. You're not safe with him."

"W-we'll try and stop you," Sira says over my shoulder.

"That would be foolish," Vor says. He sounds bored with us. "Kel is just waiting for my orders to shoot. Though I wouldn't be surprised if she just starts shooting whenever. Not the greatest rule follower."

"So, what now?" I ask.

"Maybe our interests align." He points an innocent finger up to the brightstorm. "No? What are you planning, Clayson? You've been up there so comfortable under the shield. And how did you move it without Ara? Mysterious. You must have some scheme, some plan to"—he makes quotes with his fingers—"stop me."

"Maybe. Tell me what you're planning so I can just do the opposite."

"Predictable."

"Okay, say we want some of the same things. Maybe to free the champions from their dungeons."

He stops pacing. "Ah, there's something."

"Then what?"

Sira's hands tighten on my bicep. She whispers, "Clayson, no."

Vor's smile is hard and dangerous. "Then we work together, Clayson. It's that simple. I let your friends go and we solve all the problems with the world, with *Loamin*. That's what you want, isn't it? Answers?"

"Will you let people go back to their lives? If all you want is answers..."

He weighs this uncomfortably. "Someone's gotta pay for my years of pretended servitude, Clayson."

"The council wasn't good enough?"

He shrugs. "It was a start. I have the mithrium"—he tosses it again— "I have Kel. Be easy to make something powerful. You could help, Clayson, with the recipe. Jailbreak the heart of another dungeon. Maybe we'd even find Erikzin Brightstorm among the Dura.

"I've been gathering them—the other Dura. And once I figure out a way to free them from their prisons, they'll know what I did for them, and we'll take our place at the head of the table."

"And all the Loamin?"

His lip curls as if he's tasted something bitter. "Eh."

And here's the real Vor. I'm a tool for his revenge. Giving him more power, even if I might agree about the other dungeons, hurts everyone. "I won't help you tear down this world."

Vor nods understandingly. "Right, no, of course you won't. And why—"

The ground shakes. A jagged crack spreads between us. Behind me, golden light bleeds into the sky. Sira shrinks into my back. The whispers connected to the brightstorm, to Ara's shield, suddenly dial up another octave, deafening and sharp. I clench my jaw, my ears ringing. I can't deal with this and Vor at the same time.

The brightstorm is not the source of the golden light.

A rich voice, like the embodiment of my personal sense of justice, calls out to Vor. "Vor!" It's my father. "Lay aside your crown and have your darksmiths set down their craft. This ends here."

Hundreds of conjurers toting guns and swords flank me. A handful of craft-welding Loamin standing shoulder-to-shoulder with them, brandishing fire, vines, and gears. A shorter man holds a glowing ball of mercury.

My father soars above them, iron skin wreathed by heavy red stone boulders that become more and more molten as they circle him. His oath with the conjurers has been cast aside. He's chosen to use craft again. And I know my father. He did it because Anda-lynn is dead.

He's left his oxygen tank far behind him in taking his ring back from Mom. Nothing encumbers him. After years of seeing him weak and months of watching him consistently set aside any power he could take to himself, my mouth drops open in shock.

"Therias Brightstorm," Vor sings. He rolls his eyes at me as if my father is being predictable. I, for one, didn't expect to see him like this—ever. "And you've brought—are those guns? Swords? This is... Sira, what would you say? Cute? Naïve."

"I won't tell you again, Vor," my father shouts. "Lay aside your craft. We've played this out to the end. This victory is ours. We're reclaiming our cities, and you will face the consequences of murdering the council and taking unlawful control of our world."

"You mean what's left of this world. Look around you, Therias. Your hopes of making something of this underground wasteland are shattered. The brightstorms are failing—or whatever—the Loamin are in retreat. Your own son exposed the dungeon system for what it was—a prison! There won't be anything left to destroy or to build. Nothing. There are only scraps now, garbage."

Mom and Jeiah emerge from the crowd of conjurers. I glance at Jeiah.

She nods at my unspoken question. She's done the math. We would win this fight. But I see the growing tears in her eyes. She doesn't want this. I follow her watery stare to her brother, Brig, frozen in place. Kel is aiming at them. Lagnar's eyes are closed. He's accepted his fate. They all have.

Mom has a look of sad determination screwed on. Does she think this sacrifice is worth Vor's end? Is it? This whole world, even the way people think, was forged in the fallout of the Mithrium War; Gythanstyan, becoming a wasteland, becoming an oasis, becoming a wasteland again. And the cycle won't end today.

I don't accept the balance of death they've all settled on.

"Vor." My voice is barely a whisper. "We want the same things. I'll help you. We'll open the dungeons together."

A few of the conjurers gasp. The light from Jeiah's beholder wavers but then steadies behind me. Lagnar opens his eyes and squints at me, his head only slightly shaking no. I think I hear a soft growl from Rusela.

I take another step toward Vor.

Sira releases me and scrambles behind the line of conjurers.

"Clayson, don't!" my father's amplified voice stretches out like hands trying to clamp over my mouth. But all of this—this ridiculous showdown—has to stop.

I call out to Vor. "Agree to my demands; let my friends go, and I *will* help you. That's all you want, isn't it? I'll help free the other Dura. The dungeons will be gone."

Vor waits for a beat, shakes his head, and then laughs. "No, Clayson. See your father, Sira's father. They have always been right. Craft must end. All of it. But not before I'm satisfied with the personal cost that some of these Loamin must pay."

"Ara now!" my father yells.

Suddenly she's behind Vor in the circle with Lagnar and the others. She yanks Icho from the grasp of the darksmith holding it. Immediately, a shotgun appears in Lagnar's hand, and he empties a round in Grimflail's direction. One of Grimflail's masked subordinates turns the bullets into water and charges forward. Lagnar sends another useless volley toward Grimflail and then switches to another object. He flicks a coin toward one of Grimflail's captives, and they blink away in a puff of brown light.

Rusela lunges for Grimflail, but the line of conjurers opens fire.

A dozen arrows rip through the air. Hemdi and Winta hunch over Echel. Quilgist Brightkeeper throws himself between them and Kel's arrows. I watch in horror as a feathered shaft pierces straight through his heart, and wind from the ironcraft in the arrow tears his body apart from the inside. He doesn't even scream as his body twists sharply around itself.

Quilgist, who led us through the mines to find the cradle. Quilgist who was afraid of everything. Quilgist who I barely even knew. The boy who sat on the council and supported me and my sister. He's gone.

Before I can even process what's happening, my father roars and hurls a massive boulder right for Vor. Vor's eyes go wide, but he budges before the rock hits. The shockwave sends me flying backward, but Jeiah grabs me.

"Come on," she says. "Let's get you out of here."

That's when the lights turn out.

A sharp, final whisper from the brightstorm sends a ripple down my spine, and I feel it ripped away from above us. How? What could move a brightstorm? The mithrium shield glares like a single headlight, and the only other lights come in bursts of craft, but all of those fade to nothing. The weight of confusion settles on everyone, darksmith and conjurer alike.

The earth groans and someone screams in the dark. Above us, the golden light from my father's craft returns to full power.

His voice reverberates through the darkness. "Vor! What is this?"

My father still thinks Vor is manipulating the brightstorms. There's no answer.

It could be Vor. Maybe I'm wrong, and this was all a trap. He's been building something in Everfalls with the power of millions of foilgrips.

Where did Vor go? He budged just before the boulder hit the ground. He wouldn't leave. In answer, another glaring light—Vor's crown and the third piece of mithrium—appear at the top of a pile of rubble behind Ara. Vor floating in the darkness.

"Grimflail! Kel! Don't let them take this from us!" It's a desperate growl. That's when I add everything up. His question to me, his threats, the fear in his voice even now—he has no idea what's happening to the brightstorms. It must be connected to the Dura wraiths. Maybe Hemdi and I *did* break something when we rebuilt part of that tree. Vor could be right. It could be my fault.

A large figure appears next to me. "Koglim!" He has Icho.

"Koglim!" An aching voice cuts through the dark. I don't recognize it, but Koglim must. His head snaps up, searching for the source. A reflection of light off Icho reveals his trembling chin, a sob threatening to erupt.

"Brude?" Koglim murmurs. Icho dips in his hand.

When he tries to step away, Jeiah pulls Koglim's arm back. Then Mom is there, yanking Icho from Koglim. "Clayson, we have to get you out of here."

"Where?" Jeiah says.

"Anywhere!"

A sliver of gold appears a few feet away, and the clean blue light from Jeiah's beholder paints the scarred surface of Brude's mask.

"Please," he says softly. "Don't leave me."

These words send a shockwave of warnings cascading over

every nerve of my body. It's a trick. Mom is going to budge us any second.

"Ara!" I shout for her. Mom's right, it's time to retreat, but I need Ara to come with me to Edium Fiarie. We have to get to the protodungeons.

"No time," Mom hisses.

I don't feel the craft when we budge. I squint as light bleeds back into the world. Morning rays filter through the trees, but the trees themselves are wrong. A dozen sets of long glass wind chimes dangle from the pines around us. The gravel under my feet is wrong. Where are we? We didn't return to the cabin. There are picnic tables and...

"Is this... this is the same park Dad took me to when..." I look back at Mom.

"It's the first place that came to mind. Dad and I use it for emergencies."

Koglim plops down on the scattered pine needles. "Brude." He drops his face into his hands and starts swearing through his tears. "We just left him there."

Jeiah wheezes from the surface effects but circles around our group in slow, deliberate footsteps. "Something traced our... brick! Azbena, budge us. Now!"

Mom's eyes go wide. "I should have... Vor knows this place."

My eyes go back to the trees, to the glass wind chimes. To anyone else on the surface, they would only look like beautiful artwork. I should have realized.

Koglim looks up at the trees. "Foilgrip."

I pull a whole set of chimes down from the trees. They shatter against the dry ground.

"That can break the foilgrip," Koglim says, his tears drying up.

There's a brown flash of light behind me, and Mom gasps.

A cutting voice says. "Koglim. There you are." Bhogda Grimflail's voice is as sharp as whatever cuts the scars into the masks he forces on people. Brude and Hardkeeper and another half dozen gold-masked slaves stand on both sides of him, with enough combined craft to melt us all into the dirt.

"I'm going to kill you," Koglim hisses.

Grimflail tsks. "And take Brude along with me?"

Koglim's voice wavers, but he says, "Better than being your slave."

We all look at Brude. Whatever freedom he was given only moments ago must have been manufactured. The boy is completely docile now, awaiting orders.

"Mmm. I don't think I'll give you the chance. I've been waiting for this for a long, long time. Do you know what it's like in Palecloak, what you and your friends did to me?"

"You earned that," Koglim spits.

Jeiah is still scanning the air around her, searching for a way out. Mom is crouched on the ground fiddling with the broken foilgrip. But I don't think either of them has a solution. Where's one of my father's guns when I need it? I could put a bullet through his mask.

Koglim must have the same thought. He rushes forward. Grimflail hisses and the masked figure that turned Lagnar's bullets into water glows red. Gray swells of mud capture Koglim's feet, but his momentum doesn't adjust, and he slams face forward into the ground. The thick mud—no, concrete—slides up his body slowly suffocating him.

Jeiah charges them, pulses of static popping in her hands. Hardkeeper grabs her, forcing her to the ground.

"Stop!" I yell.

Grimflail bends closer to Koglim. "Once I'm done with you, it won't be hard to find Hemdi and Winta. Their new... addition has them moving slowly. And Rugnus, I know he didn't come out of that dungeon alive. It's a fitting end for him. Though I would have liked the pleasure of killing him myself."

Since we first encountered Grimflail, Rugnus had been looking for a way to stop him. My fingers roll up into fists. Grimflail's attack in Brightstorm Dungeon forced our hand; because of that, Rugnus and Andalynn are gone. Time to deal with this guy permanently. I could charge him, maybe peel the mask from his face. But what would that do to his captives? Beside me, Mom winces.

Grimflail is still gleefully focused on the cement enveloping Koglim. He waves a floppy hand. "Kill the other two. We'll bring Clayson back to Vor."

Mom stands. Her hands are filled with golden blood. She holds the small tin she used to protect me—to change my face—when I needed to hide out with Rugnus last year in Tungsten City. The blood pools in the ring box, trickling over the side. Her shoulders sag, and her strawberry blonde hair shifts in the light, looking almost as wild and ferocious as Yinzar's shock of orange hair.

"Maybe you've forgotten who you're dealing with, Grimflail," she says. "I am Azbena Bloodsmith. Whatever form of goldcraft you even *think* you can wield against me; I can tear through it like paper."

Grimflail stands, looking annoyed at being interrupted. No wonder he and Vor get along so well. "Hardkeeper, show the *former* queen what we do with Monarchists."

Hardkeeper barely takes a step forward before the box transforms in my mom's hands. The metal stretches out. The gold blood hardens and extends upward until a hilt is cast in her hands, rising to a deadly point. Below her, a few pieces of the broken foilgrip are stained in gold. She must've used them to cut herself—deeply.

In one swift motion, she blurs forward, shoving the golden sword clean through Grimflail's torso.

At her feet, Koglim screams. He's said it before: Grimflail can't die without killing everyone under his masks. When he and Rugnus removed Valifra's mask, it killed her. But mom saved Rusela Whitechin. Hope spreads outward from my thudding heart.

The last glimmer of life in Grimflail's eyes bleeds away, and his golden mask falls to the dirt. Koglim looks to Brude, muttering what I can only guess is a prayer. Hardkeeper is closest to me. I watch as he reaches up and pulls the mask from his face. His skin is chalky. The moment the mask comes away, he falls to his knees.

"Impossible," Hardkeeper turns the mask over in his hands, and then his attention centers on Grimflail. A cruel smile forms on the old keeper's face as Grimflail slides off Mom's golden sword and crashes to the ground. Grimflail's face is drained of color and nothing pools beneath him on the ground. The sword must have absorbed all his blood, all his evil.

Grimflail's other gold slaves start removing their masks.

Hardkeeper stares at Mom. "Grimflail's masks are... how did you do such a thing?"

Mom takes a shuddering breath. "I wasn't going to... let him take... my son from me."

"Ide keep us," Hardkeeper whispers.

"Koglim?" Brude has his mask off. He can barely stand but presses his fingers into the cement around his friend, scraping and peeling as best as he can. One of the others, the woman who presumably made the cement, liquefies it and, for good measure, shoots a blast of water over Koglim.

Free from the cement, Koglim grabs his friend and pushes their foreheads together. "I thought I'd lost you, buddy."

Weakly, Brude responds. "I was grabbing a carton of noodles from Tinny's, and then Vor..."

Koglim squeezes his friend even harder. "It's over, my guy. It's over."

The sound of a shotgun pumping into action tears me away from their reunion.

"Hey, y'all," Lagnar drawls. "Did we miss the—" He stops dead, staring at the golden sword Mom's still clutching. Rusela, Yinzar, Brig, and my father appear in a flash of light behind him. Rusela takes one look at Grimflail's body and her face hardens. She spit on him.

My father and Yinzar rush forward as Mom collapses. Her body convulses. Yinzar holds his daughter gently, but her body won't stop shaking.

Dad looks at me, desperate. "Clayson, help!"

I scramble to her side. A network of golden veins pulses along her neck and forehead. Her skin is cool and damp. The golden veins begin to discolor into a deep orange. But without craft, I have no way to help her.

"Someone, please." I search the group for Hemdi. Or— "Where's Ara?" But she can't come to the surface. I know that.

"I sent her to Edium Fiarie," my dad says. "That's where I thought you would go."

Mom sucks in a breath, arching her back, then her eyes dim. Her head rolls back onto my dad's forearm. Color returns to her cheeks, but beneath her skin, there is still a dull glowing orange in her veins. She drops the sword to the ground. It isn't returning to the shape of a box. Whatever she did with goldcraft, I think it was permanent.

"Come back," Dad cries, "Bena. Please."

And as if my dad's words were an order, she opens her eyes. She exhales a breath of golden smoke glittering with flecks of metal. After a few more breaths, she says, "Had to destroy the ring box."

He grasps the sword, placing it in her hand. "You did it."

She nods weakly. "I did. I saved our son."

"What can I do? Bena."

"I think I'm okay, but I feel strange, distant."

Dad helps Mom to her feet. Her eyes have changed color. They're almost golden. She attempts to stand by herself but wobbles. I catch her arm and motion for Jeiah to help. Mom swallows hard and closes her eyes, but she takes a step. We lead her to a picnic table and help her sit.

Koglim follows us excitedly. "I don't think I'll live to see anything so powerful again. And, oh man, I had a front-row seat to the end of this piece of trollbrick. My eyes were literally glued to the whole thing. Serves this latcher right." Koglim looks down angrily at Grimflail's body, disgust warping his smile.

Hardkeeper calls out. "Therias Brightstorm," he gestures to the gold ring my father wears. "Have you returned to your position?"

A flick of annoyance bristles under my father's skin. "Not exactly," he calls over his shoulder.

"Then Queen Everbloom must return to her place, so we can cast for new keepers, and reform the council immediately."

My father faces Hardkeeper. "My daughter is dead." I can tell by his tone that he's accepted this, and fresh tears threaten at the corners of my eyes.

Hardkeeper almost growls at the news. He was never a great supporter of my family, but he valued the traditions of Whurrimduum. "Then the work I must do is even more important. Please, Therias—you have always sought to protect this kingdom. Do so now. Speak with me."

"Will you be okay?" he asks Mom.

She nods, but I see fear deep in her eyes.

Hardkeeper and my father walk together away from the group.

I glance at Jeiah. "Is Brig safe?"

"He's with Winta and Hemdi."

My head throbs. "And the other question—the big one—what happened to the brightstorm over Geum Ide? It just disappeared."

Koglim turns back to us, interested. "Maybe Vor—"

"It wasn't him," I say. "I think... what if when we went to Gamgim, to the Forest of Ide... I don't know. It triggered something. Or what if the Dura wraiths are upset that I escaped them? They could be doing this."

Jeiah shrugs. "Your guesses have been startlingly accurate in the past, but I don't know about that one. There's something missing."

"A lot of somethings."

I cast an eye at Grimflail's other victims. They look exhausted.

Most of them are simply sitting in the same spot they were standing when Grimflail met his end. Rusela is speaking quietly to the other woman. Koglim nudges Lagnar into our circle.

Mom grabs my arm and whispers, "Clayson, if Hardkeeper finds out you went to Brightstorm Dungeon, he'll hold you to your oath with the council."

I scoff. This can't even be a concern right now. "What council? Didn't you see? Quilgist is gone. Hardkeeper and Lagnar are the only members of the council left."

Mom's breath quickens. "Quilgist is... everything happened so fast. He was too young... None of this should've happened." Hardkeeper calls for me, but Mom tightens her grip. "Take everyone you can and get to Edium Fiarie. But not your father and not Hardkeeper. You hear me?"

I don't know what to say.

She turns to her father. "Protect my son."

Yinzar nods.

Mom coughs, and a few golden particles dance into the air.

My father tries to wave me over to them this time. Rusela joins them.

Mom's eyes flicker for a second, and a breath catches. I reach for her, but she puts up a hand. "It's nothing I can't handle. You need to go."

Lagnar sidles up to Jeiah. "And where might we be going?"

"Catch up, Emberfence," Yinzar says. "We need to get to the protodungeons to find something to defeat Vor, via the doorway in Edium Fiarie, using the key Clayson got from Brightstorm Dungeon, which he was led to by the Dura wraiths in Gamgim, who stole his craft."

Lagnar rolls his eyes and checks the sights on his shotgun. "That's a mouthful, but nice summary."

Koglim is quick on the draw. "Take care of Brude?"

"I will," Mom says.

With one last glance at my father, I nod at Koglim.

"Don't let Dad do anything stupid," I tell Mom.

"Says his equally rash son."

I take her hand. "I love you. You're sure you're okay?"

"As good as I can be. Go."

Yinzar squeezes his daughter's shoulder. "Rest."

We're a strange group. Yinzar Mithriumbane, who forged his own fake dungeon. Lagnar Emberfence, the formal general of the Kingdom of Rimduum. Jeiah, my girlfriend, Paladin of Tungsten City and Bluebottle Dungeon. Koglim Felsight, a professional dungeon raider. And me, the Loamin with the strangest, most confusing résumé in the history of the Rocky Mountains.

"Clayson, what—" Hardkeeper starts toward us.

Koglim, back in his element, smiles and brushes off Icho.

We budge.

Two conflicting lights greet us: the shimmering blue from the Foundation of ice on our right and a never-ending sea of lava at our left. Obsidian lays under our feet. Koglim points further down the wall toward the House of Ide, Edium Fiarie, where two hulking figures block the way.

"Wraithspit," Koglim says. "Trolls."

These are the first real trolls I've ever seen. Twice the height of a Behemoth mech, fissured with red pulsing veins between flesh-like rocky skin. They hold no weapons. They are weapons. One of them smashes its massive, spindly claw against the wall, tearing away a block of obsidian, and hurls it in our direction. It comes at us with the speed of a freight train.

We're dead.

Then a bright light nearly blinds me. It's Ara. A wave of power eddies outward from our little group. The sheen of light enshrouding us isn't circular like my typical shield but jagged, flaring with wild pulses of light. It's raw power. The hunk of obsidian ricochets back toward the troll.

It growls, which sounds more like it's vomiting mashed-up syllables. It bats the rock away with a whip-like motion, and the stone zips off toward the glimmering Foundation of ice to our right, skipping on the surface.

"Hey, Ara," Koglim says in a squeak.

"What now?" Jeiah asks.

Lagnar hums. "Old fashioned standoff, I guess."

"Probably," Koglim adds.

The troll charges us. It has no weapons, but one hand is a four-foot claw, and the other is a stump of spikes. It swings both against Ara's shield. The light flares and a shock wave of pressure pushes down on me, shifting a hundred-pound burden onto my shoulders. But the shield holds, and the troll's arm quivers above us.

The second troll flexes its rocky flesh, which seems to charge its red veins like it's been plugged into a power source.

Another sickening growl.

The first troll renews its attack, pressing against Ara's shield with all its significant might. When the second brings down its hammering arms, I'm pushed to my knees from the strain.

But Ara slips her feet into a wider stance, holding steady.

I torque my head toward Jeiah. "This... is not... going... well."

"I'll try to push back," Ara calls over her shoulder. With a groan, she takes a single step forward. Suddenly, as if someone opens a release valve, the pressure against me dissipates. I suck in an enormous breath.

The troll, who had seemed to charge itself, swings again and again and again, undeterred by Ara's resistance. "This isn't getting us anywhere," she growls.

Yinzar is crouched next to me. In his hands, the wolfstaff begins glowing copper. He winces but doesn't let it go. A mighty howl splits the air behind me, and a wall of fur passes over my head. Frrwelhst, the feral wolf who greeted me in front of Wolf-staff Dungeon, bounds into the first troll, her teeth latching onto its bicep.

Koglim's whoop of excitement nearly drowns out the fierce yowling of the troll as it tries to shake Frrwelhst off its arm. The troll's massive club arcs toward the wolf's head, but at the last second, Frrwelhst releases one arm and catches the clubbed appendage in her teeth. She whacks the second one with a flick of her tail, throwing it off-balance.

Ara and I see the opening between the trolls at the same time. She gathers the shield's energy at the front of our group, shouts for us to follow, and charges the second troll. Frrwelhst flips the first troll off the bridge, and at the same moment, the shield contacts the second one right at center mass.

The troll looks surprised, then angry, as it reaches out for something to grab onto, but Frrwelhst bats its face with a huge paw, and down it goes, crashing onto the icy Foundation. Its body sizzles, and a long bellow reverberates toward us.

Jeiah steps next to me, watching Frrwelhst carefully. "What is she saying?"

"I can't hear her." A piece of me shrinks. I can't communicate with Frrwelhst. Our minds were once connected. It must be one more thing I lost in Gamgim.

Frrwelhst licks her chops. She was the guardian of Wolfstaff Dungeon when I went for my summation. If she's here because I destroyed that dungeon, I might as well say my goodbyes.

Yinzar eyes me. "Frrwelhst says she can still hear you, Clayson. You shouldn't fear. She guarded the wolfstaff, not the champion. She wonders why she can't connect with you."

Jeiah tilts her head. "Yinzar, see if she will defend the door as we go into the House of Ide. The trolls won't stay down there."

With a glance over the battlements, I find a lava-covered troll climbing toward us. "They can survive lava?"

"They can't be killed," Koglim says. "Just broken into troll shards."

Yinzar pats Frrwelhst's side, and the feral wolf growls hungrily. "Sounds like our protector would love to oblige."

Frrwelhst circles to the back of our group. That's our cue to get moving.

The House of Ide grows larger as we pass row after row of burial chains used to lower the dead into the lava. I can't imagine where the entrance will be for the protodungeons. I've only been inside the House of Ide once. Rugnus found us a ticket into Whurrimduum using body bags. Other than that, I don't know much about the place. We're entering at the opposite side that we came from during that visit.

As we reach the sprawling entrance of the House of Ide, a troll erupts over the side of the wall. It loses no momentum, charging toward us. Frrwelhst wheels around to face it, yelping when the troll flicks a wad of lava toward her.

We can't leave the wolf here to fight for us.

The second I try to stop, Jeiah pulls my arm. "She came to protect us. Let her."

Ara agrees, grabbing my other arm. "Come on. A few more rooms in, and the trolls can't get to us. Besides, I think Frrwelhst is enjoying this."

I suddenly get a picture of me playing fetch with Frrwelhst using the massive leg of a troll. "Yeah, okay."

The obsidian lobby opens in six directions: two stairs leading up, two hallways on the same level, and two staircases going down. The familiar scene makes me think so much of Rugnus that my heart aches. Something heavy settles in the center of my body, but I can't think about them now. Stay focused.

"Which way then?" Koglim says.

I dig out the key. It's lifeless in my hand. But maybe... "Ara?"

She takes it. Nothing happens.

"Try passing the shield to Clayson," Yinzar says. "Maybe it's interfering."

All the normal rules for crafted objects are breaking into a jumble of unconnected pieces, so this is as good as any other guess.

The moment I take the shield, Ara's eyes go wide. She holds the black key out like a compass. "I hear... voices."

"Voices?" I scan her eyes. Are they the same voices I'm hearing?

Ara squints. "It's all mixed up. No, wait. Down. We need to— here!" She points to one of the descending staircases.

As she leads us down, the red light from the lava fades. The wall to our right holds dozens of slotted windows allowing crystalline blue light in from the Foundation. We follow the hallway to a strangely cut gap in the floor, bleeding the same azure light. We step over it.

"Whoa!" Koglim says.

As I follow him, pillars of fog descend along the side of the corridor between the slotted windows. When the fog clears, a long line of thirty-foot statues towers along the side between the windows. All are carved from obsidian in skillfully chiseled detail.

"Where are we?" I ask.

"The Hall of Champions," Jeiah and Yinzar say.

HEAL A SCAR

THE GLOSSED EYES of the statues watch us as we tread over the black stone. Searching their faces, I find some that I recognize. Challozil Silverlamp. Bearcloak, Grimspoon, Wolfstaff. The others tread lightly out of some reverence for the champions, but resentment colors my thoughts. Maybe these are the villains. Halfway down the hallway, I stop in front of the larger-than-life statue of Erikzin Brightstorm. He looks like my father but wears a metal cap and a vest embossed with golden thread. The historical clothes remind me that he's Blackmug's contemporary.

Koglim's voice deepens. "Impressive. Most impressive."

I ignore the movie reference. Everything keeps dragging me back to that cottage. Erikzin and Exralt meant for the key to be irretrievable. They couldn't have guessed that two of their descendants would find it. It was a dangerous secret. And with that thought, the statue of Erikzin Brightstorm seems a thousand times more like my father.

I'm mulling this over when suddenly, the rock comes alive, uncrossing its arms. "Welcome. Worship in whatever way you see fit."

Koglim catches me when I stumble back. "Forgot to tell you they speak," he says. "It's silvercraft and iron craft. Silver at the core of the rock, automated to give you greetings if you get close enough."

"Clayson, we need to hurry," Jeiah says, watching a nervous Ara waiting for us to catch up further down the corridor.

We leave the row of strange statues, thundering down a short flight of stairs only to be faced with two more flights of descending stairs.

"How far do we have to go?" I ask.

Ara shakes her head. "As far down as we can get."

After two more sets of stairs, one made of long shallow steps and the other deep, roughly gouged ones, we enter a room wider than I would have thought possible given the size of the House of Ide above. The rock must spread out the deeper you go. It makes me wonder how all these passageways and rooms were carved in the first place.

The room is filled with a maze of half walls. As we search for another door or stairway, we finally climb up on the walls, jumping between them. Along the periphery, we find no other exit. The whole time Ara is fixated on the maze, treading the pathways as we walk above her along the walls.

Koglim hops to a wall close to me. "I don't get it. There's nowhere to go." He leaps toward Ara. "Hey, Ara, which direction?"

Her speed is slowly increasing as she paces. "Down. It's below us somewhere."

We spend the next few minutes searching the pathways of the maze. Everything is solid stone beneath us. There's no pattern, no sense of direction, just a hundred sharp corners, and no other way out. Koglim retreats to the side of the room and sits. He squints, his face almost comical in concentration.

Jeiah waves the beholder in weird patterns.

After another few minutes, Koglim stands and shouts. "Wait!"

A second later, Jeiah calls out from the far corner. "Got something."

As we gather around Jeiah, Koglim announces his idea.

"Floors can be pressure-sensitive or sensitive to an element. Something like that."

"Probably accurate," Jeiah says. "And look."

I bend toward the corner where she points, but I don't see anything.

Jeiah flicks a lighted diagram into the air. "There." The diagram shows a long pin-needle opening between the exterior wall and one of the short half-walls. "It's the only anomaly in the whole room. There may be a switch at the base of the pinhole. Anyone have something thin enough to—"

Lagnar clears his throat and passes a crumpled wire to her.

When I look at him, he shrugs. "I can't be the only one that carries wire."

"Winta carries wire," Jeiah confirms.

Lagnar approves with a nod. "Smart girl."

Jeiah unfolds the thin strip of metal and jams it into the tiny opening. It hits a snag, and she wiggles the wire until it moves forward. "Brick!" She jumps back, shoving her finger in her mouth. "I think I hit something. It's hot."

With a loud pop, the other corner erupts with lava. It sputters for a moment, clearing a bit more rock and air until it overflows and begins filling the pathways of the maze. A bead of light appears on top of every half-wall. Slowly, the lava creeps toward us.

"Knew it!" Koglim punches the air with his fists.

A second corner of the room breaks open, adding another flow of lava into the maze. I glance at the corner behind me, letting out a buzz of protective energy from the shield. We're surrounded. "Not sure we're going to like what comes next," I say.

Ara races to the center of the maze, where the lava flow hasn't reached yet. "Here! There's a new opening."

We all rush forward, but as we do, fissures open above us, letting down columns of lava. Behind us, lava flows from both remaining corners. Everyone crowds around me, and I encircle them with protection. The power nudges the lavafalls away from us. It feels good to be able to keep them safe. I'm useful again. And yet, something simmers at the edge of my awareness. This is not exactly craft. The whispers I heard, first from the shield when I was on the surface, then from the brightstorm, now seem to rise from the earth itself.

Lagnar is the first one next to Ara. "Ever been to a playground, Brightstorm?"

I stare down at the open hole with understanding. It slants away into nothingness, like the top of a terrifying slide.

Koglim whistles. "I'd prefer a budge, but this might be fun if I don't get stuck."

Lagnar slaps him on the back. "Why don't you go last? I don't wanna get stuck behind you."

"Whatever we do, we have to hurry," Ara says, eyeing the swell of lava, only kept at bay with the shield. "Clayson will have to go last."

"And if we need the shield at the bottom? You know, to break our fall or something?" Koglim asks.

"Have to risk it," Jeiah says.

Ara steps to the edge of the hole. "I'll go first."

"Great," Jeiah says. "Ara, then Lagnar, Yinzar, me, Koglim, then Clayson."

We follow her orders exactly. By the time it's my turn, the whole room is flooded with lava, pressing against the shield. I sit on the edge of the hole and push myself in.

The hole grips me like a vortex and yanks me downward. Whatever light from the lava I expected to follow us gets lost after the first twist in the slide. I'm barely staying on. I can only feel the stone beneath me, but I hear Koglim whoo-hoo-ing not far away.

Good. Maybe we live through this. He shouts a few more times. I imagine him putting his hands in the air. I don't. I keep my center of gravity fastened on the slide. In the dark, I'm terrified my head will smack against a rock while going fifty miles an hour.

A square of blue light hurls toward me, and just when I think I'll be flattened, I tumble into Jeiah and Koglim in a heap on the floor. Everyone is rising to their feet, but I take a moment to catch my breath, still on my hands and knees. If Erikzin or Exralt created that torture slide, it's another reason to hate them. Unless it was the Dura wraiths, Ide itself, or whoever else might be overseeing my universe today.

When I finally reach my feet, Ara is already at the center of the room, the key in her hand. There's a pedestal with a glowing blue base, and her hand hovers over it. The top of the pedestal is an obsidian bowl, the inside of it gleaming.

Yinzar is keeping his distance from the pedestal. "We should—"

Ara drops the key into the bowl.

The blue light vanishes from the pedestal and reappears as dozens of two-by-two glowing squares evenly spaced along the floor.

Ara's shoulders sag, and she steps away from the pedestal. "That was... It was almost like I had no choice. Like I wasn't myself."

"Like you had to," Lagnar whispers. His voice has a strange quality about it, darker. Afraid. He reaches out to the pedestal, his face pale. A sheen of sweat appears on his forehead.

Ara takes the shield back from me just as Lagnar's hand touches the pedestal. He collapses to his knees and moans, almost weeping. "Anything but that. Please."

I watch him without understanding. What craft is affecting his emotions? "Lagnar? What is it?"

When I rest my hand on the pedestal, a wave of emotion hits me. I feel off. As if my limbs are pinned under a ton of granite. I'm stuck. Not physically, but my heart is so heavy that I put my hands over my stomach as if I'll have to catch it when it drops.

Past the pedestal, one of the glowing squares sends up a bright column of light.

Without any of my own will, I help Lagnar to his feet. "Come on."

"What's happening?" Jeiah asks. She tries to step between us and this new destination. We can't let her. We're moving how the pedestal wants us to.

Lagnar's grinding his teeth now, but I slip an arm under him and help him walk forward.

"We have to go into the light." I gesture my head toward the brighter glowing square.

"Into what?" Koglim asks.

I slow, fighting the pull of the pedestal. "You guys don't see the column of light?"

Yinzar's old eyes become wary slits. He marches to the pedestal and lays a hand down but shakes his head. "It's only affecting the two of you. I'd say it's craft, but there's no metal. And you can't even use craft anymore."

"I don't like it," Jeiah offers. Hesitantly she places her hand on the pedestal, but nothing happens.

"I feel... off," I say. "Like Lagnar said. I've gotta fix something. Is that weird?"

"No more than usual," Koglim says. "I hope it'll let the rest of us through once you do."

Lagnar digs in his heels. "Please. Clayson. I cannot do this. I can't."

"Lagnar, what—"

"Not this." But he's drawn forward, and I have to follow him. We're like moths to a flame. When our feet reach the lit square, it expands, washing out everything else. The sensation of being weighed down, hurting, subsides.

Lagnar and I appear in a familiar room.

A man sits at a desk. It's Drail Brightstorm, the King of Rimduum, my grandfather. How is that possible? It's like something off Bluelink but more real. I recognize him from everything I've seen in old footage.

Lagnar stands across from Drail. He's completely out of place in the old room, his shotgun leaning against his shoulder. There's a dazed and disheveled look on his face. "This ain't... Why am I here? I-I—"

His face abruptly slackens, and he turns to Drail, snapping to attention. It seems too formal for him, too obedient. "My King. You sent for me?" Lagnar's accent softens, making him sound more like his cousin, the one I met at StoneYoke, the former Bluekeeper.

"Hey, Lagnar?" When he doesn't answer me, I wave a hand in front of his face. Nothing.

"Yes, General." King Drail doesn't look up from his desk. "I need you to accept a new assignment."

I look back and forth between them. "Is this a memory, Lagnar? Lagnar!"

He only responds to Drail. "Have I done something wrong? Everything is ready for your visit to Hngaal. Security is set to—"

The King unclips the lid of a small box on his desk. "Hngaal is exactly what I want to discuss. And I need your loyalty now more than ever."

"I... my King, of course. Kingdom is stone."

"Good." He lifts the lid of the box, and light dazzles the room. "The mithrium?"

Lagnar stares dumbfounded at Drail. He raises his eyes to his King, but the King is staring down at the mithrium. "Sir, what is this? What does the mithrium have to do with Hngaal?"

"During my speech, I want you to detonate this. Protect yourself, of course, but combine it with anything you see fit. This needs to be done right. You're the only person I trust with the task. Do you understand?"

Lagnar's mouth widens. He stammers. "N-no, my King I-I don't. Hngaal—"

"Is an enemy kingdom." Drail covers the mithrium again.

"But the speech... the peace talks. I thought—"

"An illusion. As we speak, they are planning an invasion."

Lagnar shakes his head. "Surely, I'd've heard—"

"But you didn't. Kingdom is stone. Those are your own words. Will you refuse my order?" Drail still doesn't look at Lagnar directly. Something's not right. And a thought, like an itch, crawls along the base of my skull.

I clap loudly. "Lagnar! What is this?"

Watch. The word is clearer than any other whisper or impression I've ever had with any craft. The voice is female, frail, and forceful at the same time.

Lagnar is quiet for an impossibly long moment. With one last attempt to meet the King's eyes, he says. "Hngaal has its share of revolutionaries, its terrorists, but its people are innocent. Sir, I thought we were trying to rebuild. There hasn't been a mithrium event during my time as general and for ten years before that. Besides Whurrimduum, there are only eleven cities left. How can we—"

"You'll refuse then?"

Lagnar shakes his head. "I didn't say that, but I'd like to know—"

"Good, take it."

Drail waves a hand, and the gesture is familiar. Dismissive, inattentive. And again, Drail can't meet Lagnar's eyes. A strange thought, a suspicion, returns to my mind. This isn't Drail at all. A realization hits me square in the chest. Something Vor claimed on the bridge. That he caused the Mithrium Wars. Brick.

That's not Drail Brightstorm. It's Vor. Somehow, it's Vor.

Lagnar steps forward and lifts the mithrium off the desk, sealing the box. His face is hard, unreadable. "Somethin' else ya want from me, my King."

The King—no, Vor—nods. "Our conversation stays in this room. Secrecy must be maintained in this matter. There are spies everywhere."

"I understand how to take orders, my King."

Lagnar had told me about this. He claimed the King had ordered him. Even if this is only something in his memories, I can't let it happen to him again. The uncomfortable feeling from the pedestal returns in full force. This is why Lagnar didn't wanna face this. Had he known?

He needs help. I slam my hands on his chest, willing him to hear me. "Lagnar!"

Lagnar blinks and looks around the room.

"Lagnar!"

He sees me. Confusion fills his face. "Brightstorm?"

"It's not Drail!" I yell. "It's Vor."

Lagnar snaps his attention back across the desk just as Drail launches toward him. Instantly, I know that this isn't part of the memory. Lagnar drops the mithrium and catches Drail by the throat. In a sheen of golden light, Drail transforms into Vor. The illusion is done. Lagnar screams and Vor tries to scrape his hands away from his throat, but his legs flail. He can't get a grip. Lagnar's smile is cruel, satisfied.

"Caught you."

The edge of the world seems to ripple with blue rainbow light. Whatever we're doing, it's working. Vor struggles against him, his long legs finding leverage against the wall. The blue light gathers around them, collecting like static against Vor's skin.

With a loud cry, Vor pulls at the light in his hands. The room rattles with thunder, and the two men are thrown apart. Everything dematerializes except Lagnar's crumpled form leaning against empty space. Opposite him, the small cavern opens against a wall of blue rainbow energy. It's the Foundation. Constructed by the destroyer, the very thing that fueled the mines, giving Loamin the power to craft metal filled with power. All this time, the destroyer's great act could be readily seen, its frozen surface glimmering with blue.

But we must be almost under it. This gash of Foundation isn't part of the memory.

It's working. We're opening something.

The wall pulses and I turn my face away from a chilly rushing wind but step forward, pressing my hand to the Foundation. The room from Whurrimduum returns, but it's different. The desk has been knocked askew. It's nighttime. Paper flutters through the air. Lagnar is sprawled out, a large burn across his chest. Another memory.

The disarray in the office can only mean there was a fight here. Whatever happened, it wasn't pretty. A figure rises from the other side of the room.

It's me. That can't be right, but there I am. I'm dressed in a regal uniform like the Ironheads but in silks instead of rough cloth. Gold and iron festoon my jacket. A cape hangs from my neck. Am I older? Is this something in the future?

My stomach drops. That's not what this is. It *is* a memory. And that's my father. Therias Brightstorm.

Lagnar trembles on his knees. One hand hovers over the burnt flesh on his chest. His other extends outward. "Therias, please. I won't fight you. You need to hear this from me. He asked me. H-he ordered me to—"

"Even if that were true," Therias says, rings of red around his eyes. "Why would you do it? Who cares what he asked?"

"Ordered." Lagnar slowly stands. "He ordered me to do it. Kingdom is stone. Your words. Am I wrong?"

Therias swallows. His eyes are red, his face is hard. We look so much alike that I can't help but think about how others might see me. The only thing that can cause this much hurt and anger is the mithrium. Rugnus and Andalynn paid the ultimate price because of it. And here I stand, watching it break even more of the world apart.

Lagnar's face twists and his eyes fill with tears. I understand what he must be feeling. He's mourning for his friend, his kingdom, and what must have been tremendous guilt for what he had helped to do in Hngaal. I've seen the bluelink footage. The mithrium bomb used to kill the King and Queen, to destroy that city, was made from ironcraft that turned the whole city to ash. There was nothing left for the surveyors to recover.

With a cold calculation I have never seen in his eyes, Therias levels all his hatred against Lagnar. "You're banished. You'll go to the surface and never return."

Lagnar's desperation morphs into something like polar ice. "You can't banish me for doing what your father told me to do."

"You should be executed for treason. Or thrown in Keelcrawl."

"Treason? I-I was following orders!" The words thunder from him, his fists like stones shaking the air, at Therias, yes, but at the whole world too.

"Then consider this an order from the King. Leave. Never come back. I'll keep what you did from the council, but I don't want to see you again. I don't even want to hear your name."

"We're friends, Therias. Don't do this. The surface is harder on me than most. You know that. Azbena wouldn't—"

"Leave her out of this."

"No. You know she wouldn't approve of this."

There's no coming back. He's made his decision. "If you try to stay in the Kingdom, I go to the council, and banishment will be the least of your worries."

"Wraithspit, Therias. See reason."

Therias gathers fire into his hands. "I'm within my rights to kill you here."

Lagnar shakes his head. He bends to the ground and picks up a jacket. "Alright. Okay, you win. But..." He hesitates and, after a long minute, doesn't finish the sentence. He turns around, hurt and anger sharpening his face.

I can't let him leave this memory, either. Like the one with Vor, it requires a better resolution. "Lagnar wait."

Halfway to the door, he turns and searches the room. He finds me, eyes narrowing. "Brightstorm." He looks between Therias and me. "What's happening? This isn't... it's a memory, then?

Right? This place is stirring up all these melted emotions. I feel like I'm losing my bones."

"Right," I say. "I think you need to change this one too. The last time we opened part of the wall. I-I think you have to face this. I'm sorry, Lagnar. It's like the key to this puzzle is strong emotions. Regrets, maybe."

"Plenty of those to go around."

The room rumbles. The wall behind Therias cracks and a seam of blue light appears. We need to open it all the way.

"Good," I say. "Lagnar, look, I'm sorry this happened. I'm sorry about what you were made to do. And I'm not sure if it's my place, but I forgive you. I mean, I think you should have forgiveness. Accept it."

He shakes his head. "You're just not getting this, son. You don't understand. You can't be made to do something like that. Like what I did."

"In Hngaal? The mithrium bomb?"

Lagnar touches his nose and points to me. "Yeah, that. I could have turned away. I could have chosen differently."

I don't wanna justify his actions, but he was barely older than I am now, and it's not his responsibility alone. This is on Vor. It's on generations of kings and rulers. And the only thing that comes to my mind, the only thing I think to tell him, doesn't make any sense. "Kingdom is stone. That's what you were taught."

The frown lines he cuts into his face are deep and well-worn. "But it ain't. What I did was wrong. I can't block it out. Believe me, I've tried every craft I know." Again he looks between Therias and me. "Man, oh man, you boys look alike."

"I think," I say, "you'll have to face this. Face him."

"He's stronger than me."

Therias is frozen in the memory, waiting there with his hands filled with fire. His face is all rage and sadness. He lost his parents, and it was Lagnar's fault. He didn't have to follow that order. How many of the cities of Rimduum and all the other king-doms are gone because of choices like that? How could this world, over hundreds of years, keep making the same mistake over and over?

What would Rimduum have been like today without it?

Once we fix the world, maybe we can rebuild more of the cities. The shield can be moved. Its effect can heal more ruined places. Heal the brightstorms above a hundred different citybarrels. But Loamin must stop fighting.

"I didn't say fight him," I say. "I said *face* him."

Lagnar's head bows. He looks anywhere but at Therias. The memory un-pauses. My dad draws his hand back, ready to attack. Lagnar lifts his face. "Therias. Every time I think about this day, I know what I forgot. I was so busy thinking about how hurt I felt."

Lagnar sets his jacket down. He drops his shotgun and slowly steps toward Therias. My young father makes no move to stop him. "I'm truly sorry, my friend. Truly sorry. Turn me into the council. I'll stand trial. Put me to death. I'll do anything to repair what I've done. Anything to get your friendship back."

The fire fades. Therias' hand drops slowly. A breath forces its way into his lungs like he's coming up for air. Then all at once, the back of the room cracks open. The icy Foundation is fully visible, with three new doors outlined against the blue light. The office, my dad, they're both gone.

Lagnar picks up his shotgun and leans it against his shoulder. Tears shine in his eyes. "There you have it. Got a good view this time, Clayson."

"It was Vor who gave you the order."

"He said as much on the threshold of Mithriumbane. Just didn't know it was that direct. Must've used someone's goldcraft to change his appearance. Come on. Let's get outta here."

The three doors open into three strange locations. The doorframes are all cracked, pieces scattered on the threshold. But these don't look like dungeons; they look like scenes from the surface, with stretched-out skies visible through each. The first looks like a stone quarry. Through another, a stretching ocean. Last, a forest packed with towering oak trees.

The shattered doors give way to the blue ice of the Foundation, pulsing with waves of energy. I reach out to touch the ice, and Lagnar grabs my hand. "I'd be a slight bit more careful. They say the Foundation hurts worse than trollshards."

I wave the shield. "I can handle it."

When my hand touches the Foundation, it dims. Voices sound behind us.

"That's weird," Jeiah says.

"Wondrous," Yinzar says.

Everyone has reappeared. We're back in the same room with the pedestal. The squares on the floor are gone. The three doors are no longer framed by the Foundation but in stone. The key worked.

Ara approaches the door leading to the forest, but she stumbles, blinks, and holds a hand to her head. "This is it." Her voice is bleary. "I know, somehow. This is—was—my dungeon. I was trapped here. But the memories of the dungeon are... broken."

"It looks like the surface," Koglim remarks.

"It's supposed to," Ara says. "Clayson, I think...."

I finish the statement for her. "...you lived on the surface."

SACRIFICE TO IDE

LAGNAR AND JEIAH have different approaches to investigation. With her beholder in one hand, Jeiah stands before the door that opens to the quarry, her other hand scribing Bluelink notes invisible to the rest of us. Lagnar loads his shotgun to capacity before unloading it against the doorway leading to the ocean.

Each blast disintegrates on contact.

"Can you please..." Jeiah says to him, voice raised.

He feigns being offended.

Ara is transfixed by the third door—the dungeon she once resided in.

Jeiah murmurs as she lowers the beholder. "They *are* thresholds, that much I'm sure of."

Koglim tries again to push his foot through Ara's doorways. It pushes back. "But we can't get in?"

"That about sums it up," Lagnar says.

Ara takes another step toward the dungeon. "Even when my mind was here in the dungeon, before Exralt retrieved Ergal, before I inhabited my Dura body, even then, my thoughts were always broken."

"Broken?" Jeiah asks.

"Yes. After Clayson made the shield, after I took it from Geum

Ide, everything came back to me. But it was a jumble of strange experiences. Imagine being a champion inside a dungeon. You're not truly aware of everything you're doing."

"You're not?" Koglim asks. "I always imagined the champions behind every door, making choices, rewarding me, or preventing me from going forward."

Ara swallows and shakes her head. "It's nothing that concrete. I was a shadow always reflected off surfaces. A piece of myself here, a piece there. Never truly me. The memories of my life as a Loamin were like ashes scattered over the stone. That's how Vor and I know we were once Loamin, but everything else is like seeing through crooked mirrors."

"Any ideas about how to get back in?" I ask Ara, but Jeiah responds.

"Actually, yes," Jeiah says.

Lagnar stows his shotgun. "Please share this wisdom with the rest of us."

Yinzar offers, "The relics, correct?"

"Okay, so admittedly this is a guess," she says with a glance at me. "There are three thresholds, therefore three protodungeons. The thresholds are destroyed. We believe they were destroyed when the hearts of each dungeon were removed."

There are nods from everyone, then all eyes settle on me. Figures. The reminder about how I destroyed Wolfstaff is unwelcome, but the truth about the protodungeons and the origin of the three relics is like a strong pat on the back. I was right.

Yinzar considers this. "Exralt Blackmug took the heart from each of them. The ring Ergal, the knife Onrix and..."

Koglim springs to life with the next piece of the puzzle. "Icho!" He takes it out. "Maybe it can help us here."

"Sure, that all checks out," Lagnar says. "Try it."

Koglim comes to the door with the ocean, leading with Icho. He pushes it into the doorway, but the doorway pushes it back. "Nope." He moves to the door opening onto a quarry. Icho isn't rejected. Koglim's hand gets part of the way through, and we all step forward. Koglim winces and groans. His whole arm shakes until it suddenly flies back. Icho whips over our heads and bounces off the far wall, ricocheting against the ground with a metallic clang.

Koglim throws his hands up. "Ide keep me. It's like it doesn't want to go back..."

Ara's voice is barely a whisper. "It doesn't."

"But that is something," Jeiah says. "We're closer. That gave me more information." She moves her whole body as if weaving through the invisible code using some type of dance. She reaches the far wall and spins around. "All three of the dungeons are connected."

Something I read on bluelink months ago stirs my thoughts. Two dungeons were connected. But I can't remember which, and I can't remember why. "Connected how?"

"Like Strongmask and Jadehammer Dungeons?" Koglim said.

"Exactly like," Jeiah says.

"Oh," Lagnar adds.

I'm still left without understanding. "Oh, what?" Everyone looks at me again. "I hate when you look at me like that. There's something I don't know. Just tell me." When Jeiah, Yinzar, and Koglim share a look, somehow, it's even more unnerving than waiting for this information.

"Strongmask and Jadehammer were killed in the same place at the same time," Yinzar says.

"I was murdered," Ara says. "We all were. How did I forget?"

We're all silent.

Yinzar starts pacing. "All three champions came to this place, deep below the mountain. It would have been a time long ago when Loamin were only just understanding how to deal with the effects of the surface. It took generations to move below granite, the slow-forward grinding of civilization. Early Loamin didn't stay in the Rockies. They left for other places, other mountains. The trolls, the wolves, wormkind all drove them away during the exodus."

"Loamin didn't return here for thousands of years," Jeiah says. "No one would have remembered they were down here."

"Maybe no one even knew," Lagnar says. "Champions are rare. The first three could have been the only three before the exodus. No wonder Icho can beat nearly everything.

"Not only were they forgotten," Jeiah offers, "but locked away."

The scar along my back burns. "And Exralt got the key from the Dura wraiths. Could they have killed them? Could Jassin have left Gamgim?"

"The world was wilder back then," Yinzar says. "Anything is possible."

I swallow. Again, the rules, the narrative, shift. Ara, Vor, Tas were once Loamin. When they died—apparently murdered—three dungeons sprung up, filling the void. The Dura wraiths made some type of lock and hid them away. Then Blackmug, a wraithborn, got the key and came here. He freed the three Loamin Champions, and they became Dura. Then he hid the key in Brightstorm Dungeon. A key that required even more death and sacrifices to get out.

"If that's true, why would the Dura wraiths give Blackmug the key?"

No one can answer this.

Ara's eyes are as wide as moons. With a long clear breath, she raises the triangular shield made from mithrium and Ergal. Before I can stop her, she steps toward the door, her free hand finding a long crack in the stone. The rubble at the base of the threshold shudders and flies upwards. The arch reassembles itself. The smell of spring rain fills the cavern as the doorways come alive. Cool wind tickles my skin.

"You did it," I say.

Ara closes her eyes. "Yes. I did it."

Koglim says what we're all thinking. "Then explain why you look like someone put trollshards in your soup."

"Once I cross the threshold... being back inside this place... I think... it won't let me back out."

I'm stepping up to the door when the realization drops like a rock into my stomach. She can't be right. She was freed from this place when Blackmug took Ergal out. Just like when I took the heart out of Wolfstaff Dungeon. It wouldn't be possible to go backward. Would it? And if she did, could I get her out again—an endless loop of destruction and repair?

"How can you possibly know that?" Yinzar asks.

Ara sighs. "I just know. Like when Ergal called to me. Though I don't feel drawn inside. I just feel... afraid."

"Well," I say. "Then you're not going in there."

"Now, hold up," Lagnar says. "We came all this way... to what? *Not* do anything? I don't think so. We need this. We need Vor dead and the world back to the way it was."

"Look, I get that. I do. But I'm not letting Ara consign herself to some... dungeon."

Ara looks right at me. "Thank you, Clayson, but it's okay. I'll do it. If it means an end to Vor, a way to stop him, then I will do whatever it takes."

Koglim's found something interesting to stare at on the ground. Lagnar's hand is around his back, probably on the trigger of his shotgun. Jeiah is looking between Ara and me.

"I'm with Clayson," Jeiah says. "We can't ask her to go back in there. To become a slave of the dungeon once again."

Koglim tries to run past Ara through the threshold, but he smacks into a wall of energy and bounces backward. He stumbles but doesn't fall, just shakes his head hard like a dog drying its hair.

"Ouch," Lagnar says.

I steady him. "Can we just think this through?" I demand. "There has to be another way."

"Hmm." Jeiah scans the doorway again but also passes the beholder over Ara. I can tell there's something on her mind, but she doesn't wanna guess an answer. It's the way she gets when there are too many working variables.

"What is it?" I ask.

"I... I don't know..."

"Make a guess."

She frowns. "Okay. Yeah, maybe it doesn't want Ara exactly. Maybe the dungeon wants Ergal. Though there's so much wrong with that. A dungeon only *wants* because it holds the spirit of the champion. So, without Ara in there, it can't have a mind of its own... still."

If the Dura wraiths can see inside each dungeon, maybe there *is* something alive in there. Or the destroyer, who- or whatever that may be. I step closer to Ara. "Can I see the shield?"

She keeps one hand on the door but slides the shield down her arm.

When I take it, I expect the door to crumble again, but I step away, and nothing changes. Ara's presence is holding the door open. But will it let us through with the shield? "Only one way to find out."

"I disagree," Jeiah says, then she slips a hand in mine. "But if you're going to step across another threshold, I'm coming with you."

"We all are," Yinzar says.

Koglim settles a hand on Jeiah's shoulder. Yinzar on mine, and finally Lagnar, but not before adding his two cents about this being the stupidest idea ever.

"If this works, Ara," Jeiah says. "The door might close behind us like a regular dungeon. We'll do our best to find what we need and get out."

Ara gives a curt nod. "Do what you must. I'll be waiting."

The breeze picks up as we march over the threshold. The sweeping countryside is alive with a blustery wind. My hair whips my face, and I squint, but the cool air is rich with earth and plant life. Once we're all through, the doorway vanishes.

A small altar with a large, embedded bowl fills its place. The simple stone bowl reminds me of a crucible I might use forging. But there's no heat source, no ingredients, and no metal.

Yinzar drags a hand through his white-orange hair, his crow's feet expanding when he squints at the altar. "What have we here?"

A soft sound over the neighboring hillside turns all our heads. A small lamb scrambles up a boulder. It looks nervous and skittery. "Maaaa."

Koglim's eyes light up. "Keep Ide! Look how cute." The word cute is just a laugh.

"Probably eat our faces clean off," Lagnar says.

"Hey, that's no joke," Koglim says. "I've been half-eaten in a dungeon before. It was no cow roast, let me tell you."

Yinzar is crouched down near the altar, wolfstaff in his hands. He runs a finger along the inside of the bowl. "Curious."

Jeiah has the beholder sweeping the area. "Hmm. Guys, I think I know why that lamb is on the boulder instead of the ground."

I stare down at my feet and then back to Jeiah. "What is it?"

She shakes her head. "Not sure exactly, some seismic activity beneath the hills."

"I've got a bad feeling about this," Koglim says in a smooth voice. Then he smiles at me because I know he's quoting a taffy movie.

"Trollbrick," Lagnar points his shotgun at the ground. "Couldn't we just get a nice simple puzzle to solve?"

Yinzar finally stands and looks out toward the forest. "There's something familiar about this place. I can't put my finger on it."

"Just be on the lookout," Jeiah says. She cuts past me heading for the lamb and the boulder.

"I'm going to stay here and try to figure this out," Yinzar says. I hesitate only a second near the altar but follow Jeiah, Lagnar, and Koglim.

The closer we get to the boulder, the more Lagnar curses. Koglim counters this by describing how cute the lamb is. "I mean, just look at it. Its little legs are shaking, and... did it just yawn? Aww, I want to take it home. Know anything about raising lambs, Clayson?"

"A bit. Though, everything we raise at the cabin is used for food."

He gives me a sidelong look. "How dare you, sir."

The lamb bleats loudly, casts us a wary glance, and backs away. It freezes when we reach the boulder.

"Easy, fella," Koglim says. "We're not here to hurt you. We—"

The lamb bleats once more and scrambles down from the rock, bolting for the forest.

"Oh, come on!" Koglim calls after it.

We step on the flat boulder and watch the animal flee.

Koglim sighs. "I just wanted to pet the little—"

The ground between us and the lamb tears open. Dark creatures, the size and shape of small wheelbarrows, crawl from the earth, mandibles clicking.

"Keep Ide! What are those things?" Lagnar says, fumbling with more shells.

Jeiah is scanning the air. "Oak beetles. Hunt in packs. Live only twenty days. Exoskeleton is like armor, and they're impervious to many types of craft."

I ignite the shield.

Koglim jumps from the boulder and runs toward them. "And they're about to eat my new friend."

"Koglim, wait," Jeiah calls.

My feet leave the boulder, and without thinking, I follow Koglim. I shout back to Lagnar and Jeiah. "We've got to protect that thing!"

"We'll have to catch up then!" Jeiah shouts, already running ahead of me.

Yinzar is watching us from afar, but he doesn't follow. What is he doing?

The field is alive with movement as more and more beetles break through the ground, their pinchers clicking and their backs slick and shimmering. I barrel through a pair of them with the shield. "Koglim! At your feet."

One of the oversized beetles extends its pinchers, but Koglim is quicker. Without looking back, he jumps straight into the air, and the thing passes right under him. In less time than it takes me to reach him, he clamps a golden shackle around his calf, making both of his feet and calves double in thickness and glow with power. He steps down on the closest beetle. I hear a crunch, and Koglim pulls his leg away coated in slime. He crushed the thing's head.

He's never had a clear strength in goldcraft, but it's a perfect example of how variable and creative he is in a dungeon.

"Not impervious to craft!" he shouts.

Jeiah catches up to me as I skid to a stop. "That's—"

"Gross," I finish.

Koglim smiles and retracts his foot, rushing forward again. "Come on. Jimmy went into the forest."

"Jimmy?" Jeiah asks. "Did you name that thing?"

He pumps a fist into the sky. "For Jimmy!"

"Wait for us!" I say.

Jeiah sprints next to me, and we charge through another group of beetles. They tumble off the side of the shield but right themselves. At least they've stopped emerging from the ground. A quick count shows more than a dozen.

There's a blast from Lagnar's shotgun. I find him weaving through the bugs, eyes wide. The shot didn't do anything to the bug's outer shell. Lagnar curses, frantically dodging the pincers of another two of the beetles.

"Slow down," Jeiah says.

Instead, I stop completely until Lagnar catches up to us. Once he's near the shield, we resume our charge toward Koglim. He's disappeared into the grove of trees after the lamb.

Lagnar mutters, "Jimmy."

"At least we're faster than the beetles," Jeiah says. "We'll catch it first."

"And then what?" Lagnar says, nearly out of breath.

I nudge another beetle from its path with the edge of the shield, bringing us ahead of all of them. Jeiah was right. We're faster. But as we hit the trees, we slow down, scanning for Koglim and the lamb.

For a split second, I think I see a swirl of dark hair and light-shaded skin, but it dissolves behind a tree. Ara?

"Koglim!" Jeiah shouts.

Koglim calls, "Here! I've got him cornered!"

We trace Koglim's voice around a trio of oaks, but the lamb dodges him. I almost laugh at the picture. Koglim's muscular arms try to grab the white blur of motion, the small animal bleating and dodging him. It cuts between his legs, and Koglim isn't flexible enough to grab him.

He throws his hands in the air. "Come on Jimmy, this is for your own good."

Jeiah stumbles to a halt, scanning the oaks, the lamb, and Koglim. "Why does something feel familiar?"

The small lamb bolts in front of Lagnar. He holds out his hands to calm it. "Whoa there, fella, just calm down." The tone of his voice is anything but calm. That could have something to do with the clicking sounds behind us.

The beetles have caught up again. Jimmy peddles behind a tree and slips away into the path of the beetles. Koglim must seem like a bigger threat.

"Come on!" Koglim chases after it, waving us forward.

"Stay put!" I yell after him. "Let's get him under the shield."

The beetles veer straight for the lamb. Koglim kicks one to the side. Lagnar puts a slug into the underbelly of the thing, and it explodes into a shower of goo.

"Got 'em!"

"Around that side, quick!" Jeiah says, shoving me right. She and Lagnar go left. Koglim, reckless, jumps over a fallen log, his feet barely clearing it. We surround the lamb again, but this time the beetles are everywhere. One of them climbs onto the log and hurls itself at Koglim. We're too spread out for me to get the shield around everyone.

"Watch out!" I yell.

Koglim spins and punches outward with one motion. The beetle drops to the forest floor, twitching. He stomps the thing repeatedly for good measure. "Leave. Jimmy. Alone."

They may have been slower in the field, but on the forest floor, they quickly surround us. There are too many of them. Jeiah sweeps a large stick from the ground and swings at the closest one. I throw the shield up and charge for the lamb.

Koglim, completely frantic, stands with his back to the trembling lamb, screaming unintelligibly at the beetles. He kicks and punches the air, keeping the beetles at a distance.

Lagnar howls in pain. One of the beetles has a pincher around his ankle.

Jeiah swings her branch, but the beetle she's fighting with catches it in its jaws and pushes her back. She tumbles backward over a thick branch. Panic grabs me, and I sprint for her. Koglim yells for the shield, but I'm focused on Jeiah. She's scrambling away from the closest beetle. It will reach her before I can.

It leaps, a deep squeal issuing from its body like a demonic pig. Lagnar's shotgun goes off, and the beetle erupts in a splatter of sticky ooze. The spray from the shotgun rains on the shield, but the goo sails past me.

Breathing heavily, I reach for one of the trees. My hand slips over the slime-covered bark. "Eww." I shake the goo from my hand, then scrape it back onto a dry part of the bark.

A connection fires in my brain. I know what we're supposed to do. "It's the oak. Jeiah. Remember that slimy oak from Yinzar's ingredients?"

She's already closing the distance between us. "Of course. The recipe for the mithrium objects. Why didn't I see it? We knew Yinzar found items from the protodungeons in Exralt's notes."

"Come again?" Lagnar asks.

"The lamb, too," she says. "The bellows for the forge were made of lambskin."

Without another word, I sprint back to Koglim, weaving between the beetles, which seem too distracted by Koglim and the lamb to pay attention to me. I follow behind Koglim, who's chasing the lamb through the trees away from the beetles.

The second I catch him, I throw a shield around us. "We've got to calm this thing down. We need it."

"How are we supposed to do that?"

Behind Jeiah, in a clearing almost fifty feet away, the same dark-haired girl I thought I saw before drops to her knees and puts out her hands. I step around Jeiah, but the figure vanishes. It wasn't Ara. It couldn't have been. Maybe a reflection of her? Or a memory? I shake the image from my mind, but it prompts an idea.

"We need to get down to its level," I say. With the shield at my back, I sit down. "The beetles can't get through the shield. We need to just slow down. Try to get the lamb—"

"Jimmy."

"Try to get *Jimmy* to stay inside the effect of the shield."

I call out to the lamb. Jeiah copies me while Lagnar and Koglim try to corral it inside the radius of the shield. It takes them another half minute to get the lamb inside, but once inside, it follows my voice.

"That's it. Come on. I won't hurt you."

"Unless we have to use its skin," Jeiah sings out, keeping her voice inviting for the lamb.

"I heard that." Koglim sings back. "We're not doing that."

Jimmy bleats again, but he's within my reach. Still, I let him come right up to me before resting a hand gently against its woolen side, patting it a couple of times. "There." I draw Jimmy into my arms. The beetles are in a frenzy, but they can't combat the power of the shield.

I walk back toward the oak tree covered in slime, including Lagnar and Koglim in the shield. Jeiah stomps on a deadened branch at our feet and pulls a piece of the oak from the debris. She coats it in the beetle goo. "That should work."

"Will someone tell me what's going on?" Lagnar demands.

"Yinzar's recipe," I explain. "He said they had something to do with the protodungeons. All these things are from Blackmug's notes. That's how Yinzar made it work."

Jeiah scans the slimy oak with the beholder. "It's a match. And I think I know where we need to place this stuff."

"The altar." I half laugh. "Ten to one, Yinzar has it figured out."

Koglim strokes Jimmy's head. "We can't."

"Alright so we mosey back out to the boulder," Lagnar says. "And"—he gestures like he is choking the lamb—"You know."

I hand the lamb to Koglim and tighten my grip on the shield. "I don't know."

The beetles make every effort to prevent us, but the shield holds as we march from the forest to the field. By the time we reach the rock, half of them have lost interest, digging back into the ground, and the other half wander out of sight through patches of tall grass.

Yinzar folds his arms across his chest. "Ingredients, right?"

Jeiah nods, setting the pieces of slimy oak down into the oval bowl.

"Alrighty," Lagnar says. "What should we use to kill the little thing?"

Koglim draws Jimmy closer to his chest. "Ide keep me if any of you try to kill Jimmy, I'll—"

"Come off it," Lagnar says. "The lamb is a construct of the dungeon. It needs to play its part."

"The dungeon can melt itself for all I care," Koglim says. "Bunch of trollbrick anyway."

From the day I met Koglim, his life has revolved around chasing power and objects in any dungeon he could get into. He's the most knowledgeable person I know when it comes to dungeon-related statistics and history. The way Koglim squeezes

Jimmy in his arms, the determined look of pain mingled with grief and protection. His reaction has more to do with losing Rugnus than with the small bundle of wool in his arms.

But this melted thing is pretty cute.

Jeiah breaks through my thoughts. "It may be enough to place the lamb in the bowl. We don't know all the connections to the recipe. But the lambskin was used as a bellows." She gestures around at the wind. "Plenty of wind if we consider the effect of the bellows."

Koglim squints at her. "Yeah, that's true."

"Everyone, sit around the bowl," I say. "We have to keep Jimmy calm. Look as non-intimidating as you can."

We all sit, and Koglim gently rests Jimmy down in the bowl. He stays.

When nothing happens Lagnar says. "Am I missing something? Were there other ingredients?"

"Amethyst, peat moss, ice water in a silver bucket, and quartz."

"Maybe we have to go looking for those things as well?" Jeiah offers.

"Or maybe we're just blocking the wind." I create an angled shield above us. It catches and funnels the gusting wind down into the bowl. Blaring light erupts behind me.

Lagnar stands up and inspects two new doorways. "The other two dungeon thresholds are back. You were right, Paladin. They're all connected."

"I gather," Yinzar says, "there will be other bowls waiting in these two other dungeons. We collect everything and see what happens."

"Or," I add. "We find something in Vor's dungeon we can use against him. We don't have to just blindly follow the track the dungeon has set out."

"Sometimes," Jeiah says, "the dungeon leaves you no choice."

Lagnar heads toward the quarry. "We split up and get the ingredients. Which ones will be through here?"

"We're not splitting up," I say. I stare through the doorway to the quarry. "I can see the onyx stone right there. We also need amethyst, peat moss, a bucket of ice water, and gypsum."

"There's your ice," Koglim says with a gesture to the other threshold.

The ocean stretches far into the distance, but Koglim's right: there are slivers of ice skimming the surface. Yinzar eyes the door again and frowns.

"Looks inviting," I say.

"This is how we work this," Jeiah says. "Onyx, amethyst, and gypsum could all be connected to the mine. We do that one first. Then we go together to the last one."

I nod at the ocean dungeon. "That's got to be Vor's former dungeon. The bucket used in the recipe was silver and so is Onrix."

"That's a fair extrapolation, but let's not get ahead of ourselves," Jeiah says.

Lagnar is reloading his shotgun. "Into the quarry then."

Koglim nods to Jimmy. "See you around, little guy."

Jimmy turns in a few tight circles and lies down against the stone.

"Either choice seems fair at this point," Jeiah adds with a frown toward Lagnar. "As long as we stick together, we should be fine."

Lagnar sweeps a hand in front of him and says, "Paladin, lead the way."

Jeiah purses her lips and casts her eyes upward but steps toward the door without starting an argument with Lagnar. From across the threshold, the glow of the white onyx is almost as brilliant as the sun glaring through the puffy clouds. She passes through.

Lagnar rounds his shoulders and follows her across the threshold. The next second, the onyx dims, and the light from the doorway flickers and winks out.

I panic and leap forward but hit a barrier.

"Brick and spit," Koglim says, rushing forward, pounding his fist against the barrier. Jeiah and Lagnar get a couple of bars in, only to stop and turn toward us. Jeiah curses, but I can't hear it through the barrier.

The threshold vanishes and the fear inside my veins becomes something like needles. Ara's mind doesn't guide this dungeon. The dungeons are like some twisted force of nature, delivering wave after wave of destruction. This is more proof of the evil in these dungeons.

"I guess we split up," Yinzar says.

Koglim growls. "Latching dungeons can get melted."

ECHO THE DEAD

"WE HAVE TO MOVE FORWARD," Yinzar says.

Koglim still stews in his frustration. He's wandered back to sit with Jimmy curled against his leg. It's as if this was the final setback for him, the last time he was willing to let a dungeon trick him. His meaty hands are fists, his mouth set hard. Something about this broken raider draws a circle around my thoughts and yanks me down into my same old anger at the world.

I sit next to him and say nothing. We stare into the woods, the sky, across the field, but there's nothing to grasp. Nothing left to believe in. Maybe that's what I've been looking for—something permanent. But is this place even real? Are any of the dungeons?

Yinzar's shadow fills my vision. "There's no need to despair. Lagnar and Jeiah are competent raiders. My guess? Vor's dungeon lies across this other threshold."

Koglim slowly stands. He jabs a finger at the remaining threshold. "Then I'm going to tear it down piece by piece."

We can't know for sure which one is Vor's threshold: the one Jeiah and Lagnar just disappeared into or the one before us. But something about the ice and the cold makes me think that Yinzar is right.

I stand and cross the threshold. Koglim stands beside me,

"

Yinzar like a sentry behind us. "Somewhere in there, we'll find a way to defeat him," I say. "The sooner we find it, the better."

Koglim walks through, and Yinzar and I follow him, a new sense of determination forming a seal over my heart.

An endless sea of gray-blue water rises to meet us. I cross my arms over my chest and hunch my shoulders against the frigid air. It's a manageable cold, somewhere just above freezing, and my breath trickles out of me in a great plume of mist. I whirl around as the threshold door dissipates into fog. Behind Yinzar, the dark snaking line of a distant shore slowly comes into focus.

Koglim hops on the ice at our feet. "At least there's something to stand on."

The sheet of ice must extend a couple hundred feet in every direction.

"The cooling agent," Yinzar says. "The recipe used a silver bucket of ice water."

That's the ingredient we're gathering here. A giant silver-lined ceramic bowl sits in the middle of the sheet of ice, expecting a sacrifice.

"Easy," Koglim says. "Let's just break some of this off and—"

"The ever-living ice isn't typical ice," Yinzar explains.

Koglim eyes the bowl like he's determining whether he could break it. "Of course not. Why would it be?"

"How did you get the ice before?" I ask Yinzar. "From where?"

"From the caverns under Lake Onthratia. The strange ice forms in the waters where the Great Smoke swims."

How did I know it would've been someplace dangerous? But I've made it to the bottom of that lake before. My eyes dart to the surrounding water. "I'm guessing the source is the eel, not the cavern itself."

"Indeed. If I'm not mistaken, we've found ourselves in the ancient domain of the Great Smoke or its kind."

Yinzar and Koglim share a long, wide-eyed stare at the water.

Koglim shivers. "I thought the Great Smoke was the last of its kind."

"Ah," Yinzar holds up a finger. "But if these dungeons are as ancient as we believe, and Vor and the others lived on the surface..."

"There could be giant eels right below us."

"A host of them."

Koglim rubs his face thoughtfully. "Shouldn't we be able to just skim it off the water then? Last time I checked, ice floats on water."

"In this case, no. The ever-living ice described in Exralt's poetry sinks like a stone. But never fear—"

A wave hits the ice floe at our feet—no, not a wave. Something bumped us. We tip toward one side, then back to the other until the ice finally settles. I hear a splash behind me and whirl around, but the ice floe is too large to scan the water. Yinzar closes the distance to the edge.

"Get back here!" Koglim hisses. "Are you crazy?"

Yinzar waves him off. "The Great Smoke cared little about my presence in the cavern. Well, until I started collecting the ice."

I follow him to the edge and stare down into the water. "You're thinking about going down there."

Koglim is backpedaling to the other side, trying to balance out our movement toward the edge. He shouts, "You want to go into the water? Of all the fizzblooded—you've got to be kidding."

"He's right," I tell Yinzar. "And if anyone should go, it's me. I have the shield."

Yinzar twirls the wolfstaff expertly. He looks me in the eye and laughs. "You're young, Clayson. So, I'll excuse that. Besides the fact that you can't use coppercraft, I know what the ice looks like. I know the type of ground it typically rests on, how to dislodge it, and so on. Do you?"

"I—"

"No, indeed you do not. I see the concern on your face. You think I'm too old to make the dive?"

He narrows his gaze on me, highlighting the flare of crow's feet banding his eyes and the wrinkle on his forehead. The orange hair I came to know him by in the visions is streaked pale. He is nearly sixty. In Loamin years... well, he has relatively few left. I can't let him go down there. If I don't bring him out of this dungeon, I'll never be able to look my mom in the eye.

I lunge for the edge of the ice, but suddenly, my weight shifts backward. My heels slam into the ice, and my back follows. Wind rushes from my lungs. One second. Two seconds. I gasp for air.

"What just—"

Yinzar grins down at me, aiming wolfstaff. "Maybe someday you'll have my reflexes. You forget I am peerless in coppercraft. I have trained and tamed this world's wildest beasts and been in the deepest places with the most dangerous threats. I can hold my breath for nearly nine minutes, and that's without craft. Keep Ide, I forged my own dungeon and returned even from that. Stay on the ice with your friend, *grandson*. I'll be back with the ingredient before you can spell Onthratia."

I ease myself up, and as my breathing evens out, he transforms into part wolf and dives from the edge of the ice floe, disappearing beneath the surface.

Koglim comes to my side, his mouth open in a grin that travels all the way up to his eyes. "That was the funniest thing I've ever seen." He lifts me to my feet. "Don't look at me like that. You've needed a good humiliation for a while now. Besides, it improved my mood tens-on-tens."

The gray-blue water has calmed, and we both stare after Yinzar. "He said nine minutes, right?"

"Yep."

After an empty half minute, Koglim says, "How *do* you spell Onthratia?"

I ignore him, moving back toward the sacrificial bowl. As each minute passes, I try to push away the thought of Yinzar deep in the water beneath us. I stamp my feet and pace to stay warm.

My teeth chatter and Koglim squeezes me in a bear hug until I can't breathe. "I'm good." I push away. "The air temperature is warming up." I scan the horizon again and find the dark shoreline is even closer. "Koglim, if we're moving..."

"Then Yinzar is..." we both look toward the opposite horizon, where we may have left Yinzar a distance behind us.

In a rush of water, twenty yards from the edge of the ice, Yinzar's head burst into view. A split second later, his arm comes up, and a small, glimmering shape comes flying in our direction. The ever-living ice. Koglim backs up and catches the white globe.

Koglim peels his fingers back. "He got it!"

I blink, and Yinzar is pulled back under the water. "Wraith-spit." I back up, not thinking, about to leap off the icy platform when Koglim's arm hits my chest.

"Wait, check it out!"

Yinzar bursts from the water again, this time speeding toward us at an impossible rate. Beneath him, a scaly shape breaks the surface. Then Yinzar's pulled back down.

"No, I'm not waiting," I say, charging toward the edge.

"You don't have craft!" Koglim shouts after me. "What are you going—"

Yinzar appears again, this time much closer. I can see his hands pulling back on the edges of the eel's mouth, just out of contact with its teeth. Then he goes back under with the eel dragging him past the edge of the ice beneath us. The whole ice floe careens to one side, and my feet slip out from under me. Before I can slide off, the floe tilts the other way, and I twirl over the ice toward the bowl.

I scramble for a hold, but the ice tips again, this time leveling slowly until I can get my feet beneath me. When I scan the ice, Koglim is gone.

Suddenly, I can't breathe. A scream builds inside my throat. I've lost them both. No. I force a gasp of air into my body and stand. The ice is slick with water, and my feet won't move fast enough. I slip again, trying to run toward the edge of the ice.

"Clayson!" A gurgled cry for help reaches my ears. I make it to the edge where Yinzar is treading water. The second he sees me, his hands emerge from the water, stretching for me. I reach for them, but my feet fly out from under me, and I hit the ice hard.

"Disperse... your weight," Yinzar says, unable to catch his breath. "Spread out."

I flip to my stomach and pull myself toward the ledge. Yinzar's arms find mine, and slowly, even with his arm slipping away, I draw him out of the water, and we fall in a wet heap. I can't spare another second. Maddeningly, the slippery surface of the ice refuses to let me stand without being hunched over, but I see two dark arms frantically clawing at the edge of the ice.

"Help me with Koglim!"

Flattening out on the ice again, I grasp his meaty forearm. "Got you." One of his hands stays in a fist, refusing to grab on. "Both hands!"

With a groan, Koglim opens his fist and half-pushes half-throws the globe of ever-living ice closer to the bowl. I tug on his arms, but he's too big, too heavy. Then Yinzar is there, and we hoist the massive raider back onto the ice.

I nearly collapse, but Yinzar shakes his head, grabbing my shoulders. "We must keep moving—Koglim and I especially—or we'll freeze. The air is warmer than the water, but we need to warm up."

"The... stupid... ice stuff," Koglim says, nearly in tears. "Put that wraithspit... into the bowl."

Yinzar blinks, but I'm faster. I scoop the ice from the ground and drop it in the sacrificial bowl. The moment it hits the bowl, the ice floe takes another massive hit from an eel and tips to the side. A giant barb tail rises from the water and smashes down on the ice.

Yinzar grabs Koglim's feet before he can spin away, and I grab Yinzar with one hand and the bowl with the other. This time the ice floe doesn't settle back. We stay perched at an angle, but there's a sudden burst of acceleration.

"What's happening!" Koglim yells.

I blink and look toward the horizon, past the water. Where there's a slash of dull green. "I think it's pushing us toward land."

The wind whips my face, sucking at my damp clothing. Koglim and Yinzar have it worse. Both soaked completely through.

Koglim growls through his teeth, "I can't hold on."

Then my hands are yanked free from the bowl, arms nearly wrenched from their sockets, and we all tumble over the edge into the water. It's less of a shock than I expect. I glimpse Koglim sinking below me. Instinctively I flip toward him and scissor kick. My hands support him under his right arm, and I swing to his side, kicking, my shoes impossibly heavy. But Yinzar comes to the other side, and we push upward.

The ice floe is above our heads, so we have to swim further. Then I see a wall of submerged rock. We cut through reeds and gasp as we break the surface.

"Drag him forward," Yinzar commands.

Koglim sputters and pushes us off. "I'm okay. Ide keep us. We're out of the water. We're out of that spit and bones water." He keeps repeating this, adding new curses each time.

Yinzar searches the horizon. "The air temperature has improved, but we have to find a way to warm up."

Koglim flops his hand landward. "There's a fire pit."

He's right. There's a rough circle of broken stones only twenty feet away.

Yinzar shakes his head. "How did you see that?"

"That's Koglim's real craft," I say.

A grin spreads on Koglim's face. "Power of observation."

With a moment to catch my breath, I take in the shoreline again.

It's a harsh world made from cold mud—rocky, with a brush of green and red shrubs clinging to the earth. Fog hangs over reedy pools of surface water.

"Smells bad," Koglim says.

"It's a bog," Yinzar says, stating the obvious. "You're smelling the sulfur and methane gasses that build up here. But a bog also means—”

“Peat moss,” I finish. “Another ingredient.”

Yinzar nods, still shivering. We’re all shivering, so we move to the firepit and find a heap of charred ash. Next to the pit, there are bundles of dried bushes laid carefully in even piles. I stir the ash gently, revealing a few dull embers. It takes little effort to start the fire, but I know the bundles will burn quickly.

We huddle against the growing flames, smoke licking our faces, caught in our eyes. I pile more tight bundles on the fire, and we fall into a pattern of strengthening the fire and rotating our bodies. I try to use the shield to trap the heat around us, but it traps the smoke also. Koglim and Yinzar both wring out their clothes the best they can. The chill never disappears entirely, but the warmth is enough to fight the cold in my hands and ears.

“What now?” Koglim coughs. “Can we harvest the moss?”

“Maybe,” Yinzar offers, “But peat develops over a long time. It’s usually dried and stored. Perhaps—” His next word hums on his lips as he stares through the fire, out into the bog. “Has that always been there?”

I follow his stare through the mist. A rough mud-cracked shelter sits perched on a swollen mass of rock. There’s a single empty entryway without a curtain or a door. A bone-sticky dread coats my insides. Yinzar’s right: this is Vor’s dungeon. Something of him remains in this place. I’m not sure how I know, but that’s what this feeling is—the hollowed-out fear that Vor is watching us.

An involuntary shiver runs over me.

“If,” Yinzar says as if testing the air for a reaction to his words, “this represents the place of Vor’s origin, maybe we can find what we need to defeat him here. In there. But I feel some craft coming from this place.”

I glance back to the shoreline, where the ice floe still clatters against the rock. The bowl awaits another ingredient. “The peat moss is in there.”

Koglim comes around the fire and looks at me expectantly. "Forward then. Like Yinzar said. I'll be melted before I go back into the water."

Yinzar shrugs his brawny shoulders. "Something's a bit off. The moment I noticed the building, I felt... uncomfortable. It must be craft."

Koglim nods but says, "I would say the champion of the dungeon could be manipulating us, but these protodungeons— their champions have already left the dungeons, right?"

"I saw Ara in that forest. I know I did. A reflection of her. Maybe this place—these places—somehow contain an echo of their champions."

"Or memories that never left with them," Yinzar offers.

Koglim gulps and then rounds back his shoulders. "Then Vor could be in there."

"No," Yinzar says. "Only a shadow of what he once was."

"Some shadows are dangerous," I say. But in the forest, Ara didn't interfere with us. The dying fire no longer provides any stopper for the cold, and the bundles of kindling have burned to ash. I step around the pit and point my feet toward the structure. "Let's get this over with."

Koglim and Yinzar follow me warily. In the quiet, I can almost hear their fears in their soft footsteps. We reach the large slab of stone and change the direction of our approach. The structure is longer than we thought, maybe forty feet in length and fifteen-foot wide, an oversized muddy coffin with a door.

For a brief second, I glance to my side, expecting to see Rugnus nod his approval to enter. For Andalynn to smile knowingly and place a kind hand on my shoulder. I was always the shield, but they carried that shield.

The rebuilt strands of my heart quiver, and a shaky sigh passes my lips. I can't do this without them. Then Yinzar is there like a steady mountain, cutting away the fog of a long morning. "I'll go in first."

I whisper a hoarse 'thanks' and follow him through. The darkened doorway leads to a room rank with the putrid smell of animal corpses, so strong it makes the sulfurous bog seem like a pleasant park. Curtains, stitched together from small white-brown pelts, run from the floor to the ceiling at every angle. The mud caked inside of the walls seems fresh enough to breed flies. A string of fish loops across the ceiling from one side to the other.

The whole room draws shivers across my back.

"Wraithspit," Koglim mutters. "Guess we know why Vor is so messed up."

Yinzar shrugs. "I wouldn't say that. By all appearances, this is what his life was like. It would have been an efficient and useful livelihood in the bog. Nothing out of the ordinary, except to our modern eyes, so trained to look away from death."

Koglim eyes Yinzar with disgust. "Anyway, I don't see any peat moss."

Curious, I push through a set of curtains only to find more of the same, with the addition of a coarse wooden table. My eyes grow wide. The table holds a host of intricate sculptures: a blossoming flower, an eel perched on its tail, a couple of trees, and even a man's face, bearded with hollow eyes. All of these things are carved from tiny bones.

Yinzar makes a small grunt from his throat. "I stand corrected. *That* is somewhat morbid. The bog must be overrun with lemmings, but this seems a strange hobby."

I glance from the table to the next curtain of small furs. Yinzar is right about the lemmings. When life was simpler, my dad and I lived alone in the cabin, and I watched a whole series about animal life in the tundra. Herds of lemmings roved the craggy bogs. Is that where Vor comes from? Isolation? I try not to think about this new similarity between us. Though I never made curtains from squirrel pelts or anything.

The need to prove myself unlike him pushes me forward.

And in the next long room, he's there. He's standing at a worktable, his sing-song voice muttering something. Even though it is him, the figure is much shorter. He's Loamin at this moment, so it must be a memory. His facial structure is wider, eyes less narrowed.

The light from a single slim window near the ceiling slants across the space and falls on the floor in a clean rectangular shape. Next to him, sitting on the ground, there are two large woven baskets lined with fur and packed with dried peat.

Koglim parts the curtain behind me. "Is that..."

"Vor," I confirm. "Ara didn't see me. I don't think he will either."

Passing through the streak of blinding light, I come close enough to Vor that he could reach out and grab me. His silver knife is in one hand, and a lemming in the other. He continues to hum as I take one more step and scoop my hands into the peat moss.

I cup as much peat as I can in both hands and step away slowly. That's when Vor stops humming.

I hear Koglim curse as I turn toward Vor. It's strange not looking upward. He's shorter than me now, but the silver knife still glimmers in his hand. What would happen if I tried to take the knife? If this is an echo, is the relic even usable? Yinzar must sense my thoughts in the air.

"Get out of there," Yinzar hisses.

But Vor takes a sharp breath, his eyes flicking from side to side. Can he see me?

He frowns, then mutters something in the same ancient language. But I hear the words in my mind. "Shadows again, Vayris. Only shadows." Vayris? Was that his name? I can't help wondering if this event truly happened to him. I shake this off.

"Go back to your work," I tell him, a new feeling pushing me to dare him.

He squints harder, tightening his fingers around the knife, and turns back to the table. "The things I make are important. Creation is death. Death is creation. I'll find them. And when I do, I'll make something new." He slices deeper into the lemming.

"Come on," Yinzar hisses again.

I slide through the curtain. The weight of fear and anger balled up in the center of my body loosens. We flee Vor's workshop, and the hold these emotions have on me declines with each new step until, somehow, I'm standing at the edge of the shoreline, peat moss in hand, about to walk out on the ice floe to where the sacrifice bowl waits.

"How many will this make?" Koglim asks.

"Four," Yinzar says. "The oak, the lamb—"

"Jimmy," Koglim says.

"—the ice, and now the peat moss. I don't think we will find the amethyst, onyx, or quartz here."

"If I'm right," I say, "Jeiah might've already found those."

I march across the ice and dust off the handful of peat moss into the bowl. What could Vor have been talking about? What did he mean *find them*?

A threshold appears, showing the quarry. "One more door."

The moment we cross the threshold, the temperature rises fifty degrees. Heat like the inside of an oven radiates from the hallway of cut stone surrounding us. Koglim groans with pleasure like he's sinking into a warm bath. Yinzar takes a deep breath, though his eyes stay fixed on the walls of quartz around us.

The bright disk of the sun wavers in the sky, almost an illusion. The sacrifice bowl stands close by. It holds a piece of quartz —which must have been easy to find, seeing that there are shards of it all around—and a broken hunk of gypsum.

"Looks like they only need the amethyst."

"Clayson!"

Lagnar and Jeiah are rushing toward us. Lagnar clutches his chest. Even from this distance, I can hear his sharp wheezing.

"Don't touch the walls!" Jeiah shouts.

At that, Koglim and Yinzar jump closer to the bowl at the center of the path.

A wall materializes behind Jeiah and Lagnar, and they move faster. Jeiah almost plows into me. Lagnar, a rough cut on his arm and a large bruise on his face, drops something shimmering purple into the bowl. The amethyst!

From out of nothing, white crystal gems fly into place, forming a small arch. Thick birch limbs weave through and around the crystals, leaves blooming from green shoots. The wood and crystal remind me so much of the Forest of Ide I can't force away a shiver of terror.

The gateway pulses once and then lights with the power of a thousand brightstorms. I turn away. This can only lead to the destroyer. The Dura wraith were right.

Koglim gazes downward, murmuring the sacred name of the earth itself—Ide keep us.

"In!" Lagnar yells, looking over his shoulder.

The wall that had formed stands and strides toward us. Fat feet hold up the stone wall like something out of a video game.

"Uh, guys?" Koglim says.

"What's that thing?" I ask.

Yinzar squints at it. "I do not know this type of beast."

Jeiah pushes me toward the door. "We don't need to understand. Go!"

The walking wall accelerates. Jeiah's right. No time to think about this.

Lagnar growls. "Alright then, I'll go first." He marches through the blazing light.

Koglim seems fixated on the bottom of the door. Jeiah and I each grab an arm and pull him along with us.

Koglim mutters, "Not supposed to go into the light." He gives us half a laugh.

Through the door, we find a stretching gravel path skirting away in both directions. I can't help but think of Gamgim. I look up, expecting to see stars. But above us and in front of us is a wall of fog. Unsearchable. Unknowable. Another mystery inside another mystery.

"This place seem familiar to anyone else?" Jeiah asks.

"Kinda like Gamgim," Yinzar offers. "Do you think there's a connection?"

Clear stone borders the fog. Behind us is a wall of slate, curving away into the distance. "I have no idea at this point."

A low buzz draws my attention to the right. A figure rounds the bend.

It's a woman with long, tangled hair. Her brown shawl is knotted along with her hair. Her skin is cracked and dry, like the dehydrated surface of a long-dead lake. She carries a pole over her shoulder, but as she draws closer, I see the pointed end of a thick, rusted scythe, almost more of an ax.

She's humming, chanting, in drawn-out ghostly vowels.

I press against the slate wall, giving the frightening women room to pass. Her humming pauses. Her lips crack open, this time chanting a string of foreign words. Suddenly she stops, the ax-scythe at her shoulder bouncing upward as she straightens. Her mouth pinches, her jaw grinds, then she opens again as if the very act will hurt her.

"I do know"—her accent and inflection are so thick I barely understand her—"this lan-gu-age of the Loamin."

Jeiah slips her beholder out, holding it down but still scanning.

The woman cranes her head toward me. "Have you come to des-troy me? Hm? Clayson Brightstorm." She gestures at me awkwardly. "Then I show you how." She slices her ax-scythe through the air, and behind her, thick rays of sunlight punch into the fog. A forest, gleaming and ancient, appears as the fog dissipates.

With a smile, she says, "And I show you why."

STUMBLE ON THE ROOTS

"DESTROY YOU?" My voice feels as dry and cracked as her skin. "We don't even know who you are. We're looking for a way to defeat—"

"Vor, yes. I know." She laughs, and the sound is like an engine trying to turn over. "I am Idulel." This is some final statement of proof for her as if she has answered all our questions. She points a gnarled finger at her chest and shuffles to the tree line. With one great swing of the ax-scythe, she clears a few young saplings to reveal a path inward.

Yinzar has recovered enough to say, "But *what* are you?"

Idulel works her jaw open to hum. "Jas-sin told you of me, Clayson. Call me Loam-in if that is what you want. But I made all of this. Mmm? Years and years, and years and years."

Yinzar halts my step forward toward her. "Then you are the first champion?"

"No cham-pions. There are none. Yin-zar Ever-blooooooom. You of all Loam-in should know."

"How do you know of me?" Yinzar asks.

She grunts, returning to her work, chopping at the brilliantly lighted forest.

"Maybe it's because of your connection to the dungeon you created," I say.

"I just know," she snaps. "That is how it works."

Jeiah checks something on the beholder's display and frowns. She tucks the glass rod away. "What works?"

The ancient cracks in her skin deepen when she smiles. "E-ver-y-thing Jeiah-lir. I see e-ver-y-thing."

Something in the way she says these words, pronouncing every syllable, extra syllables even, the way her yellowing eyes gaze beyond me, through me—she knows the dungeons. She knows each of us. "You see into every dungeon?"

She nods.

"How is that possible?" Jeiah asks.

Idulel glances at Koglim. "Ask me any-thing about any dun-geon."

Koglim grins. "Okay. In Runearmor, what was the name of the raider who discovered the post-interior shortcut?"

She leans on the handle of the ax-scythe as if she's bored. "Lop-gren Hazel-bag. So. Many. Sounds. In words."

Koglim's mouth falls open, but only momentarily. "Yeah, what year?"

"By my number or yours?"

"Huh?"

"One thousand, seven hundred, seventy-six, primus." With this wordy statement, her pronunciation creeps closer to our own.

"You're reading my mind or something," Koglim accuses.

"Am I? Did you know? Did you know? Did you know? Lop-Gren killed Yor-nag Rock-chord to open the shortcut?"

"I—" Koglim stammers. "No... well, that's just not true. Rock-chord died—"

"Killed in the Room of Oran-ges by Hazelbag."

"She's lying," Koglim says. "She doesn't know what she's talking about."

Jeiah nudges Koglim out of the way, coming to Idulel's side. "What did you mean there are no champions?"

"There are none. Plain. Simple. Only Loamin who suffer the curse I caused. Can't dream. Can't breathe on the surface. Can't live on the surface."

Koglim chokes and sputters. "Wh-what?"

"You caused that?" I ask.

"They call me the des-troyer." She gestures toward the forest. "See for your-self."

The light from the forest pulses, bringing with it a million questions. I wanted to find something to defeat Vor, but the Dura wraiths sent me here to kill the destroyer. How can this be the destroyer? She looks as though a good shove might break her hip, shatter her paper-thin skull.

I step toward the forest, but Yinzar and Jeiah softly restrain me.

Jeiah finds my eyes. "Wait. I want more answers." Then turning to Idulel, she says, "The Dura wraiths want you destroyed. Why?"

Idulel stares at the pointed end of the scythe. "I des-troyed the world. One time. One time. When I did, they got trap-ped in the forest of creation. Prison after prison after prison."

"Gamgim is a prison?" I murmur. "The Valley of Ide."

She tries to wet her lips but puckers her mouth instead. "Flat-tering. Named it after me."

The gears click into place. "Idulel. Ide."

"A name all rev-er-ence."

"You are a goddess then," Yinzar says. "Earth itself."

"No. I am a curse. Made you, and you, and you. But first, but first... I made the Found-ation—" she chokes on the word, erupting into a fit of dry coughing.

Jeiah's eyes widen into round circles. "You made the Foundation?"

"My voice, I... just let me show you." She strides into the forest.

But we hesitate.

"Do we follow her?" I ask.

Jeiah blinks. "We came for answers."

"There's no turning back now," Yinzar adds.

Koglim shrugs with annoyance. "What else could go—"

"Don't finish that statement," I say. "You can't say stuff like that, Koglim."

"Now, who's superstitious?" Koglim levels a smile at me.

The trees are so dense that it is hard to even find a place to enter, but we weave into the light, following flickers of Idulel's brown shawl through gaps in the forest. Gamgim was much less dense. Idulel passes through a thin veil of light that seems to stretch the length of the forest. And she's gone. After only a second, I follow her through.

We enter a clearing where the bright lights dim, the canopy turns to cold bare limbs, and a sky appears above us. Buildings—skyscrapers made from towering gemstones—surround us. Broken pieces crunch beneath my feet, and I'm reminded of the field of broken shards where I found Jassin and the other wraiths. Maybe this is the same place. Perhaps destroyer is a good name for Idulel.

"Another memory of the surface," Koglim says.

"Idulel's time came even before Ara, Vor, and Tas," Jeiah says.

"Shhh." Idulel appears behind me. One bony finger extends from her shawl toward the center of the city. A hooded figure strides out from behind a glimmering wall, pacing to the center where a great tree raises heavenward. It's the largest tree I've ever seen—the same size and shape as the stump we saw in the Valley of Ide.

"This can't be it," I say.

"A long, very long time ago." Idulel's voice is kind now, like a mother teaching a child. When the figure lowers her hood, I see now—it's Idulel, though millennia younger.

More figures emerge from the surrounding city, some even stepping past us. They're bruised and bandaged. They wear wooden armor, faintly glowing in soft neons. One of them I recognize immediately. Taller than her by a couple of feet, Jassin steps to her side.

He takes a deep, slow breath and lets it out. "It was worth the cost in blood."

She nods.

I turn to Idulel. "What is this? What are you showing us?"

"The end."

The younger version of her clears her throat. "This will be the beginning."

Jassin places a hand on her shoulder, and I see energy moving into Idulel.

Jeiah stares. "That looks like sharing a craftprint, but the opposite, running from Dura to Loamin."

The ancient Idulel chuckles. "Watch."

Every Dura in the clearing—maybe thousands of them—comes forward and touches her skin, hands, face almost in worship. Each touch sends waves of energy pulsing over the ground toward us. Whatever they're doing, it's powerful, more potent, and wilder than even mithrium. The younger Idulel draws the long gleaming scythe out from under her cloak. Energy gathers along her arms and hands in bright iridescent rainbows. A foul wind stirs the whole clearing, whistling through the leafless branches. The Dura step back in wonder, and many fall to their knees, weeping like a god has been revealed to them.

Jassin remains at her side. "Do it!" he yells over the wind.

I rush forward as if I can stop this ancient act. There's something deeply wrong with what I'm seeing. Hurt and hatred echo over the forest. I can feel it in my bones, calling to me, trying to fill the hollowed-out parts of my soul, the vacuum left behind when I lost craft, when I lost Andalynn and Rugnus. "Don't!"

A whispered voice enters my ear. The ancient Idulel stands next to me. "This has already hap-pened, Clay Son Bright Storm."

With a sneer and vicious cry, the young woman brings the scythe down, and the whole scene turns white as if we've passed into some type of afterlife. The five of us, with Idulel hovering between us, appear like an overexposed photograph. Slowly the world returns.

Jeiah stumbles toward me. "What was that?"

"The earth was magic. In the leaves. In the trees. In the roots com-ing from the ground. It had always been that way. Humans, dwarfs, and elves lived happy. Only a few elves, you call Dura. The Loam-in feared them. Too many. A strong dwarf would die. Move on. But, but, but a new individual would emerge."

"Like the champions?" Koglim asked. "Like how Loamin become Dura."

She nods. "But... this act—des-troy the first creation." The word *creation* sounds strange on her tongue. "The broken tree becomes an awful curse. The power in my body, and I tried, I tried, to make it go back in-to the earth, but... the tree was dead. My friends, the elves, were gone to their prison. I woke up here. When the first dun-geon appeared—Tas, sweet Tas—I learned from his mem-ory about the curse."

"All that power," Yinzar says, "in what you called the tree of creation, it only became something else, didn't it? You couldn't destroy it. Energy moves, but it is never destroyed."

"The Foundation," Jeiah says.

Idulel scrunches up her face and nods. "Yes. Yes. Yes. You under-stand. All that power into the earth... frozen. Like crystal."

Jeiah rubs her face. "And from there... I see it. I see what happened. The Foundation started leaking power into the earth above, all across the world. Loamin found that power in Ide, in the very rocks. They must have figured out a way to trap it in metal."

"So, let me get this straight," Lagnar says. "You destroyed the... well, this first creation, this tree, which caused the Founda-tion to form, which allowed Loamin to print metals and use craft? Whilst at the same time, you brought down a curse on every Loamin the whole wide world over. That about sum it up?"

My head spins. The Foundation, this tree, the Valley of Ide

where the Dura wraiths are trapped. They're all connected. "You must have thought you were doing the right thing. Why?"

"Jealousy," Idulel says sharply. "Many elves feared the rise of more of themselves since they could live without end. How many could live on this plan-et? What type of power would they wield? Some of us, Jassin, disagreed. The sides fought and fought and fought. We thought: hmmm, des-troy the forest and everyone will be the same. No powers. Part of the elf, a-greed... they gave magic to us. And we won this war. We thought if we destroyed the source of magic, that it would end, and end, and end."

"You can't destroy energy any more than you can destroy matter," Yinzar says.

"But you can change it," Jeiah says. "And that's what happened. And when you did, the Loamin—dwarfs as you call them—were cursed."

"And now, Clay-son," Idulel says, "you can change things again."

"What does that mean?"

With a wave of her hand, we return to the forest inside her dungeon. But at the center of the clearing, instead of a tree, there's a swarm of festering lights. A soft wind calls to me, beckoning.

"I cannot enter," Idulel whispers. "You can. The elves—Dura wraiths—took your power. Makes you safe to enter."

"How do you know that?"

"Exr-alt Black-mug. We tested it. He was close. He was wraithborn as you. But he had his craft still. You do not."

With a deft movement, impossible for her age, she slices a nearby branch up and down. She retrieves a large piece of fallen wood and passes it to me.

I know immediately what it is, what the forest here is made of.

"Mithrium."

Koglim's mouth falls open. "What?"

Jeiah collects the piece from my hands, scanning it from all angles. She hands it back to me and then runs her hand on the closest glowing tree, squinting hard. She shakes in disbelief. "This whole forest is mithrium."

Idulel nods at this. "Exralt could open the lock, but it kept closing. So, we planned. Wake the ancients—Ara, Vor, Tas. I gave Exr-alt the mithrium to get them out. And they are out but still connected. I can't break these connections to the Foundation. You can, Clay-son."

She holds her ax-scythe out to me. I don't take it. Something is wrong with this. The itch I sometimes feel, the need to see what is next, died with Rugnus and Andalynn. I won't cause more grief.

Instead, I fold my arms. "The Dura wraiths sent me here to destroy you."

Idulel's face seems to age another year. She must understand my hesitance. "But you are un-willing to kill?"

"We came for a way to defeat Vor, not this."

"You won't help me?" Her eyes find mine, desperate, tired.

"This connection... what will happen if I break it?"

"I be-lieve craft will die. Loamin can return to the surface in peace."

Astonished cries drown out the soft wind. Koglim gulps, visibly sick. Yinzar wobbles dazed, repeating, "No, no, no."

Lagnar whistles and runs a hand through his hair. "Wraithspit."

Jeiah mutters, "You can't be right. She can't be right."

Is such a thing even possible? I close my eyes and feel air tickling my face. What would it be like for all my friends and family to live on the surface with me without the danger of magic? Without dungeons and monsters? But also... without budging to exactly the place you need to be. Without magic food that grants a peek into another's nostalgia. Without the power to bring forth a host of trees and whispering flowers. Without the touch of silvercraft that helps you finally understand a friend.

I've lost Rugnus and Andalynn, and for their memory, I won't lose Rimduum. "Believe?" I say, "Then you don't know what will happen if I break this connection?"

"Change," Idulel replies.

"Loamin have lived under the mountains for thousands of years. Will they have to leave their cities? Does their culture come crashing down? Will the Foundation melt? What happens to craft? Do you even know?"

She looks away from me. "That is kept from me. I only know that something will come next."

"Then you're just like Vor. You want me to break the world to satisfy your curiosity about what comes next. I won't do it. I came to disconnect Vor from his power. That's what the Dura hinted was here. Instead, I find you and your sales pitch to end the world. I'm gonna pass."

Idulel looks at me thoughtfully and then toward the fog. "It has been a very, very long time. So pointless. I do not know what is in the heart of this place. I do not care anymore."

Lagnar steps closer to me. "We could use the scythe on her."

She laughs. "Exr-alt tried. I tried. Older and older, that's it. No death for me until you sever the connection."

"Will I still have a choice if I go in there?"

"You always have a choice, but this is the only mys-tery left to me."

"Then, I'll go."

"We'll all go," Jeiah says.

We step forward. Idulel lets me pass but rests the handle of her scythe on Jeiah's chest. "Only wraithborn can enter. Even Ex-ralt could not make it to the center of the fog."

Jeiah searches Idulel's face. I can tell she's trying to see how much truth there is to the ancient woman's statement. She's looked at me the same way a hundred times. But there is no deceit in Idulel's words. If she could have, she would've entered the fog thousands of years ago and ended the world herself.

I level the shield and hold out my free hand. "Give me the scythe."

"And you will find the connection? Sever it?"

"No, but if I can find a way to take Vor's power..."

"There you go doing something stupid again," Lagnar says. "How do you know you can even come back from this place? If this old biddy doesn't even know what's in there—not for sure anyway. No offense."

"What's the alternative?" Koglim says.

"I'm coming back from this." My fingers curl around the handle of the scythe.

Jeiah grabs my empty hand. "Please do."

"Yeah."

She smiles. "Sure."

"Okay." I lean toward her, and she tips her head toward me.

Her cold fingers draw me in, and she kisses me gently on the cheek. "I want you to live long enough to tell me you love me."

I open my mouth to finally tell her, but the words won't come out. I know how I feel about her. Why can't I just say it?

She closes her eyes. "Come back to me."

Yinzar bows to me slightly. "'For a raider tests his strength upon the unknown...'"

Koglim huffs. "'...and breaks the universe.' The Historian of the Champions. Pival Shatterkeg? At a time like this?"

"I find the Historian is always appropriate."

"I'm not breaking anything," I say, but my voice trembles, cutting the last word short. "We've gotta see what's there. I'll sever Vor's connection to craft if I can. We came through all of this."

As I walk into the unknown, the lights shape around my body. I hear Idulel's sharp inhale. Maybe she expected to be wrong. Maybe I expected her to be. My heartbeat suddenly goes faint at the idea of walking into the most impenetrable place under granite. Even a goddess can't break through this fog. Stronger than Keelcrawl, harder to reach than the heart of any dungeon. Maybe this *is* the center of the universe.

Another step and the ground rushes toward me. I fall face-forward. Instead of slamming into the earth, I keep going, like I'm swinging down from a balance bar, attached only by the soles of my feet. I rotate a full one-eighty across the axis of the ground. The world on the other side is full of darkness. It is another plane of existence.

But the darkness isn't complete.

A tangle of softly glowing roots extends from the floor upward. At eye level, some strands and tendrils have turned into thin metal wires. The familiarity of this darkness and of the metallic strands draws me closer. I run my finger up a gold wire. It comes away holding a bead of mercury. Connection.

I can almost follow the path of this single strand. From Idulel's forest—this place—all the way into the darkness of the mountains. A strand weaving through rock and earth meeting up with its own reflection beneath Gamgim, the summation room, where the Loamin have woven these same strands into strange receptacles gathering the mercury. But the roots continue upward, bursting through the ground into the illusion of Gamgim forming the other book end of this strange magic, where Jassin and the Dura wraith wait.

Every part of this world is connected to Idulel's great act of defiance. Her hope and anger translated into the destruction of one type of world and the creation of a new one. I trace a bead of mercury as it travels a strand of copper far into the darkness, where it disappears in a wink of light.

An echo fills the space, ricocheting off a million surfaces. The dull sound of muffled screaming. Something deep and foreboding, an ancient force like a black hole, skips across my nerves.

Wraiths.

"Who's there?" No one answers. "You can't harm me. I have no craft. Show yourself!" The sound becomes duller as I push through the upside-down roots—an angry buzz of background noise, like a long cold hiss of breath.

Something shifts behind me—I feel it more than I see it, like a tingle down my spine, an evolutionary trait calling out a warning over my nervous system. I freeze. When I'm able to turn around again, I catch a thread of darkness weaving through the tiny strands of metal—and I follow it.

This winding shadow, a dancing thread of black against black, refuses to stay still.

As I push through the snaking roots, I murmur Koglim's typical words of wisdom. "Bigger the trap..."

Raiders must see what's out of place, but every second I'm in this darkness feels wrong. I circle a massive knot of roots—a wall almost—into an open area where the dark thread whirls around a long metal braid. I know at once I'm at the center. This braid sticks right up from the floor as a long ancient chain, different from this prison of roots.

I move to the side of the braid cautiously, keeping the scythe in front of me and an eye on the thread of darkness that led me here. The shadowy threat unwraps from the metal strand and hovers in the air. It wanted me to find this. Before I can think, my fingers wrap around the cord of shadow.

The darkness shatters, and sharp visions strike me in rapid succession: the sacrifice bowl, the Dura wraiths, Jassin, sculptures of tiny bones, beetles scrambling out of the ground, and the maze of quartz. Three Loamin—Vor, Ara, Tas—screaming.

This is the moment they were murdered.

I jerk my hand away. "What was that?"

Drawing even closer to the strand, I let the scythe drift to my side. The most tangible cord is made from three metals: a bright aluminum central core partially encased with an alloy of tungsten and silver. The same metals that make up Icho, Ergal, and Onrix. Combined with the visions, there is only one thing this braid of metal can be: Vor's connection to his craft. But not just his; it belongs to Tas and Ara as well.

I grab the shadow one more time. The visions clarify. I see all three of them in their native homes, in a time before they were trapped in their dungeons before they became champions. I watch Ara herding other Loamin safely through the forest, her eyes wary for beetles; I see Tas moving stones, budging them out of the quarry; I observe Vor enticing a group of lemmings into a trap he's set for them.

But next, he lures Tas and Ara. Vor entices them deeper under the mountain toward a fire he set. This flashes back to something earlier—Vor and Jassin making an oath. Vor would lead them to their deaths to help further lock Idulel away. Vor brought them all to a mountain of obsidian that will become the House of Ide. They travel deeper and deeper. There are a few more Loamin with them, but they are not champions. They will die with these three and become wraiths in their dungeons. Jassin had said Exralt brought other wraithlings to him.

They come to the location of the thresholds and Vor engages the trap. They are all eaten up by flames and shadows. Their death carved out the first three dungeons, sealed under the obsidian. I let go of the shadow.

Vor murdered them.

The three dungeons are inseparable. The meaning of this place, the millions of strands, this metal alloy cord, comes into full focus in my mind. These are the lives of every Loamin under granite. And this central cord is the joint lives of Ara, Vor, of Tas. I can't destroy Vor without ending Ara's life alongside his.

I won't do this.

The second I turn from the braid, the scythe trembles in my hands, then lurches me back around. I reverse away from the cord just as the scythe sails across my vision, still in my hand, missing the cord by only an inch.

A whisper pierces my mind. "Destroy it!"

It's Idulel. Bringing the scythe with me has brought her with me. The weapon slips in my hands, but I grab it, reigning its lurching movement.

"Stop! You can't cut it. Ara will die. The Foundation will unravel."

The scythe burns in my hands, but I frantically tighten my grip. If I let go, it will cut the metal braid. More lives are in my hands. More death. Even if it kills Vor and the pendulum of the world swings in the opposite direction, I can't let this happen.

I try to pin the handle underneath me, but it jerks free. I hinge at the shoulder and fall backward, trying to drag it back. "Stop!" I try to dig into the floor, but it's polished smooth, almost slick. I reach for something to grab but just as I come close to a few of the thin strands I stop. What if these are more lives to be snubbed out if they're severed?

Vor believes me to be a wrecking ball. But I won't let myself be used.

I hear the familiar muffled scream of the wraiths. But they're nowhere to be seen. The sound came from...

The single dark thread that led me here floats closer. It stretches down to the floor and coils like a snake. If the strands are the connection of the Loamin and champions, then what is this dark thread? Something that wants to help me calls out for my acceptance. I glance at the metal cord representing the first three champions, then back to the dark twist of shadow.

I let the scythe pull me closer to both strands. "I've made my choice!"

When the scythe tries to fly forward again, I let it, but this time shift my weight just enough to bring the blade whirling down, slicing through the dark thread. The two pieces whip away from each other, the spot where I sliced through bleeding fog and rainbow light. The room swells with it. I hear my champion's name hissed from every direction.

"Wraithking. Wraithking. Wraithking."

The shadow held every wraith in every dungeon. And I've just released them.

I run, pushing through the upside-down roots. At the edge, I fall forward once again, crossing the axis of the world, and I snap back into the glowing mithrium forest. Idulel stares at me, seething. The swirl of lights and fog are still in place behind me.

"You did no-thing! You came all this way. In every dun-geon, I watched you de-feat every-thing, and you give me this?"

"It would have destroyed all three of them."

Yinzar and Koglim step toward me as I walk out of the lights.

Yinzar steadies me. "What does that mean?"

"Severing the connection would kill Vor. I'm sure of it. But killing Vor also means killing Ara and Tas. I won't do it. We'll find another way."

Idulel points a heavy finger at me. "Wouldn't Ara want this?"

"I wouldn't care if she did. We can't kill her to save everyone else."

I scan the three faces closest to me. Yinzar's face is pinched together in concern. Koglim's anger only draws closer around him, his shoulders bunched, fists at his side. Jeiah taps her beholder on her leg, most likely judging me.

I snap my attention toward Idulel. "The wraiths. Not the Dura, but all the others. There was a black swirl, a cord. I think... I severed their connection to this place. Will they—"

"Die? They are al-ready dead. But... I do not know what will happen."

"Clayson," Yinzar says softly. "Was there no other way?"

I shake my head. "We should go. This was a waste of time."

"You can't," Idulel says, and for the first time her eyelids part wide enough to see her soft blue pupils. "I don't want this. You must des-troy me. Please, Clay-son."

"We're not doing that," Koglim says. "You made the Foundation. The curse on Loamin that keeps us under the mountain... it's our way of life."

Idulel stares through Koglim. "What did you do in Brightstorm Dungeon?"

This stops me in my tracks. "What did you say?"

"I cannot see what is happening. But you sense it, do you not, Clay-son?"

"The whispers?"

"More, but more what? I cannot see?" She closes her eyes and shakes her head.

Forget this.

"There's one more thing we should do," I say, ignoring the itch to get more answers from her. "We need more options to defeat Vor." I move to the closest tree on the rim of the clearing and whip the scythe upward. A branch flops to the ground. Then I cut again a clean piece that can fit in a person's hand.

Yinzar picks up the fallen piece of wood. It glows in his hand.

"We'll make something to stop him," I say. "And if we need more, we can come back."

Jeiah steps to the pile I've created. "Are you sure about this?"

"Do you see another way? We need something strong enough to defeat Vor."

She nods but takes the piece of mithrium from a reluctant Yinzar.

Idulel begs us to sever the cord, but we march from the forest out to the circle where the threshold waits.

Koglim goes through first, then Lagnar and Yinzar, then Jeiah.

Idulel steps out of the forest. "There's not another way. You'll have to destroy this place to stop him, to bring the world back into balance."

"Balance? That's what you thought *you* were doing long ago, but in the end, you traded one curse for another. I'm not willing to see what happens next. I've done enough damage to this world."

She hangs her head as I cross the threshold.

Ara stands right next to the threshold where we left her. But she knows. Somehow her connection to this place helped her to see what happened. She eyes the mithrium in Jeiah's hands.

"It's okay, Clayson. It's okay."

I close my eyes and swallow a breath to stop my fears and worries from rushing out. Whatever this is, it's not okay.

PLEAD OUR CASE

ARA SEARCHES for a way around me. "I'll do it. I'll go back in and—"

I block the threshold, hands up. "No. Ara, please just hang on."

We've already spilled the messy creation story on the floor like a jigsaw puzzle. Two sides fighting over the earth. Idulel's destruction of the Tree of Creation and her hasty construction of the Foundation to hold the world together. Vor working with the Dura wraiths to lock Idulel away even further.

Ara knows everything we know. I don't keep secrets. Still, she wants to enter the dungeon, find the metal braid that connects her with Vor and Tas, and cut it down. Her eyes are wide, furious almost.

She tries once more to step around me. "You don't—you need to—" in her anger, she can't even complete a sentence.

"Ara!" I back up closer to the threshold. "I understand, I do."

"No, you do not understand, Clayson. Not this. You should have done it! Saving all of this... all of you... it's worth whatever sacrifice Tas and I must make. He would do it."

Lagnar scoffs. "Then why did Tas join Vor, hmm? Explain that one. We had him at the bridge. Until Kel and Vor—"

Ara barely glances over her shoulder. "You could never know what it's like to wake up after what we went through." Then more softly to me, she says, "Tas is afraid. I've felt it through our connection. And my connection to Vor. And Clayson, Vor's not wrong about freeing the other Dura from their dungeons. He's wrong about everything else. We have mithrium now. If you won't let me back in that dungeon, we should use that to wake up the other Dura."

I focus on Ara. "That's gonna have to wait. We don't know what side any other Dura will be on. What if Vor convinces them to—"

Ara's face hardens. Part of me knows she's right. It's unjust to leave those people trapped in their dungeons. The room feels smaller, I pick up the key from where Ara dropped it, but the three threshold doors remain in front of us.

The opening from the slide we came down is gone. In its place is a long stairway. No one speaks as we trudge up the stairs. I can feel Ara's heavy footfalls. Everyone's on edge.

Returning to the Hall of Champions seems wrong. Once we're all out, I expect the stairway to seal, but it stays open. A gaping maw of some awful predator. What would Vor do if he found this place?

"It's not closing," Jeiah says.

"I don't think we can do anything about it," Lagnar says.

We wait another minute. Finally, I shrug. "I guess we leave it."

We walk past the larger-than-life statues, the symbolic items that allow the false worship of these Loamin—these Dura—trapped in the dungeons. I stop dead, staring at a statue of Torlina Wolfstaff wrapped in stone-carved furs, a metal staff gleaming, and a fierce hard look in her eye. Kel.

The group stops behind me. You could hear a filament of lead drop against the stone. I meet Ara's eyes, searching, hoping, wanting different words to come out of my mouth than the ones I'm thinking of. The hard unmovable stones fade away from her pupils. She knows where my mind is at. The path forward is as clear as a day under the brightstorm.

"I was able to free the heart of Wolfstaff Dungeon," I start, "because part of the mithrium was in me, trapped there when Yinzar forged Mithriumbane. And with the mithrium, Exralt reached the heart of your dungeon, Ara. Long before he left the ring in Wolfstaff Dungeon for me to find, he took Ergal, and it broke you out of the dungeon. He did the same thing with Vor and Tas. With Onrix and Icho." I stop there, letting my words sink into everyone's flesh. "But at first, you didn't even remember being in the dungeon. All you remembered was—"

"My life as a slave."

"Exactly." I pause, pulling the mithrium from my shoulder bag. "But when I was in your dungeon, I think... I saw you. You were helping to guide other Loamin on the surface. You were good."

Jeiah taps her fingers against her leg. "Where are you going with this?"

"We have mithrium, yes. And we could use it to craft something using the recipe, true, but the only objects to combine it with are Kel's staff..."

"Yeah, no. Don't do that." Lagnar says.

"...and Icho. Which belongs to Tas."

Koglim groans. "We can't trust him."

Yinzar weighs this. "Why? He and Sira helped me escape."

"Maybe we can," I say, "and maybe we can't, but I want everyone's opinion. If Ara was good in life before Vor murdered her, then couldn't there be other champions who would help us? Who was known for being kind, trustworthy, and brave? There has to be someone."

Yinzar and Koglim glance at each other. Jeiah shifts her eyes as if I don't wanna hear what she has to tell me. A soft warning goes off in my mind.

Ara answers, "Erikzin Brightstorm. His creation was designed to bring Loamin together, to help them become one. He loved the people. He was much like Rugnus that way."

I force myself past my anger toward Brightstorm Dungeon. In the same way Ara was not the one who manipulated us in her dungeon, maybe neither was Erikzin. "If you think we can trust Erikzin Brightstorm..."

Ara's face brightens with hope, enough to loosen up the last of my reservations. "If Vor's not there to poison his thoughts when I get him out, I think he may help us. But this must be more than that, Clayson. We can't do this out of... I don't know, trying to get something out of it. We do this because it's the right thing to do."

"You think?" Lagnar growls, now pacing. "Whole damn world's falling apart, and we're contemplating adding more of your friends. It's ridiculous!"

"Lagnar," Jeiah says, "hold on."

He gives her a withering look.

"Please," she says. It's a calculated word when Jeiah uses it, but she means it.

Lagnar throws up his hands, cursing under his breath about how no one listens.

Jeiah looks at me, and I continue. "With the key from the Dura wraiths, you can get into any dungeon. And with this," I hand her the mithrium, "You can rescue him."

Jeiah shakes her head, drawing in a deep breath. "Clayson, you have the best intentions here, but I'm not sure this is right. Particularly now. How can we trust that another Dura will be on our side in this fight?"

"We can't. But I can trust Ara."

Ara takes the mithrium from me, and I give her the key.

"Don't force him to help us," I say, "Just... tell him—"

"—that he's free," Ara finishes. "I will. If I can find him."

"I'll go with you," Yinzar says.

Yinzar takes the mithrium, and Ara holds the key. With a sad smile, they disappear, leaving me behind to face those who are left. The spectrum of light from the Foundation washes everyone out in a dozen shades of blue.

I'm focused on Lagnar's fists, tightening and untightening. He smooths his vest and takes a deep breath. When he turns back to me the flicker of anger in his eyes changes to fear—wide-eyed horror. He raises a finger and points behind me through the window.

Koglim and Jeiah stumble back. I barely have time to turn around before I understand what they're seeing. The same thing everyone fears—every Loamin but me. A massive cloud of fog and flickering light expands outside the long window.

"The wraiths," Koglim says.

I lead us down the hall at a sprint. We emerge from The House of Ide onto the wall that separates the Foundation from a sea of bubbling lava. The blood-red light competes against the blue light of the Foundation. But the radiance of the wraiths shines all the brighter.

"Wraithspit!" Koglim says.

Lagnar cowers behind everyone. "Bad choice of words."

Jeiah stands behind me. She whispers, "There has to be... I don't even know how many."

Floating over the Foundation, stretching at least a hundred yards in each direction, including upward, an incalculable number of wraiths swirl. Their fog and lights press against the far stone in a hurricane of terror. With a rush of wind, the wraiths smash together, and I see hundreds of wraith faces.

"Ide keep us," Koglim says. "If that's even a thing anymore."

More faces emerge, more arms and shoulders, until an army of wraiths materializes before us. I can't see the back of their ranks, there had been thousands of wraiths trapped in not even a hundred dungeons.

"How can there be so many?" I ask.

"A few dungeons held armies, Clayson," Koglim says. "The champion commanders during the Mithrium War died in battle."

A wraith steps forward. The homespun cloth of his tunic and

the shards of metal woven along its seams, show him to be a highly decorated Knight of Shale.

He bows to me. "Wraithking Brightstorm. We, the tortured, are free. I am General Baxa Songborn, son of Ylidarala Flatkeeper and Mart Songborn. We crave the craft of all who would stand in our way." He eyes Koglim like he's sizing up a meal.

Koglim swallows but bravely comes to my side, not quite rising to his full height. "We're not afraid to lose our craft!"

"We're not?" I ask with a side glance.

"There are worse things." I know he's thinking about Rugnus again, and I agree with him.

General Songborn's lower half becomes a cloud of light again. "My soldiers and I serve at your command. Turn us against your enemies, and we'll drain them of their strongest craft. Will you give us orders, or shall we start with you?" His skeletal face contorts in anger.

"Orders?"

"You freed them. They want to serve you, Clayson," Jeiah says.

Lagnar lowers his rifle. "Bricks and beards. That could work."

It dawns on me as Lagnar speaks. The crown still renders Vor untouchable, but the darkmages aren't immune to wraiths. The wraiths could take their strongest craft. "We could use the wraiths to stop the darkmages."

Lagnar taps his nose. "Exacta mundo."

"But..." Koglim says. "What about Vor's crown? He could still control us."

I shake my head. "We wait for Ara. Last time Vor had help, this time... when the shield and the crown cancel each other out, there will be no one to help him. And shieldcraft always has a slight advantage."

"Then we can kill 'im," Lagnar says.

"Stop him," I correct. I face the host of wraiths. "How do I call for you? I have a need, but I'm not ready."

The loose skin around the general's mouth tightens into a

cruel grin. "Our connection is strong. Think of your request and we will come. Until then, Wraithking, may Ide keep you in power and glory." With a twirl of his wrist, he signals the host of soldiers.

They burst back into fog and fly off over the Foundation.

Lagnar slaps my back and yips. "This is gonna work, Brightstorm. Wipe that worry off your face. Scary as a cold swim on the surface, but it's gonna work."

"He's right," Jeiah says. "It all adds up perfectly. And no one else will be hurt."

"It's gonna work," I whisper. I let myself dream for only a second, and the hope expands inside of me. An unexpected gift, but a gift that I'll cling to for now. We have a way forward where no one has to die.

"Let's go find everyone else. There's a lot to explain."

Jeiah flashes a light from the beholder. "They're back at Lagnar's hub."

Lagnar's eyes widen. "The darkmages overran my place."

After another gesture, Jeiah shrugs. "Therias Brightstorm has issued an encrypted call to all current and former knights to assemble there."

"Is it a trap?" Koglim asks.

"I don't think so?" Jeiah says.

Koglim nods, producing Icho.

Something reaches into my chest and squeezes. Rugnus and Andalynn aren't here with us. They're not coming back. I know that, but every time I see Icho, all I can think about is the all-consuming fire that destroyed my friend and my sister. Suddenly, I don't wanna see my dad. I lied to him. Hurt him on purpose, and I'm not sure we can make it back from that.

"Clayson," Jeiah says. "You're thinking about them?"

Koglim looks away from me.

I blink away the thoughts. "No. We can—we can go."

Koglim nods, and we're standing in front of an aluminum chain-link fence. Through the diamond shapes, the concrete building of Lagnar's hub is framed by the muted dusk. Lagnar immediately needs support, but Koglim and Jeiah only look slightly ill.

"Why didn't you budge us in the safe zone?" Lagnar says.

Koglim takes a wheezing breath. "Something weird threw me off. I—it's the fence."

"Where did this come from?" Lagnar says, scanning a padlocked gate.

"Must be an update from Therias and Hardkeeper," Jeiah says.

"Hold on," Koglim says. A second later, we're inside the fence. Lagnar, Koglim, and Jeiah react like fish being thrown back into the river. "See. Can't stop Icho. I'm just still getting used to it."

Lagnar whistles. "What'd they do to the place?"

The large utility door of the old radio station swings open, and Hemdi and Winta step out of the building, light from the hallway behind them stretching out their shadows on the ground.

"Finally," Winta says. She steps into the light of dusk and takes us in. "Where's Ara?"

Hemdi holds Echel on his hip. He squints. "And Yinzar?"

"Long story," I say. "I take it my dad's here with you?"

Hemdi and Winta share a quick look. She sighs. "You might as well come see for yourself. He's pretty much running the show now."

"What does that mean?"

Hemdi shifts Echel to the other side, gesturing for me to enter.

I pass under the light and squeeze through a set of heavy glass-looking pylons—transparent aluminum.

Koglim grunts a little trying to push through them. "What are these?"

Winta steps through, and Hemdi passes Echel to her. "Therias had the knights install new anti-budge."

"The knights?" Jeiah says.

"When Vor left Tungsten City, there were a few people who

escaped to the surface, including a whole battalion of knights. Your dad found them over bluelink, and now they're here."

"Won't that make it easier for Vor to find this place?" Jeiah asks.

"He's too busy with Everfalls," Winta says. "He tried to break in with his darkmages again, but they couldn't get past the anti-budge and shieldcraft. Well, that and the hellfire your dad called down on them," Winta says.

"He's still using craft?"

Winta looks back at me. "I'd say."

The interior of the hub feels like a military command center. Massive screens and holographic displays cover every wall, surrounded by chattering Loamin, some pointedly arguing. Work surfaces are cluttered with crafted items. Two thick glowing chains strung from floor to ceiling rotate around each other. A dozen or more smiths cut out chunks from the chains, pulling the glowing metal over to corners, banging the metal with sledge-hammers against massive anvils.

Knights and conjurers intermingle everywhere. The knights test and train with crafted objects, and the conjurers clean and prepare a frightening arsenal of assault weapons. In the back of the room, behind a newly erected wall, I see the flash of gunfire.

My father stands regally at the center of it all, spinning a map of Tungsten City, zooming in here and there to point out various weak spots for Hardkeeper. When they see us, my father rushes toward me and sweeps me into a hug. Hardkeeper steps down toward us, warier.

"You made it back," my father says. "I-I'm sorry about your sister. I'm sorry about what I said. I can't imagine what you must be going through. I understand why you lied to me. It's okay." He glances at one of his attendants. "Go find the Queen."

It's not just the room that's transformed. My father is no longer the closed-off, cautious man I had to keep alive at the cabin. That person is gone. There's only Therias Brightstorm, King of Rimduum. But this transformation leaves me feeling empty as if the person I knew growing up was all just an act. I know that's not the truth, but that doesn't erase the hurt I feel.

"Where's Ara?" he asks.

I begin telling him everything. My father brings us all to a workbench and orders a few people to give up their stools. I start with how we opened the door with Lagnar's memories but glance at Lagnar. These are his stories, not mine. With a sigh, Lagnar picks up the story and explains all that happened. He seems to feel marginally better as he tells the tale, eventually standing fully upright and meeting my father's gaze.

When he finishes, my father drops a hand on Lagnar's shoulder. "My mistake was far greater than yours. I'm sorry."

Lagnar shakes his head, and the two men test strengths. "Water under the bridge, my friend."

Mom clears her throat. She steps toward my father. The men release each other, and my father encourages her to sit close to him. He adjusts his chair near hers. Her skin is yellowing, worse than when I left her. Her green eyes are still speckled with gold.

"Don't let me stop you," she says weakly. "What happened next? Where's my father and Ara?"

My account of the protodungeons takes only a minute. When I reach our encounter with Idulel, the destroyer, Hardkeeper places his hand on his chest and gasps. My father is speechless.

Mom asks, "How could one Loamin create all craft?"

"The power of the Dura. They gave her everything. It was like she absorbed the craftprint of thousands of Dura at the same time. It almost destroyed her."

"And her request?" Hardkeeper asks. "You didn't honor it. You chose to keep her alive."

"I wasn't going to end everything the Loamin have built over ten thousand years. Would you have ended the curse?"

Hardkeeper scowls. "I would not have."

Lagnar adds. "It was so long ago. To change it again? It'd just be a different curse."

For a brief second, caution returns to my father's face. "Then craft comes from Ide itself. Earth is the power. We've never needed metal."

Hardkeeper shakes his head. "Your majesty, our best plans won't work without Ara."

"Of course," my father says, coming back from his musings. "Where is she? You said she couldn't go in the dungeon. She didn't go back in, did she?"

"No, no," I assure him. "We—I took another piece of mithrium from the protodungeon. And Ara—"

"You let her go free?" Hardkeeper accuses. "With the mithrium?"

"And the key," I add. "Yinzar went with her to free Erikzin Brightstorm."

My father catapults to his feet. "What?! That's... what did you do? We can't know—"

"Ara believes he will help us."

"We can't know that!" Hardkeeper shouts. "What if Vor finds him first?"

"I needed Ara's shield," my father says. "We were going to begin the attack the moment she arrived."

"The attack?" Jeiah and I say at the same time.

Mom places a hand on my father's arm to steady herself, but it steadies him too. He takes a deep breath. "With Ara's shield, we can level the playing field with the darkmages."

The command center comes into sharper focus. The map of the city center. The knights and conjurers are training. "You're going to war?" I ask. "You're going to attack Tungsten City."

Hardkeeper grants me a smug grin. "Not without Ara. But yes. We have Vor backed into a corner."

"What does that mean?" Jeiah asks incredulously.

"He's not controlling anyone in Tungsten City," Mom adds.

My father acknowledges this and adds, "And he's voluntarily made his way to the bottom of Everfalls. He can't budge past the anti-budge monstrosity he's built there."

"That's a trap, folks," Koglim squeaks.

"Maybe," my father says, a sense of caution returning for a moment. "But it's our feeling that he miscalculated."

"That's a leap," Jeiah says, echoing my thoughts. "We should wait for Ara."

"We don't need her," Hardkeeper says. "Attack pattern fourteen is my suggestion, King Brightstorm. If Ara adds another Dura to the equation, we don't know what that could do. We should move forward with the alternative."

My father nods. Turning to another attendant, he says. "Bring the vacant out."

The harsh words make me take a step back. I stare at my father. Has he ever used *that* word when talking about the Dura? I sense the rage eddying out from him. I've never, ever seen him this way. And now, witnessing the danger and power in him when he leans into his role as the true King of Rimduum, my whole childhood pivots in an unexpected direction. This is what he had been avoiding—becoming this.

It was more than just hiding me. He could have kept in contact with the knights. He didn't have to swear off craft. But he did. He did it out of fear of becoming this.

The attendant reappears with Tas. From another room, I hear a sharp yell then a door smashes open. Sira stamps out furious. "Don't treat him that way!"

The woman ignores her, pushing Tas to his knees before us in shackles.

"Tas!" Sira charges us, but the attendant blocks her path. "Let him go! He's a good person. Like Clayson." She pleads with my father. "Please. He helped me escape Vor. And—" She sees me. "Clayson, do something."

"Are you not the girl that controlled the Queen and me?" My father's voice is cool and unforgiving. "Who forced us into Silverlamp, who betrayed us on the bridge in Geum Ide?"

"Yes," she whispers. "I did those things, those bad things. I made those awful choices, but... I..."

"She was scared, Dad," I finish. "Vor raised her."

"And you can judge her real intentions now? Her character?" Hardkeeper asks.

"She wants to help us. And you shouldn't treat Tas this way."

My father and Hardkeeper share a look, and then Hardkeeper continues, "What does your intuition say about Tas? He's offered to help us as well."

"Attack pattern fourteen," Jeiah says, eyes narrowed. "What is it?"

My father clears his throat. "Tas stated that with Sira's craft-print he could counteract the effects of the mithrium crown for perhaps five thousand people. It would give us an attack force that Vor would find hard to repel."

"Yes," Tas says. "It will work."

Sira looks at me, pleading. "See?"

"Clayson," my father says. "I trust your judgment. You are the future King of Rimduum. You must help me make this decision. Can Tas be trusted? Can we use his power to do this?"

Tas' eyes plead that I believe him. I refuse to internalize my father's comment about me becoming King, but I nod. "I trust him. But Dad, there's a different option. No one else needs to get hurt."

Hardkeeper folds his arms across his chest. "There's no scenario where—"

My father silences him with one hand and nods at me. "Let's hear it."

"After I cut the dark thread in the protodungeon, I—we were about to return here when General Baxa Songborn showed up."

"General Songborn? Trollbrick." Hardkeeper says. "He was killed when... when..."

We all watch the wheels turn in Hardkeeper's eyes.

Koglim nods encouragingly until the lights turn on. "Now he's got it!"

Hardkeeper says, "But that would make him—"

"Correct," Jeiah adds. "He's a wraith."

I continue. "When I cut the dark thread, it released the wraiths."

"From Flathand Dungeon?"

"From every dungeon."

"Ide keep us," Hardkeeper murmurs. "They could destroy everything. And... wait, you said you had another plan. You can't mean..."

I square my shoulders. "I *am* Wraithking. They will heed my command. We can go to Tungsten City, but not with this... this army. Not to kill everyone. But the darksmiths, we can take their strongest craft. Forever. It will give us an advantage. Vor will have no one to—"

My father shakes his head. "But it could backfire. The wraiths could take our craft. Or—how do we know they wouldn't help Vor. That is a big risk."

"And this isn't?" I ask.

My father draws himself to his full height. "If you believe Tas is being truthful, then we follow attack pattern fourteen. Jeiah. You are a paladin with a high AMP score. What is your assessment of Tas' plan? Can it succeed?"

Jeiah opens up her connection with bluelink and connects to the hub. "I've already looked at it. It has a higher likelihood of success than any other pattern without Ara. But you could wait for Ara, and the plans combined would—"

"People are dying," Tas says. "Every minute we wait..."

Jeiah shakes her head. "But Clayson's plan—"

"I'm not leaving this matter up to wraiths," Hardkeeper states. "King we—"

My father holds up his hand once more, and this time Hardkeeper growls. I hold my breath. My father's thoughtful for a second, hand over his mouth. "We can't count on wraiths. And who knows when Ara will return or how this new vacant will change the balance between Vor and the people. We're going with pattern fourteen. Using Tas' power, we will bring our group to Tungsten City and attack Vor within the confines of the

Everfalls."

"Mom!" I say, turning to her. "You can't agree with this! Change his mind."

But she looks helpless next to him, her face gaunt with whatever sickness she's still fighting from her confrontation with Grimflail. For a second, I see the normal fire in her eyes, but it fades quickly. "I don't know, Clay. There's so much danger in setting the wraiths free."

"Danger? More dangerous than the darksmiths? Than Vor?" I glance at Lagnar. "You were a general. What do you think we should do?"

There's a pain in his eyes. He wants to help me, but he has just repaired his relationship with my father. "Don't look at me. I don't make these kinds of decisions anymore."

My father places a hand on my shoulder. "We've been preparing for many options, Clayson, in case Ara didn't come back. We can do this. And with you by my side—"

I pull away from him. "By your side? As you lead even more people to their deaths? This is atrocious. Can't you see past—it's like y-you only see through this lens of destruction. All of you!" I raise my voice over the room. "You grew up at the end of a war and it colors everything you see. You try to fix things, but you just keep amplifying the destruction. I-I can't let you do this."

Hardkeeper scoffs. "You have no choice."

"Don't I? I can call a legion of wraiths to my side," I say, and I'm shaking now. "I could stop you and the darksmiths and Vor all at once. Forget this. Koglim. Bring us to Tungsten City. We're ending this the right way."

My father whispers something sharp to Hardkeeper. There he is—my secretive father. But whatever he's planning has little to do with protecting me.

"You got it, boss," Koglim says.

The second he gets Icho out, his body jerks forward. Starting at the top of his head, particles flake off his body until he's made only of mist. Everyone jumps back. Hardkeeper steps forward, and Koglim's ashes swirl around his hand—no, they're entering the round iron sphere in Hardkeeper's hands. A husk.

Then my hands start to dematerialize. Hardkeeper already has another husk out, pulling me in.

"Therias, stop this!" Mom reaches out for me, but it's too late.

There's a strong itching sensation behind my eyes. I squint. When I try to open them again, I only see ash. I'm a mass of carbon atoms, and then everything goes black.

A cold, black, iron prison.

That's it.

Time enters a place that has no meaning. My thoughts are sharp, angry, but unfocused. I imagine flashes of a battle in Tungsten City. Vor's slippery silver crown. Bright gunshots echo like firelight competing with the neon backdrop of the city. The darkmages pull down buildings while my father's metal fire rains from the brightstorm above.

How could I let this happen? What had my father whispered to Hardkeeper? Capture them? Did he say the word husk? Is that what I heard? Hardblaze Dungeon is known for its connection to silver slavery. Maybe I *should* have torn down the dungeons, torn down all the craft when I had the chance.

REAP THEIR FEARS

AN ITCH BUILDS, impossible to scratch. Light and substance bleed back into the world like poured paint. Half of my body has reformed. The lower half is still coming together when I see Yinzar standing alongside Hemdi and Winta.

Yinzar grabs a husk on the table and crosses the room. With heavy tongs, he drops it into a fire. I try to speak, but I'm still disoriented. The command center is empty. Has everyone already left to face Vor? The first clear word from my mouth is, "Brick."

Hemdi comes to my side. "You okay?"

"No."

Yinzar brings the super-heated husk closer to us and smashes it on the ground. Koglim slowly reforms next to me. Yinzar grabs the next husk.

"Yeah," I say. "How long was I—"

"About two hours," Winta says. "And thanks to you, your father locked us up when we refused to go with them. Yinzar broke us out first. Don't worry. Jeiah is around somewhere."

I rub my face. "Two hours? Where's Lagnar?"

Hemdi frowns. "I'm not sure what happened in the protodungeons, but he and your father are getting along. Though Lagnar did try to convince him of your plan.

I scan the closest Bluelink display. It shows Tungsten City and thousands of red and blue dots. "So, everyone…"

"Attack pattern fourteen. The fight is mostly going our way. Tas and Sira are hiding out in the forge district. Sira gave Tas her craftprint, and he's protecting the knights. The assault is happening all over the city. A bit hard to keep track of, but the darksmiths are budging everywhere. They're holding some citizens hostage, trying to run out the clock on Tas' borrowed craftprint. Meanwhile, your dad and the conjurers are attacking Vor's position at Everfalls."

Jeiah appears from out of a hallway. She spots me. Relief hits her visibly, and she rushes to me. I draw her into a hug. "Hey, I'm sorry they—"

"Nothing to apologize for. You're right about this. There are already mass casualties on both sides, including some of the hostages. It's bad. The wraiths are the only way to stop this."

"But Ara—"

Yinzar interrupts. "Ara sent me away. We did it. Took the cup from Erikzin's dungeon. She just… budged me here."

Every fear my father and Hardkeeper voiced hurtles toward me. What if I was wrong about Ara too? "What happened?"

Yinzar shakes his head. "The dungeon opened right to its heart. It must be the key, or maybe Erikzin Brightstorm wanted us to free him. It's like the dungeon needed to be destroyed. She went to search for Dyn."

"Dyn?"

"That's the Dura she believes to be Erikzin Brightstorm."

A tickle of recognition pulls the back of my mind. Dyn. I know that Dura. He was in the park when Sira and I went to breakfast, performing water acrobatics. And I saw him again in the water tank in the VIP lounge at StoneYoke. How could I have come so close to him and not known him?

I gather all this information and let it fly away. Ara will have to deal with that—far away from Vor and the Everfalls. There are more important things right now. "Jeiah, what's the status update for Tungsten City?"

"Vor's using his crown, predictably. But not on everyone. Maybe he's still trying to get them to think he's vulnerable, I don't know, but we should still be able to piggyback off Tas' power for a moment. There were five thousand under his—well, Sira's—protection at first but there have been hundreds of casualties. All the knights and conjurers were implanted with these silver coins. If we're going to Tungsten City, we'll need to do the same. And they need to be monitored. There are some disruptions to the craftprint when people budge."

"I can do that from here," Winta says. "Everyone ready?"

Koglim shrugs. "Sure. Why not? We're just bringing an army of wraiths down on the last remaining city under granite and trying to wrestle an overpowered, mithrium-forged crown away from a maniacal sentient Dura. What's the big deal."

We all snort, then Jeiah turns to Hemdi. She tugs the collar of her shirt to one side so he can slice her skin. He pushes in the silver coin, quickly healing the cut.

"Sorry," he offers.

Koglim goes next.

Then Hemdi comes around to me. Koglim can budge me using Icho, but the coin is direct craft—skin to metal. "I'll have the wraiths. If Vor tries to control me, just budge me back here."

Jeiah voices her discomfort with a grunt.

"It's the best we've got. Besides, if I'm right, Vor is waiting for me at the bottom of Everfalls. But he doesn't know about the wraiths." I look at Koglim. "Let's go."

"Hardkeeper is gonna pay for putting me in that husk," Koglim says, readying Icho.

"He's on our side," Yinzar says.

"We're going there to stop this permanently," I say. "There are no sides. If Hardkeeper gets in the way, I'll have General Songborn take his craft too." I nod to Koglim, who smiles back.

Immediately, we appear in a large field in the apex. Yinzar on my right, Koglim and Jeiah on my left. The brightstorm over my head fills the entire sky. How can it have grown so large? A searing pain floods the space behind my eyeballs. The whispers return in full force.

Clayson. We're here.

At first, the words are so clear but immediately get lost in a sea of whispers. If Vor's not responsible, and the Dura wraiths aren't responsible, then what triggered the change in the brightstorms? The answer I keep circling is a dangerous one: Brightstorm Dungeon. Something we did, something Rugnus and Andalynn did. But even Idulel couldn't see what it was... if she was telling the truth.

All I know is that I need to hurry.

Ahead of us, there are flashes of craft. A group of knights sprints from the tree line blasting a larger group of darksmiths with all the craft they can bring to bear. One of the darksmiths falls prone and doesn't move.

I step away from the others and stretch my arms outward. "General Songborn!"

There are a few seconds of quiet. The darksmiths spot me. Against the power of the gathering brightstorms, a mass of sparkling clouds rises. It swarms over the trees. One by one, all who had been trapped in the dungeons as wraiths appear in the clearing.

"Follow me and drain anyone who gets in our way."

Over the gunfire in the clearing, I hear the whispers of my champion name on the lips of every conjurer, Knight, and darksmith alike—Wraithking. Halfway across the field, I pass a huddled group of knights crouched behind a large boulder. A charge of lightning scores the other side of the boulder forming a black scar.

When the attacking darksmiths see me, the jagged bolts of lightning immediately swing my way. I stand tall, my body rigid with confidence. I have neither craft nor relic, but I have anger. The wraiths around me breathe in my rage like craft itself. The wraith cloud washes over me, absorbing the elemental attack, and when it swirls back around, the darksmiths are curled up on the ground.

One of the knights peeks out from behind the boulder.

I shout at them. "How far away is my father?"

"He's at the turbine on the lake!"

Another one shakes his head. "The assault would have started. He's halfway to the bottom of Everfalls by now."

I step back toward them as General Songborn appears behind me. "One of you will lead me there."

All three knights shake their heads, terrified. One of them speaks. "Just... please. D-don't. H-he should be easy to find. He's the King. Ide keep me."

"Through the trees, there," another manages to point a wary finger, holding his arm close to his chest.

The General sneers at them. "If only I had the power to make soldiers weep like this in life. I could have shortened the Mithrium War by centuries."

"Leave them," I order. "We need to get to the turbine."

I search behind me for Jeiah and Koglim, but they keep a large berth between us. Yinzar is the closest. "Can you avoid the knights and the conjurers? I need to know they will be safe around me. And my friends."

Brief discomfort shows in what's left of Songborn's mouth, but he gives me his acceptance with a drawn-out nod. He is my General, and I am his King. He will follow orders.

I call Jeiah, Koglim, and Yinzar, but they don't move. I'm surrounded by wraiths. I tell the General to hold his position and run back to them. "Jeiah, there's a turbine ahead. Can you pull up a map and lead me there?"

"Uh, yeah. I can probably get a read on your dad too. Hold on. Winta, did you catch that?" Jeiah makes a quick adjustment to the public volume of her bluelink connection. "Can you repeat that?"

Winta's voice blares, "He's down there alright. But you can't just budge. He's got all the foilgrips in the world." There's a low buzz of sound, then she says. "Are you guys catching the reading from the brightstorm? What the brick is going on?"

Jeiah scans a long line of floating text, then tosses her head back. "The brightstorm is nearly fifty times denser than it was a month ago. There are all kinds of strange signatures. It's not just one brightstorm."

I feel it again. That familiar tug in my stomach. Geum Ide. Its brightstorm didn't disappear. "They're all budging into this one."

"That is what I've suspected," Yinzar says. "The question is: how?"

Jeiah's eyes widen. She scrambles through a dance of gestures, and then her mouth drops open. "The signature for Geum Ide's brightstorm. I can't believe it. That's why the signatures are all out of whack for Tungsten City."

"Guys wait," Koglim says. "Do you get it? I can't be the only one."

I look at him blankly. "I thought I did."

"It's all of them. Every single brightstorm, from every fallen city. Everywhere, maybe even as far as Zal Kakraja or Dashen. Who made them, guys. Who made them?"

"Fizzblood," Jeiah says. "If Ara found Erikzin Brightstorm..."

I shake my head. "But this was happening before Ara destroyed his dungeon. And it's calling me. Whispering. I don't wanna believe it, but what if Vor was pretending not to know anything about it? The brightstorms are combined above the Everfalls, a creation he's been forging."

"Interesting," Yinzar says. "But I will point out that if Vor is the one behind this—whatever he's planning—we are wasting time."

Jeiah shrugs, looking overwhelmed. "A wraith's cradle, then."

We return to General Songborn, who takes my orders without further question. We fly toward the outer ring of trees. The brightstorm tugs again at my heart as we pass under the sparse foliage. Will this brightstorm fail too? What is Vor's plan? But the pieces won't click together.

I force my legs to move faster. Koglim and Jeiah easily keep pace with me. The moment we break through the trees, I skid to a halt, taking a deep breath. At my feet, a cascade of stairs leads to the edge of a pristine lake, bordered in metal—a perfect, flawless oval stretching a few city blocks.

At the center of the lake, there looks to be a deep ravine where the water drops into the underbelly of the city. Bordering the ravine are dozens of towering brown buildings with neon yellow stripes. Somehow the beauty of this place raises a surge of freight deep inside me, and a wave of hopeless anger growls somewhere in my throat.

"Everfalls," Jeiah says.

"The greatest anti-budge in all of Loamin architecture," Koglim adds.

"Made a hundred times stronger by Vor," Yinzar offers.

"And the turbines?" I ask.

"In the buildings on the edge of the falls."

I shake loose feelings of dread and fear. "Then we budge to the buildings with Icho."

"Can't," Jeiah says. "The anti-budge extends to the lake's edge. You can only pass that boundary with the lamp posts."

I follow her finger down the stairs to the edge of the lake. A short lamp post sits unlighted, poking from the ground like a stretched-out fire hydrant. I turn to General Songborn. "Can you physically carry me to the center of the lake?"

"Of course." He orders two of the undead knights to my side.

My grandfather, Koglim, and Jeiah pound down the steps, perhaps to avoid the host of wraiths transforming back into a cloud of fog and pulsing light.

When Koglim touches the lamp, there's a brilliant pulse of brown light, and Koglim folds into himself. I haven't seen a budge like this one before. Yinzar goes next. Jeiah waits for a second, staring up at me. She opens her mouth to call out, but then she sighs and shakes the words from her head.

I open my mouth to speak, not knowing what will come out. "Jeiah—"

"Don't." Abruptly, she places her hand on the lamppost, blinks, and folds inward. She becomes almost two-dimensional.

I'm never going to be able to tell her how I feel.

"Onward." The two knights seize me, and I'm absorbed into the cloud, surrounded at once by muffled screams as we fly forward. Almost as fast as a budge, we materialize on a long pier overlooking the falls, thundering water roars in my ears. Half of the myriad of waterfalls are overlaid with transparent aluminum foilgrips floating in the void.

Jeiah, Koglim, and Yinzar emerge from a building at gunpoint flanked by conjurers. More knights pursue them out of the building. I expect my father to appear—blood rises to my face, and I square my stance to face him—but it's not him. He's sent Hardkeeper to deal with me. A few other men and women flank him. Most of them I don't know, but Lagnar is with them, looking anywhere but in my direction.

None of the others look happy to see me. And, with one look at the wraiths, the crowd of knights at the edge of the group stutter-steps backward. I expect my friends to join me, but even they come only so close.

"Clayson Brightstorm," Hardkeeper's voice is amplified over the rush of water. "Disperse your wicked force and surrender."

The General appears on my left. "Shall we take their strengths, my King?"

The glimmer in his dead eyes sends a chill down my spine. I could so easily release them to attack Hardkeeper, but what would the conjurers holding guns do in the few seconds it will take the wraiths to reach them. "Hold General. Wait here for my orders."

I walk close enough that Hardkeeper will hear my voice over the water. "Where are my parents?"

Hardkeeper glances toward the ravine, and for a second, I think he means he threw them in, but he speaks. "Vor is deep in the ravine. We have him trapped there. Your father and mother went in with a company of knights. The orders are to eliminate him on sight."

I step even closer, and the knights adjust their stances. The conjurers tighten up on their rifles. "Hardkeeper. I... we can help."

"Get it through your head, son. You're not needed here. This is working. Sira and Tas are secure. They're providing us plenty of strength in this fight, enough to overpower the darkmages. And might I remind you of your broken oath with the council. You've entered multiple dungeons since that time. That will have to be a part of any future discussion I have with, or about, you."

"How many casualties?"

Hardkeeper's face sets like cooling metal. "As many as are necessary to end this battle."

"Then let me help. I can send the wraiths out into the surrounding area. Without their strength, they will be easier to subdue. They'll surrender. No one else has to die. See reason."

One woman next to Hardkeeper speaks up. "Reason? Our valiant soldiers would rather lose their life than their craft."

"They will lose both if you don't let me help. General Songborn and the wraiths are under my orders to attack only darksmiths. Hardkeeper, we don't have to argue. We're wasting time. You're taking the focus off Vor."

Hardkeeper pinches the bridge of his nose and speaks with the group around him. They hold up their fingers like they're voting. That's when I realize that these aren't just random Loamin. They're keepers. Lagnar Bluekeeper is part of the council. He's reforming the council. Tradition must return to its honored place.

Hardkeeper pushes his way to the front of the group, pauses for a second with an eye on the wraiths, and walks over to me, extending an arm. "Your wraiths can engage with the darksmiths out in the city, the ones hunting for Tas and Rensira Silverlamp."

I grab his wrist and pump his arm to test strengths. "Good, now—"

"But keep them away from here. And for every knight or conjurer they drain, you will spend one year in Keelcrawl prison, Clayson Oathbreaker."

The air temperature cools twenty degrees. "Fine. General Songborn, you have your orders. You understand what to do?"

"Orders received *Wraithking*."

The cloud whirls above me again. It takes flight over the whole group, nearly skimming their heads. One of the conjurers fires into the cloud in complete fright. Two of the knights send out white shields over the group.

"Hold," Hardkeeper yells. He turns around and says, "Follow."

Inside the building, a makeshift command center clutters the marble floors and walls. Along the outside rim, a half dozen bluemages stand manipulating bluelink data. At the center of the only room, the floor is cut out, revealing a massive turbine churning the water beneath us. A railing protects people from accidentally tumbling over the side. Darkness frames the turbine. The shaft appears to extend to the bottom of the ravine.

"Brightstorm!" Hardkeeper barks. "Get over here."

I step into the circle made up of the council members and generals. Nasur Lavalock—my grandmother's faithful conjurer lapdog—looks completely disgusted by my presence. I nod to him with a smile, and he nearly chokes.

Hardkeeper turns to a glowing map of the ravine. It's a complicated system of tunnels and stairways, crisscrossed with swift-moving rivers and pounding waterfalls. Large flashing brown drains at the bottom show how the water loops back to the edge of the lake and keeps the whole system continually running. But I can tell what Vor has added. Large, mismatched planes of glass float in thousands of places. He must have found every foilgrip in the city—no, every budge—and made the people install it all here.

"Vor is here." Hardkeeper points a finger at the bottom center. "Your parents and the knights are closing in on him." He shouts over my head to the bluemages. "I want tracking data on these wraiths."

The same council member from before speaks up. "And the darksmiths?"

"Everywhere. The knights have come across three separate pockets of—watch."

The lights representing the knights and my parents blink and flash as they engage another group of dots. Hardkeeper replaces the map with some type of body camera footage.

A stutter of light flashes. The camera angle breaks from its first-person viewpoint and zooms above the group. My father steps into the frame as a darksmith draws blackened plants out of the surrounding water. The plants seize two knights by their necks and drag them under the water. My father is covered in the scarlet light of ironcraft. A long tendril of the plant whips forward and snares his leg.

The darksmith's eyes widen, and his face goes ashen with fear for two seconds. I think he might untangle the web of plants around him and fall to his knees. Instead, from the top of his head, red fissures appear, splitting his face with volcanic cracks until, all at once, he becomes flecks of firelight and smoke. Obliterated.

The light leaves my father's body. "Forward!" he orders. The live footage retreats into a small box next to the map. "See," Hardkeeper says. "With the return of your parents to the throne, balance is restored. Individuals like these darksmiths can have no purchase in the world."

This is why my father left the throne. After years of taking care of him, I simply can't recognize this other person. He killed that man.

Then my mom's face crosses the frame, and I step back. Her

skin is chalk pale, lacerated with broken veins of gold and a sickly orange. This is the cost of killing Grimflail and freeing everyone under his control. Using craft is killing her. One more reason to get down there as fast as I can.

Against the drumming, and quickening of my heartbeat, an alarm chirps over the whole room. Another section of the command center hums with frantic energy.

"Status!" Hardkeeper calls. One of the knights sprints toward us.

"Sir. Tas and the Silverlamp girl are under siege. We think—"

"What?"

The man tries to continue, but more frantic yelling comes from the section with the alarm. "Sir. Sira is gone. The darksmiths have her."

"What? How? Where are the wraiths?"

"All over the place. Dozen of the darksmiths are fleeing, but Sira—sir, it was Kel. The other Dura. We didn't see her coming. She—"

"Wraithspit!" Hardkeeper thunders. "Curse that vacant hound." Hardkeeper nearly shoves me backward. The crowd of leaders coalesces around him as I'm pushed to the side. "Get this under control right now!"

"The darksmiths are gone, sir. I—they seem to... Tas is dead."

Cold fingers pull me away from them. "Dead?"

Hardkeeper shouts. "I need options! Now! Can Vor control us?"

After more commotion, another bluemage pipes up from across the room. "I'm not sure what I'm seeing. Something else is balancing out the crown. Our craft readings say it-it's equal to the crown."

Hardkeeper whispers a name. "Ara."

I spin back to my friends.

Koglim is bouncing on his feet, ready for a fight. That's when the whole building cracks from floor to ceiling along one side in an ear-splintering boom! Behind them, the wall burst outward, and a flood of darksmiths charge in, lit by the colors of their deadly crafts. Koglim, Hemdi, and Jeiah are knocked to the ground.

Icho flies out of Koglim's grip.

The conjurers respond with a wall of bullets, forcing me to dive to the ground just in time to catch Icho from tumbling into the turbine well. Hardkeeper rises from the ground, and for a moment, I think it's some goldcraft like my father. But it's one of the darksmiths. Hardkeeper's body is stretched limb-to-limb until something pops. He goes limp, plummeting to the ground.

We need the wraiths, or none of us will survive this attack. My voice rises through the air. "Help!"

Seconds later, a dozen wraiths spin through the opening, draining the darksmiths. Their angry cries fill the air, but when the wraiths withdraw, their anger becomes understanding and wrath. The wraiths can only take a single craft. I had been relying on their fear of losing craft to the wraiths, but for the wicked, anger is stronger than fear. The newly angered darksmiths switch to secondary crafts and continue their attack.

Helpless, I crawl toward Hardkeeper; Jeiah and Koglim are too far away. Where's Yinzar? Shouted commands and raging battle cries tear through the air. I reach Hardkeeper's body, but he's dead. Jeiah and Koglim are facing off against the darksmiths, a sheen of soft shieldcraft white around them. It won't last.

Hands claw at my shirt, and I find Yinzar before me, shouting. His words are drowned out by breaking concrete and a thunderstorm of gunfire. He has one of Hardkeeper's husks in his hands, pointing and shouting to the well.

"What?" I shout.

"...down the well. You and the wraiths. If I'm right, Ara will not be far behind." He shakes the husk again and shoves a rifle at me. "I can time it just right."

"You want me to go back into the husk? Are you crazy?"

"Most of the time. And don't tell your mother I did this. You are our brightest hope, Clayson. I couldn't be prouder of my grandson."

"But—"

"No more discussion."

He slides a piece of the husk into place, and the same strange sensation from last time hits me. I become immaterial, sucked into the husk. It's worse than a bad budge. I try to count to thirty, but the numbers don't make any sense. Not that anything could. It's a good thing I don't need craft for other people to shove me in a box or budge me everywhere.

It's with that thought that I burst back into the world. I'm still five feet away from the surface, and I hit a walkway hard, sliding off and tumbling through a spray of water into a pool of crystal blue. I left my breath at the site of the impact.

The rifle slips from my shoulder, and I dive after it, holding my breath. Just as my fingers wrap around the barrel and pull, a rain of stones hits the waterline above me. What's happening? The stones drop unnaturally, forming into something with jagged teeth and a snaking body. It lunges.

Wraithspit.

I fire off the rifle, sending lines of spinning metal through the water. It does nothing. My legs frantically kick toward the surface. It lunges again, and I dodge to one side, rock scraping a gash in my leg, but I make it to air, taking in a gasping breath.

Blood clouds the water at my feet as I scramble onto the walkway. I look up past long stairways and a hundred waterfalls and sheets of glass. It's an impossible, fantastic view, and on a good day, I could find the beauty of this place without all of Vor's unsightly additions. I catch a stream of misted clouds drifting downward. A wraith forms from the cloud, and at the same moment, an avalanche of stone rockets out of the water and lands on the deck, this time forming something on four massive paws.

I command the wraith. "Find the darksmith responsible for this!"

The wraith flies through the waterfall behind the rock monster.

A lump forms in my throat as I try to swallow my breath. The jaw of the rock monster stays slack, exposing a sharp, cruel line of teeth still dripping with bloody water. It's got a taste for me.

I run.

As fast as I can, I sprint in the other direction. The monster explodes into action leaping over me to block my path. So much for running. Turning again, I try the other direction. Would I be better off in the water? No. Then the whole walkway trembles. I don't stop running. On my right, I see another walkway through a waterfall and jump for it, landing hard on the metal.

I twist around, expecting to see the monster, jaws ready, prepared to cut through my flesh. But nothing happens. I side step the waterfall and look back. The stones lay in a pile on the walkway. The wraith is briefly visible before returning to a vapor.

"Help me find my father!" I call out.

It moves past me on the walkway, and I chase after it.

Two more darksmiths block the way ahead. One of them dives out of the way as we come crashing through, but the other takes the full weight of the wraith. I see the cloud transform into half a person, latching onto the woman and inhaling. She screams, but it's just swallowed up in the waterfall's roar.

Before she can switch to another craft, I leave her there. A descending stairway spirals to our left, and the wraith careens down to the base. I hurry down the stairs, adrenaline pumping into my heart and out to my limbs, but I feel the tug of the brightstorm again. The whispers.

Together.

I force them away from me. I have enough of a timer.

At the bottom of the stairs, I stutter to a stop.

Sira.

Another darksmith—claws like a lion—has her wrapped tightly in his grasp. We're close. I know Vor is ahead of me. The wraith glances at me, unsure, awaiting orders. Attacking the darksmith will mean attacking Sira. I bring my sights up.

"Let her go!" I shout down the barrel of the rifle.

"Your wraiths don't attack if we are close enough to our hostages. Drop your weapon, and I won't burn her pretty face."

"Clayson, please! Just—" her last word is cut off as the man squeezes her throat.

"Shut up!"

Two more wraiths materialize. General Songborn is one of them. Somehow his cheeks flush for a second, and a gray-brown tone returns briefly to the broken flesh. His appetite for Loamin craft is insatiable. "We need more!"

"Wait," I order, but I can feel my control slipping away.

"This is foolish," he says. "Your enemy is ahead of you. Free us to help you."

"No!" I tighten my aim.

"Shoot him!" Sira screams. But the man clamps down on her neck again.

I have to stop this. With a roar, I squeeze the trigger.

Nothing. The gun is jammed.

"You're wasting time," General Songborn says. "Your allies are willing to sacrifice themselves. I can taste it in the air. Forward."

The rifle nearly drops from my hand when I reach out for the General's arm, but he's vaporous again. The place where the darksmith stood with Sira is shrouded in light and smoke. In only a second, Sira emerges from the cloud, sprinting toward me, but I know it's too late. The wraiths were all over her. Silvercraft—her strength—will have been taken from her. I was powerless to stop them, just like when Hemdi lost his tincraft.

Twenty feet from me, Sira is knocked backward by a burst of wind. Kel, winged from whatever craftprint she has absorbed, drops between us, copper tattoos pulsing over her body. Reptile skin covers where her hair should be. Her forked tongue slips over pointed teeth, and she snarls.

"I felt it, you know!" Her voice drips with poison. She is more Torlina Wolfstaff than Kel in this moment.

Confusion settles over me. "I don't understand."

"I felt when my son died. Landred. I may not remember much from my life, but he came with me into my dungeon, and he died with your name echoing in his mind. For that, you deserve to die."

CAST OTHER SHADOWS

Sira screams as Kel's claws dig into her arm. Kel's split tongue tests the air, basking in the fear of this prey. "I'm bringing you back to Vor."

My fingers itch against the rifle's trigger, trying once more to squeeze. Nothing. I let the lifeless weapon clatter to the ground. I have the wraiths at my side, but they are useless against Dura. Dura use craft differently than Loamin, so there's nothing to take. The only thing I have left is to reason with her.

"I didn't kill Landred. I helped him."

"Lies."

"No, listen. We found him on the surface. He needed our help to get to Gamgim. But I didn't know what would happen. I couldn't have known."

Kel looks behind her as if Vor could be right there listening. She shakes Sira. "I'm supposed to keep this one alive, but if you don't tell me the truth…"

"I'm telling the truth. We went to Gamgim. The wraiths there killed him. Kel, I know you're angry, but you've gotta understand Vor doesn't care about anyone but himself."

"You think I don't know that!" Kel shouts. "I'm happy to help him. The Loamin deserve every punishment we give them."

This isn't working. "What about Tas? Is he really dead? They said he was. Did you help with that? I can't imagine that killing other Dura is what you signed up for."

"Enough!" she snarls. "Tas was helping you, helping Loamin. Now listen. Get in front of us and follow my directions. If you make any other move, I will kill her. Then I will kill you, despite what Vor wants. I'm not the best follower of orders. And don't think we don't know you were emptied of craft. Vor knows."

I move slowly across the bridge, taking a position in front of them. She orders me deeper into the center of Everfalls. Darkmages flank me. We move under bridges, past gurgling ponds, and over a walkway painted with blood spray and broken vines— where my father killed that darkmage. My heart grows heavy. The bodies of a few conjurers drift by in crystalline rivers, rifles still strapped to their backs.

At the largest waterfall yet, a darksmith raises the drumming water like a curtain. Another one pushes me forward, laughing.

At the center of a large basin, Vor stands, hands clasped in front of him.

The whole basin is a massive floor drain, and I have to step carefully, or my feet could slip through the grating.

Kel flies over me and lands next to Vor, still clutching Sira.

Vor meets my eyes and steps to the side, pointing with his crooked sword. My parents lay unconscious in glimmering silver chains at his feet. Mom's blanched skin reveals the gold-orange sickness that has only worsened. Behind them lies a glowing forge. The mithrium glares from a large crucible, already liquified.

"A bit early," Vor says. "I thought it would take you longer to reach the bottom. Using a husk was clever. But I'm ready anyway. I had a few of the darksmiths start the forge, and everything is prepared to finish making my next cool thing."

Torlina's staff leans against the forge. I scoff. "You think you can make something of the staff?"

"Well," Vor glances at Kel. "That was a thought. But not my real plan."

Kel cast him a venomous stare. Her mouth opens, but Vor cuts her off.

"Patience, Kel. All in good time."

Her face hardens. "That is the only other piece of mithrium we have. You can't—"

"I can!" Vor thunders. He groans with exasperation. "See, Clayson. This is why we have to make the crown stronger. Sure, we can make something out of the staff, or—I see you have Tas' useless relic—Icho could make a fun little tool, but no. No, there's a better Idea. It's always Ara's shield versus my crown—Ergal versus Onrix. Well, no longer. We're going to add another piece of mithrium to my crown. It will be twice as powerful. Beautiful. I might even be able to control other Dura with it."

I give a pointed look to Kel. "You can't seriously want this."

"Don't bother with that, Clayson," Vor says.

"And how exactly do you think we can use the recipe without opposite energy?"

Vor laughs. "Oh, I didn't think you were that thick. You didn't figure it out?" He lifts his arms in some grand display, gesturing all around him.

Everfalls. The new foilgrips. He's been filling this place with energy to counteract the recipe. It was never meant to be a prison. I think of the filament from the graybulbs we use to extend the shield. All we had to do was wrap the tungsten around the shield, and it absorbed some of its power. "The foilgrip uses the energy from the brightstorm. That's why you forced the Loamin to build more of them. That's why you're gathering the brightstorms."

Vor scoffs. "Partially right. The foilgrips, yes, but the brightstorms... I got to hand it to you... whatever you did to get them all gathering together—even if we can't figure it out—it's only making the foilgrips stronger. So, thank you."

"Why wait for me? Anyone can drop an item into the mithrium using the recipe."

Vor shakes his head. "No. Didn't you use someone peerless?"

I look at the crown. "I'm not peerless in silvercraft."

Vor strides up to Sira, pulling her from Kel's arms. "She is. And we were almost ready with the foilgrips... but she ran off. Raising teenagers is tough. Give them an inch..." He sighs. "You think this was about you? Nope. You're powerless, I hear. You are less than that, just an assurance that Sira will do what I tell her. She loves you, Clayson, and love is a more dangerous weapon than any craft. Well, and I wanted to see your face when I did this. Ego, I know."

But Sira's tears have dried up. She's laughing. The pure sound rises over the echoing water deep down the drain. The giggle turns into something sharper, victorious.

Vor doesn't look amused. "Stop it, Sira. What's wrong with you?"

"It's weird," she says, her canines visible through a smile. Her freckles dance on her face like starlight. "I was so afraid of losing my craft to the wraiths. I was already a near null in budgecraft, so without silvercraft what would I be? Nothing. But I was wrong. I'm stronger now. You can't control me."

"What are you talking about?" Vor snaps.

General Songborn materializes with a dozen wraiths at the side of the drain. A few of the darksmiths shrink back, but most of them tighten their grip on whatever objects and relics they have left, perhaps already drained of what makes them the most dangerous.

"She lost her silvercraft to the wraiths," Kel says.

I stay silent. We were never sure that someone peerless was needed to craft mithrium objects. It's nothing that Exralt mentioned. But I was peerless in shieldcraft when I forged something from Ergal, and Sira was peerless in silvercraft when she made Vor's crown. If it's not true, it still causes a much-needed distraction.

Vor simmers in anger. "You think that matters? I'll make her do it anyway."

Kel steps between Vor and the forge. "Stop! You'd waste the mithrium just to slake your anger?"

Vor pushes Sira to the forge. "Out of my way, Kel!"

Kel straightens. In one beat of her powerful wings, she knocks Vor across the basin. He flies past me as she rushes forward, claws glistening. He rolls out of the fall, bringing his sword up to meet an attack. But his crown lies upside-down.

I glance at my parents, lying still. Are they even breathing?

If I can use Ara's shield, then maybe... no thinking. I surge forward to grab the crown. Kel slams into Vor, and he stumbles back, kicking the crown with his heel. It tumbles toward the darksmiths, and they scatter. The forge is at my back now, Sira at my side working to undo the chains around my parents, but unable to break the silvercraft. I can't get to the crown without going through Vor.

Vor rams his sword through Kel. I blink. No. Her body becomes a luminous form against the waterfall, and I have to look away, but not before I see Vor's sword being drawn out. He killed her.

When the light clears, there is only a pale mark on the metal drain, sun-washed and blank. She's gone. One more in a long line of Vor's victims. Kel maybe even deserved this, but I won't let him kill again. That's an oath I must keep. A hot fury simmers somewhere inside of me. It's good Jassin emptied me of all my craft; it leaves more room for this growing anger.

Vor lifts his crown from the ground. With a disgusted head shake, he says, "It did not have to be that way, but... it's done. Clayson, I don't care who makes it at this point, but one of you will cast a new crown for me. You don't have a choice."

I glance at Sira. "We always have a choice, Vor." I throw her Icho.

Her jaw sets. She drops Icho into the crucible with the liquid mithrium.

The second it hits the mithrium, it melts like butter. I find a lever on the crucible and turn the whole solution over into a long mold, enduring an ear-splitting whistle like the falling of a nuclear bomb. If Vor is wrong about the opposite power of the foilgrips, we'll all be dead. I take comfort in that fact as much as I can. Vor can't shield himself from a mithrium bomb.

At my feet, the water begins to reverse from out of the drain, pulled toward the mithrium-filled mold. Sira and I step back. I drag Mom further from the forge, and Sira drags Dad, the chains still wrapped around them. Vor screams at us to stop, but his crown is still useless. Somewhere out in the city, Ara is blocking him. I wish she had been here with us.

The waterfalls around the drain reverse direction now too. Darksmiths are fleeing in terror. As they should. The mold pulses with bands of electricity. My hearing ebbs and flows until every sound is absorbed into the vacuum of the mithrium object. The world buzzes and shakes. My vision blurs. Then all at once, the sound returns with the obliteration of thousands of transparent aluminum foilgrips—undoing everything Vor had made and more.

The sand-fine particles of the foilgrips join with the waterfalls, cascading in a brilliance that competes with the brightstorm. A mist swells from the ground. Inside it, the mold is dark. When it finally bursts, the swollen outline of a sword hovers in the fog.

Time and space seem to stretch out.

I step forward, thinking only of Rugnus, who didn't live to see what Icho would become. What would he think of what I did? When my hand finds the sword's grip, the fog glitters away. Vor stares at me. Sira and my parents are behind me.

Through the power of Icho, now resting in the mithrium sword, I sense a network of budgecraft. Lagnar. I sense him. His intentions are the most prominent. He has dozens of knights at his command, trying to budge to us. Koglim, Jeiah, Yinzar are all trying to budge here as well. I prevent them all. No one else needs to face Vor today.

He paces the drain floor, his sword scraping against the metal, ticking like a bomb. I tighten what was once Icho in my hands. If

I can't get justice for Rugnus any other way, I can at least use Icho to defeat Vor.

We don't get the chance. A light swells between us.

"Ara?"

The mithrium shield shines on her arm. Next to her, Dyn stands with a soft smile. The mithrium we freed from the Forest of Ide is in his hands. For a second, I only see the man from the park the day Sira and I first met, and the acrobat in the water performance in the VIP lounge at StoneYoke. But he smiles, and dimples form on his cheeks. Maybe he is Erikzin Brightstorm.

He bows slightly with a satisfied smile. "Hello, Clayson. Don't be alarmed. Ara explained everything: who I truly am, the Dura, the creation. I'm sorry. At first, I didn't want to come to you. But I'm glad Ara helped me see the truth."

Vor scoffs. "You found more mithrium. Good. I don't know what Ara told you, Dyn, but—"

Dyn holds up a hand to Vor. "I don't need to hear your side of things, thank you. Ara was kind enough to give me this." Dyn extends his hand, holding a mesh cup made of every metal. It's like a summator, the baskets used to call people into the dungeons for summation, but it's also similar to the cradle, the birthplace of the brightstorms.

Sira whispers confirmation. "The cradle."

Even deep in this ravine, the light of the brightstorm reaches for me. No, not the brightstorm, the *brightstorms*. New whispers bloom in my mind, and I can almost sense Andalynn and Rugnus next to me. They had died in Dyn's dungeon, and now it's destroyed. With the dungeon truly gone, any hope of finding them alive is gone with it. Though I've known that, the hurt is somehow newly fresh. The scar opens back up, and I let in more pain. I saw their bodies consumed in the flames of the hearth.

Then a familiar fear of the unknown pricks at my mind. Too much is changing. Too much is falling apart around me. I can't see the path ahead of me. There's a danger in the gathering brightstorms.

Vor adjusts the crown on his head. "This isn't over. I've worked for hundreds of years to end the Loamin. I'll keep waiting."

"That's why I'm here, Vor," Ara says, passing me a wary look heavy with implications. "What if I told you there was a way to destroy craft, but I need your help to do that?"

"What is that supposed to mean?" he spits.

"We found the source, but Clayson didn't tell you."

Fear coils around my stomach like an approaching rattlesnake. "What are you doing, Ara?"

She frowns. "After all my years with your father, Clayson. After all those years with the conjurers, I've come to believe what they always have: That Loamin shouldn't draw power from the earth. Maybe it's something more natural that can't be conjured out of anything. If Vor agrees, then we go and break the strand together."

With every bit of determination I have, I keep the look of confusion off my face. There's no lock blocking the entrance to the protodungeons. Maybe Ara is planning something else. Either way, leading Vor into the protodungeons is too dangerous. "Ara, you can't do this."

Still wary, Vor steps closer to her. "What source?"

"You don't remember much from your life, do you?" Ara asks him.

"Same as you. Bits and pieces."

"Yes, we were Loamin. But before that, Loamin and Dura lived together on the surface. Loamin had no craft of their own. It seems—like us—they borrowed craft from Dura."

"Impossible," Vor says. He glances at me with narrowed eyes.

"But with that craft, they borrowed," Ara continues, "they cursed that world, creating the Foundation and everything that goes with it. Dungeons, wraiths, craft, metal. We were the first ones to suffer the fate of that curse. You, Tas, and I became the first champions."

This can't be happening. Vor is the one that made the deal

with the Dura wraiths, whether or not he remembers. "Ara, please. What are you doing? You can't trust Vor with this. You know what he did."

"What is he talking about?"

Ara shakes her head. "He thinks you made a deal with the original Dura, the wraiths trapped in Gamgim because of the curse. He thinks you murdered us and created a seal that blocked the door to the person responsible for this."

"Did I?"

"Even if you did, how were you to know you would stop people from finding their way to the destroyer?"

Vor's eyes narrow even further. "And you want to lead me to this place?"

Ara nods. "We would go together. You want a way for the Loamin to be powerless. This is it."

There's one thing she's holding back: he and Ara will have to die to end this world. They will have to sever the cord… if they can even reach it. But something tells me that once they go back into their dungeons, they will find a way to Idulel, the Forest of Ide, the thread that holds the world's most powerful curse.

Ara makes eye contact with me, a sad smile on her face. There was once a time she couldn't look at me. Before she had the shield. She's been burdened with this curse just as long as Vor has. She means to do this.

"Don't," I say, but the words fall between us without hope or meaning.

Vor smiles and gestures for Ara to lead the way.

"Everything will be okay, Clayson."

The three powerful Dura budge far away from me. Through the mithrium sword, I follow Ara's intention. They're going to Edium Fiarie, the House of the Dead. She had meant every word of what she said.

"I have to follow them."

"But your mother." Sira kneels next to her. Mom's eyes are closed, her chest barely rising and falling. Whatever Grimflail's power did to her, the chains Vor bound her with have made it worse. Craft is tearing her apart.

Maybe it's the mithrium sword's connection to every type of craft, but I sense all the nearby objects. I close my eyes, concentrating. I can feel every object as far as the sword's power extends, past the outskirts of the city. I refocus on my parent's chains and budge them miles away.

Dad immediately stands, breathing sharply. Anger rises to his cheeks. "We have to stop Ara. We can't let them—"

"Dad!" I grab his arm. "Wait. How do we... what can we do?"

He looks down at his wife, stammering. "I don't know. I—"

Sira shakes her head. "She's been trying to say something."

Mom's body shakes. Her eyes snap open again, and she gasps.

"Mom? It's okay. We're here—"

"No," she hisses. "I'm not... my AMP, Clayson."

Sira's hand hovers around my mom, but she's too afraid to touch the swollen golden veins and her papered skin. "What does that mean—her AMP? Not what?"

"It happened on the surface," she says. "No one would have heard it."

"Heard what?" Dad says, dropping to his knees next to her.

Tears spring into her eyes, and her mouth twists into a knot. She chokes. Only an edge of pink remains on Mom's usually rose-blossom cheeks. The sunburst of her strawberry-blonde hair is flat and faded.

She's dying.

Her next gasp is weaker still. "Go, Clayson. Get away. You can't... you can't be here... if I..."

Sira squeaks. "Oh, no."

Dozens of wraiths appear behind me. Songborn's hands become solid, and he tries to drag me away. I fight against him.

"This is not safe," he pronounces. "You can't be here."

"What's happening?" I'm desperate to understand, for someone to rescue her. If I had Ergal or the shield, Mom wouldn't be struggling for breath, but I can't do anything to help her. I should have forced Ara to stay. I should have understood how close to death Mom was.

"Her AMP," Sira says, "She was always so close. The sword she made to kill Grimflail. She must mean—"

Mom nods hard. Then looks at me, her mouth open, unable to speak. She presses something into Dad's hand. Her AMP is crystalline and transparent. Only champions have crystal AMP scores. She reached sixty-three AMP. If she dies here...

Sira stands, searching both directions. "We'll be wraiths."

Dad seizes Mom's hand. Every thought of stopping Ara is gone from his mind. "Go!" He orders us.

"It is too late," Songborn says.

I reach out to budge Sira and Dad away, but Songborn—with a hundred wraiths now—is interfering with the sword. They howl around me in fury. I try to break free of the cloud, but hands materialize and restrain me. "We will protect you!"

"No! No! Protect my dad. Protect Sira."

"They don't matter."

Seconds later, the cloud of wraiths lifts, and the world is painted in dripping gold. The entire drain, the forge, up every wall for a hundred feet, everything in the radius of my mom's death has transformed into gold, still dripping as if it were made of her very blood. Sira and Dad are nowhere to be seen. The door to her dungeon stands solitary. It's the same door from her chambers in the castlestack of Whurrimduum, but it's made of solid gold.

Azbena Bloodfeign is gone. There is only Bloodsword.

The echoing call has a clear source—the brightstorms above. For a moment, the voice is old and parched. It's Idulel.

My mother is gone. Bloodsword Dungeon has risen in her place.

I don't think. I pull open the door and enter. If I can rip the heart out of Wolfstaff, I can do the same to this unholy creation. With Vor gone, I see the villain I know best loom up before me: It has always been the dungeons.

CUT THE WORLD

MY MOTHER IS DURA. Somewhere outside of the dungeon, her new form has appeared like Ara and Vor. Like Tas and Kel and Dyn. Their bodies were transformed, appearing in the world with only a spark of life. Their minds were trapped in their dungeons. Unless someone destroys a dungeon... and I will.

Two seconds past the threshold, vines surround me, squeezing, but I squeeze back. Finding purchase against a thicker vine beneath me, I push upward. I squirm through the vines. I climb because that is something that is always within my power. Climbing upward, dragging and pulling myself toward the unknown, I stretch a hand toward the light but catch hold of a thin vine instead. Still, it works. I hoist myself up and tear through the top layer, spilling out in a bath of sunlight.

I blink a few times, and with each blink, the lights become less sharp, changing color from stark white to a sharp blue, and settling on a cool green wash I would know anywhere. It's the brightstorm over a Whurrimduum night. My eyes stay open, and I'm standing in Everbloom Garden atop the stacks in Whurrimduum.

But it's not Whurrimduum. It's a dungeon. And all around the garden, instead of the city skyline, there is only a pale green dimness.

"Hello?" I test my voice. "Mom?" A whisper follows. "Help me to find you."

But I don't trust that she can hear me.

As I pace over the walkway, the whole scene glows with familiarity. I've been here with Andalynn and with Hemdi. Even Winta and Rugnus visited with me once to see the famous spread of green foliage and the rainbow of colorful blossoms. But Mom never came here with me. She'd been trapped in Geum Ide with Dad or with me on the surface.

My only remembrance of her in this place is from Yinzar's memory garden. He had brought her here to tell her about his intentions of taking the mithrium to make something powerful. To make something that could never be used to destroy. She had been a fearful daughter then, expecting her own child.

Okay, so technically, I have been here with her.

Rounding another corner, I come face to face with Glaris. My mother's mother, the leader of the conjurers before Vor destroyed their settlement months ago. But she's dead.

"Glaris?"

She says her name along with me. "Glaris?"

She moves her hand in sync with mine. When I blink, she blinks. That's when my peripheral vision catches up with me. Her form is framed with a blurry rectangle. She mimics my exact moves as I walk to the side. I reach forward and feel the lip of the long sheet of glass. I peek behind it, and Glaris is gone.

Stepping back in front of her, I say, "It's a mirror."

She says the same thing. Her eyes narrow in confusion—my eyes.

"Okay," we say together.

After pressing on the mirror, even trying to break it with a rock, I give up and resume wandering the garden. A minute later, I find Dad blocking my path.

I rush toward him. Maybe he didn't become a wraith!

But when my arms come up to seize him, he copies me, a mirror as well. This mirror could be of me in some distant future. We've always looked alike, but I feel it more than ever as I stare at what should be my reflection.

I find nearly twenty mirrors with various people. It's Mom's mind or consciousness, and the only thing I can think is that these are all the people that are important to her. Lagnar, members of the council, Yinzar, my father's parents—the former king and queen of the Kingdom of Rimduum. The hardest reflection for me to look at is Andalynn. My face feels pinched as I hold back tears. I can't stay in front of her for longer than a couple seconds.

I leave the established walkways, wandering into the plants and bushes, searching the flowers and the leaves for anything that could give me a clue about what needs to be done here. I'm looking for the Bloodsword. That will be the heart of her dungeon.

But my mind can't bypass the terrible truth of what's happening, and I find myself unable to focus on solving this challenge. I circle the paths. My feet moving me, but my mind is fuzzy, and my body prickles with cold despair. Why? Why did any of this happen to me? I feel pressure in my jaw and realize all my muscles are tense. My hands are fists.

Finally, I take a breath, and it's as if someone presses a button. I sit on the path, wrap my arms around my knees and bury my head.

I stay like this for a long time. Nothing comes in my mind to counteract this fear, this despair. The universe contains no answer to any of my questions. Is there ever an answer to these questions?

Why am I the son of these two people? Why was my life so different from anyone else? The moment I think this, I know the answer—I'm no different. But my challenges are.

That's what pushes me from the ground, the realization that I'm the same as everyone else. My status as Wraithking, the craft taken from me by the Dura wraiths, and even my ability to use mithrium objects, dosen't define who I am. I'm just me. And *just me* needs to get up off the ground and find Mom.

With a long breath, I rise from the path. Maybe I'm seeing more clearly, but in between the plant life, off the established trails, splotches of the grass hold a film of gold.

Examining the paths, I see clear patterns and shapes. The smears of gold paint are rabbit tracks. The sight of golden liquid conjurers up the memory of my mom's touch, of the night we escaped in the camper when she put her golden blood on my face to protect me from being spotted. If I can find something gold, it will lead me forward.

Then, like a bolt of electricity, something strikes my mind. The night I came here with Rugnus and Andalynn. The night we tried to free my mom from Keelcrawl prison. There was a bush with blossoms that dripped with what seemed like golden paint.

I push past the lilac trees, following the small tracks as they wind around the garden. As they cross a short section of the path, the same set of tracks crosses this one. It loops around ahead of me, so I turn in this new direction.

I find the rabbit around the next turn, sniffling and chewing on a thick green leaf.

"Hey, buddy," I say.

The rabbit freezes for a moment and then darts past me. I turn to catch him, but his footprints no longer leave behind the golden paint. I search the whole area, hoping to find the bush with the golden fruit. Nothing.

That's when I notice the footprints fading into the ground. Of course. The rabbit wasn't leading me to something. It came from the bush. I jog back, following the tracks, trying to keep up as they disappear, which happens in increasingly large sections. Around one bend in the path, I find the mirror with Andalynn waiting.

No. I can't focus on her right now. I return to the trail, just catching the footprints as they disappear behind a purple and silver-leafed tree. Behind that, lemon-yellow vines trickle over a golden trellis. I remember this plant—it was nearby the golden one.

I duck around the trellis and grin. It's here. A large tin pot holds a towering bush. Gold-webbed leaves poke through slits in the tin pot, dripping with a golden paint-like substance. The flowers themselves are nearly black. Splashes of gold dot the ground below it.

Relief washes over me for a second, then I return to the task. Unsure of how much to use, I let the golden drops accumulate in my cupped palm. I don't have a way to use this craft, but I try anyway. Scooping the liquid up with the fingers of my other hand, I rub it across my cheeks and forehead.

Nothing happens. Would the dungeon present me with a challenge I can't do? I can't use craft. Maybe I was wrong about the gold plant, but the tracks led me here. That can't be a coincidence.

But her paint doesn't just work for her. It works on others. Could I use it indirectly? The mirrors were trimmed with gold.

Keeping some gold paint in my hand, I search for the mirror. Andalynn. I notice that she's smiling faintly—that I am. It's hard to see her staring back at me, even if it is just a reflection. There's a birthmark on her right cheek she doesn't have. If that's not out of the ordinary, I'm not sure what else to look for. I take some of the paint, steady my face near the mirror to steady hers, and dab it on the birthmark.

Her image vanishes, replaced with a doorway. I'm about to step through when I stop. Would Mom's memory of Andalynn lead to the heart of her dungeon? I know immediately it won't. As much as she loves her daughter, as much as she needed Andalynn all those years, there's only one person who captures more of her mind and heart. It doesn't take me long to find him.

Dad looks at me intently. No. I'm looking at the mirror intently. Searching for the thing about him that is off. That's when I catch it. His eyes are a deep brown. I take two fingers of paint and dot the mirror. I align my eyes with the paint as it drips down the reflective surface. The transformation is instantaneous.

The passage opens into another room, darker, without any hint of plants. It's a room in the castlestack of Whurrimduum. Her home. She raised Andalynn there. She met Dad there. This has to be the heart of her dungeon. But the walls are empty of tapestries, and the large windows are filled-in. As I step through, the sound of my footfalls echo on the floor. Where there are usually rugs and furniture to absorb sound, there is only gray stone.

A dim, ghostly figure sits facing away from me on a lonely granite bench. The figure is colorless; its long hair could belong to anyone.

"Mom." My voice finds all the edges of the room coming back broken into a dozen pieces. "Is that you?"

As the figure flips her hair toward me, the long strands turn to vapor around her face. There are a few bursts of silver, iridescent light. A wraith. The stream of vapor settles back into hair, framing a girl's face. Not my mother.

Cold fingers pull my heart in a dozen directions, and I gasp, "No."

Sira's voice is a hiss. "It's okay, sweetie. It's okay. It's kinda nice, actually. Quiet."

"What did I do?"

"You didn't do anything, Clayson. Grimflail killed your mother. She was suffering. Now she's not. But... I am sorry. Oh, Clayson, this must be hard for you."

"Me? She died, and I'm... here I am. Nothing. Nothing happened. Songborn and the other wraiths protected me somehow."

"Then"—this voice behind me is deeper— "you can still leave this place and find Ara." Dad floats beside me, his bottom half a swirl of clouds.

Sira glances down. She's holding a small golden ring box. The sword has reverted to its original form.

Dad stares at the box. "I sense your mother. She doesn't understand what happened to her or who she is. I think that's what happens when you enter a dungeon as a champion; Your memories are scattered throughout the dungeon, hidden even from you. But I remember everything about her. More even. It's like, as a wraith, I hold the key to those memories."

"I do as well," Sira says. "Maybe together, they're all still there."

"You're communicating with her?" I ask them.

"Kind of. I'm trying to introduce myself," Sira laughs softly and her face blurs for a second with fog. "She's vulnerable right now. She's weak." Sira thrust the box toward me. "You should take this. Leave the dungeon. Set your mom free."

The choice hits me center mass. I look between Sira and Dad. "Why aren't you free? I destroyed the connection wraiths have to the Foundation, to the curse."

Dad shrugs. "Perhaps cycles merely start again."

Sira laughs. "I guess it kinda feels like the thread wants to regrow. Like it could repair itself. Does that make any sense?"

"No."

Dad glances behind me but resettles his stare on me. "This dungeon was created after you made the cut. Right?"

The reality of my choice catches up to me. "If I take that box, you'll both be free. But you'll be like Landred was after Wolfstaff. When he left the dungeon, he was distraught, dangerous even."

Tears come to Sira's eyes. "But what happens if you don't? I stay here... for eternity? I don't want to do that either."

"I agree," Dad says. "Whatever comes next, at least we won't be trapped."

"I'm sorry I couldn't stop this."

Dad shakes his head, tears coming to his eyes. "Seeing more of your mother's memories... I wish there had been a way for all of us to stay together. I tried as hard as I knew how. I'm sorry for so many things, but not our time together at the cabin, Clayson, even when it was hard to be on the surface. I have always loved you, my son."

The resentment I have for him gives way to pity. I didn't want this for him. I've been so angry with him the last few months, and as justified as I felt, none of it matters now. I try to peel away his role as the King of Rimduum. I let in his consummate parental love, the thousands of good memories we had together on the surface.

"I love you too, Dad."

"Clayson?" Sira says. "You never thought I was bad. You gave me a lot of chances to walk away from my fears and my worries. It's okay that—" Startled, she looks at Dad. "The box!"

Dad's eyes widen, and they both transform into clouds. The box clatters onto the stone floor.

"Come back! What's happening?" The walls shake, and the ground cracks. I charge forward into the cloud, falling to my hands and knees, searching for the box. My fingers rams against the bench, but I find it.

Who are you? It's Mom's voice. *The other champions want me to help you. But it hurts. You can't take that. It hurts so much. Tell me who you are?*

My fingers tighten around the box. "I'll find you, Mom. I swear I'll find you."

Sira screams, and part of the cloud becomes her again—her eyes, with that smattering of freckles across the bridge of her nose. She looks to my right, and the fog parts briefly. The stone under my feet has changed to a path, and there's a brightness I recognize behind me. I stand and turn around. The Forest of Ide. My mom's dungeon is destroyed. I think back to when I first found the mithrium in the dreamwell in Silverlamp Dungeon. I have heard so many of the champions.

It hits me like a stone. "The dungeons are all connected."

Here is the entrance back into the first dungeon, back to Idulel. I'm not sure how, but does it really matter? If Vor and Ara have already reached the thread, maybe this whole place would be gone, maybe the Foundation would be melting, or maybe the world itself would truly come undone.

The tree trunks try to hold me back; the branches try to wrestle me from the center of the forest. I fight through them, holding the mithrium sword in one hand and the box in the other.

Five people stand near the center of the forest. Idulel sees me first and then Dyn. If Dyn is here, Ara and Vor are already in the fog. The three others... it can't be. Jeiah, Koglim, and Yinzar stand next to her. Are they real?

"What is this?" I murmur.

Jeiah spins around. "Clayson!" Her face lights up, and she plows toward me. I nearly drop the sword as she hugs me.

"How is this possible?" I stammer. "Can this even be real?"

"I was going to ask you the same thing?" Koglim says, squeezing us both together.

"Mom..."

Yinzar steps behind Koglim. "We found the threshold and guessed what happened. But Vor was gone, as was Ara." Yinzar's voice is subdued. He understands what the box in my hand means.

I hand it to him. "We *will* find her. But I've got to stop Vor."

"I knew you would make it here," Jeiah says. "Somehow, I guessed it."

"You guessed right. The dungeons, mithrium, the curse, the thread, everything is connected. The moment I found the heart of her dungeon, I appeared here. I think she understood where I wanted to go."

Jeiah pushes me toward the fog. "Then put an end to this."

They can't come with me. I'm gripping the mithrium sword like I intend to break it. This must end here. It must. But I don't wanna leave anything behind. I don't know what will happen.

"Jeiah. I'm coming back."

"No more promises," she says.

Koglim slaps me on the back. "I'll take that bet. Now get in there and save the world."

Dyn and Idulel watch me carefully, but they don't stop me. Neither can enter.

The fog absorbs me. Once in the center, I let my body fall into the void, turning on an axis until I'm in the dark world of metallic roots. Beads of mercury travel up from the tangle of metal. My heart is racing. Whether with anger or fear or with adrenaline, it's all the same. It all moves my feet and drives me forward.

Vor will be at the center of everything, trying to destroy the thread that holds the world together. I'm not halfway there when I hear Ara's piercing scream.

There's no way to run in this maze of metal. I scramble, squeezing through thin layers of roots. I feel a cut across my cheek and more on my hands.

Another scream, this time more desperate.

As I skid to a halt in the open space around the thread, Vor swings his dark blade. A loud twang pulses outward. Ara, who had been on her knees, shield raised, collapses to the floor. I run to her, glancing at the thread. One of the three pieces is frayed, one split in two. The bottom half is coiled on the floor, and the other hangs from the nothingness above us.

Vor looks manic, unblinking, his lips in a satisfied snarl. "It's too late for her—for any of us. Whatever is next is on its way. You can't stop the world from crumbling this time."

Ara is barely responsive. "It was the only way." Her eyes lock on mine, the black space of this place a dim reflection against them. "We tried everything else." Her head rolls to one side, and her eyes droop close.

"Ara, stay awake. Stay with me. You're going to be okay."

Vor's gleeful voice changes instantly. "Are you serious? It's over, Clayson. You're so... infuriatingly stubborn. Guess I shouldn't be surprised. If you've known as many Brightstorms as I have..."

Ara's shield slumps toward the ground. If she couldn't stop him, how will I be able to? But I have the mithrium sword. I slip the shield from her arm and onto mine. I direct all its power to the thread, and a barrier of white energy sizzles around it, expanding enough to push back at Vor.

He steps backward but keeps his sword leveled at the thread. "What do you think the end will be like, Clayson?"

"I should have killed you."

"Mmhmm, mmhmm. Probably would have been smarter. But answer my question. You're not curious? Even after learning how this whole world was created, even with all your illusions stripped away, you don't wonder if maybe cutting this thread is right?

"I remember the oath I made with the Dura wraiths. The Foundation was pure chaos, Clayson. Idulel couldn't control it. It was tearing the world apart. Jassin sent me here to create a tether. I was a hero. Sacrificed myself, Ara, and Tas. The first three champions. And we made this tether, stabilized the Foundation. Can you believe that? Without me, there is no Loamin world. But... maybe the world is better in chaos."

In that moment, I see into Vor's mind. Not by craft, but it feels that way, an illumination of the truth. "That's complete trollbrick Vor, and you know it. You're not doing this because of some sense of justice. You're doing this because of your hatred for Loamin. You want to see the world come crumbling down. Who are you to say this isn't the way it's supposed to be? Who are you, or Idulel for that matter, to call this world cursed? Was the world before it better? From what I saw, the Dura and the Loamin were at war before the Foundation. Is that what you're returning this world to?"

He shrugs. "Doesn't matter. This is where we are now. Two swords. The thread. You. Me. And there's no going back."

"You're right." I laugh. "There's no default to go back to, no glorious time without fear and anger. You destroy craft—then what? You have a choice. We have a choice. Destruction isn't creation. It's just terror. Like what you did to StoneYoke. Did that change anything? Did that rebuild something? You keep saying idiotic things about destruction and creation being the same, but what if they're not?"

Vor lowers his sword an inch. "Fair point. Fair point. But I don't care. I don't. And neither should you. You don't even belong to this world. Do you want to live in a world held together by nothing but a thread? Chaos. Let me do this. Let me break this one... little... thing."

For a second, I think I might be sick. A shiver runs down my back. The temperature of my blood must drop ten degrees. I tighten the shield around my hand. "You've broken enough of this world, Vor."

The shock on his face as I charge him only fuels my body to move faster. The shield hits him with the force of all my failures. I couldn't keep my parents alive, my sister, or Rugnus. I made the very crown Vor uses against the Loamin world. But I push back.

The two swords clang together. I lose my grip. But so does Vor, screaming wildly as he flails backward. I didn't expect his body to give way so easily, and we land next to each other. The shock on his face wears off quickly, and he lunges for his sword. I clamp my hand on his leg, pulling him back toward me.

"Get. Off. Me. Now!" He lands a few kicks to my shoulders and face, but I refuse to let go. I could use the mithrium shield for protection, but it would leave the thread vulnerable. Instead, I swing the shield down like a hammer. The triangular tip pierces his leg. Now *his* scream echoes through the air. Then his sword whips toward my head. I parry the blow, barely, still unwilling to drop the protection around the thread. He comes back around and hacks at my other hand, the one around his ankle.

The blade hits us both. A large gash opens from the bottom of my thumb along the side of my wrist, and I lose my grip. Vor pulls himself to his knees and crawls forward, but his ankle is bleeding freely. Next to the thread, he stops and looks at me. I switch the shield to my bad hand and push myself up, accepting what healing it offers.

"Stop. Just stop, Clayson."

With heavy breaths, I say. "It doesn't matter. You can't get through the shield."

He glares at me, his face falling. A second later, he looks up, smiling. He holds up the Dura key in his other hand. "Ara gave me this."

Before I can blink, his sword slices through the white layer of protection and severs the tether he made so long ago. It will kill him. It will kill Ara. And unlike Idulel's wish, it won't restore the balance of this world. Pure chaos is unleashed, and the world will fall apart. It's over.

A blast of cool air, heavy with electricity, washes over me. Vor's face starts to transform. I can't understand what I'm seeing. I turn to Ara, and the same thing is happening to her. It's not a transformation; they're disintegrating.

"No." My mouth is dry, heavy with the only word I have left.

Vor tries to laugh, but his face turns to ash, and the crown falls from his head.

Above Ara's bright cheeks, her eyes still hold a light, but it's fading. I hear only the breath of what she says to me. "It's okay." And then she's gone. Ash in the wind. Scattered over the roots of a world growing rapidly colder and harsher.

The last of Vor drifts away from circling the thread. At that moment, a stroke of lightning strikes above me, and freezes. Fear numbs the spot on my back where the Dura wraith stabbed me. Darkness no longer clouds the world. Instead, I see the metallic roots twisting away to an impossible height. Swirling around the roots, a host of wraiths. Jassin and the other Dura. This place was connected all the way back to Gamgim.

Their prison is open.

I grab the key, still holding the shield. I gather the mithrium sword and the crown.

When I turn to run, the world flashes away. I'm back in the

forest of creation. All around me, the trees are blazing with black fire. More ash. More destruction.

Jeiah, Koglim, and Yinzar are facing away from me, watching the forest in shock. Dyn is gone. Idulel is sobbing in joy as the correction of her mistake tears the Foundation from the earth.

I try to yell at them, but my voice doesn't work. When I am right behind them, I find it again. "Run!"

They spin around.

"Clayson?" Jeiah says. "What happened? What's going on?"

"It's the end, isn't it?" Yinzar says. "Ara and Vor?"

"Gone. And the Dura wraiths are free."

There's a massive tremble, and the ground rolls behind my feet.

"They're coming for me," Idulel says.

"We've got to go!" I yell. I pull them toward the burning forest.

Jeiah plants her feet. "Through there? We'll be burned alive."

I hold up the shield and throw energy around us. "Still works."

"For now," Yinzar says. "Let's go."

But before we can even take two steps, there's another mighty tremor of the earth and fissures open all around us. Dura wraiths crawling from out of the earth, blocking our way. A figure rushes past our heads and materializes in front of me. Jassin.

He holds out a hand. "Give me back that key."

I shake my head. "Does it even matter anymore?"

He produces the long knife he used to stab me. "It does to us."

"No. I don't know what that will do."

A hand pulls on mine, trying to take the key. Idulel. "Go," she says. "They don't care about you. They just want the key."

I shake my head. "But what if—"

"The key no longer has a function. Can't you feel it, Clayson? The Foundation is dying. Craft is draining away. You should get somewhere safe. If there is such a place." She backs away.

Jassin eyes her carefully. "We started this together. It's time we ended it."

The Dura wraiths weave past us, following Idulel into the center of the clearing. The ground rumbles as an army of Dura wraiths continue to break from the ground. Without a glance backward, we crash through the trees into the outer circle of the dungeon. The threshold awaits us. We cross into the ruins of the three protodungeons. The moment we're through, all three doorways become a pile of rubble.

But the world keeps shaking. The obsidian walls and floors shake as we return to the House of Ide and make our way through the hall of champions, dodging raining pieces of obsidian.

At the top of the second stair, we cross under the arching doorway of the House of Ide out to the great wall that divides the Foundation from the scorching power of the lava. We stop at the edge and stare. It's filled with a river of molten rock, steaming and hissing as it contacts the Foundation.

"Look!"

I follow Jeiah's finger out to the Foundation. Above the glittering shine of all the shades of blue light, the cavern is melting. Raindrops, all of the molten metals from the mines above the Foundation, fall from the rock like a hellish maelstrom.

"It's over then," Yinzar says. "Craft is dead."

The sword. I feel its power still. "Maybe not just yet."

"What will happen now?" Koglim yells.

"I don't know," I say, hefting the sword. "But we need to leave."

A second later, the world is filled with starlight and muted leaves.

Yinzar asks where we are, but I know our property best. It's on the southern edge near the orchard. "We're home. Come on."

"Do you feel that?" Koglim asks.

"Feel what?" I ask.

"Nothing."

I glance at him. He's breathing normally. Everyone else is breathing normally too. "It's the shield. Same as always. See." I hold up the shield for Koglim to see.

"Koglim's right," Jeiah says. "This feels different. No surface effects. No fizzblood."

We follow a bead of a path winding through the forest. My mind is scrambling to understand what's happening. The mines fall to pieces, the Foundation leaches light, the thread is cut. The curse is broken, and nothing will be the same ever again. For now, the powers of the shield, the crown, and the sword still work, but what will happen to the Loamin stuck under miles of rock?

When we reach the gravel road at the exit of the grove, I spot a tall figure walking along the road. Everyone freezes. My eyes are glued to her. Impossible. The moment her strawberry blonde hair catches the moonlight, my heart takes flight. I can't believe it. My mom is here. Of all the places her Dura body could appear, she came here.

She's muttering the way Kel did, the way Tas did. And though it's not quite her voice, not as severe, it's one more piece of evidence I can use to confirm my hope. It *is* her.

"Bena," Yinzar stammers.

Confusion softens her face. "Connection?"

Yinzar sets the golden box in her open palms.

"Oh," she says.

GATHER TOGETHER

MOM REMEMBERS nothing of her life. She barely remembers the two wraiths—Dad and Sira—and my incursion into the heart of the dungeon. She doesn't remember me at all. Though, she seems most comfortable with Yinzar. Kel had been different. She had a thousand years with Landred. Her memories were all connected to his life, a ghostly reflection. Mom doesn't even have that. She and Yinzar sit on the cabin's porch steps, speaking softly.

"It will be okay," Jeiah tells me.

Koglim purses his lips. The truth is more evident on his face. Mom is gone, and again she won't remember anything about me. Not only that but there's a hole where Dad should be. How can I help him? Or even find him?

"I'm not sure you should be so optimistic, Jeiah."

She shrugs. "When you don't have any evidence, there's always hope. Guess where I learned that?"

Koglim raises his hand, smiling. "Ooh, I know. Clayson."

Jeiah nods. "Yep."

I take a deep breath. And then another. If Koglim can still find something to smile about as his whole world comes crashing down, and Jeiah can find hope in the future, then there's a way to move forward.

Voices call out from the shop. Winta, Hemdi, and Brig come out to meet us. Rusela and Lagnar behind them. Winta has Echel slung on her back in a carrier.

"Found you!" Brig says, "And just in time."

"In time?"

Winta points a thumb back to the shop. "You better see this." We follow them past the cabin and into the clearing where the shield once stood. Winta steps next to me. "When the foilgrips came down, Jeiah told me what happened. You gonna be okay?"

"Depends on what's happening."

She frowns.

Brig rushes ahead to hold the door open, and we all file in. The screens are shouting taffy news. Winta mutes it, but not before I hear phrases like *massive earthquake, unprecedented eruption,* and the worst one... *the end of the world.*

"Winta." A warning edges my voice. "What's happening?"

"We budged before craft stopped working," she says.

"See," Koglim says. "Before we got here did you guys feel any different?"

Brig lifts an eyebrow. "If you're asking about the surface effects, yeah. They were gone before Clayson showed up with the shield. And that's why we have to hurry. The Loamin down there, it was a complete reversal. My guess is something about the elevation and the pressure from the mass of the mountain. Ide keep us."

"Brig," Koglim says, "I love you, but never say that again."

They start arguing, but I tune them out. I feel the weight of the mithrium objects in my hands. I know what I have to do. Placing the crown on my head, I say, "I'm going back down to Tungsten City."

Everyone looks at the shield, then the crown, then the sword.

Jeiah shakes her head. "We don't know how long even these mithrium objects will last. If there's no craft—"

"Okay, we vote. But we don't have much time. I won't go if there's no agreement."

There's silence. Even Brig ponders my statement. Maybe I've shocked everyone because I'm not rushing to the rescue.

"It's reasonable," Yinzar says. "The mithrium objects are currently working."

"No one else can do it," Brig says. "And Clayson could bring us with, but at what cost. He might be able to shield us, but we won't be able to help him."

"Melt everything," Koglim says. "Get as many survivors as the sword will let you budge. And hurry."

Everyone else agrees. But Jeiah weighs everything. "Yeah. Sure. Okay."

"Translation," Koglim says. "She loves you. Don't die."

"I got that," I say.

Then, overwhelmed with losing her, I pull Jeiah toward me. Softly, I kiss her, and it's so much like our first—filled with hope and promise—that I almost don't wanna leave. But when she pulls away, I'm ready.

"I love you," I say. The words are easy now like I've always been saying them. "I'm coming back."

She smiles and adjusts the crown on my head. "Find them, Clay. Every last person and budge them to the surface."

The budge is instantaneous.

I'm at the top of Bluelink tower. I look over the whole of Tungsten City. There are no more floating buildings. The brightstorm has expanded over the entire citybarrel, eating into the sidewalls. The white light washes out the whole city, making it hard to find familiar shapes and places.

But the whispers return. I don't know how many brightstorms are converged on this one—maybe all of them—but the voices are deafening. Who they belong to and why they exist are mysteries that I'll never solve. Once this is done, no one will ever return here. And for that, my heart breaks. Rugnus loved this city. It was a living, breathing thing.

I take a few precious seconds and mourn for this place I barely knew. I regret staying on the surface when I could have visited every strange place under granite. I could have used goldcraft to soar through the sky, silvercraft to know its people and understand their lives. Roamed the city as a lynx. I could have protected them all so much better than I did. Andalynn experienced this world. Rugnus experienced this world. I was always just visiting.

I open my thoughts. For a moment, it's like I feel someone else reviewing everything, sorting my hopes and fears by how badly they've hurt me. Vor. My mom. Sira, Andalynn. Rugnus. The loss of a whole way of life. The end of ten thousand years of craft. The end of these two last cities underground.

Above me, a flare whips out from the brightstorm, and for a moment, I feel like Rugnus is next to me, guiding me on how to use Icho like he did when I first arrived at his vault nearly a year ago. I miss him. I miss my sister. And then it's like Andalynn takes me by the hand and helps me see everyone.

The city comes alive with people. They can hear my thoughts, my commands. I project out to them. *This is Clayson Brightstorm. I'm getting you out. Get ready to budge.*

A wave of agreement rises from their minds. I imagine them at the cabin, Lagnar's old radio station building, and the convenience store in Denver. Even places I've only ever seen on TV, the world's cities glimmering with familiar landmarks, then I send them all over the world.

My concentration shatters, and my knees bend as a wave of movement hits the tower. I hear a million breaking windows, and the brownstone building next to us splits along its masonry, half of it slipping off and tumbling into the park below. At the edge of the city, a whole section of the skyline is eaten by the ground. A chasm appears where Everfalls had been.

I need to leave.

"Hello, Clayson." The voice spins me around to face the roof of Bluelink tower.

It's Dyn. He's holding the piece of mithrium I brought out of the Forest of Ide.

"Dyn. What are you doing here?"

"Are you up for one last task?"

"What does that mean?"

Dyn laughs, and it's as bright as his champion's namesake—as my namesake. He smiles, and dimples form on his cheeks. It reminds me so much of Dad that emotion fights to the surface. "You don't think Ara would just leave you without a choice, do you? That she would destroy the world on a whim."

"I don't understand."

"It's been hard for you to listen to them." He points to the brightstorm.

"To who?"

"You have most of the pieces." He holds out the mithrium. "Just two more. And everything that has happened, everything that should come next, will click together, forge the world into something amazing."

He steps forward, but I step backward.

Think, Clayson. It's what you're good at.

The voice settles over me like strong craft. "It can't be."

"See?" Dyn says. "When Ara found me, and I touched this"— in the other hand, he holds up the cradle— "Something else whispered to me. Exralt left a mark in my dungeon when he forged that puzzle."

My mind spins, flashing with insight. "The cottage. Exralt made that challenge with the mithrium."

Dyn nods. "He brought the mithrium to the heart of my dungeon. He could have freed me, but I wouldn't let him. He wanted to do exactly this: bring an end to the world of Loamin. I didn't want that. He came to me again and again, and I grew weary of him. Finally, I agreed to a compromise. We'd make a puzzle so unlikely to be solved it would take centuries to find it and even more to uncover the truth."

"But we found it. Rugnus, Andalynn, and I."

"By that time, I had seen your connection to the dungeons. I knew the risk. I knew that the tether to the Foundation might be broken, and perhaps, with it, after all this time, the Foundation itself would collapse".

"But Vor made that tether when he murdered the first champions."

"Yes. Exralt hadn't made that connection. So, I presented you with the challenge. By the time Ara woke me, Rugnus and Andalynn had already gathered most of the brightstorms."

"The whispers I've heard..."

"The champions, the wraiths, but yes... also your friend and your sister."

I feel like I can't catch my breath. "How do I—"

Dyn holds out the mithrium again. The cradle too.

There's no hesitation as I grab them. My connection to the brightstorms becomes an overwhelming force. The minds of the champions sear into mine like hot coals. The whispers of thousands of wraiths compete for my attention. But I know what I'm looking for. The clearest voices have been theirs. I crane my head back to stare at the brightstorm. I sense Rugnus' strength and Andalynn's compassion forged together. For a second, I sense them as one being, but no. Andalynn is there alongside Rugnus. Their will is made of fierce determination and a warmth of love that could melt a brightstorm.

I tighten my hand on the mithrium sword and pull.

"Finally," Rugnus says at my side.

Andalynn rests her hand on my shoulder and puts her head against mine. "You did it, Clayson. Now let's fix this together."

The spark of hope I had kept kindled for them erupts in laughter. They're actually standing here. In front of me. Not ghosts or wraiths. They've returned more alive than ever. I grip them in a bone-crushing hug.

"Gonna be okay there, latcher," Rugnus says. "We've got a world to piece together if you haven't noticed. May I?" He reaches for the mithrium sword.

"No one can use it unless—"

"...unless they don't have craft? Earth to Clayson—craft is gone. I've got plenty of room for this." He eases the sword from my hand and sighs. "I missed you Icho."

"Don't get too attached," Andalynn says with tightened lips.

"How is this possible?" I gasp.

"Still stuck on that?" Rugnus says. He turns to Dyn. "Don't be offended Erikzin—Dyn—Clayson can be a little slow on the uptake sometimes, but his heart is in the right place."

"Clayson, the crown," Andalynn says.

I pass it to her, bewildered. As we stand shoulder to shoulder, Dyn takes the cradle from me. Rugnus has the sword, Andalynn the crown, and I have the shield and the last piece of mithrium.

Another section of Tungsten City drops in the cavern, and Rugnus growls.

"Focus," Andalynn tells him.

"How does this all work?" I ask, still reeling from having them back with me.

"In theory, we pull down the combined power of every bright-storm—like ever—and melt the Foundation into something more... fluid. The sword can help me move the brightstorms. The shield can protect us, and the crown... I think Andalynn is going to have to *talk* the earth into being nice. Then push the Foundation into all the cracks, use its power to seal the fissures tearing the world to pieces."

"Can we live through this?" I ask.

Rugnus shakes his head. "No guarantee on that part."

"Shall we begin?" Dyn says. We all nod. "Reach."

The shield responds with the force of a thousand bright-storms, and only now do I understand the full extent of the Loamin world. The Foundation beneath me covers an area spanning most of Colorado. But it's more than that. This beginning of creation has shoots of power extending all over the world: beneath Hngaal and Brimwok, deep under Firas Andem and Himdem, Dashen and Zal Kakraja.

When we reforge this patch out of the Foundation, every Loamin kingdom will come to its final end. I sense more Loamin hiding everywhere under granite, all over the earth.

"The people!" I shout.

"I'm on it!" Rugnus yells back.

At the same time, he reaches for every Loamin the world over, and the giant brightstorm in the sky drops toward us. The mithrium shield holds as the burning sun passes through us. It burns through Tungsten City, through the vaults, through the mines, striking the Foundation with all the might of Loamin civilization. We float above it, radiating with power.

Rugnus keeps us balanced in the void, I keep the shield wrapped tight around us, and Andalynn reaches deeper than both of us. The earth wants to give up, to give in to this force of such great power, but Andalynn wills its spirit to stay with us.

"It's working!" Rugnus calls.

Dyn sails toward us. "Hand them off to me!"

Andalynn goes first, setting the crown on his head. Rugnus is next with the sword. After all my confrontations in the dungeons, after everything the champions have put us through, I cling to the shield. I don't wanna give Dyn this power. "What will happen to you?"

"That's nothing for you to worry about, Clayson."

"You'll die?"

"I've been dead a thousand years."

Gently he pries the shield and the mithrium loose from my hands. When he has everything secure, he free falls into the melting Foundation in a brilliant flash of light.

We appear on the surface near the top of Pike's Peak. The summation chamber at Gamgim forest had once been there, but it's a flatted, glowing crater. Light from a thousand cracks over the surface is draining away. There's nothing left of Rimduum but ashes and darkness.

Rugnus hugs me. Andalynn watches for two seconds and then rests her head on my shoulder. I'm wrong—there is something left from that world. I have it right here.

"Think I'm taller than you now, by the way," Rugnus says.

I step back. He's right. They're *both* taller than me now. "Hmm, interesting."

"Interesting? That's all you've got."

"I mean... maybe you're human."

Rugnus raises a warning finger. "Not on your life, pal. Loamin, through and through." He slouches down, making Andalynn laugh.

"Well," she says, "what's next?"

"There are Loamin out there that need us."

"Refugees," Rugnus says.

Andalynn gazes down the mountain. "Let's get to work." She takes a step forward and stops. "Clayson, maybe you should lead the way. I don't know enough about the surface to be in charge. What do we need?"

"Everyone else is back at the cabin," I say, "They don't even know I'm alive."

"They do," Andalynn says. When I stare at her in disbelief, she shrugs. "The crown. I sent a quick message to Jeiah."

"Okay," I say incredulously. "But we're pretty much helpless nobodies now. We're going to need phones, transportation, and money."

Rugnus laughs. "About that."

Andalynn and I wait for him to clarify.

"That, uh, dragon guardian at Brightstorm Dungeon... I may have borrowed some ferrum from him."

Andalynn's mouth drops open. "How much?"

"A bit," Rugnus says. "And... well..."

"Spit it out."

"All that gold and silver in the vaults... I couldn't just melt it."

"What did you do with it?" Andalynn says.

I laugh so hard I can barely speak. "That's a lot of human money."

"The PO boxes weren't big enough. So... Lagnar's hub. It's somewhere close by, I think. Oh, and I thought 'the ministack could hold some of it, so—"

"You didn't?" She says, slapping his arm. "We were saving the world, and you used the mithrium sword for that?"

"You used the crown to talk to Jeiah, so don't accuse me."

"I sent some of the Tungsten City refugees to the hub," I say.

Rugnus grins. "I bet that was a surprise."

Andalynn sighs and rubs her temples. "We better get down there."

As we make our way out of the forest, the world lights up with fireflies. Tall pines give way to shrubs, and we come out to a road leading down into the valley. The lights of Denver twinkle to life as we shuffle along over the asphalt toward Lagnar's hub.

Rugnus takes a deep breath and shakes his head.

"What?" I ask.

"Surface is actually pretty nice."

EPILOGUE

RENSIRA

I REMEMBER WHO I AM, who I was. Rensira Silverlamp, daughter of Theridal Silverkeeper. I was a child, a bouncy little girl, then an unwilling servant, and then a wraith made of rainbow lights and fluffy clouds.

What am I now? I shift and feel more alive than I've ever felt before. I'm strong. Safe. How is that possible?

Wind combs through my fingers. No, silly, not fingers. My leaves. What? I tower above the other trees. The night is so deep, and the moonlight tickles my skin—uh, no, bark. It's a wonderful, pure, gentle kiss.

I miss Clayson.

But this moonlight! My whole form, each bough and limb, shiver with pleasure.

Still. What would it be like to simply step out of myself? Not that I need to move from this place. My roots are so deep and draw so much safety from the rich, black earth. But what if...

I find my hands again and push, tumbling out of the tree. My skin is translucent blue-green. I think it makes me look even cuter. I bet my freckles could kill. And I'm still connected to the tree. That's my world now, and I can't be long away.

I steal across the grass in a flash. Wow! I'm fast.

Zoom!

I reach a large tree and stop. Someone is there, trapped in the tree. The big scary oak has rough bark, but it needs help. I press my translucent hands against the surface. I'll be like Clayson, unafraid.

There's a hum of energy, and I feel how sad the tree is.

Oh. It's Therias Brightstorm in there. Well, maybe it's him about as much as I'm that little girl. What was her name again? Rensira Silverlamp. Fun to say.

The grumpy tree pushes something into my translucent hands. A glowing ball of energy. I tuck it away for safekeeping. It's important. I'm sure it is. I spend more time weaving in and out of the trees, soaking in the wind, letting the grasses tickle my feet. When dawn approaches, I slink back to my tree. Pushing my way inside, I sigh as the sunlight warms me down to the bones.

Trees don't have bones, silly.

I'm different now.

A long while later, maybe days, weeks, or years, I remember the glowing ball of energy I have tucked away. More than that, I had something stuck in one of my branches, too, something that doesn't belong to me. A little rock, a smooth tiny pebble, stuck in my bark. When I try to push against it, I feel—nope, ha! Not the right word—I *remember.* I remember everything from a long life, but these memories are not mine.

They belong to someone's mother. But it's only half the memories. That old scary oak tree gave me the other half. And two halves make a whole. I'm a pretty smart tree.

I'll put these memories where she's sure to find them. With some effort, I escape my tree. It's getting harder to do that lately. I make my way to a little orchard of pear trees.

This will do nicely. No need for me to hang on to the memories. I float down the rows, and at the end, I find a tree that's nearly dying. That won't do. I push the memories into the tree. I let it take something of the moonlight inside of me. And it grows strong fruit swelling the boughs.

Oops. A little too strong. Oh well. The little pears are safe, and the memories are in just the right spot. That's when I decide I'm allowed to be happy. I smile and race back to my tree, shivering from the tickle of dew against my feet.

⁂

CLAYSON

The light on the baggage claim carousel awakens like a siren, but I wait at the back of the crowd. It doesn't take long for the small knot of people to thin enough for me to swoop in and grab my duffle bag. Well, Rugnus' duffle bag. I borrowed it for the trip.

I swing around and find a family of four gawking at me. They're dressed for a hike up the Appalachian Trail.

The mother blinks and pats her husband on the shoulder. I acknowledge them. It's always more uncomfortable if I don't.

As I walk by, a girl about ten calls out, "I saw you on YouTube. Clayson... something."

"Spangler," the father says. "You're Clayson Spangler."

I extend my hand to the man. With the enthusiasm of a kid, he grabs my whole arm, saying, "Test our might. Is that right?"

I can't recall how many humans I've tested strength with since last year. The grocery store, the movies, the bank.

"Testing strengths," I say. "But you're doing great."

The mother introduces me to her two kids. "Clayson helps all the Loamin refugees find jobs, get training and school, so they can adjust to life on the surface."

"And he's doing a great job," the father says. "You're doing a great job."

Laughter erupts in a crowd hovering in the corridor ahead, followed by a round of loud applause.

"That's gonna be my ride." I excuse myself and walk forward.

A second later, a big figure cuts through the crowd. He sees me, feigning surprise. "Is that—that's got to be... Clayson Spangler-Brightstorm!" Behind him, the crowd gasps. I wave reluctantly.

"Koglim Felsight."

He wraps me in his arms and squeezes me until I can't breathe. "Glad you're back. How's things over at the Home Base?"

"Busy as ever."

"How's everybody else? Rugnus and Andalynn? Yinzar?"

As we talk, people stare at us, but we make our way out of the airport into the parking garage, eventually stopping in front of a black and chrome Hummer.

I eye Koglim. Another new car.

"Don't say it."

I shake my head as the lock opens. Koglim rounds the front end, turning the Hummer on with an automatic start. He grins as he climbs into the driver's seat. I open the door, and a golden cup tumbles off the seat. I catch it before it falls to the concrete.

Koglim scrambles to move the pile of fast-food wrappers mixed with various objects made of precious metals.

My eyes widen. "This is what you're doing with your share? This stuff should be—"

"Yeah, yeah, in a bank. You're the same as Hemdi. I just like having a few objects around. Even if they don't do anything."

"Rugnus didn't budge all this stuff to the surface moments before saving the world so you can treat them like old Tupperware."

"I've traded some of it in. Here look."

He combs through the refuse and pulls out a crumpled paper lunch bag.

"Do I wanna see what's in that?"

He dumps the bag. Coins jingle out with fistfuls of cash. A stack of hundreds bounces off the center console into my lap.

"Ide keep me Koglim. You look like a drug dealer."

Koglim's mouth drops open. "Those guys are bad. I'm not a drug dealer."

"Relax, I know. But this should be in a bank. Did you not even watch my last human tutorial?"

"I did. I promise I did but... the bank. I hate people who work at the bank. They look so greedy when I walk in there. Change of topic. So... did you miss Jeiah?"

My pulse doubles. I've been gone for two weeks helping Andalynn understand government paperwork in the Colorado Welcome Center we've dubbed Home Base. "Of course I did."

"More important question," Koglim says. "Will you watch rugby with me and Brig tonight?"

For the next couple of hours, we talk about a thousand different things. Every sport imaginable, Winta's growing list of marketable human skills, the Loamin welcome centers, Andalynn and Rugnus, Lagnar's online sales of metalwork. Mostly positive things. But every now and again, the conversations drift to the things we've lost. Dungeons, for Koglim. That's what he's missing the most.

We stop for gas, and Koglim emerges from the small store with a dozen bags—all snack food. He opens a full-sized bag of chips and offers me some. "Cheddar-ranch flavored."

The last few miles pass impossibly fast, not like a budge, but it might as well be. There's something comforting about being able to drive through the mountains, take a plane, or hike up a trail. A sense of progression that I never seemed to capture in the Loamin world. The trees climb around me like a welcoming blanket.

I roll down the Hummer's window and stick my hand out, feeling the warm summer breeze. The Rockies have their own pine-rich smell, but there is something more to the scent of the Blue Ridge Mountains. Something older.

Home.

When we hit the gravel road leading to my father's property—my property—I breathe more quickly. It's been a year since the end of the Loamin world. The ministack has been added to by well-paid human construction workers. We named it the *Therias Brightstorm Welcome Center*. Three stories tall, constructed of stone and long wooden logs, it appears almost like a resort, with the backdrop of the forest behind it. The tall windows invite all to come inside around a comfy hearth, Loamin culture, and artifacts on display around the main foyer.

But most of us live in the cabin.

The second I step out of the Hummer, Brig emerges from the large double doors of the Welcome Center and runs down from the porch. "Ho, Clayson. Long time no see."

He wrestles me into a hug.

The doors open again, and Echel waddles out. He's wearing a purple t-shirt, a diaper, and a pair of canvas sandals. At the top of the stairs, he points to me. "Dat's man!"

Winta follows him out the door. "Man? Hm. Sort of, buddy. That's Clayson."

Everyone laughs. Echel keeps pointing at me, smiling. At the bottom of the stairs, I say. "Hi to you too, Winta."

"Hey, latcher."

Echel grabs the railing and takes the first giant step toward me. "Latur, latur."

Koglim dies laughing as I step up and hoist Echel into the air. How is he heavier after only a couple of weeks? He yanks on my hair.

Winta comes to my rescue. "Brig, take Echel around to the playground."

Brig sighs, but Echel looks at me and says, "Sorry, I play now!" repeating the word "play" a hundred times as they make their way around the welcome center.

We all stand there awkwardly until Winta says, "Holy goodness, Clayson. Jeiah is out in the grove with Hemdi. Go find her. So predictable."

Koglim gestures to the four-wheeler in the shed. "Go on."

"Hemdi still trying to keep that pear tree alive?"

"How'd you guess?" Koglim deadpans.

When I turn the four-wheeler on, the hum of the engine brings me back to my life with Dad, taking care of the property. I take the quickest route to the orchard, stopping short when the dogs find me. I jump down and grab the closest one. I ruffle his coat and ears. "Good boy, Stone."

"Clayson." I recognize Jeiah's warm voice.

If possible, her eyes look even bluer. Her face is inviting and hopeful. There's an openness about it that I've missed even in only a couple of weeks. It doesn't escape me that we're close to where Andalynn and Rugnus made their vows. I wipe the smile off my face and straighten up. "Yeah."

"Sure. Okay," she finishes and kisses me firmly.

She leads me to the clearing, and I find Hemdi and my mom there tending to a massive pear tree in the grove. We only planted them last year, but this one is larger by three times as much.

"Who replaced the tree?" I ask, investigating the surrounding dirt. "Wasn't this one basically dead when I left?"

Hemdi smiles broadly. "Clayson. You're back. I've been trying to answer that very question. Someone must have swapped it out for a different tree. I don't know."

"No one else was working the grounds," my mom says. Her face is broader, more like Andalynn's. She's taller, but her hair is the same strawberry blond I've always known it to be. It's hard not to hope that someday she will just remember me.

Jeiah dusts off her hands. "As interesting as this might be, I'm going to go get cleaned up. Meet me at the cliff." Her mischievous smile drives a thrill into my blood.

"Sure," I say, but my voice betrays my eagerness, which she sees.

She leaves me with a smile and steals the four-wheeler.

I help Hemdi and my mom with a few more trees, but we don't solve the mystery of the pear tree. After another hour, Hemdi shrugs and picks a few pears for breakfast tomorrow. "Might as well," he says.

I take a slow walk back to the cabin and find my room.

Koglim must have brought in my duffle bag, and I quickly change into climbing shoes. I take the well-worn path through the trees. The strawberry patch is new, something I always talked about doing with Dad. The cliff is as old as time itself, steady and unmovable. I make no effort to find some obscure way up. I take the first familiar grab like the hand of an old friend.

With a slow rhythm, I climb to the top and sit on the brink. The sun is lost somewhere behind me in the trees. The horizon is a melted gray color. There's a single bright pinprick on the horizon, maybe a star, maybe Venus or Mars. I focus on that one point and let the beauty of summer wash over me.

I almost sense Jeiah's arrival at the edge of the forest behind me.

"Thinking about your mother?"

"Honestly?" I ask. "No, I was thinking about that pear tree."

Her laughter tickles the air. "Of course, you were. It's a mystery to be solved. If I wasn't tied up with relocation business, I guess I would be too. It *is* a strange occurrence." She sits down, and I put my head in her lap.

Her fingers run through my hair, and I sigh, contented. Somehow life inches closer and closer to normal the further we get from what was—to Loamin anyway—the end of the world.

We circle through every possible topic as the night encroaches. Echel's cute. Loamin are thriving on the surface with the help of the welcome centers. The human friends we've made as we've tried to forge a new life together. When we find a bit of silence Jeiah's hand moves to a spot of bare earth. She scoops some into her hands and lets it fall through her fingers.

"Now, what could you be thinking about?" I ask.

"It's nothing." She scoops the same dirt up and lets it fall again.

"I can't read your mind. Tell me."

"The tree. It's weird. It reminds me of something the conjurers believe."

I sit up straight. "What's that?"

"That craft was never meant to be controlled. To them, nature was magic. They wanted to conjure the power of Ide. They even named the city after Ide. And Geum was some type of a plant genus, I think."

"Who told you that?" I smile, but we both know it must have been Hemdi.

She slaps my arm. "I'm being serious. What if…"

"What if the plant has something to do with spontaneous craft?"

She groans. "When you say it that way…"

I settle back into place. "Sounds like a mystery we could solve together."

She runs her hands back through my hair. "It does, doesn't it."

After all the endings we've faced in the last couple of years, after all the destruction, it's Vor's words that come back to me uninvited. Destruction and creation are two sides of the same ferrum. That single star in the sky is lost behind the trees, but a mist of the milky way begins to reveal itself above us. A world of possibilities opens like the sky.

AZBENA

When Clayson asks me to help with breakfast, I go quickly to work. It's not that I need to prove anything to him, but he is my son. Something deep in my bones verifies this every time he smiles. And there's something magical in those dimples.

It's a simple salad to complement the eggs and toast. It's made with ingredients from around the welcome center: butter crisp lettuce, peas, blueberry vinaigrette, and pears—though everyone is a bit wary of eating the pears.

But that's where I find it. A small pebble. I slice into a pear, and there it is.

"How did you get in there," I say, picking it up carefully.

Understanding spreads from the tip of my fingers along every nerve in my body. I drop the knife and let the wonder of this magic fill my blood. Every second with Andalynn in the castlestack at Whurrimduum returns to me like a force of nature, a hurricane. I see my mother and father as I wait for entrance into summation. The first time Therias laughed at something I said. Lagnar's warm hand in mine before his banishment, before Therias and I...

Clayson's birth. Every detail comes back to me just as he enters the kitchen.

"Can I help?" he asks. "Wait, are you okay?"

I hold up the tiny pebble. "Everything is exactly right."

He smiles and squints, his eyes colored with wondrous curiosity.

I am forever grateful we've shared this story together.

If you enjoyed the world of RIMDUUM, please consider leaving a simple rating or review on Amazon or Goodreads. If, like me, you've fallen for the characters and setting of this amazing world, please share the news with your scifi/fantasy-loving friends. Word of mouth makes such a difference for creatives like me.

Pick up signed copies over on my website. I'll ship directly to you and stamp them with your favorite craft symbol. Don't forget to sign up for Bluelink—the RIMDUUM exclusive newsletter—bringing you deals, chances to read my work early, and free short stories.

www.loamseedpress.com

THANK YOU

There are so many beautiful and imaginative stories floating in the great void and you chose the world of RIMDUUM. Thank you so much! I'd love to hear from you. Feel free to contact me on social media. May all of your dreams and wishes come true. May you find something that stokes the fires of your imagination and leads you to be more and more human, and to treat other people the same. Go out there and build worlds of wonder.

Sincerely,

ABOUT THE AUTHOR

BEN GREEN has always been a storyteller. When he was a kid, he would tear apart his coloring books and assemble them into crossover stories with lots of drama and lots of glue. Then he discovered action figures and took to burning Cobra agents at the stake and writing/acting out whole episodes of Star Trek the Next Generation. As a teen, he wrote Star Wars fanfiction and began creating his own worlds on a Brother word processor with a tiny screen and floppy disks. Meaning he's also very old.

Though he grew up in Arizona and Nevada, Ben now lives in southern Minnesota where he puts his degrees in teaching, history, and technology to use as a social studies teacher for non-traditional students. He is passionate about teen issues and at-risk youth. This may be why he spends so much time with his four children, telling stories, working in the garden, and encouraging them to find something to be passionate about.

facebook.com/bengreenwrites

instagram.com/bdigitalgreen

goodreads.com/bengreenwrites

pinterest.com/bengreenwrites